**Double Chaser**
From *Mickey Mouse* #33, 1953
Artist and Letterer: Paul Murry
Colorist: Digikore Studios

AN' SPEAKIN' OF WILD WEATHER, THIS RAIN HAS SOAKED MUH SUPER GOOBERS SOGGY... MAKIN' 'EM ONLY A TENTH AS EFFECTIVE!

**Rain, Rain, Go Astray**
From Brazilian *Zé Carioca* #1105, 1973
Artist: Jack Bradbury
Inker: Steve Steere
Colorist: Digikore Studios
Letterers: Nicole and Travis Seitler
Dialogue: Joe Torcivia

GANGWAY!
ZOW!

**Mortgage Misery**
From Norwegian *Donald Duck & Co.* #32/2015
Writer: Lars Jensen
Artist: Joaquín Cañizares Sanchez
Colorist: Digikore Studios
Letterers: Nicole and Travis Seitler
Dialogue: Lars Jensen and David Gerstein

Series Editor: Sarah Gaydos
Archival Editor: David Gerstein

Cover Artist: Lorenzo Pastrovicchio
Cover Colorist: Andrea "Casty" Castellan
Collection Editors: Justin Eisinger
and Alonzo Simon
Collection Designer: Clyde Grapa
Publisher: Ted Adams

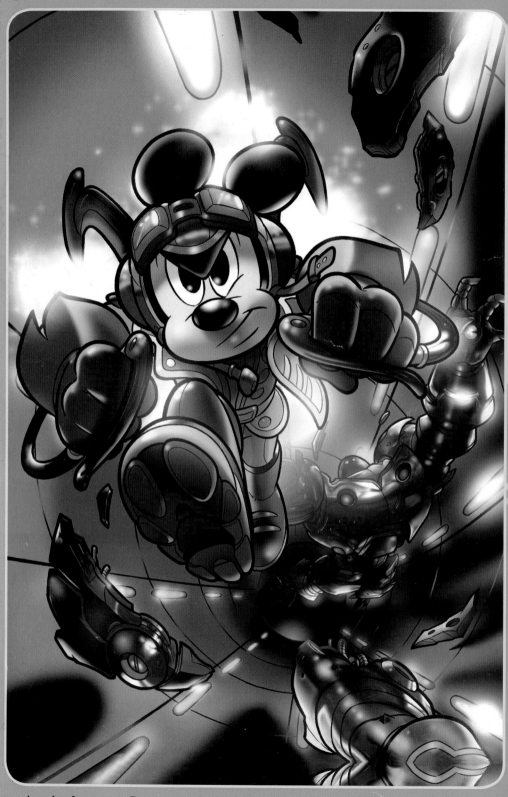

Art by Lorenzo Pastrovicchio, Colors by Andrea "Casty" Castellan

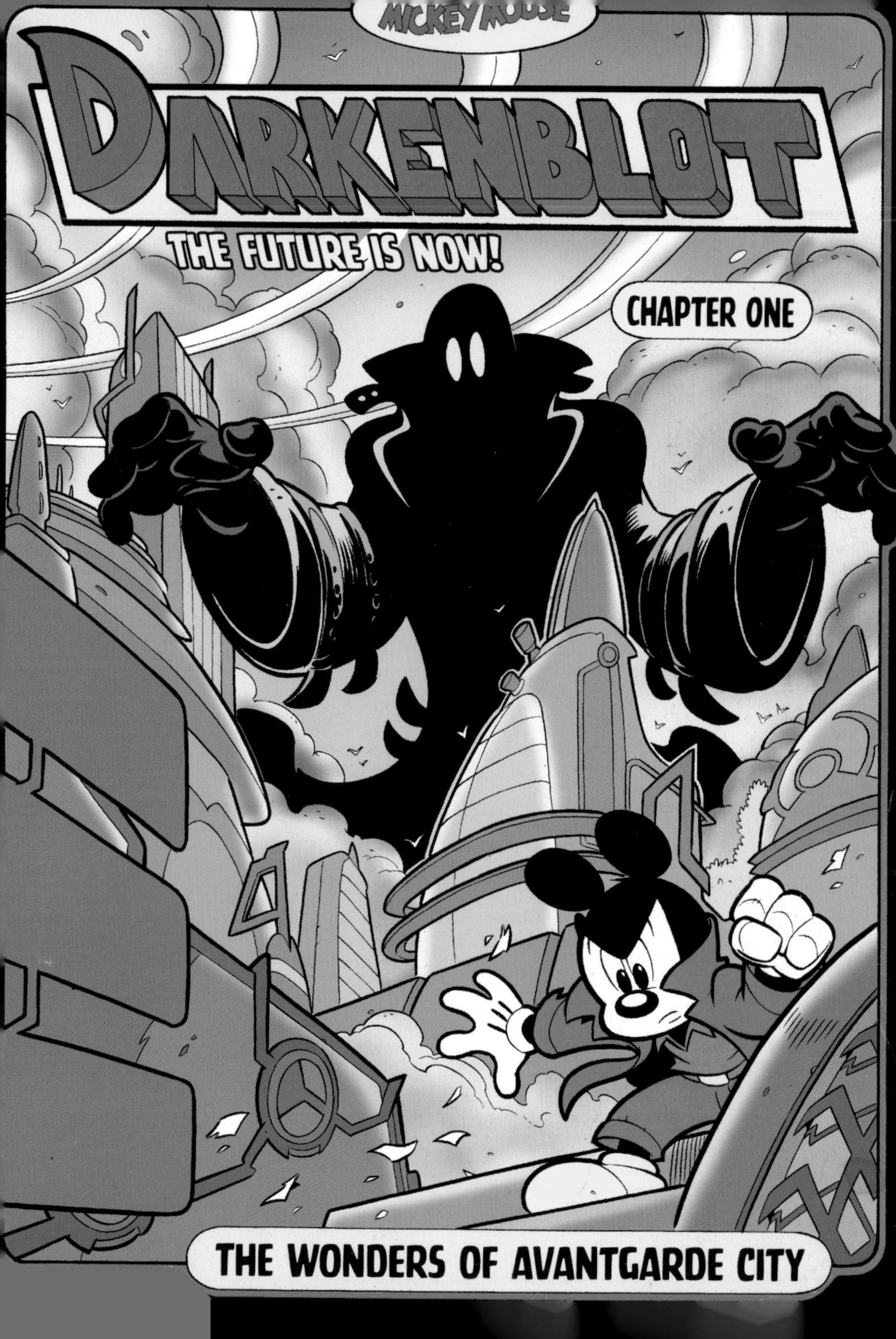
MICKEY MOUSE
DARKENBLOT
THE FUTURE IS NOW!
CHAPTER ONE
THE WONDERS OF AVANTGARDE CITY

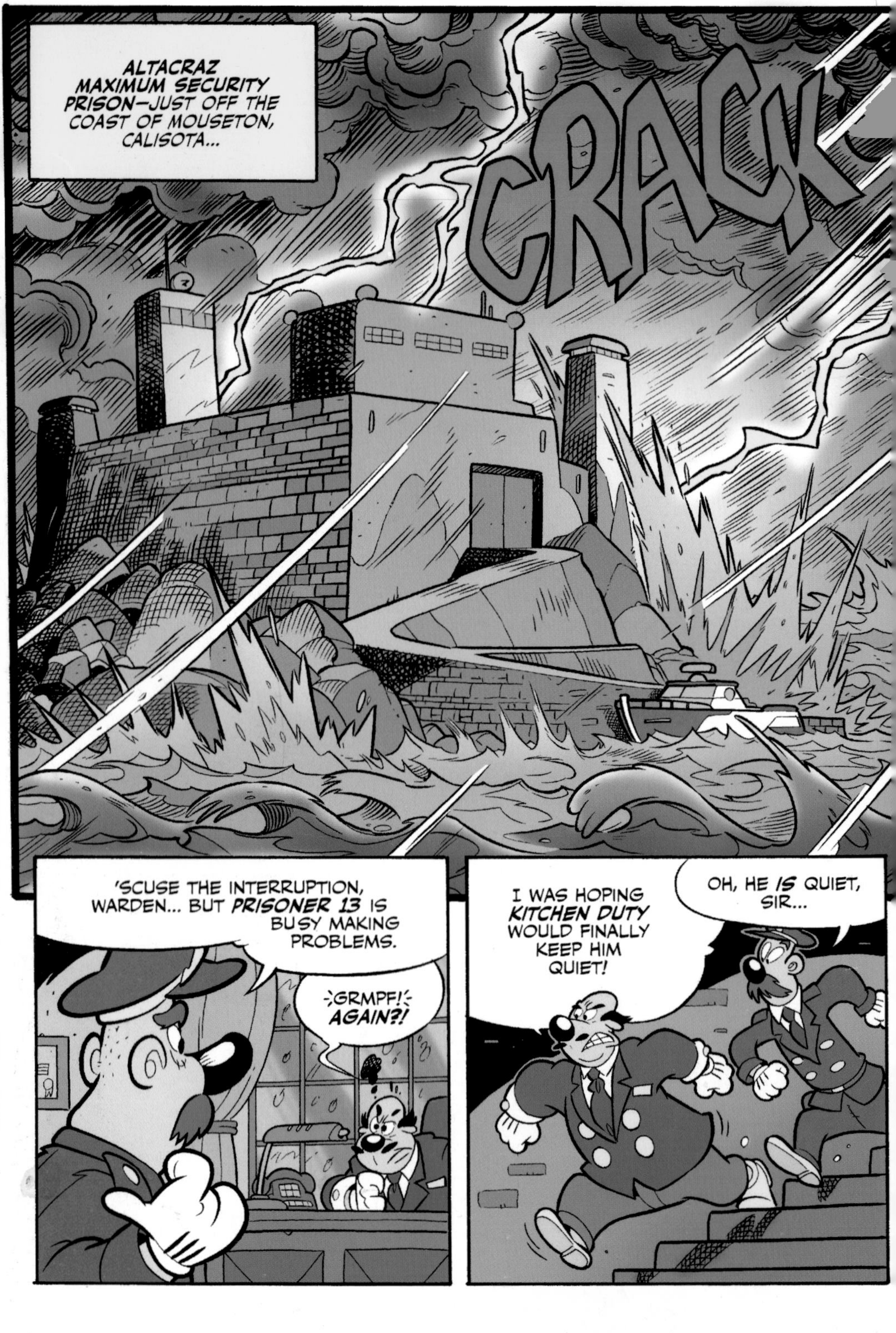
ALTACRAZ MAXIMUM SECURITY PRISON—JUST OFF THE COAST OF MOUSETON, CALISOTA...
CRACK
'SCUSE THE INTERRUPTION, WARDEN... BUT PRISONER 13 IS BUSY MAKING PROBLEMS.
GRMPF! AGAIN?!
I WAS HOPING KITCHEN DUTY WOULD FINALLY KEEP HIM QUIET!
OH, HE IS QUIET, SIR...

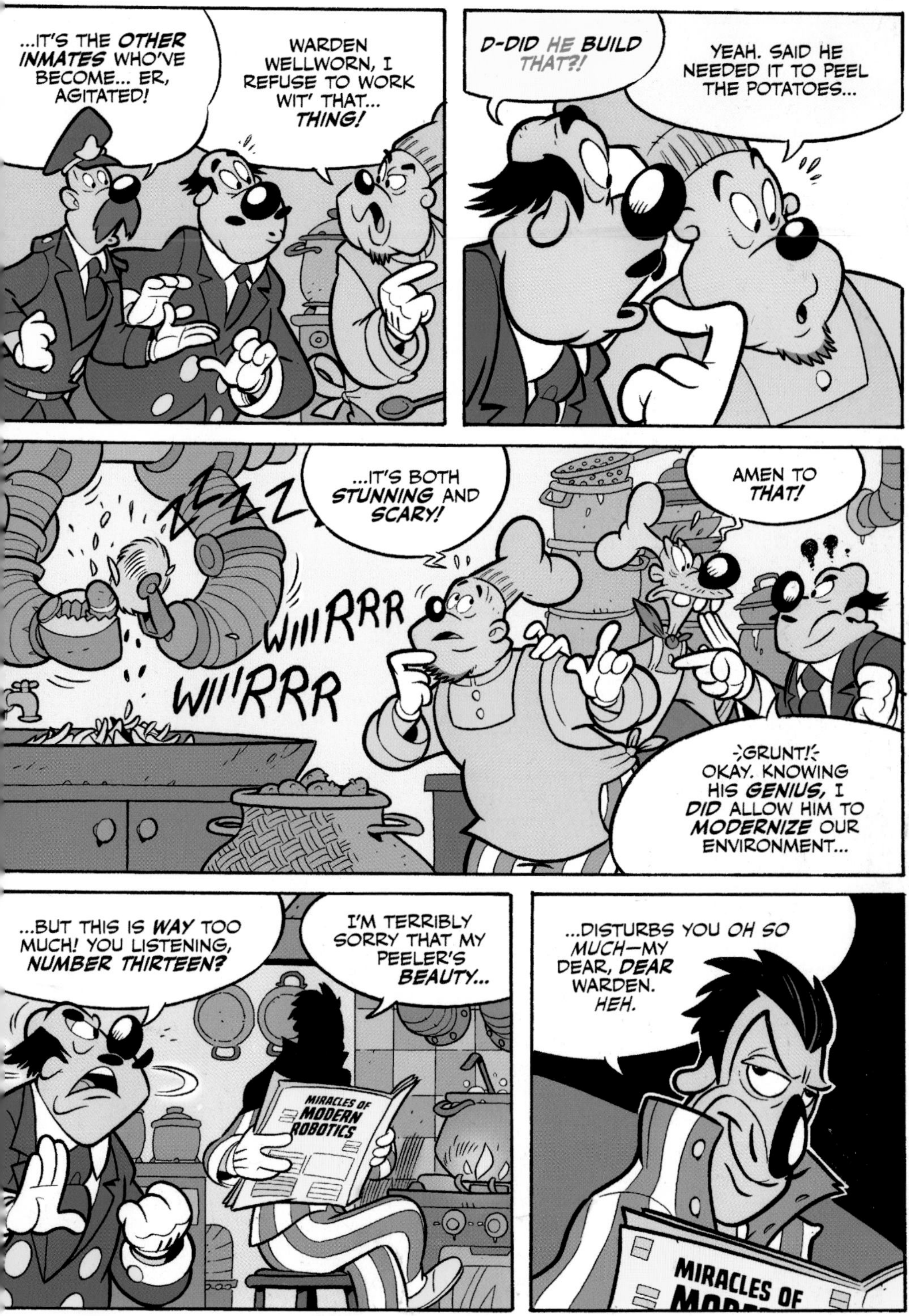
...IT'S THE OTHER INMATES WHO'VE BECOME... ER, AGITATED!
WARDEN WELLWORN, I REFUSE TO WORK WIT' THAT... THING!
D-DID HE BUILD THAT?!
YEAH. SAID HE NEEDED IT TO PEEL THE POTATOES...
...IT'S BOTH STUNNING AND SCARY!
AMEN TO THAT!
WIIIRRR
WII'RRR
-GRUNT!- OKAY. KNOWING HIS GENIUS, I DID ALLOW HIM TO MODERNIZE OUR ENVIRONMENT...
...BUT THIS IS WAY TOO MUCH! YOU LISTENING, NUMBER THIRTEEN?
I'M TERRIBLY SORRY THAT MY PEELER'S BEAUTY...
MIRACLES OF MODERN ROBOTICS
...DISTURBS YOU OH SO MUCH—MY DEAR, DEAR WARDEN. HEH.
MIRACLES OF

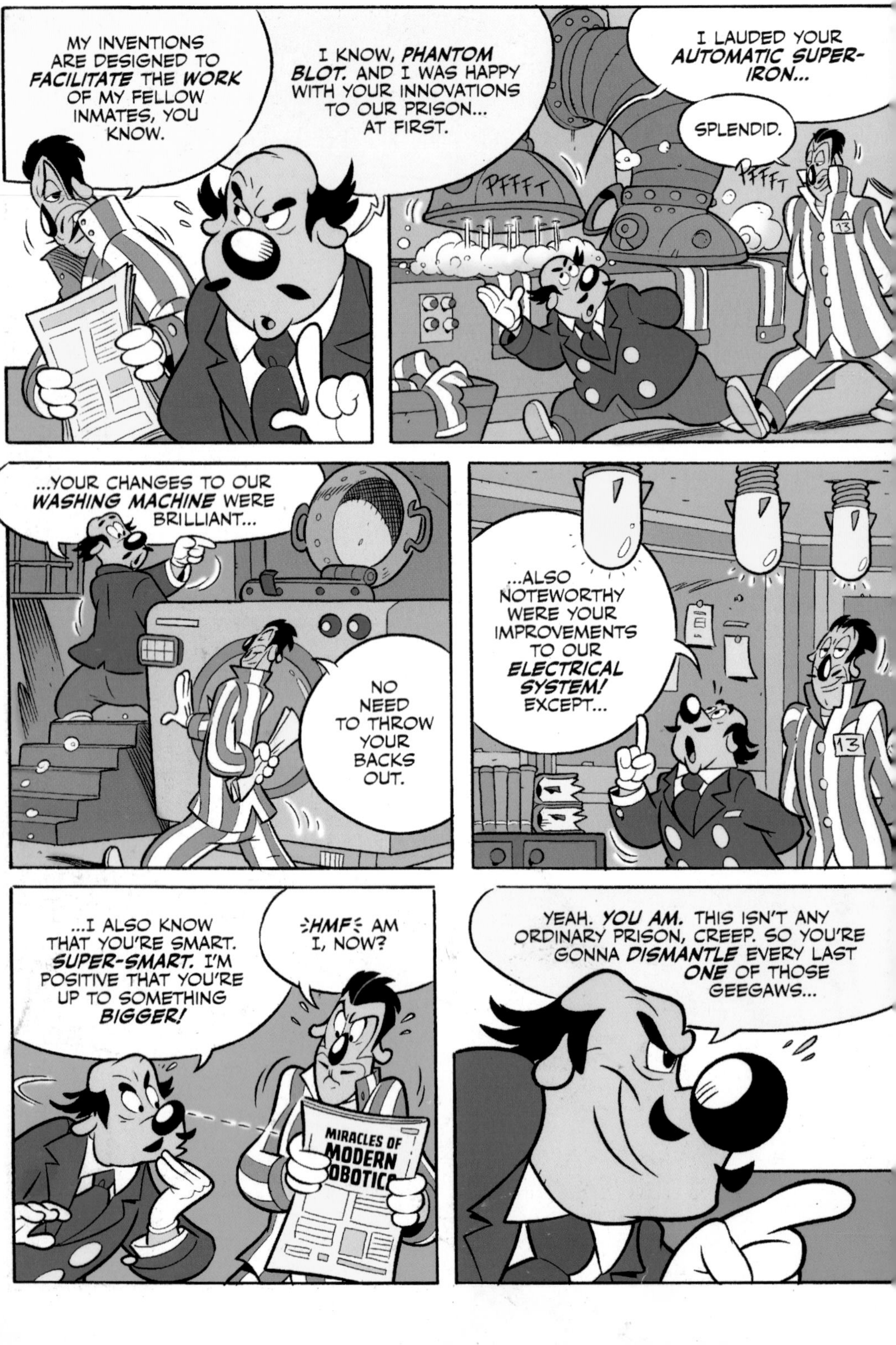
MY INVENTIONS ARE DESIGNED TO FACILITATE THE WORK OF MY FELLOW INMATES, YOU KNOW.
I KNOW, PHANTOM BLOT. AND I WAS HAPPY WITH YOUR INNOVATIONS TO OUR PRISON... AT FIRST.
I LAUDED YOUR AUTOMATIC SUPER-IRON...
SPLENDID.
PFFFT
PFFFT
13
...YOUR CHANGES TO OUR WASHING MACHINE WERE BRILLIANT...
NO NEED TO THROW YOUR BACKS OUT.
...ALSO NOTEWORTHY WERE YOUR IMPROVEMENTS TO OUR ELECTRICAL SYSTEM! EXCEPT...
13
...I ALSO KNOW THAT YOU'RE SMART. SUPER-SMART. I'M POSITIVE THAT YOU'RE UP TO SOMETHING BIGGER!
HMF AM I, NOW?
MIRACLES OF MODERN ROBOTICS
YEAH. YOU AM. THIS ISN'T ANY ORDINARY PRISON, CREEP. SO YOU'RE GONNA DISMANTLE EVERY LAST ONE OF THOSE GEEGAWS...

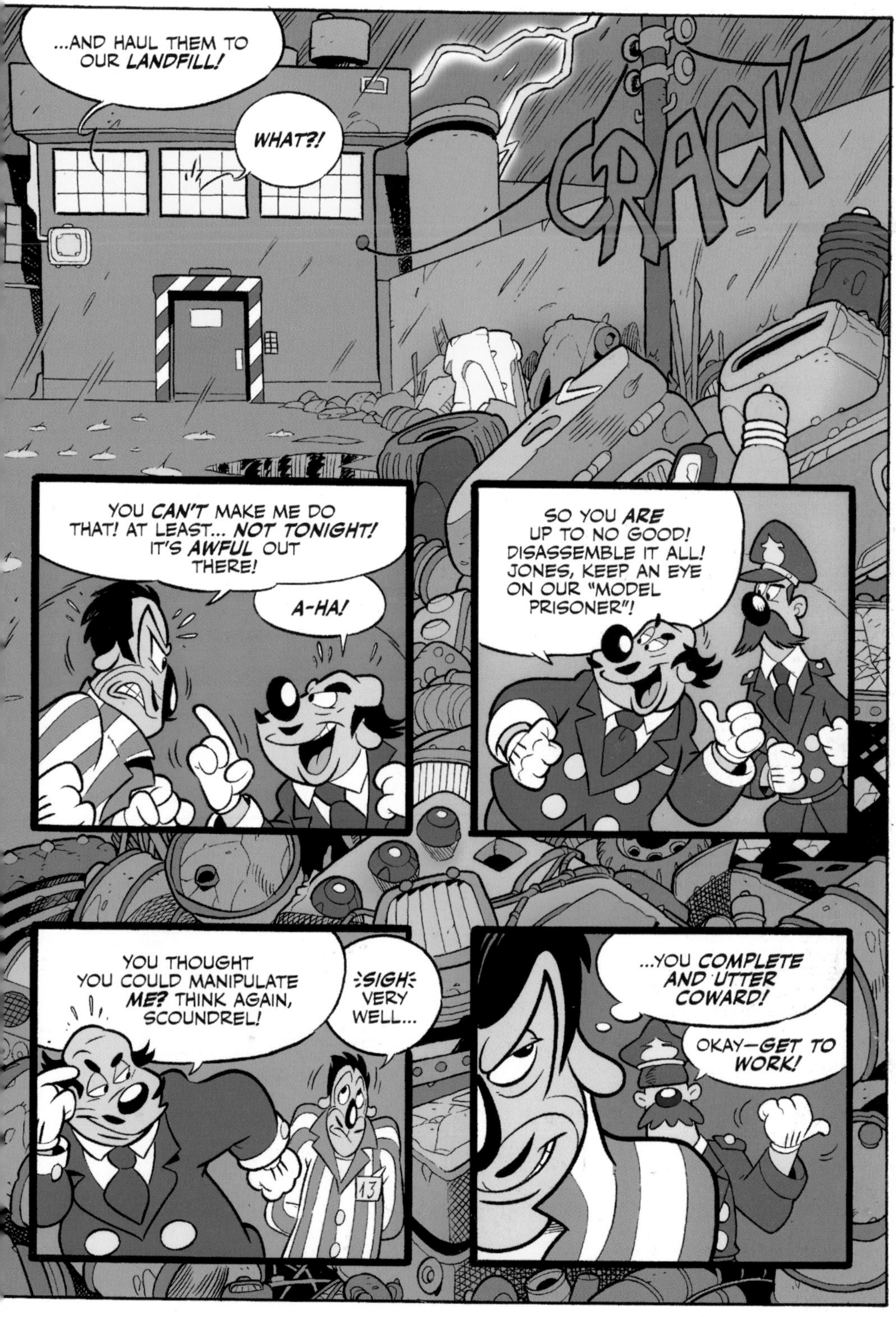

...AND HAUL THEM TO OUR LANDFILL!
WHAT?!
CRACK
YOU CAN'T MAKE ME DO THAT! AT LEAST... NOT TONIGHT! IT'S AWFUL OUT THERE!
A-HA!
SO YOU ARE UP TO NO GOOD! DISASSEMBLE IT ALL! JONES, KEEP AN EYE ON OUR "MODEL PRISONER"!
YOU THOUGHT YOU COULD MANIPULATE ME? THINK AGAIN, SCOUNDREL!
SIGH VERY WELL...
13
...YOU COMPLETE AND UTTER COWARD!
OKAY—GET TO WORK!

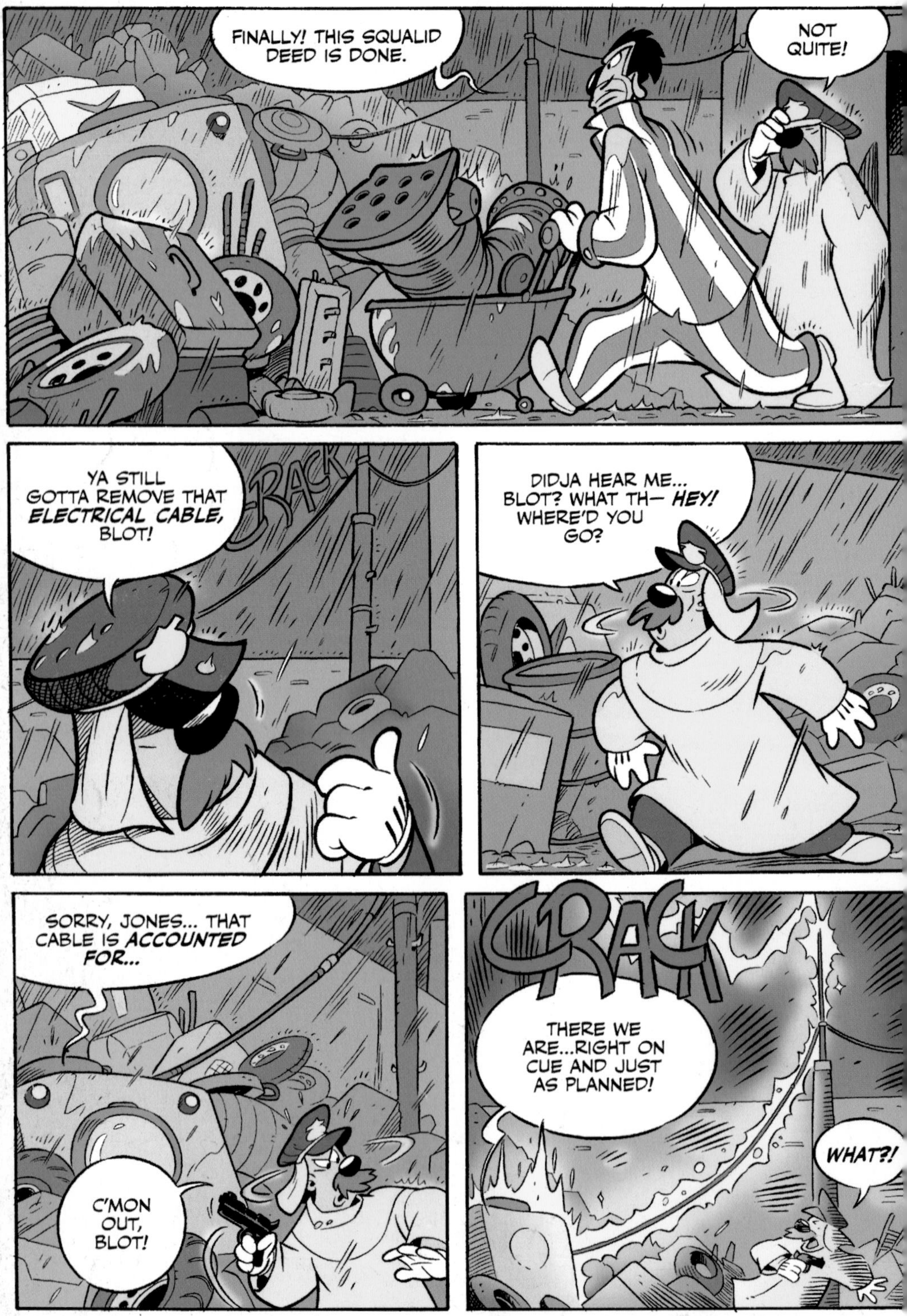

FINALLY! THIS SQUALID DEED IS DONE.
NOT QUITE!
CRACK
YA STILL GOTTA REMOVE THAT *ELECTRICAL CABLE,* BLOT!
DIDJA HEAR ME... BLOT? WHAT TH— *HEY!* WHERE'D YOU GO?
SORRY, JONES... THAT CABLE IS *ACCOUNTED FOR...*
C'MON OUT, BLOT!
CRACK
THERE WE ARE...RIGHT ON CUE AND JUST AS PLANNED!
*WHAT?!*

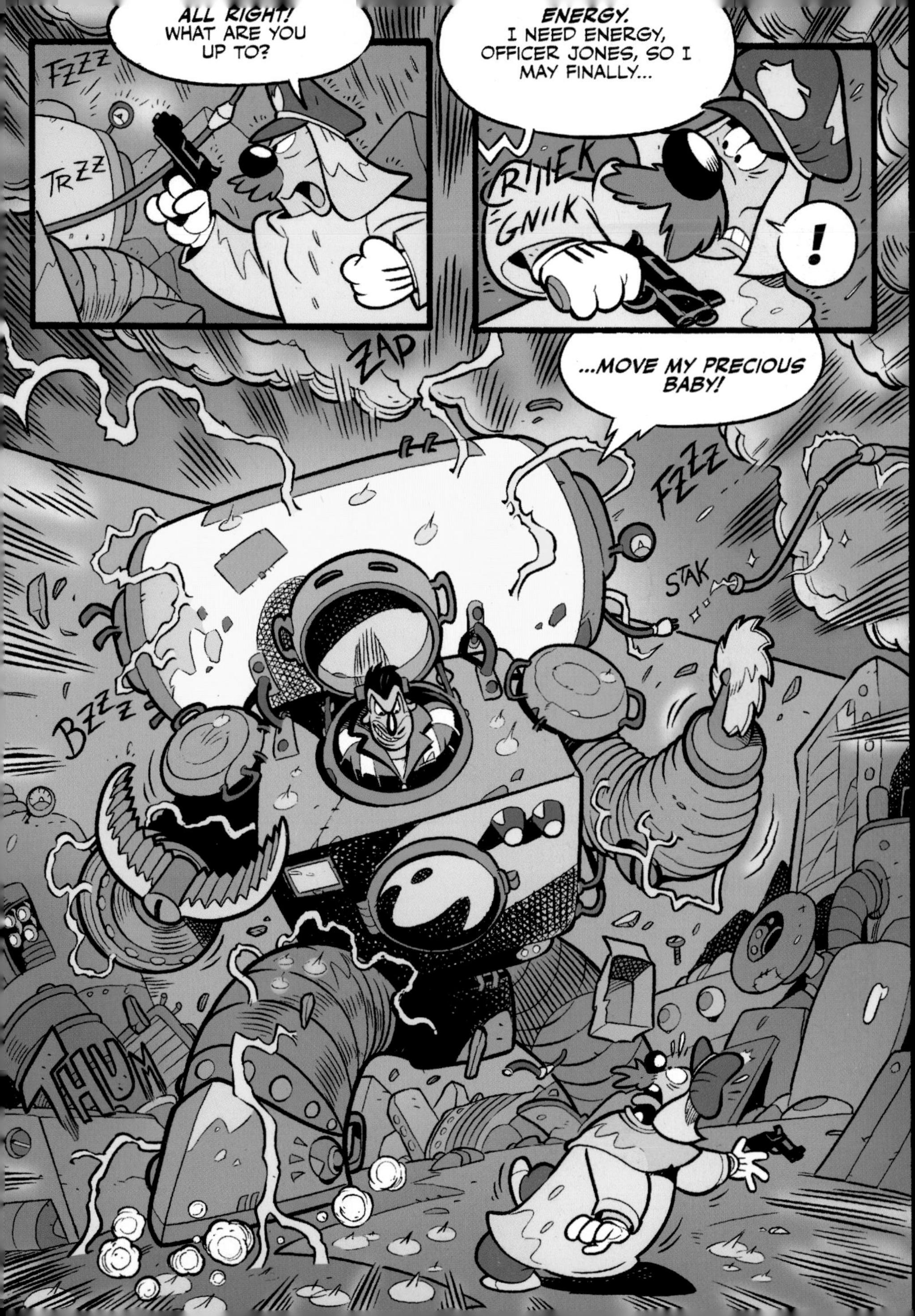
ALL RIGHT! WHAT ARE YOU UP TO?
FZZZ
TRZZ
ENERGY. I NEED ENERGY, OFFICER JONES, SO I MAY FINALLY...
CRIIIEK
GNIIK
!
ZAP
...MOVE MY PRECIOUS BABY!
FZZZ
STAK
BZZZ
THUM

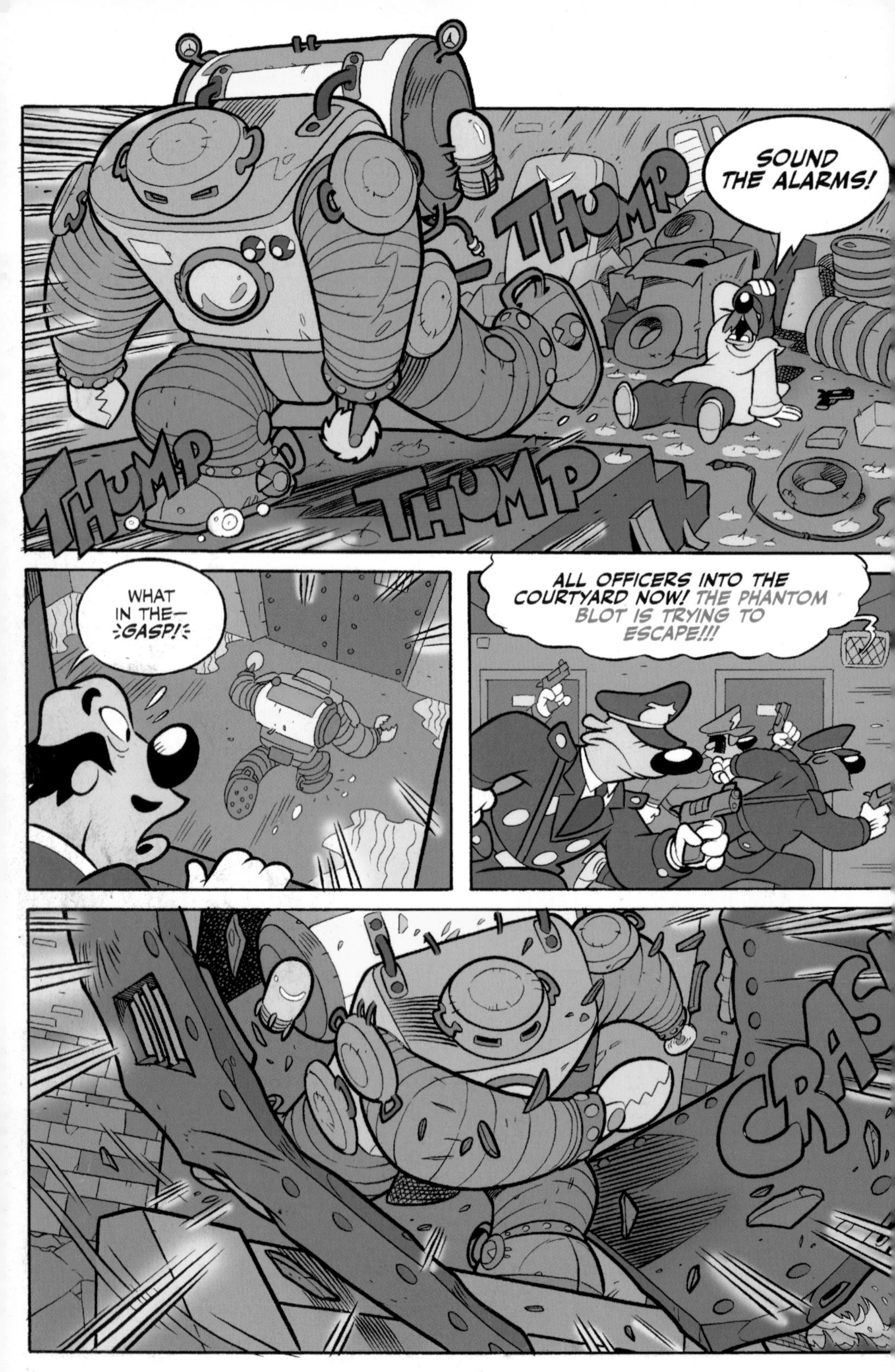
SOUND THE ALARMS!
THUMP
THUMP
THUMP
WHAT IN THE— GASP!
ALL OFFICERS INTO THE COURTYARD NOW! THE PHANTOM BLOT IS TRYING TO ESCAPE!!!
CRAS

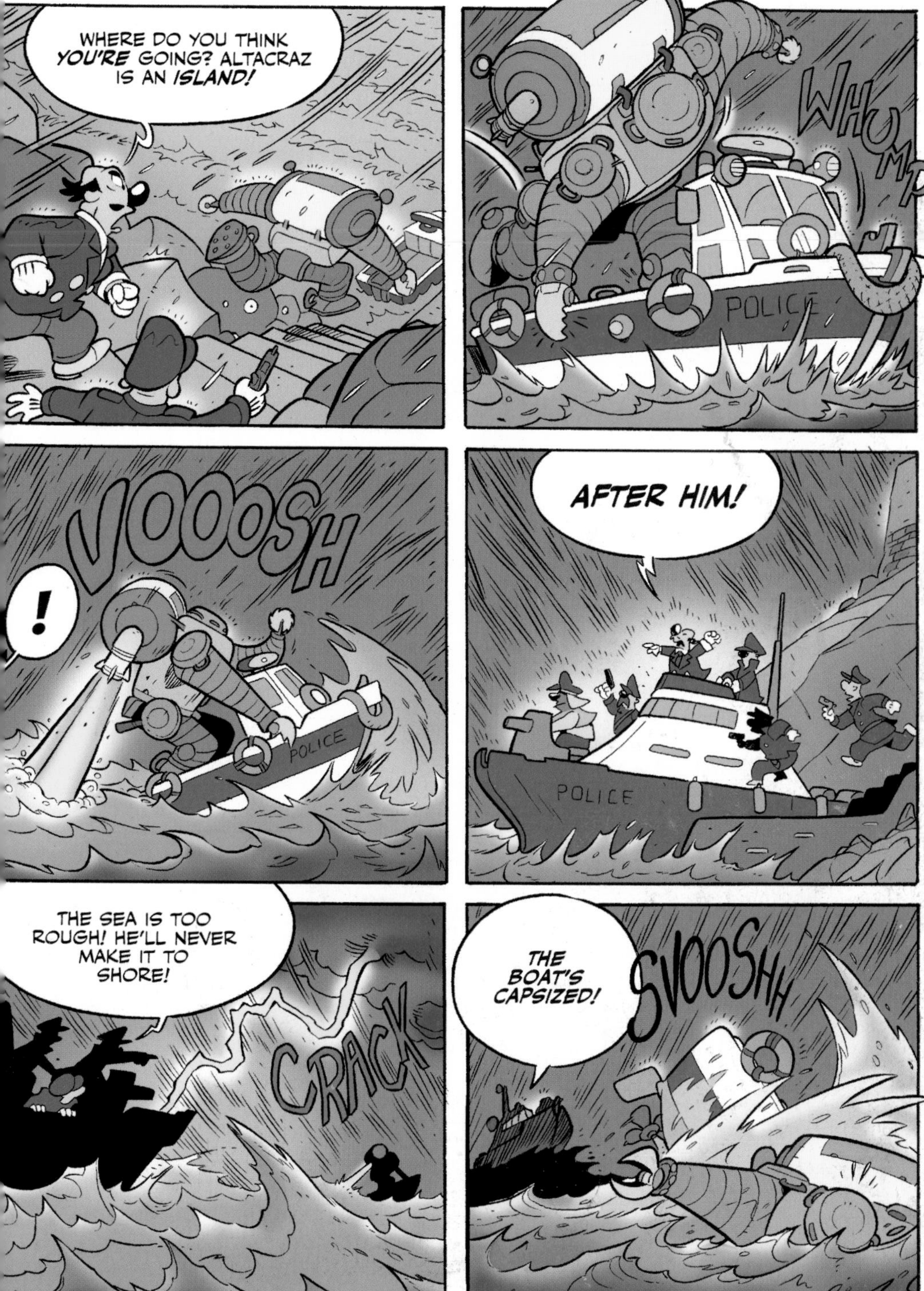
WHERE DO YOU THINK YOU'RE GOING? ALTACRAZ IS AN ISLAND!
WHUMP
VOOOSH
!
AFTER HIM!
POLICE
THE SEA IS TOO ROUGH! HE'LL NEVER MAKE IT TO SHORE!
CRACK
THE BOAT'S CAPSIZED!
SVOOSHH

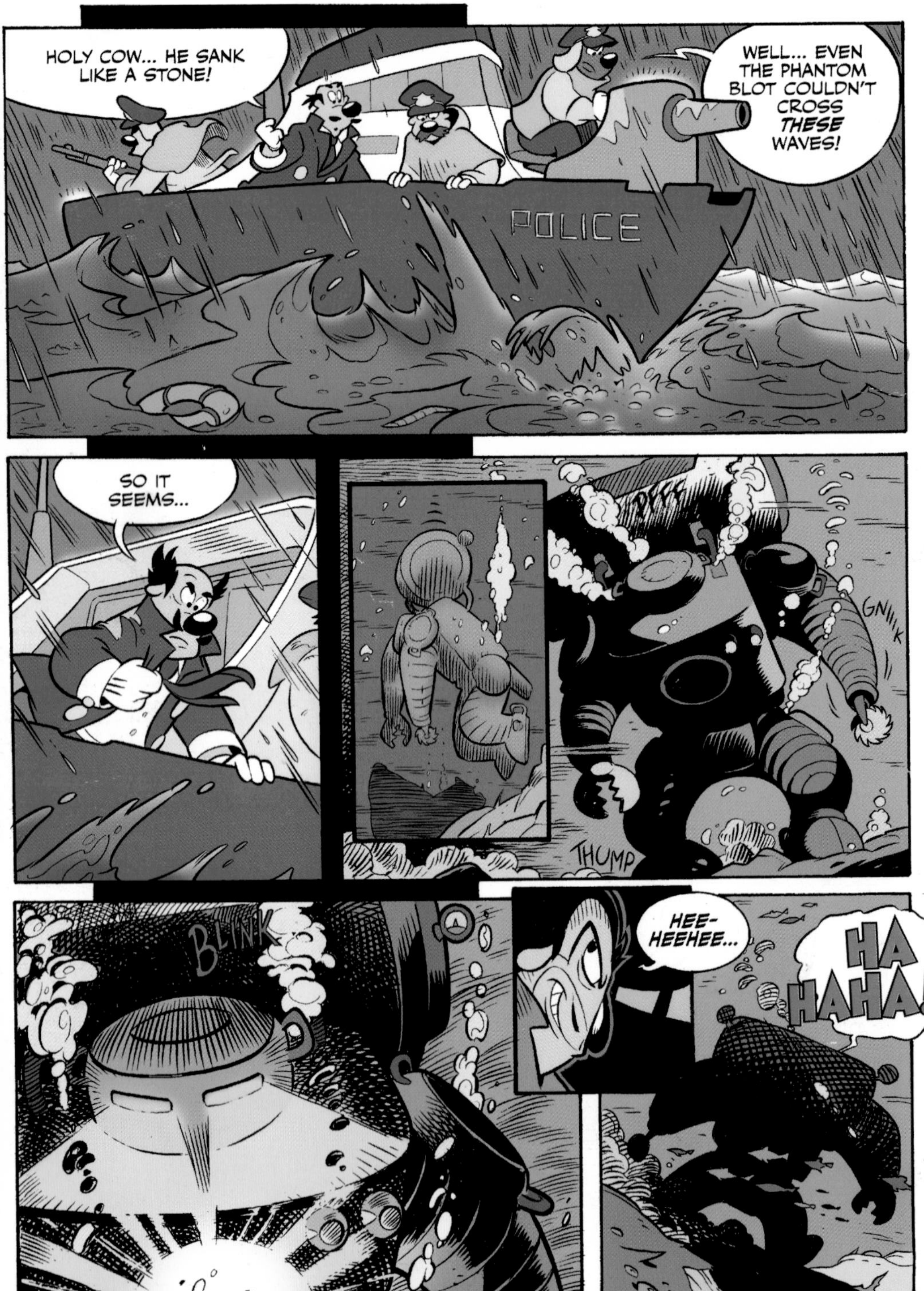
HOLY COW... HE SANK LIKE A STONE!
WELL... EVEN THE PHANTOM BLOT COULDN'T CROSS *THESE* WAVES!
POLICE
SO IT SEEMS...
GNIIIK
THUMP
BLINK
HEE-HEEHEE...
HA HAHA!

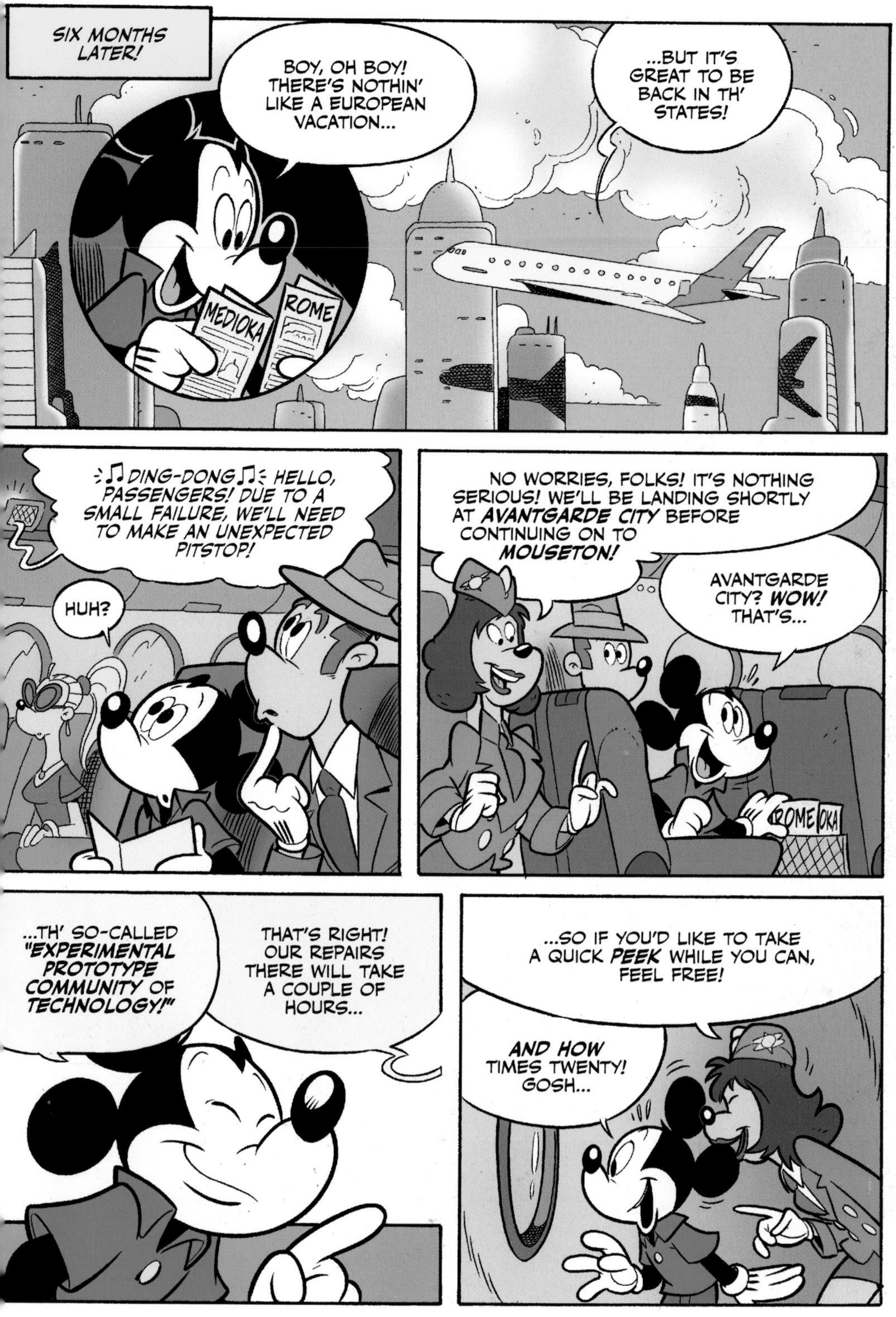
SIX MONTHS LATER!
BOY, OH BOY! THERE'S NOTHIN' LIKE A EUROPEAN VACATION...
...BUT IT'S GREAT TO BE BACK IN TH' STATES!
MEDIOKA
ROME
♫ DING-DONG ♫ HELLO, PASSENGERS! DUE TO A SMALL FAILURE, WE'LL NEED TO MAKE AN UNEXPECTED PITSTOP!
HUH?
NO WORRIES, FOLKS! IT'S NOTHING SERIOUS! WE'LL BE LANDING SHORTLY AT AVANTGARDE CITY BEFORE CONTINUING ON TO MOUSETON!
AVANTGARDE CITY? WOW! THAT'S...
ROME
OKA
...TH' SO-CALLED "EXPERIMENTAL PROTOTYPE COMMUNITY OF TECHNOLOGY!"
THAT'S RIGHT! OUR REPAIRS THERE WILL TAKE A COUPLE OF HOURS...
...SO IF YOU'D LIKE TO TAKE A QUICK PEEK WHILE YOU CAN, FEEL FREE!
AND HOW TIMES TWENTY! GOSH...

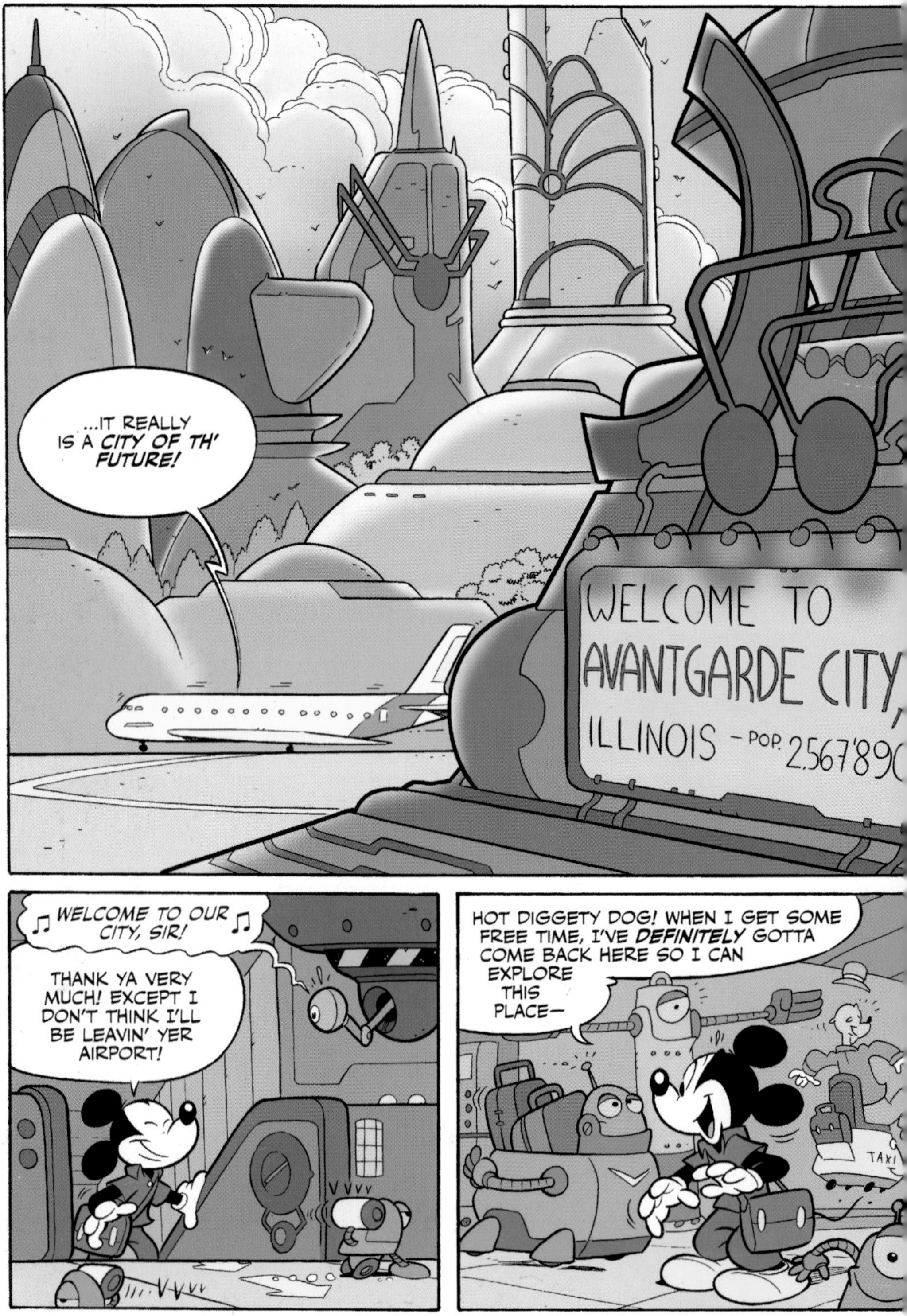
...IT REALLY IS A *CITY OF TH' FUTURE!*
WELCOME TO AVANTGARDE CITY, ILLINOIS - POP. 2.567'890
♫ *WELCOME TO OUR CITY, SIR!* ♫
THANK YA VERY MUCH! EXCEPT I DON'T THINK I'LL BE LEAVIN' YER AIRPORT!
HOT DIGGETY DOG! WHEN I GET SOME FREE TIME, I'VE ***DEFINITELY*** GOTTA COME BACK HERE SO I CAN EXPLORE THIS PLACE—
TAXI

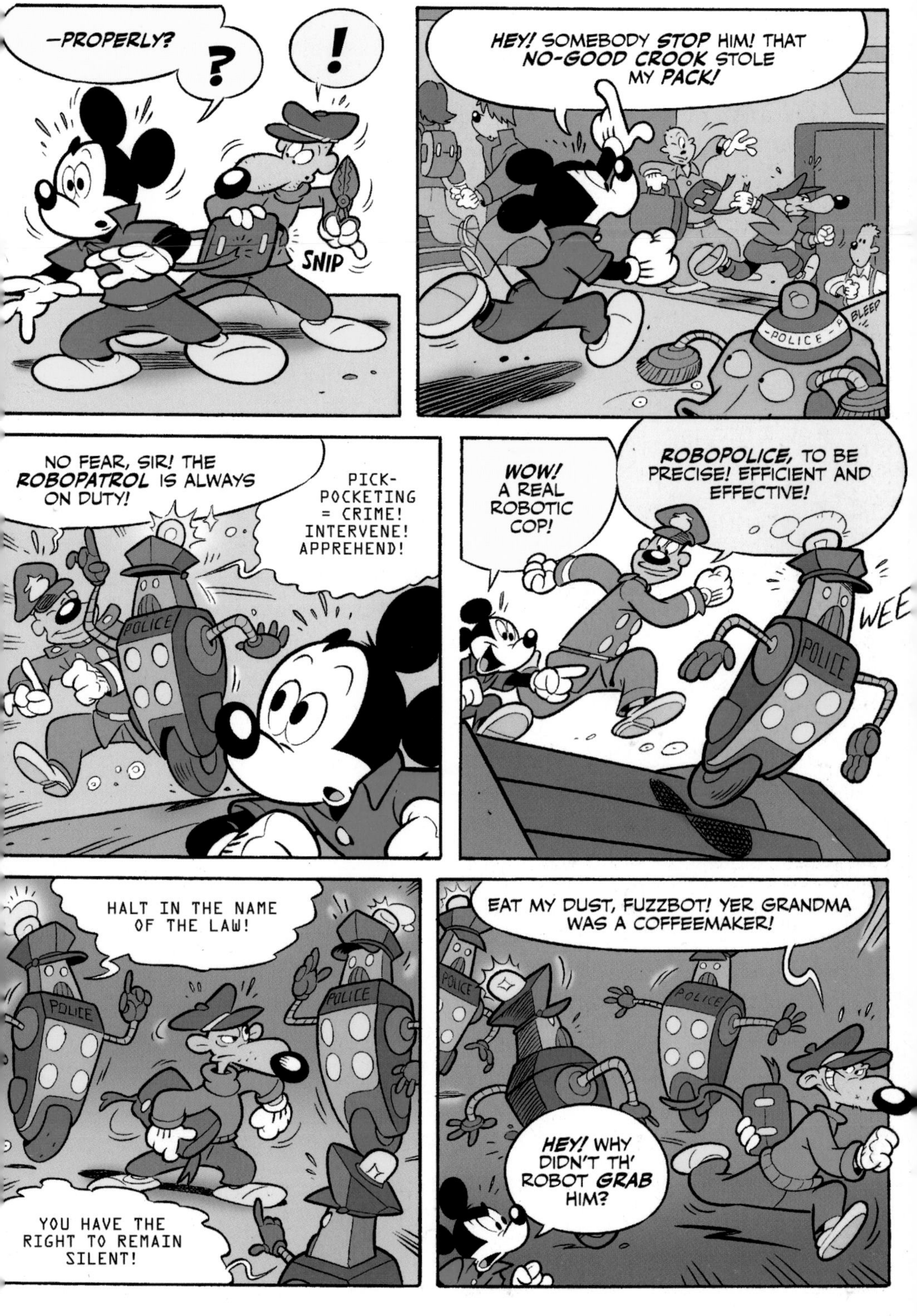

—PROPERLY?
?
!
SNIP
HEY! SOMEBODY STOP HIM! THAT NO-GOOD CROOK STOLE MY PACK!
POLICE
BLEEP
NO FEAR, SIR! THE ROBOPATROL IS ALWAYS ON DUTY!
PICK-POCKETING = CRIME! INTERVENE! APPREHEND!
POLICE
WOW! A REAL ROBOTIC COP!
ROBOPOLICE, TO BE PRECISE! EFFICIENT AND EFFECTIVE!
WEE
POLICE
HALT IN THE NAME OF THE LAW!
POLICE
POLICE
YOU HAVE THE RIGHT TO REMAIN SILENT!
EAT MY DUST, FUZZBOT! YER GRANDMA WAS A COFFEEMAKER!
POLICE
POLICE
HEY! WHY DIDN'T TH' ROBOT GRAB HIM?

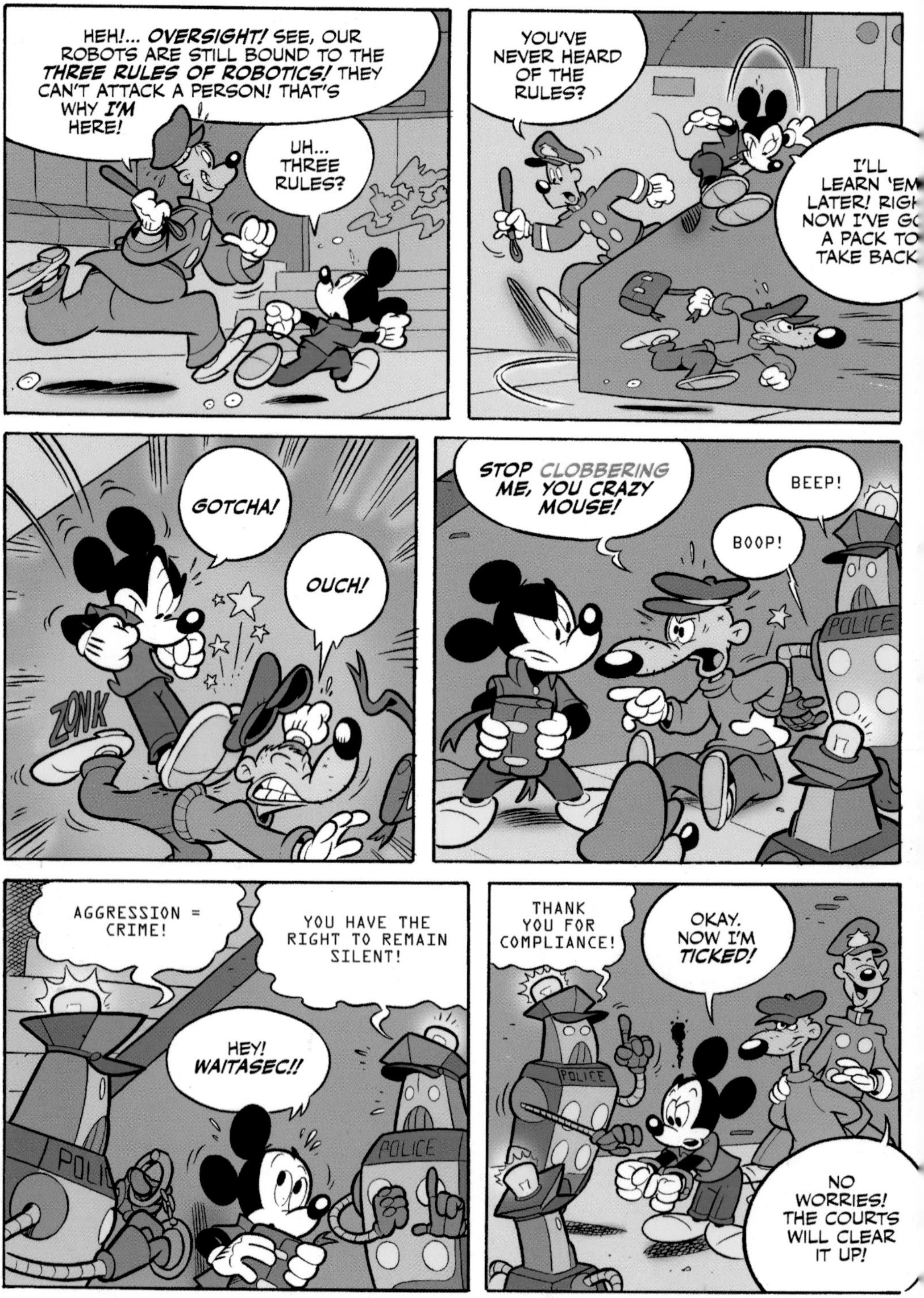
HEH!... OVERSIGHT! SEE, OUR ROBOTS ARE STILL BOUND TO THE THREE RULES OF ROBOTICS! THEY CAN'T ATTACK A PERSON! THAT'S WHY I'M HERE!
UH... THREE RULES?
YOU'VE NEVER HEARD OF THE RULES?
I'LL LEARN 'EM LATER! RIGH NOW I'VE GO A PACK TO TAKE BACK
GOTCHA!
OUCH!
ZONK
STOP CLOBBERING ME, YOU CRAZY MOUSE!
BEEP!
BOOP!
POLICE
AGGRESSION = CRIME!
YOU HAVE THE RIGHT TO REMAIN SILENT!
HEY! WAITASEC!!
POLICE
THANK YOU FOR COMPLIANCE!
OKAY. NOW I'M TICKED!
POLICE
NO WORRIES! THE COURTS WILL CLEAR IT UP!

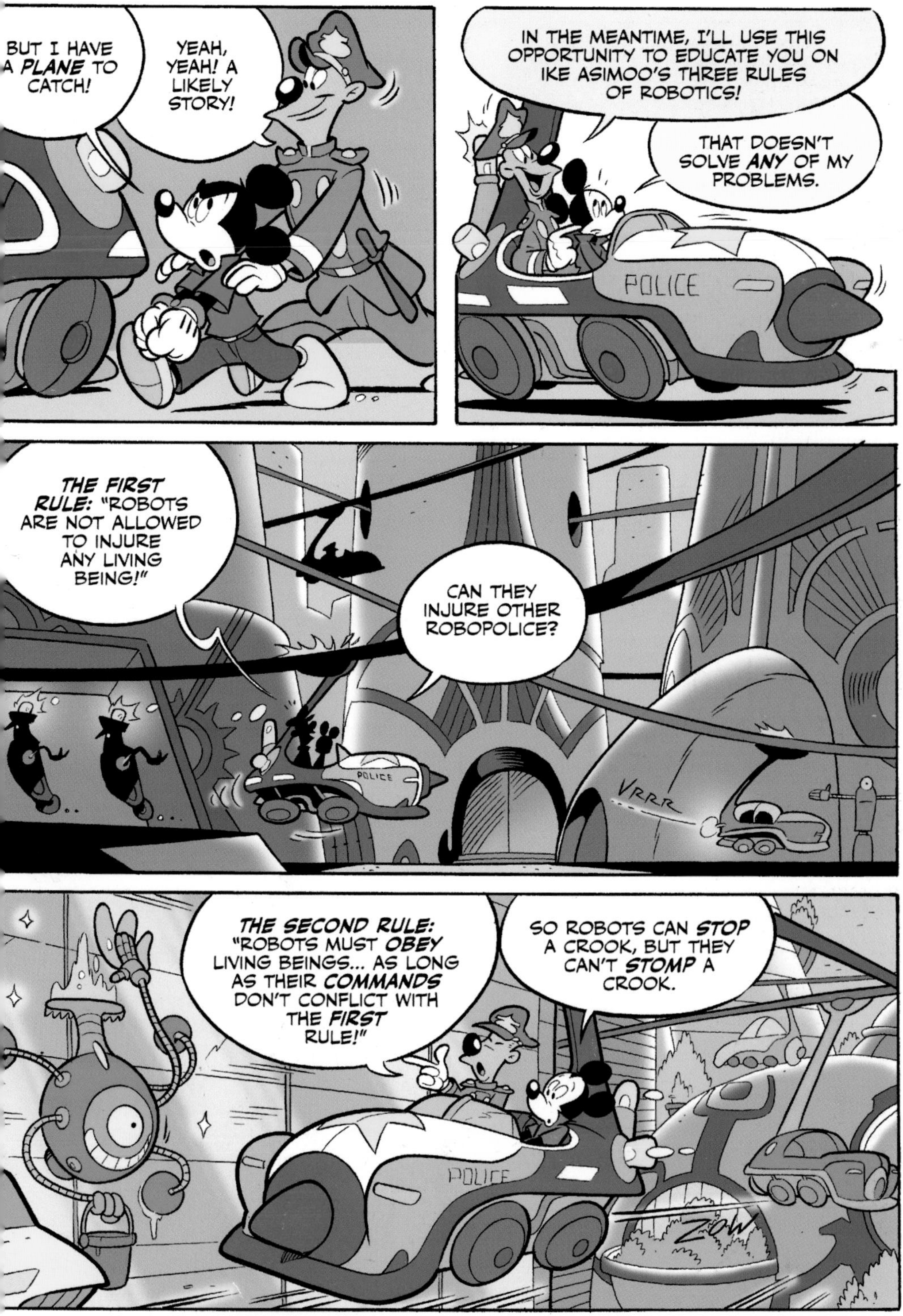
BUT I HAVE A PLANE TO CATCH!
YEAH, YEAH! A LIKELY STORY!
IN THE MEANTIME, I'LL USE THIS OPPORTUNITY TO EDUCATE YOU ON IKE ASIMOO'S THREE RULES OF ROBOTICS!
THAT DOESN'T SOLVE ANY OF MY PROBLEMS.
POLICE
THE FIRST RULE: "ROBOTS ARE NOT ALLOWED TO INJURE ANY LIVING BEING!"
CAN THEY INJURE OTHER ROBOPOLICE?
POLICE
VRRR
THE SECOND RULE: "ROBOTS MUST OBEY LIVING BEINGS... AS LONG AS THEIR COMMANDS DON'T CONFLICT WITH THE FIRST RULE!"
SO ROBOTS CAN STOP A CROOK, BUT THEY CAN'T STOMP A CROOK.
POLICE
ZOW

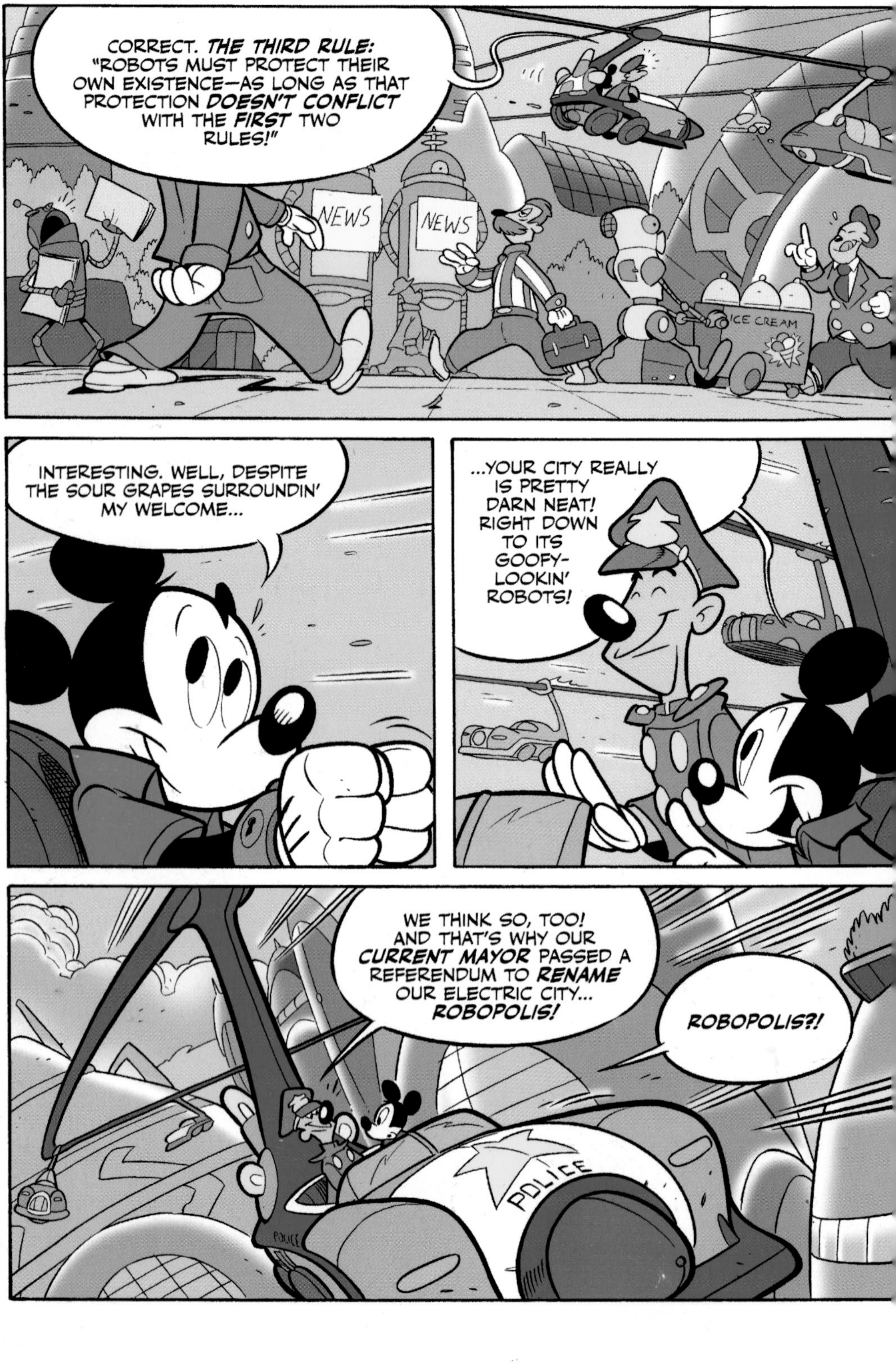
CORRECT. THE THIRD RULE: "ROBOTS MUST PROTECT THEIR OWN EXISTENCE—AS LONG AS THAT PROTECTION DOESN'T CONFLICT WITH THE FIRST TWO RULES!"
NEWS
NEWS
ICE CREAM
INTERESTING. WELL, DESPITE THE SOUR GRAPES SURROUNDIN' MY WELCOME...
...YOUR CITY REALLY IS PRETTY DARN NEAT! RIGHT DOWN TO ITS GOOFY-LOOKIN' ROBOTS!
WE THINK SO, TOO! AND THAT'S WHY OUR CURRENT MAYOR PASSED A REFERENDUM TO RENAME OUR ELECTRIC CITY... ROBOPOLIS!
ROBOPOLIS?!
POLICE
POLICE

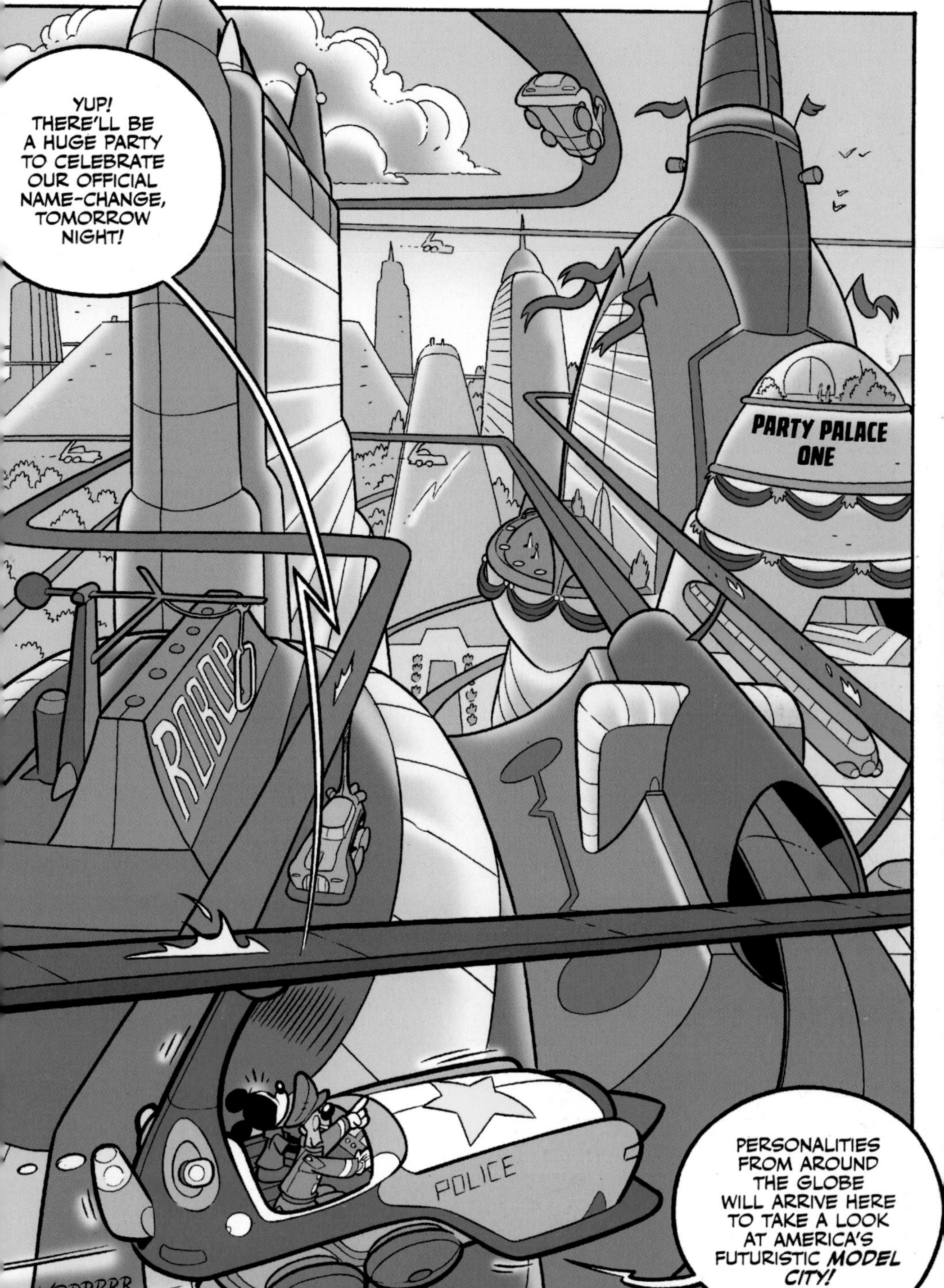
YUP! THERE'LL BE A HUGE PARTY TO CELEBRATE OUR OFFICIAL NAME-CHANGE, TOMORROW NIGHT!
PARTY PALACE ONE
ROBOPO
POLICE
PERSONALITIES FROM AROUND THE GLOBE WILL ARRIVE HERE TO TAKE A LOOK AT AMERICA'S FUTURISTIC *MODEL CITY!*
VRRRRRR

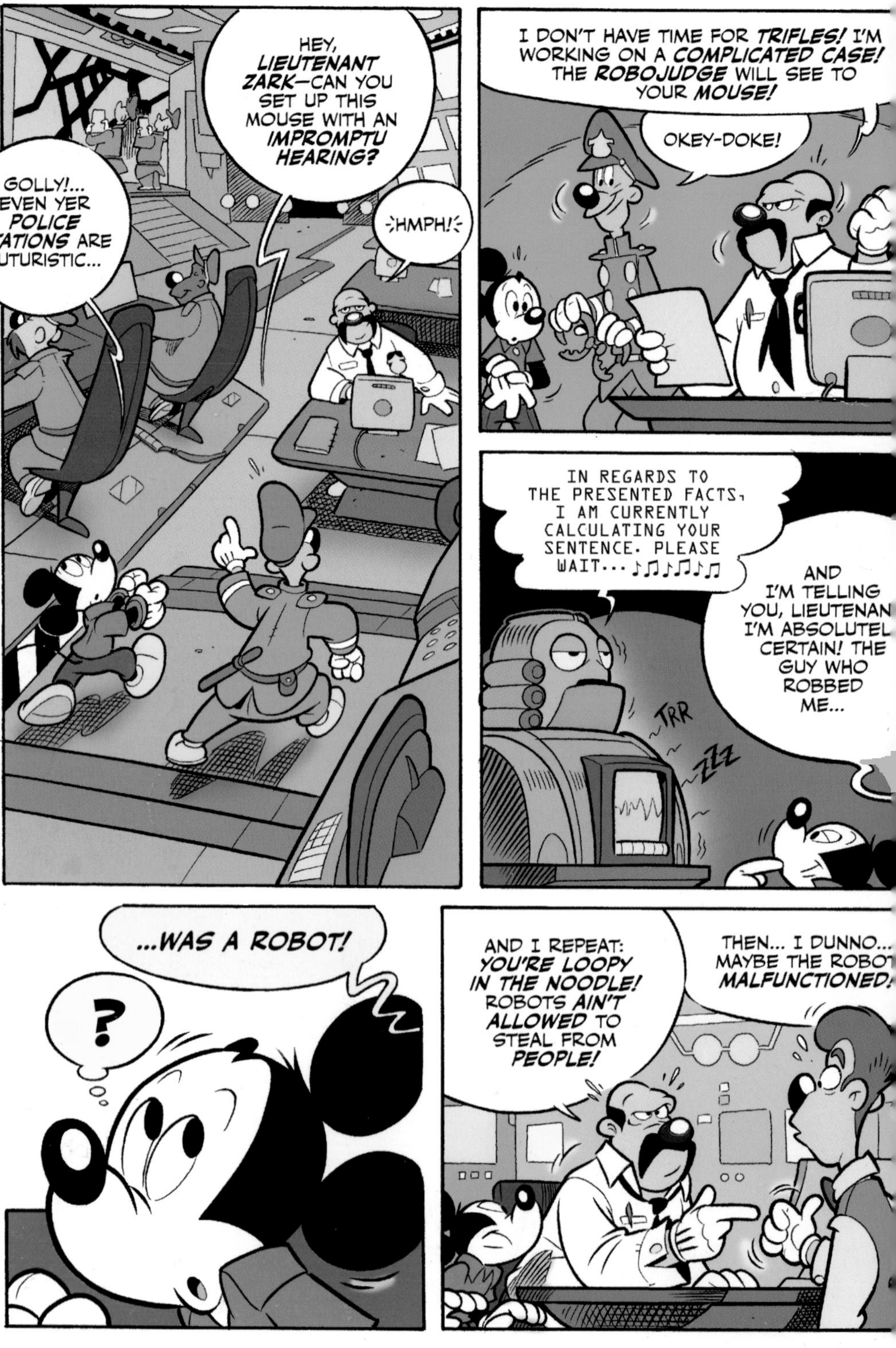
HEY, LIEUTENANT ZARK—CAN YOU SET UP THIS MOUSE WITH AN IMPROMPTU HEARING?
GOLLY!... EVEN YER POLICE STATIONS ARE FUTURISTIC...
HMPH!
I DON'T HAVE TIME FOR TRIFLES! I'M WORKING ON A COMPLICATED CASE! THE ROBOJUDGE WILL SEE TO YOUR MOUSE!
OKEY-DOKE!
IN REGARDS TO THE PRESENTED FACTS, I AM CURRENTLY CALCULATING YOUR SENTENCE. PLEASE WAIT... ♪♫♪♫♪♫
AND I'M TELLING YOU, LIEUTENAN I'M ABSOLUTEL CERTAIN! THE GUY WHO ROBBED ME...
TRR
ZZZ
...WAS A ROBOT!
?
AND I REPEAT: YOU'RE LOOPY IN THE NOODLE! ROBOTS AIN'T ALLOWED TO STEAL FROM PEOPLE!
THEN... I DUNNO... MAYBE THE ROBOT MALFUNCTIONED!

IMPOSSIBLE! THE ROBOTS IN AVANTGARDE CITY ARE WORKING JUST FINE!

ER, UH... 'SCUSE ME, LIEUTENANT!

YER ROBOJUDGE SEEMS TO BE... ON TH' FRITZ! IT CAN'T SEEM TO DECIDE WHETHER I'M GUILTY OR INNOCENT!

YES? NO? MAYBE SO?!

SORRY TO BUTT IN, BUT IT LOOKS LIKE YER ROBOTS AREN'T ENTIRELY FOOLPROOF!

HEH. SO IT SEEMS WE HAVE A WISE GUY. GOODY. WHAT'S YOUR NAME?

MICKEY MOUSE... FROM MOUSETON, CALISOTA!

EH. IT DON'T MATTER. NONE O' THIS MATTERS! I'VE HEARD O' YOU! YA SOLVE CRIMES, SAVE THE WORLD... JUNK LIKE THAT.

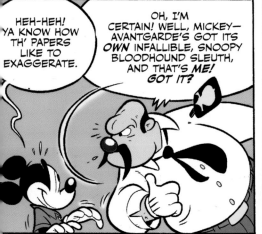

HEH-HEH! YA KNOW HOW TH' PAPERS LIKE TO EXAGGERATE.

OH, I'M CERTAIN! WELL, MICKEY— AVANTGARDE'S GOT ITS OWN INFALLIBLE, SNOOPY BLOODHOUND SLEUTH, AND THAT'S ME! GOT IT?

AND IF I SAY THAT ROBOTS DON'T GO AROUND ROBBIN' FOLKS, THEN ROBOTS DON'T GO AROUND ROBBIN'—

ER... HEY, LT. ZARK...

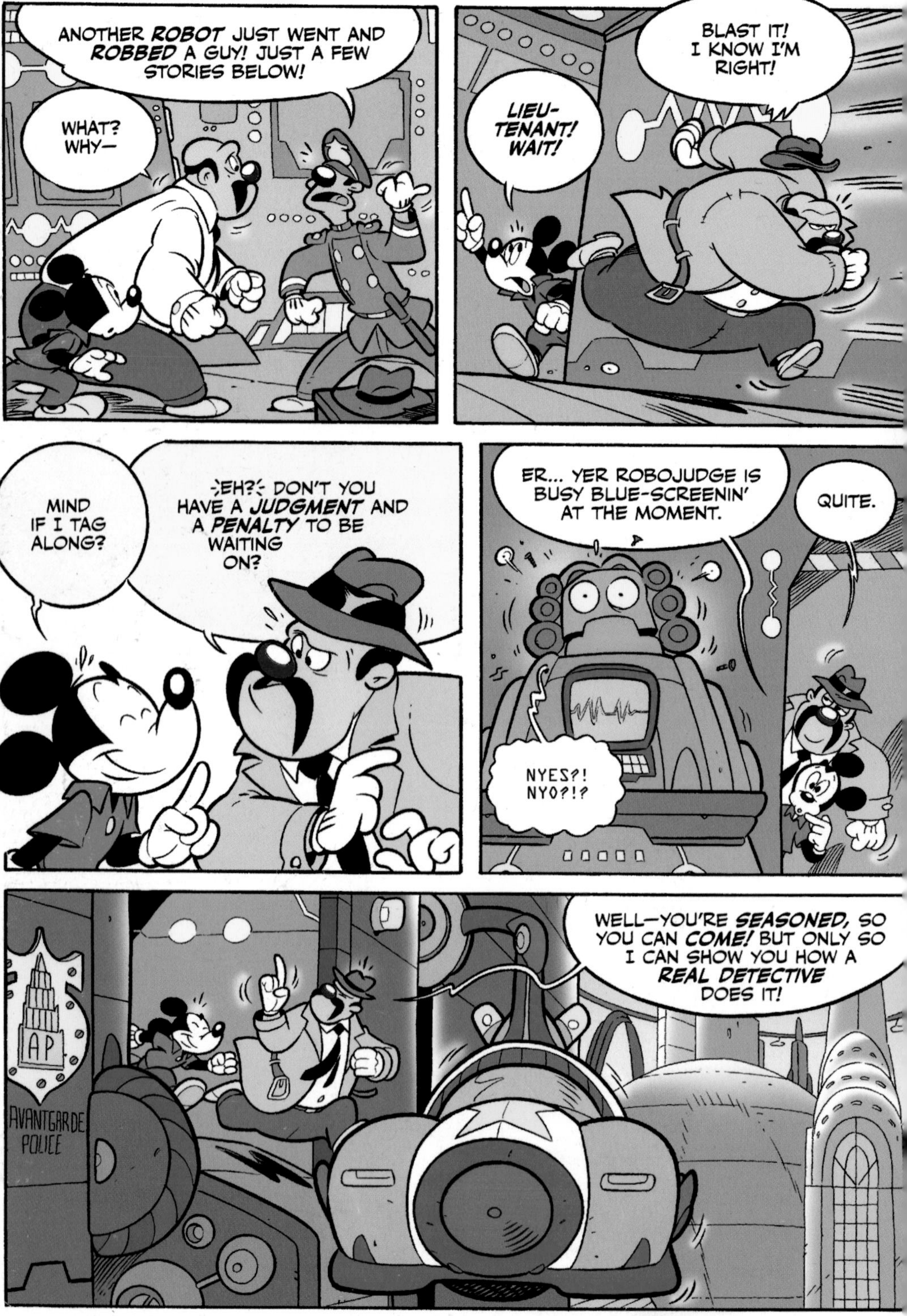
ANOTHER ROBOT JUST WENT AND ROBBED A GUY! JUST A FEW STORIES BELOW!
WHAT? WHY—
BLAST IT! I KNOW I'M RIGHT!
LIEU-TENANT! WAIT!
MIND IF I TAG ALONG?
EH? DON'T YOU HAVE A JUDGMENT AND A PENALTY TO BE WAITING ON?
ER... YER ROBOJUDGE IS BUSY BLUE-SCREENIN' AT THE MOMENT.
QUITE.
NYES?! NYO?!?
AP
AVANTGARDE POLICE
WELL—YOU'RE SEASONED, SO YOU CAN COME! BUT ONLY SO I CAN SHOW YOU HOW A REAL DETECTIVE DOES IT!

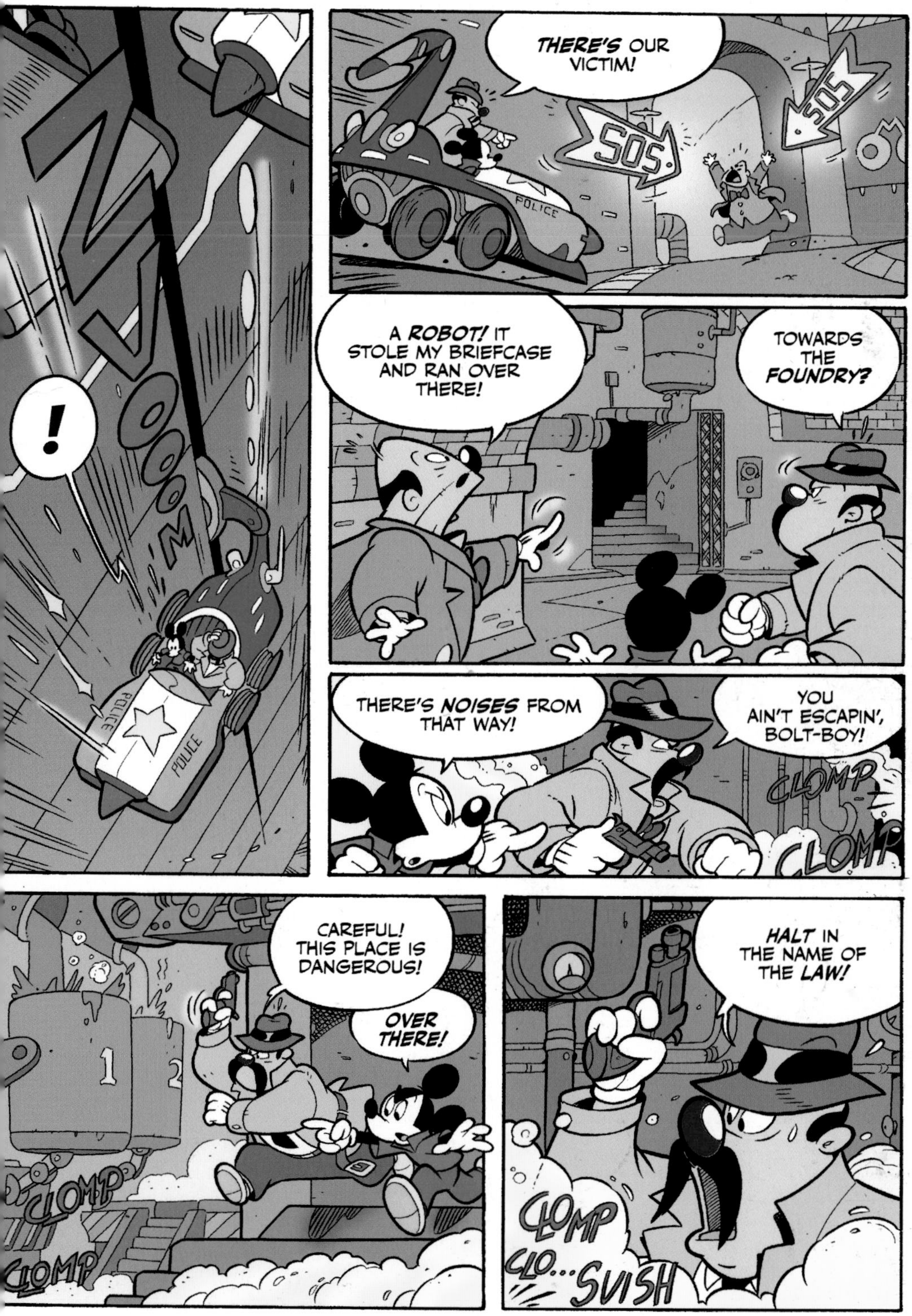

VROOOOM
!
THERE'S OUR VICTIM!
SOS
SOS
POLICE
A ROBOT! IT STOLE MY BRIEFCASE AND RAN OVER THERE!
TOWARDS THE FOUNDRY?
THERE'S NOISES FROM THAT WAY!
YOU AIN'T ESCAPIN', BOLT-BOY!
CLOMP
CLOMP
CAREFUL! THIS PLACE IS DANGEROUS!
OVER THERE!
CLOMP
CLOMP
HALT IN THE NAME OF THE LAW!
CLOMP
CLO... SVISH

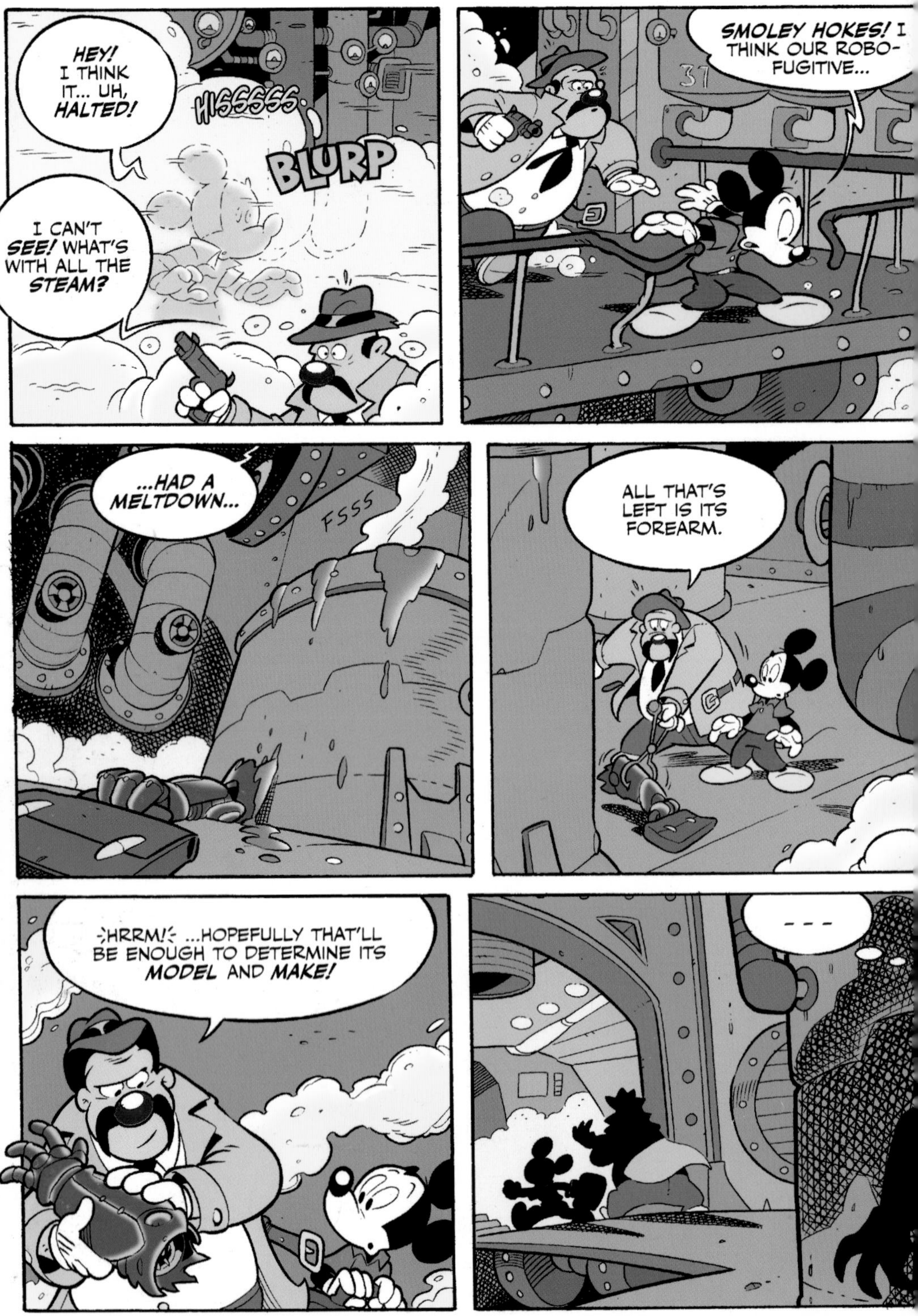
HEY! I THINK IT... UH, HALTED!
HISSSSS
BLURP
I CAN'T SEE! WHAT'S WITH ALL THE STEAM?
SMOLEY HOKES! I THINK OUR ROBO-FUGITIVE...
31
...HAD A MELTDOWN...
FSSS
ALL THAT'S LEFT IS ITS FOREARM.
HRRM! ...HOPEFULLY THAT'LL BE ENOUGH TO DETERMINE ITS MODEL AND MAKE!
- - -

THANKFULLY, IDENTIFICATION WON'T BE DIFFICULT: AVANTGARDE ONLY HAS *TWO* ROBOT PRODUCTION FACILITIES!

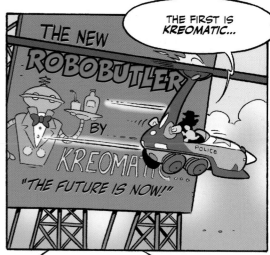

THE FIRST IS *KREOMATIC...*

THE NEW ROBOBUTLER BY KREOMATIC

"THE FUTURE IS NOW!"

...AND THE SECOND IS *GASPARD ROBOTICS...*

GASPARD ROBOTICS INC.

MEANIN' *ONE* OF THESE JOINTS IS RELEASIN' ROBOTS THAT DON'T OBEY ASIMOO'S THREE RULES?

THAT'S WHAT I AIM TO FIND OUT!

PEDESTRIAN ENTRANCE

POLICE

VRRRR

GASPARD ROBOTICS ENTRANCE

I'M *100% CERTAIN,* SIR! THIS LIMB *DOESN'T BELONG* TO ANY ONE OF OUR CURRENT *OR* PREVIOUS MODELS!

SO YOU *SAY...*

*SO I KNOW!* LOOK... WE'RE THE FOLKS WHO *BUILD* YOUR DAFFY *E-POLICE!* ENOUGH *BACKTALK!*

POLICE

E-POL THERE'S A NEW COP IN TOWN!

BY GASPER ROBOT

:OOP!:

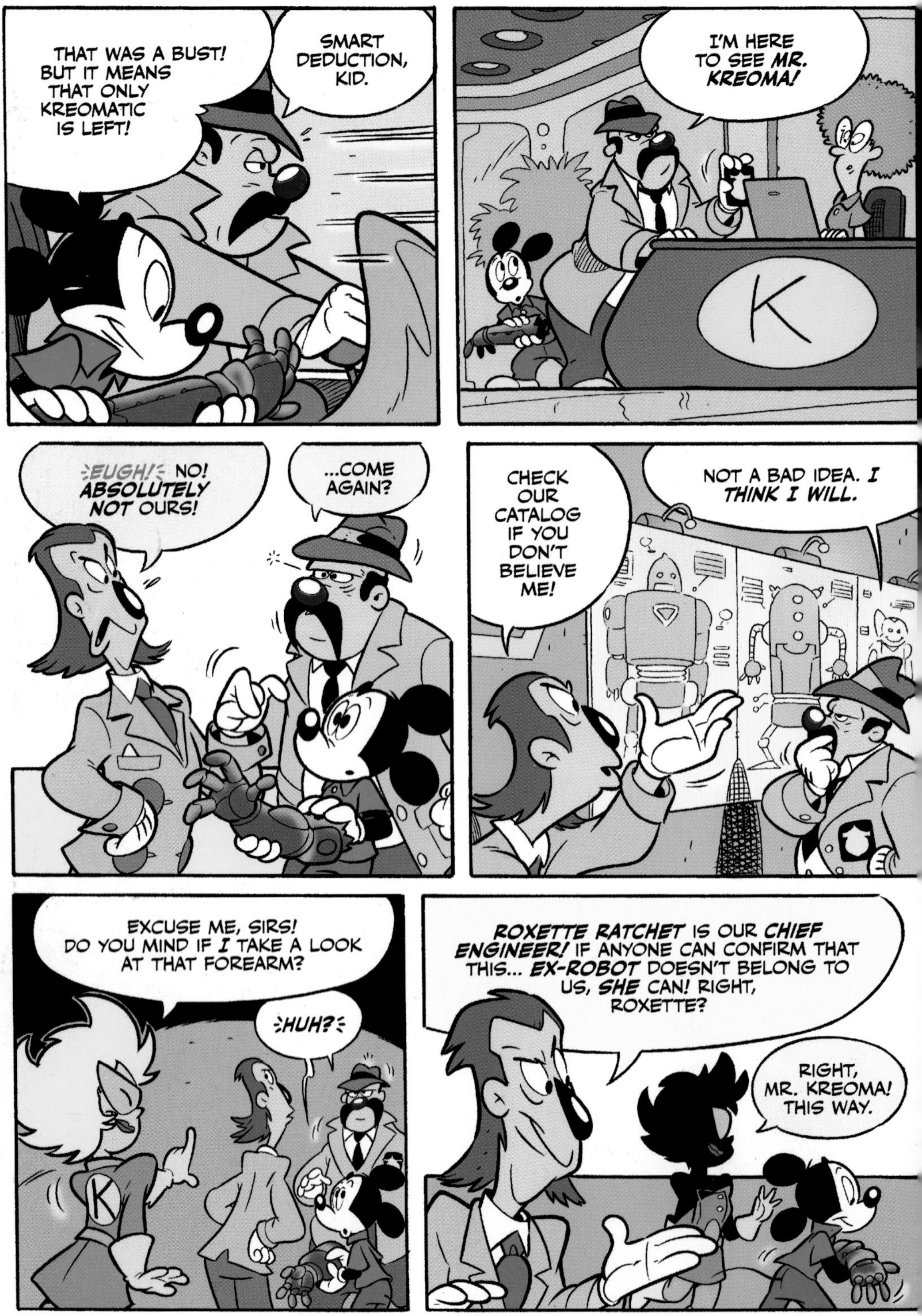
THAT WAS A BUST! BUT IT MEANS THAT ONLY KREOMATIC IS LEFT!
SMART DEDUCTION, KID.
I'M HERE TO SEE MR. KREOMA!
K
EUGH! NO! ABSOLUTELY NOT OURS!
...COME AGAIN?
CHECK OUR CATALOG IF YOU DON'T BELIEVE ME!
NOT A BAD IDEA. I THINK I WILL.
EXCUSE ME, SIRS! DO YOU MIND IF I TAKE A LOOK AT THAT FOREARM?
HUH?
K
ROXETTE RATCHET IS OUR CHIEF ENGINEER! IF ANYONE CAN CONFIRM THAT THIS... EX-ROBOT DOESN'T BELONG TO US, SHE CAN! RIGHT, ROXETTE?
RIGHT, MR. KREOMA! THIS WAY.

BIP BEEP BOOP

YES... IT'S ME. THE POLICE ARE HERE NOW... AND YOU'RE ABSOLUTELY SURE THAT THIS IS ALL RIGHT?

TRUST ME, MR. KREOMA...

...MY PLANS ARE *FLAWLESS.* IN FACT...

...*THIS* PLAN IN PARTICULAR... *IS PERFECT.*

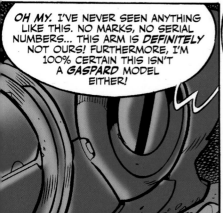

OH MY. I'VE NEVER SEEN ANYTHING LIKE THIS. NO MARKS, NO SERIAL NUMBERS... THIS ARM IS *DEFINITELY* NOT OURS! FURTHERMORE, I'M 100% CERTAIN THIS ISN'T A *GASPARD* MODEL EITHER!

*NEITHER* OF OUR COMPANIES CAN CREATE *ROBOTIC CRIMINALS!* A MENTAL BLOCK MAKES OUR ROBOTS *INCAPABLE* OF CRIME! PROTOCOLS FOR THE THREE LAWS ARE *ALMOST IRREVERSIBLY* HARD-WIRED INTO THEIR SOFTWARE AT THE SOURCE—

"AL-MOST?"

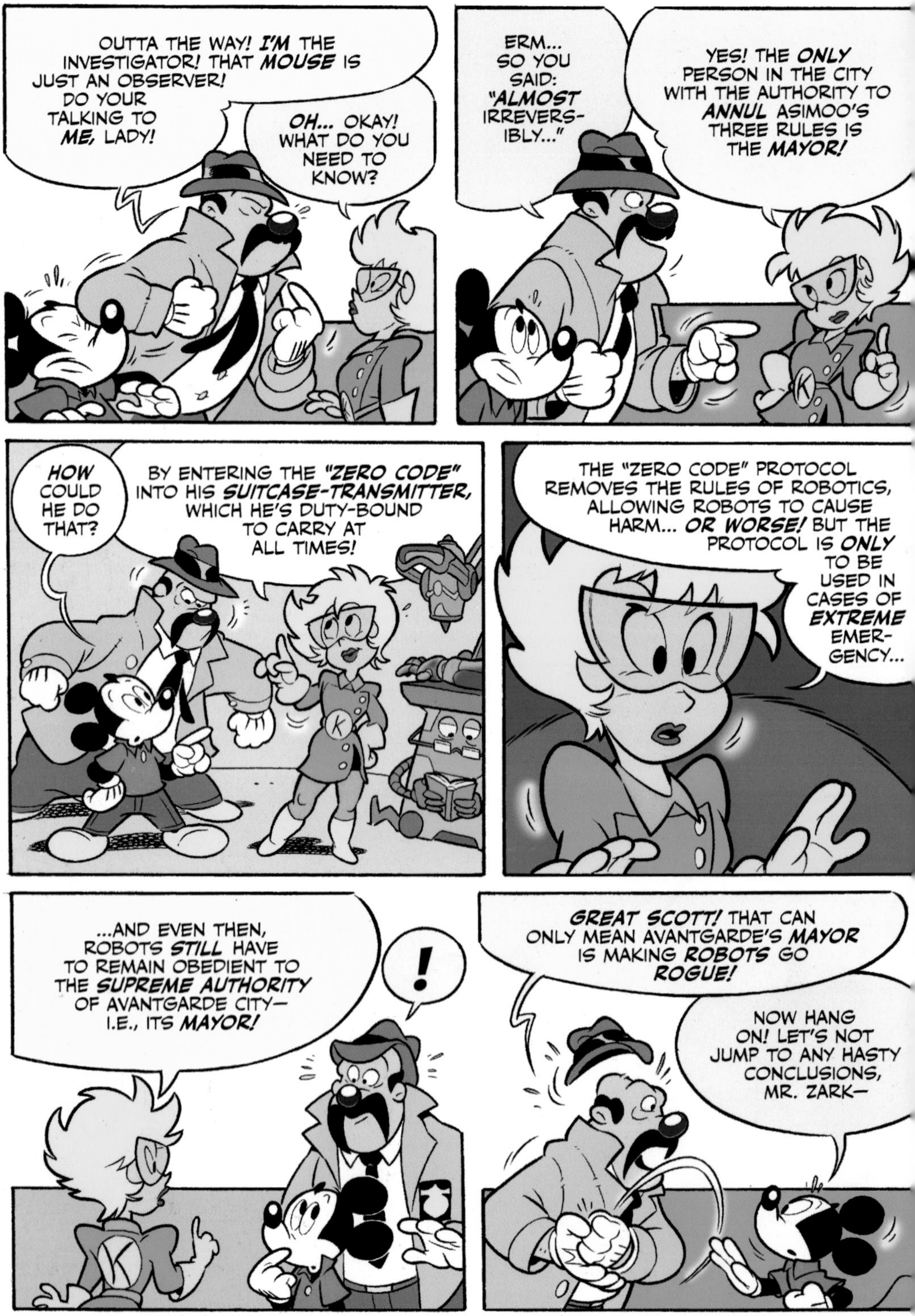
OUTTA THE WAY! I'M THE INVESTIGATOR! THAT MOUSE IS JUST AN OBSERVER! DO YOUR TALKING TO ME, LADY!
OH... OKAY! WHAT DO YOU NEED TO KNOW?
ERM... SO YOU SAID: "ALMOST IRREVERS-IBLY..."
YES! THE ONLY PERSON IN THE CITY WITH THE AUTHORITY TO ANNUL ASIMOO'S THREE RULES IS THE MAYOR!
HOW COULD HE DO THAT?
BY ENTERING THE "ZERO CODE" INTO HIS SUITCASE-TRANSMITTER, WHICH HE'S DUTY-BOUND TO CARRY AT ALL TIMES!
THE "ZERO CODE" PROTOCOL REMOVES THE RULES OF ROBOTICS, ALLOWING ROBOTS TO CAUSE HARM... OR WORSE! BUT THE PROTOCOL IS ONLY TO BE USED IN CASES OF EXTREME EMER-GENCY...
...AND EVEN THEN, ROBOTS STILL HAVE TO REMAIN OBEDIENT TO THE SUPREME AUTHORITY OF AVANTGARDE CITY— I.E., ITS MAYOR!
!
GREAT SCOTT! THAT CAN ONLY MEAN AVANTGARDE'S MAYOR IS MAKING ROBOTS GO ROGUE!
NOW HANG ON! LET'S NOT JUMP TO ANY HASTY CONCLUSIONS, MR. ZARK—

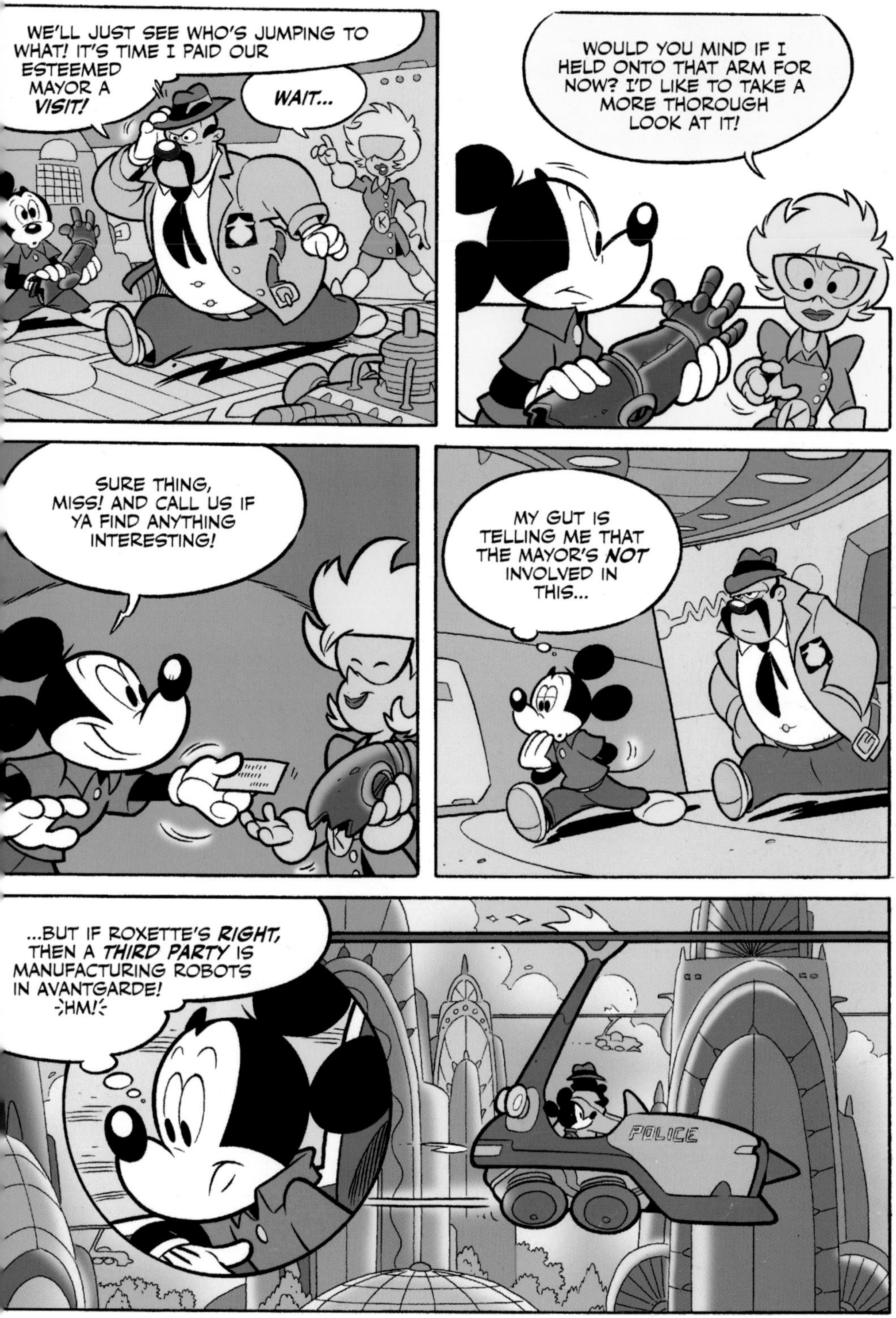
WE'LL JUST SEE WHO'S JUMPING TO WHAT! IT'S TIME I PAID OUR ESTEEMED MAYOR A VISIT!
WAIT...
WOULD YOU MIND IF I HELD ONTO THAT ARM FOR NOW? I'D LIKE TO TAKE A MORE THOROUGH LOOK AT IT!
SURE THING, MISS! AND CALL US IF YA FIND ANYTHING INTERESTING!
MY GUT IS TELLING ME THAT THE MAYOR'S NOT INVOLVED IN THIS...
...BUT IF ROXETTE'S RIGHT, THEN A THIRD PARTY IS MANUFACTURING ROBOTS IN AVANTGARDE! -HM!-
POLICE

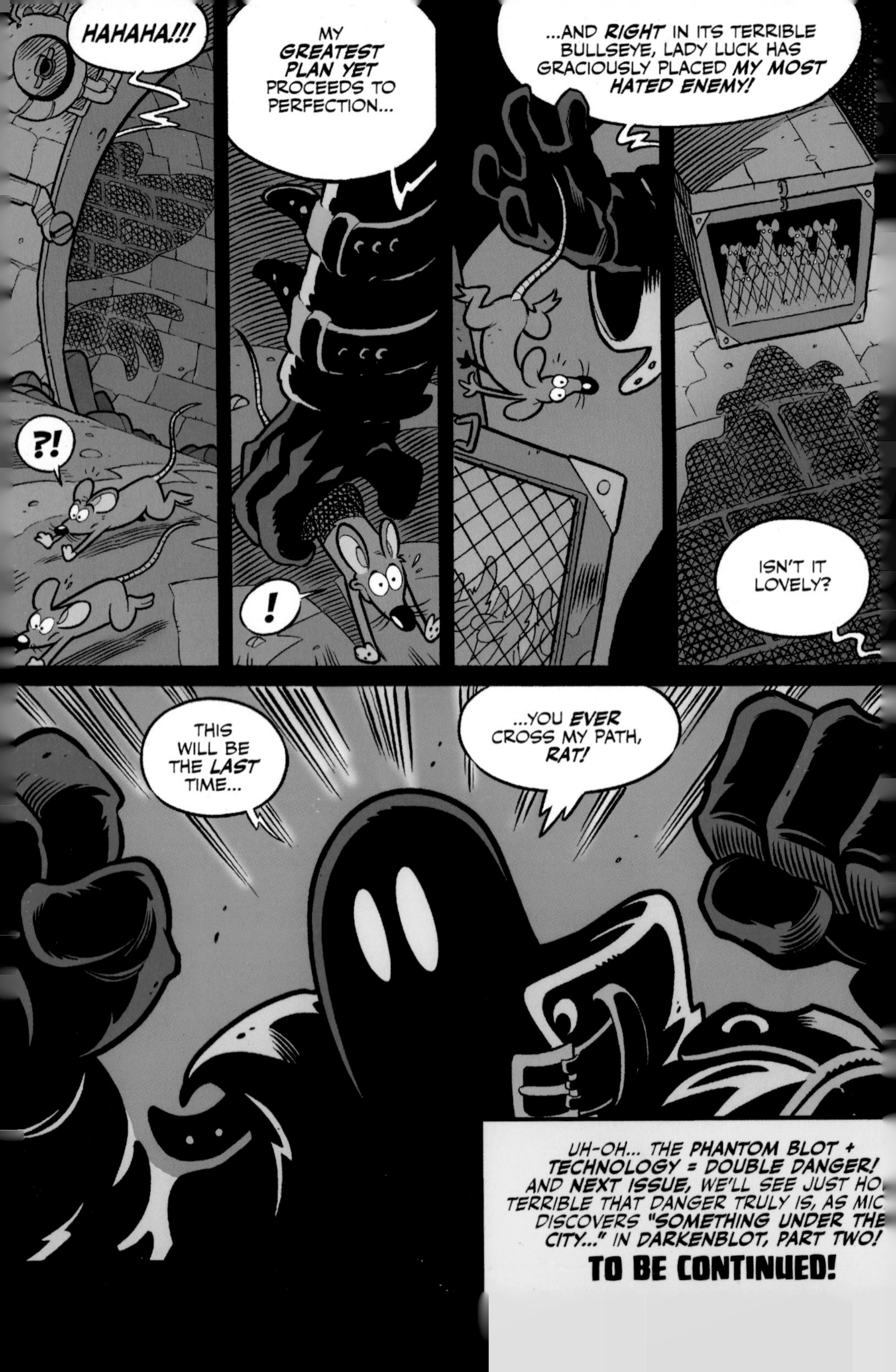
HAHAHA!!!
?!
MY GREATEST PLAN YET PROCEEDS TO PERFECTION...
!
...AND RIGHT IN ITS TERRIBLE BULLSEYE, LADY LUCK HAS GRACIOUSLY PLACED MY MOST HATED ENEMY!
ISN'T IT LOVELY?
THIS WILL BE THE LAST TIME...
...YOU EVER CROSS MY PATH, RAT!
UH-OH... THE PHANTOM BLOT + TECHNOLOGY = DOUBLE DANGER! AND NEXT ISSUE, WE'LL SEE JUST HO TERRIBLE THAT DANGER TRULY IS, AS MIC DISCOVERS "SOMETHING UNDER THE CITY..." IN DARKENBLOT, PART TWO!
TO BE CONTINUED!

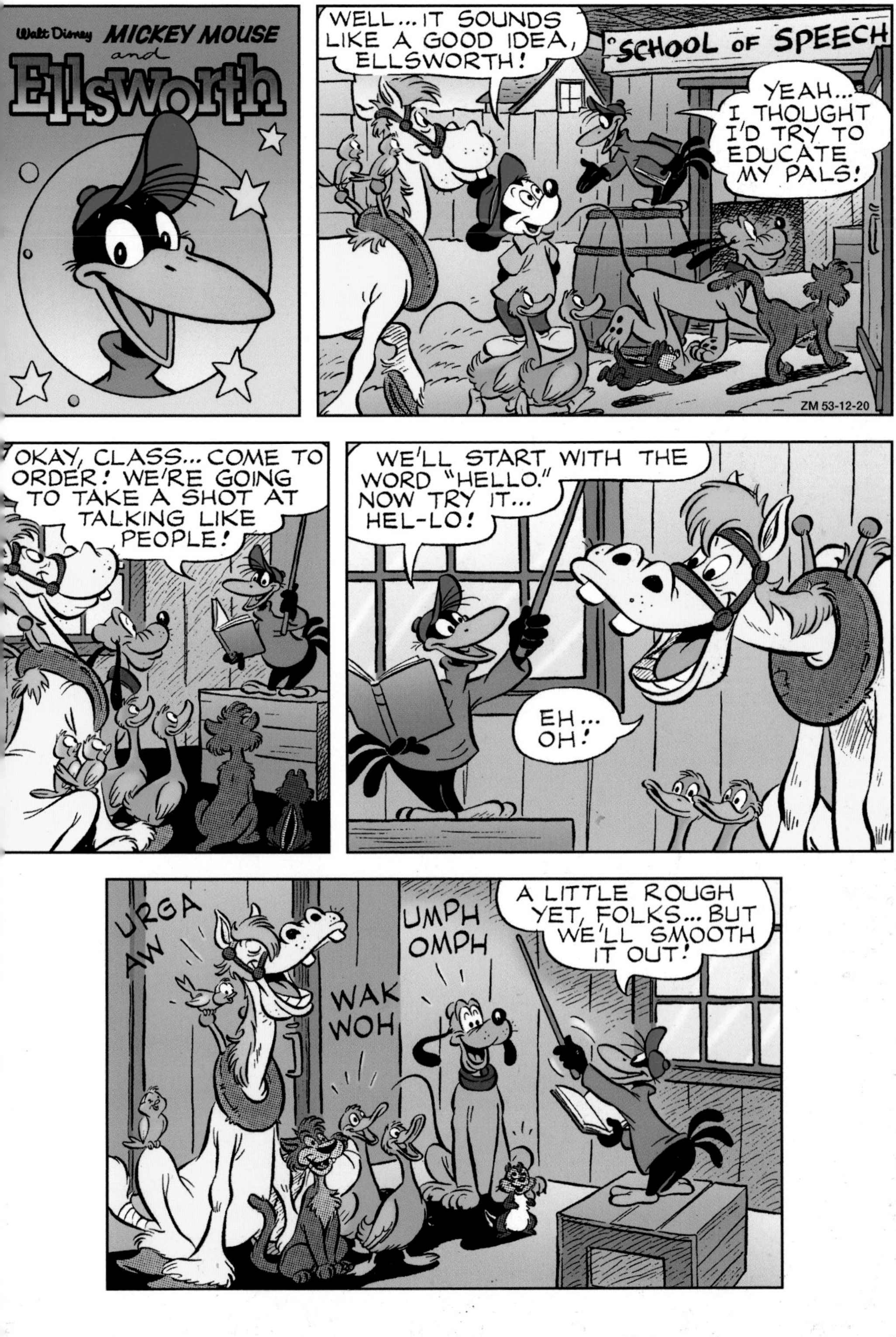
Walt Disney MICKEY MOUSE and Ellsworth
WELL... IT SOUNDS LIKE A GOOD IDEA, ELLSWORTH!
SCHOOL OF SPEECH
YEAH... I THOUGHT I'D TRY TO EDUCATE MY PALS!
ZM 53-12-20
OKAY, CLASS... COME TO ORDER! WE'RE GOING TO TAKE A SHOT AT TALKING LIKE PEOPLE!
WE'LL START WITH THE WORD "HELLO." NOW TRY IT... HEL-LO!
EH... OH!
URGA AW
UMPH OMPH
WAK WOH
A LITTLE ROUGH YET, FOLKS... BUT WE'LL SMOOTH IT OUT!

Originally published in *Mickey Mouse* Sunday comic strip (USA, 1953)

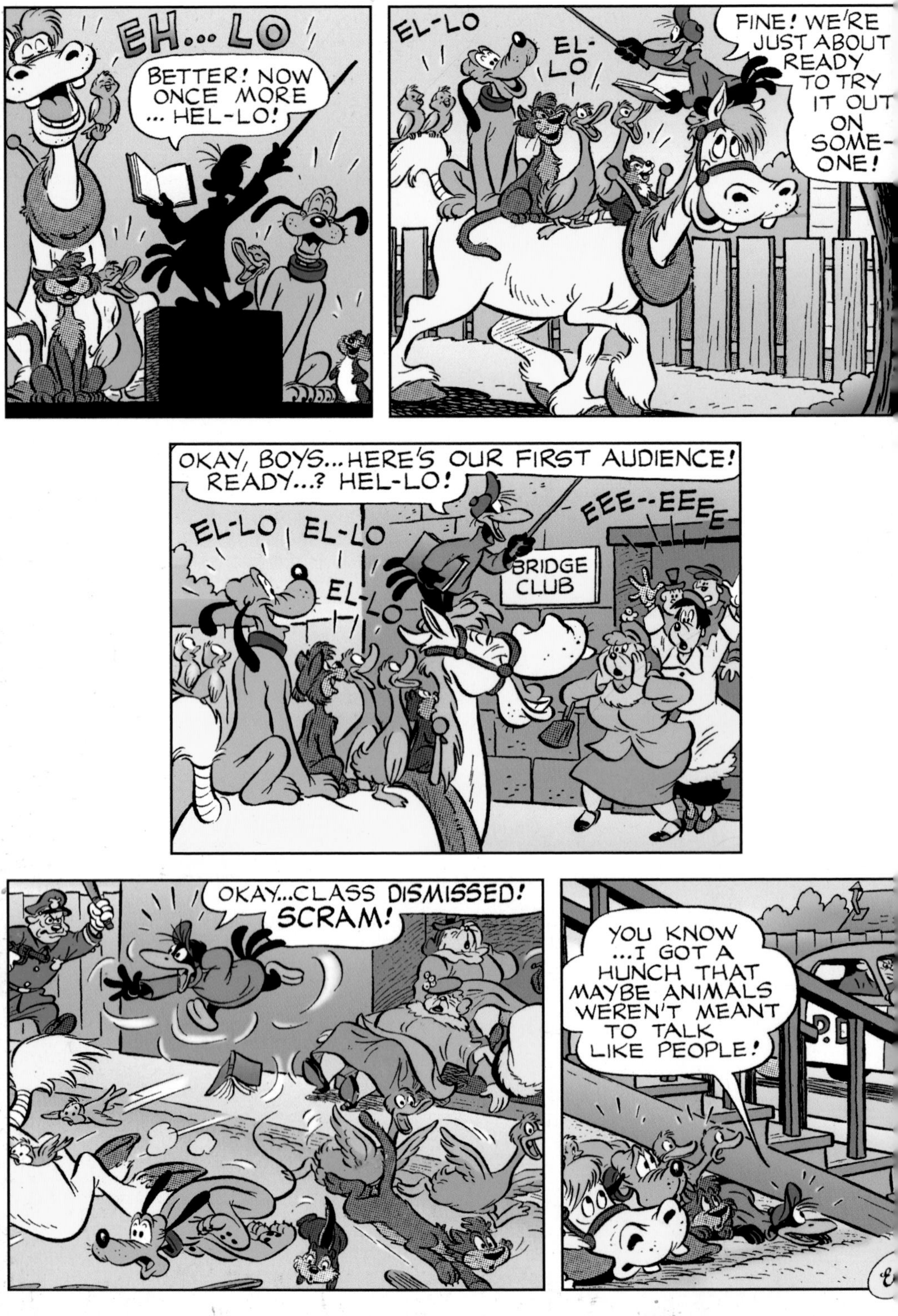
EH... LO
BETTER! NOW ONCE MORE ... HEL-LO!
EL-LO
EL-LO
FINE! WE'RE JUST ABOUT READY TO TRY IT OUT ON SOME-ONE!
OKAY, BOYS...HERE'S OUR FIRST AUDIENCE! READY...? HEL-LO!
EL-LO
EL-LO
EL-LO
EEE--EEEEE
BRIDGE CLUB
OKAY...CLASS DISMISSED! SCRAM!
YOU KNOW ...I GOT A HUNCH THAT MAYBE ANIMALS WEREN'T MEANT TO TALK LIKE PEOPLE!

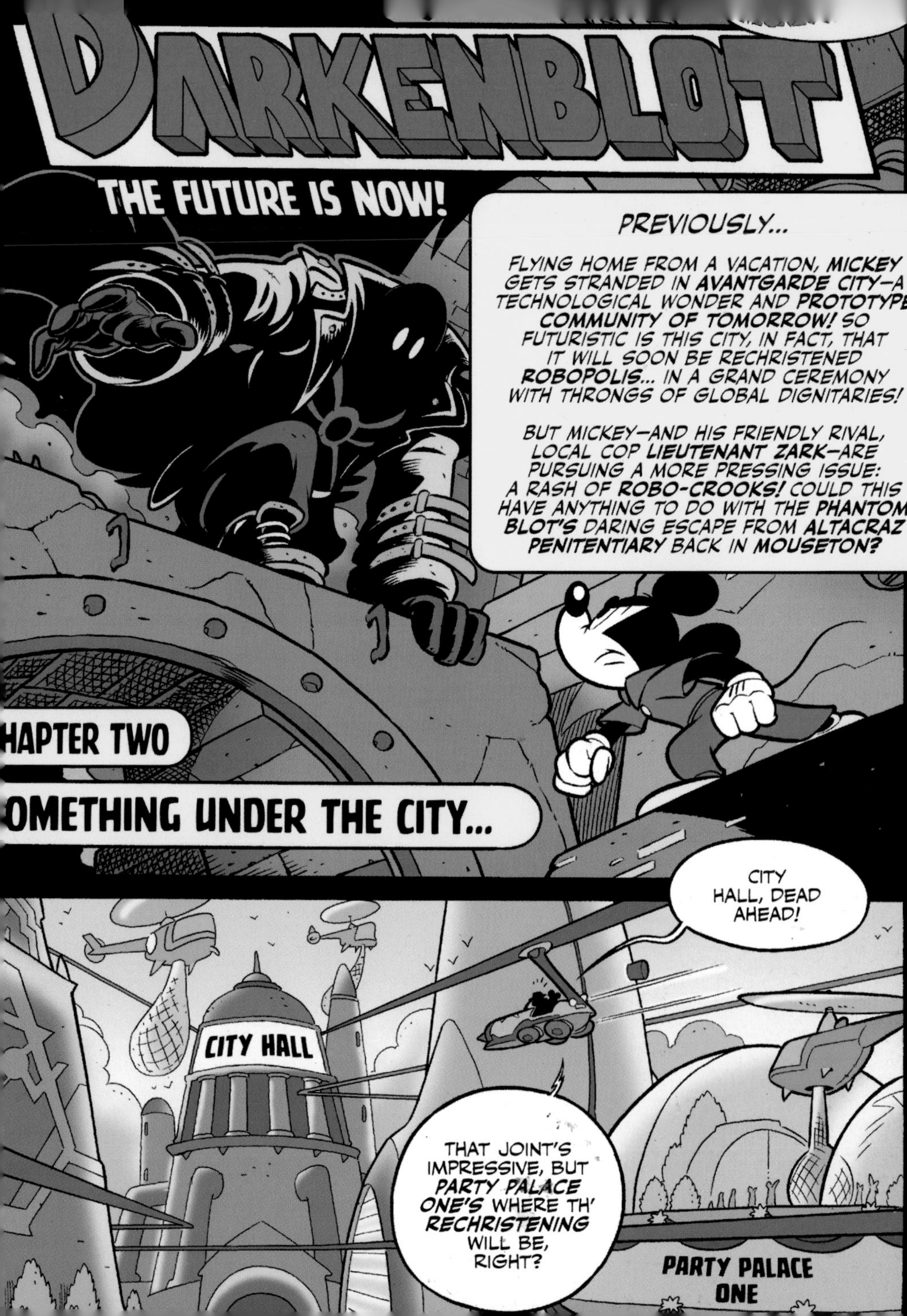

DARKENBLOT
THE FUTURE IS NOW!
PREVIOUSLY...
FLYING HOME FROM A VACATION, MICKEY GETS STRANDED IN AVANTGARDE CITY—A TECHNOLOGICAL WONDER AND PROTOTYPE COMMUNITY OF TOMORROW! SO FUTURISTIC IS THIS CITY, IN FACT, THAT IT WILL SOON BE RECHRISTENED ROBOPOLIS... IN A GRAND CEREMONY WITH THRONGS OF GLOBAL DIGNITARIES!
BUT MICKEY—AND HIS FRIENDLY RIVAL, LOCAL COP LIEUTENANT ZARK—ARE PURSUING A MORE PRESSING ISSUE: A RASH OF ROBO-CROOKS! COULD THIS HAVE ANYTHING TO DO WITH THE PHANTOM BLOT'S DARING ESCAPE FROM ALTACRAZ PENITENTIARY BACK IN MOUSETON?
HAPTER TWO
OMETHING UNDER THE CITY...
CITY HALL, DEAD AHEAD!
CITY HALL
THAT JOINT'S IMPRESSIVE, BUT PARTY PALACE ONE'S WHERE TH' RECHRISTENING WILL BE, RIGHT?
PARTY PALACE ONE

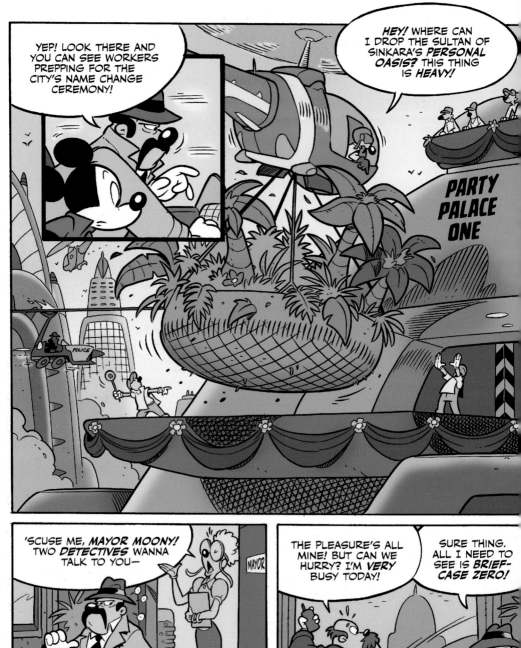

YEP! LOOK THERE AND YOU CAN SEE WORKERS PREPPING FOR THE CITY'S NAME CHANGE CEREMONY!

HEY! WHERE CAN I DROP THE SULTAN OF SINKARA'S *PERSONAL OASIS?* THIS THING IS *HEAVY!*

PARTY PALACE ONE

'SCUSE ME, *MAYOR MOONY!* TWO *DETECTIVES* WANNA TALK TO YOU—

ONE DETECTIVE, MISS!

THE PLEASURE'S ALL MINE! BUT CAN WE HURRY? I'M *VERY* BUSY TODAY!

SURE THING. ALL I NEED TO SEE IS *BRIEF-CASE ZERO!*

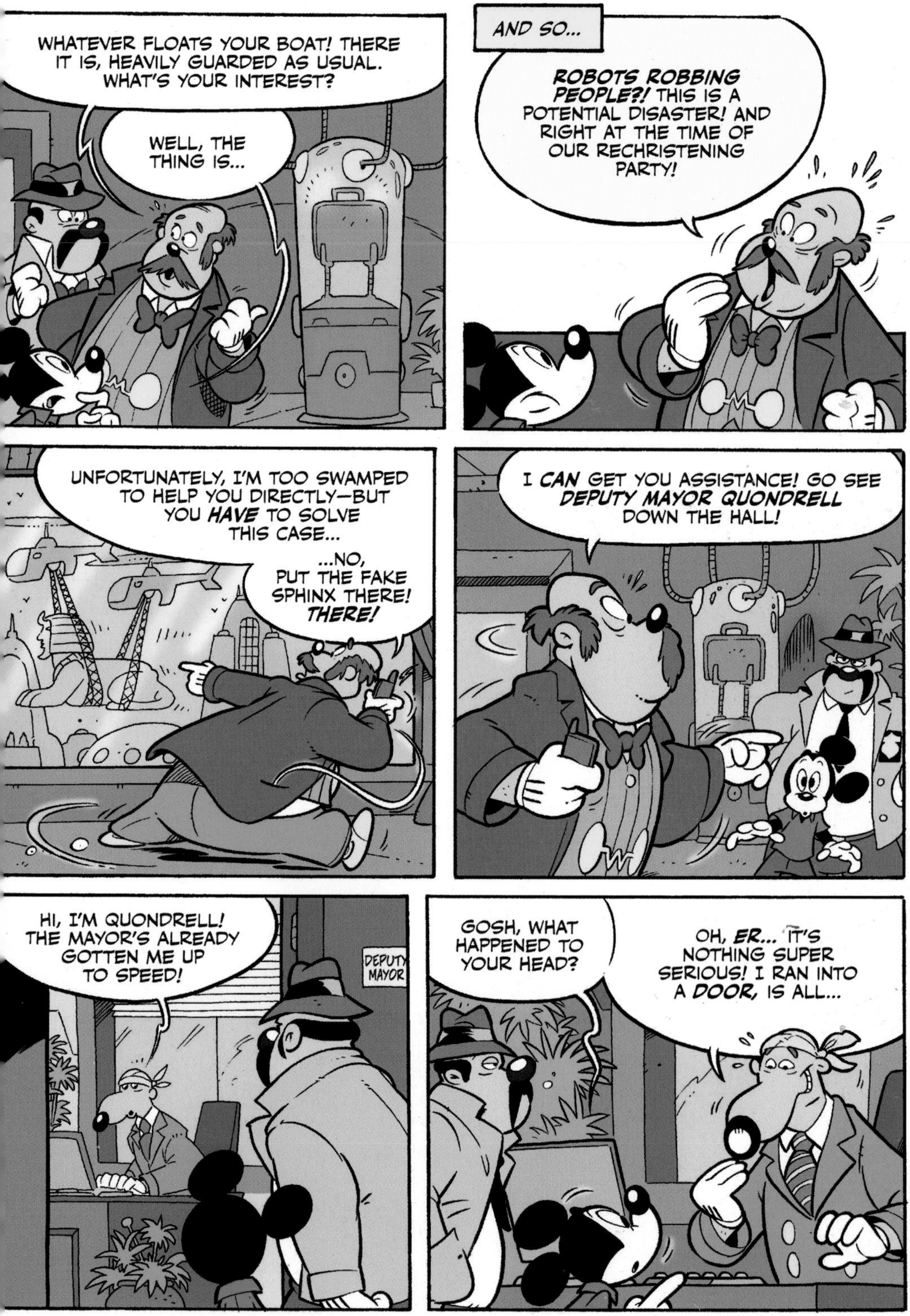
WHATEVER FLOATS YOUR BOAT! THERE IT IS, HEAVILY GUARDED AS USUAL. WHAT'S YOUR INTEREST?
WELL, THE THING IS...
AND SO...
ROBOTS ROBBING PEOPLE?! THIS IS A POTENTIAL DISASTER! AND RIGHT AT THE TIME OF OUR RECHRISTENING PARTY!
UNFORTUNATELY, I'M TOO SWAMPED TO HELP YOU DIRECTLY—BUT YOU HAVE TO SOLVE THIS CASE...
...NO, PUT THE FAKE SPHINX THERE! THERE!
I CAN GET YOU ASSISTANCE! GO SEE DEPUTY MAYOR QUONDRELL DOWN THE HALL!
HI, I'M QUONDRELL! THE MAYOR'S ALREADY GOTTEN ME UP TO SPEED!
DEPUTY MAYOR
GOSH, WHAT HAPPENED TO YOUR HEAD?
OH, ER... IT'S NOTHING SUPER SERIOUS! I RAN INTO A DOOR, IS ALL...

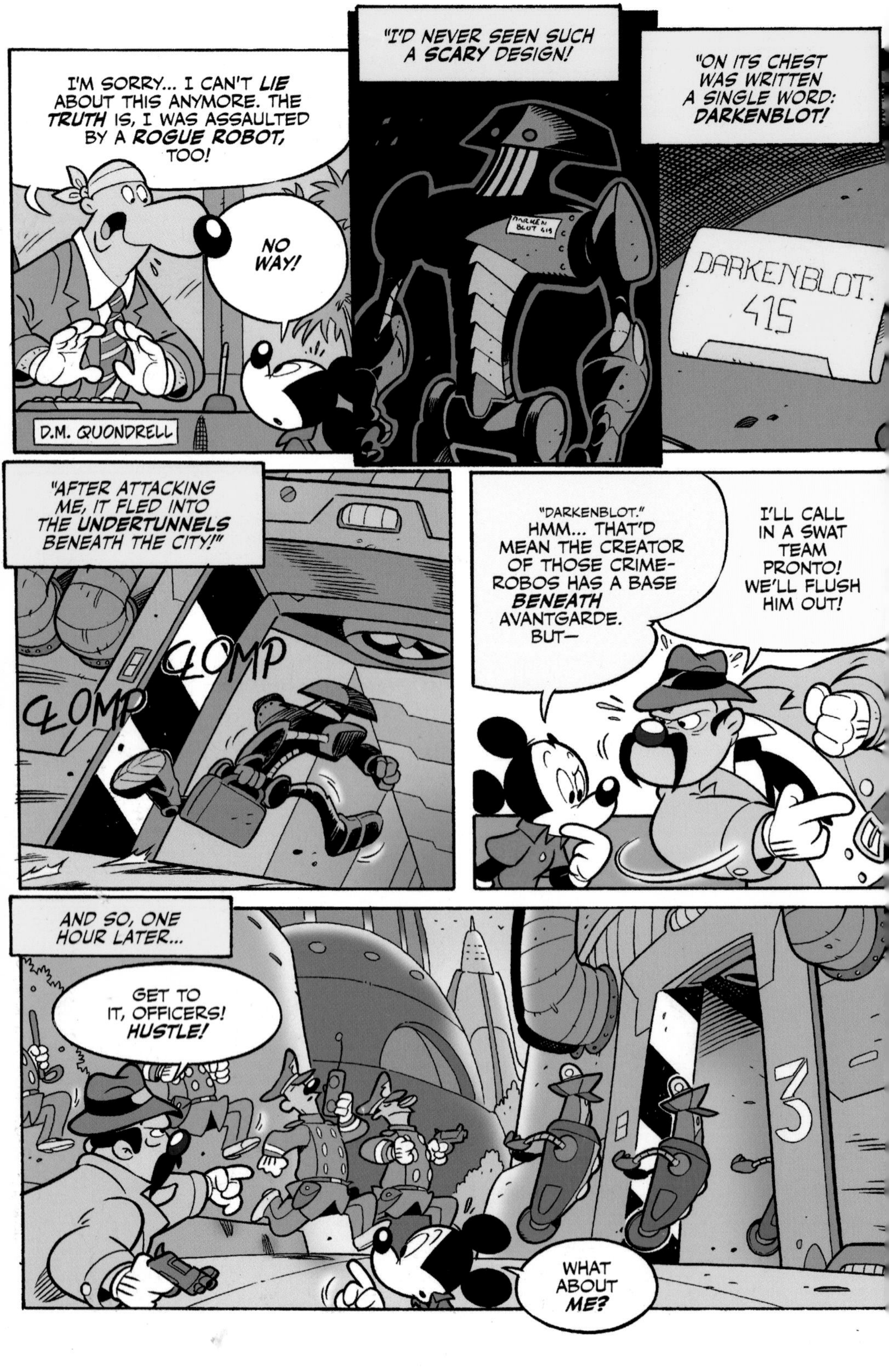
I'M SORRY... I CAN'T LIE ABOUT THIS ANYMORE. THE TRUTH IS, I WAS ASSAULTED BY A ROGUE ROBOT, TOO!
NO WAY!
D.M. QUONDRELL
"I'D NEVER SEEN SUCH A SCARY DESIGN!
"ON ITS CHEST WAS WRITTEN A SINGLE WORD: DARKENBLOT!
DARKENBLOT 415
"AFTER ATTACKING ME, IT FLED INTO THE UNDERTUNNELS BENEATH THE CITY!"
CLOMP
CLOMP
"DARKENBLOT." HMM... THAT'D MEAN THE CREATOR OF THOSE CRIME-ROBOS HAS A BASE BENEATH AVANTGARDE. BUT—
I'LL CALL IN A SWAT TEAM PRONTO! WE'LL FLUSH HIM OUT!
AND SO, ONE HOUR LATER...
GET TO IT, OFFICERS! HUSTLE!
WHAT ABOUT ME?

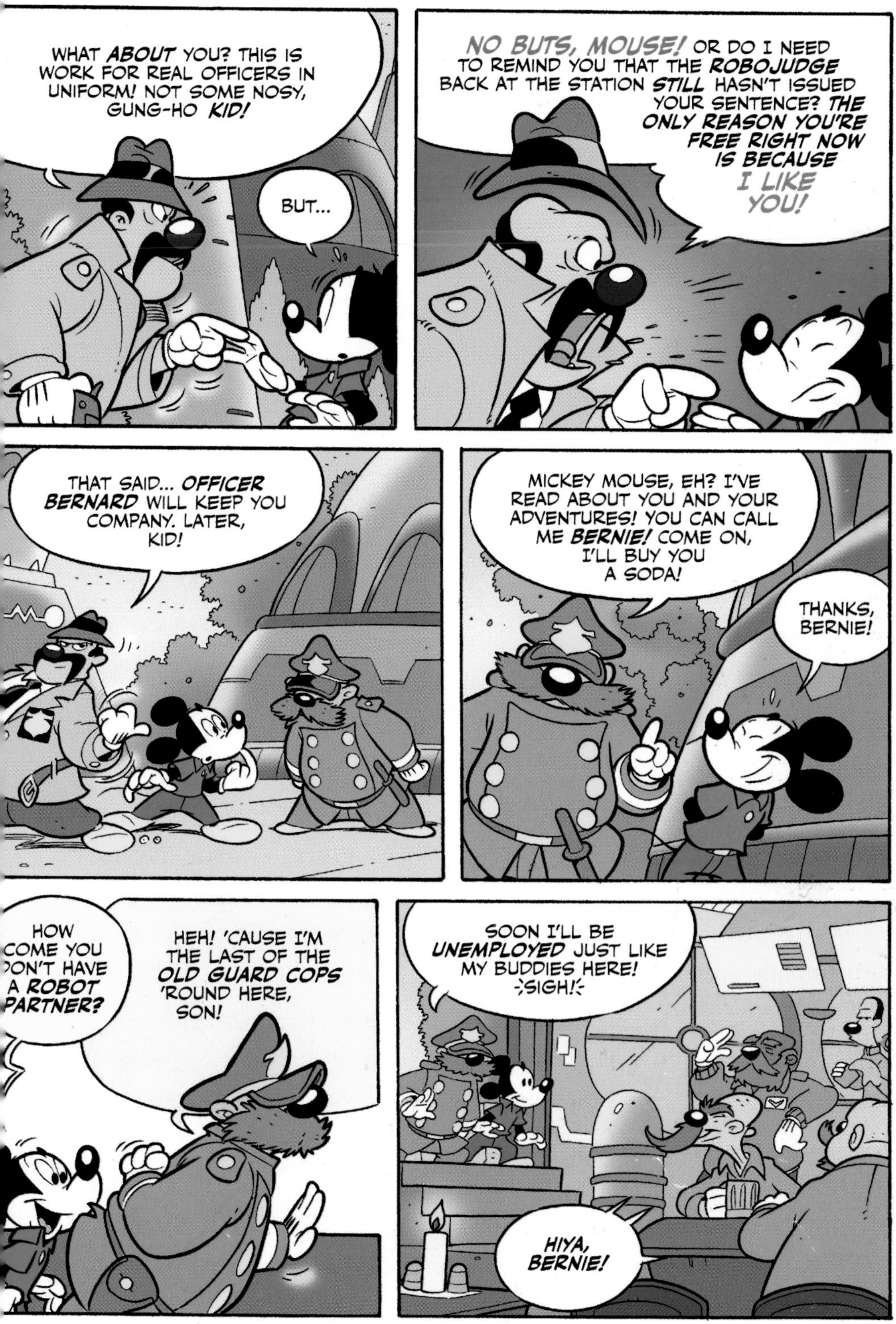
WHAT ABOUT YOU? THIS IS WORK FOR REAL OFFICERS IN UNIFORM! NOT SOME NOSY, GUNG-HO KID!
BUT...
NO BUTS, MOUSE! OR DO I NEED TO REMIND YOU THAT THE ROBOJUDGE BACK AT THE STATION STILL HASN'T ISSUED YOUR SENTENCE? THE ONLY REASON YOU'RE FREE RIGHT NOW IS BECAUSE I LIKE YOU!
THAT SAID... OFFICER BERNARD WILL KEEP YOU COMPANY. LATER, KID!
MICKEY MOUSE, EH? I'VE READ ABOUT YOU AND YOUR ADVENTURES! YOU CAN CALL ME BERNIE! COME ON, I'LL BUY YOU A SODA!
THANKS, BERNIE!
HOW COME YOU DON'T HAVE A ROBOT PARTNER?
HEH! 'CAUSE I'M THE LAST OF THE OLD GUARD COPS 'ROUND HERE, SON!
SOON I'LL BE UNEMPLOYED JUST LIKE MY BUDDIES HERE! -SIGH!-
HIYA, BERNIE!

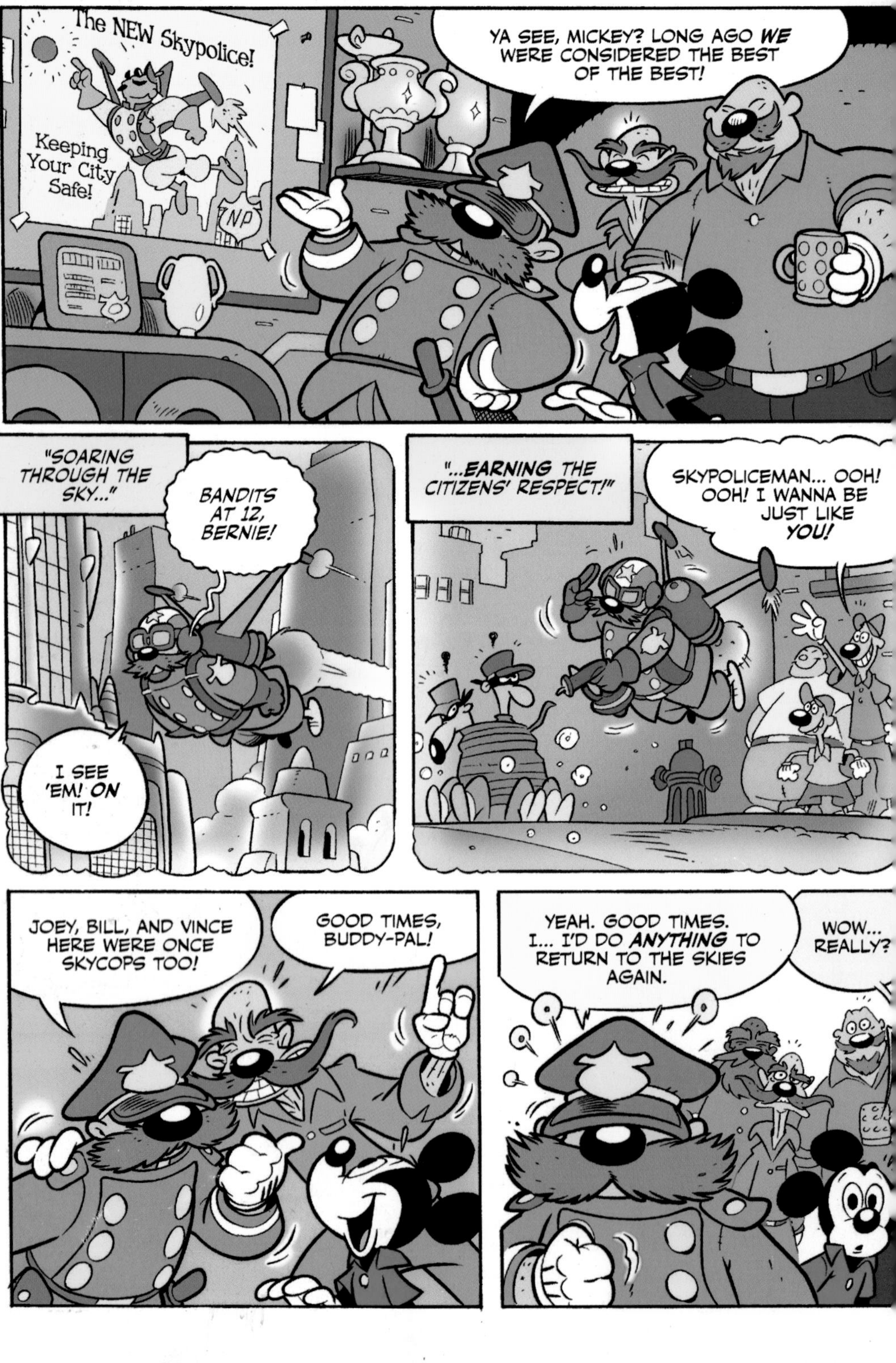
The NEW Skypolice!
Keeping Your City Safe!
YA SEE, MICKEY? LONG AGO WE WERE CONSIDERED THE BEST OF THE BEST!
"SOARING THROUGH THE SKY..."
BANDITS AT 12, BERNIE!
I SEE 'EM! ON IT!
"...EARNING THE CITIZENS' RESPECT!"
SKYPOLICEMAN... OOH! OOH! I WANNA BE JUST LIKE YOU!
JOEY, BILL, AND VINCE HERE WERE ONCE SKYCOPS TOO!
GOOD TIMES, BUDDY-PAL!
YEAH. GOOD TIMES. I... I'D DO ANYTHING TO RETURN TO THE SKIES AGAIN.
WOW... REALLY?

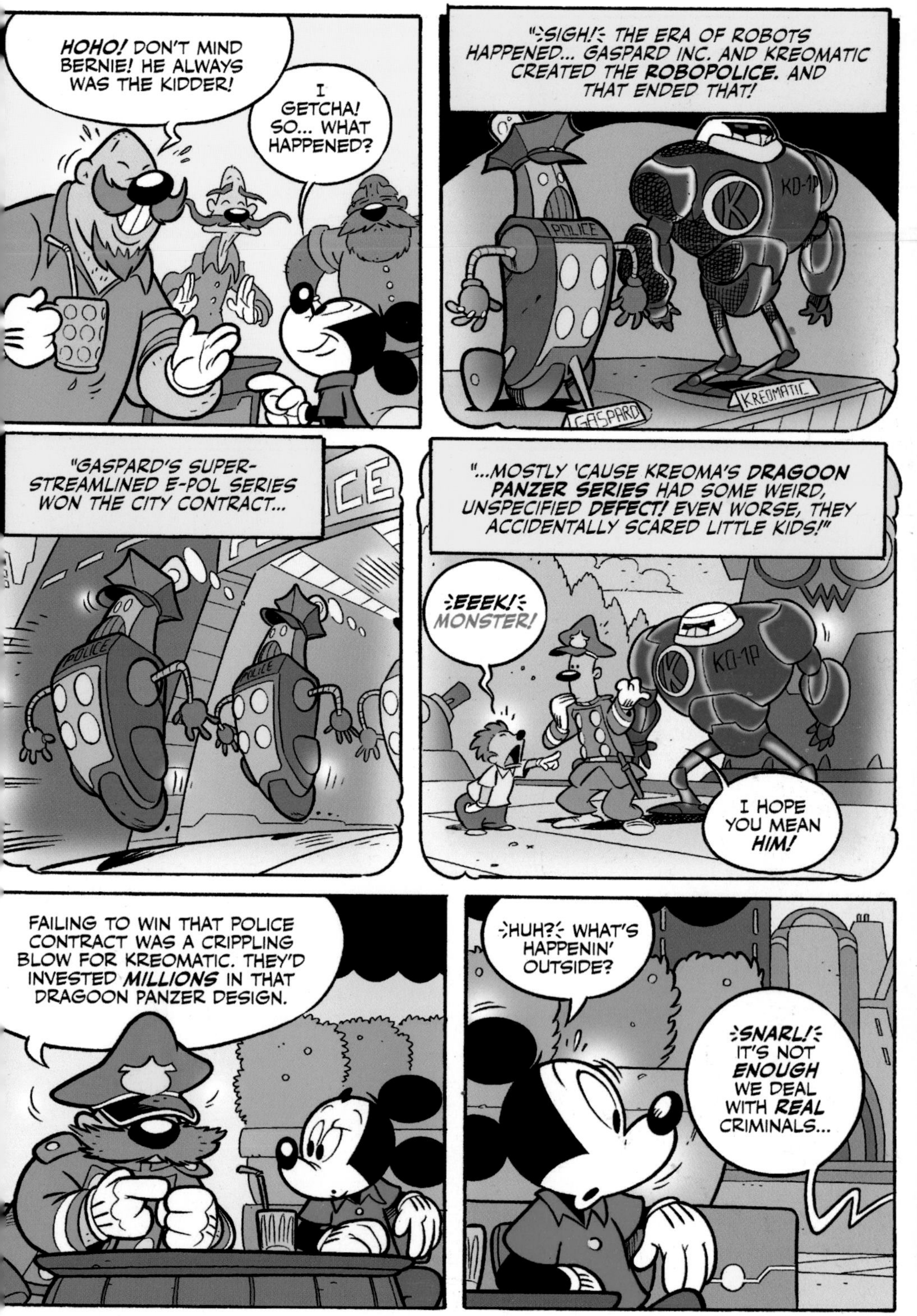
HOHO! DON'T MIND BERNIE! HE ALWAYS WAS THE KIDDER!
I GETCHA! SO... WHAT HAPPENED?
"SIGH! THE ERA OF ROBOTS HAPPENED... GASPARD INC. AND KREOMATIC CREATED THE ROBOPOLICE. AND THAT ENDED THAT!
POLICE
KD-1P
GASPARD
KREOMATIC
"GASPARD'S SUPER-STREAMLINED E-POL SERIES WON THE CITY CONTRACT...
POLICE
POLICE
"...MOSTLY 'CAUSE KREOMA'S DRAGOON PANZER SERIES HAD SOME WEIRD, UNSPECIFIED DEFECT! EVEN WORSE, THEY ACCIDENTALLY SCARED LITTLE KIDS!"
EEEK! MONSTER!
KD-1P
I HOPE YOU MEAN HIM!
FAILING TO WIN THAT POLICE CONTRACT WAS A CRIPPLING BLOW FOR KREOMATIC. THEY'D INVESTED MILLIONS IN THAT DRAGOON PANZER DESIGN.
HUH? WHAT'S HAPPENIN' OUTSIDE?
SNARL! IT'S NOT ENOUGH WE DEAL WITH REAL CRIMINALS...

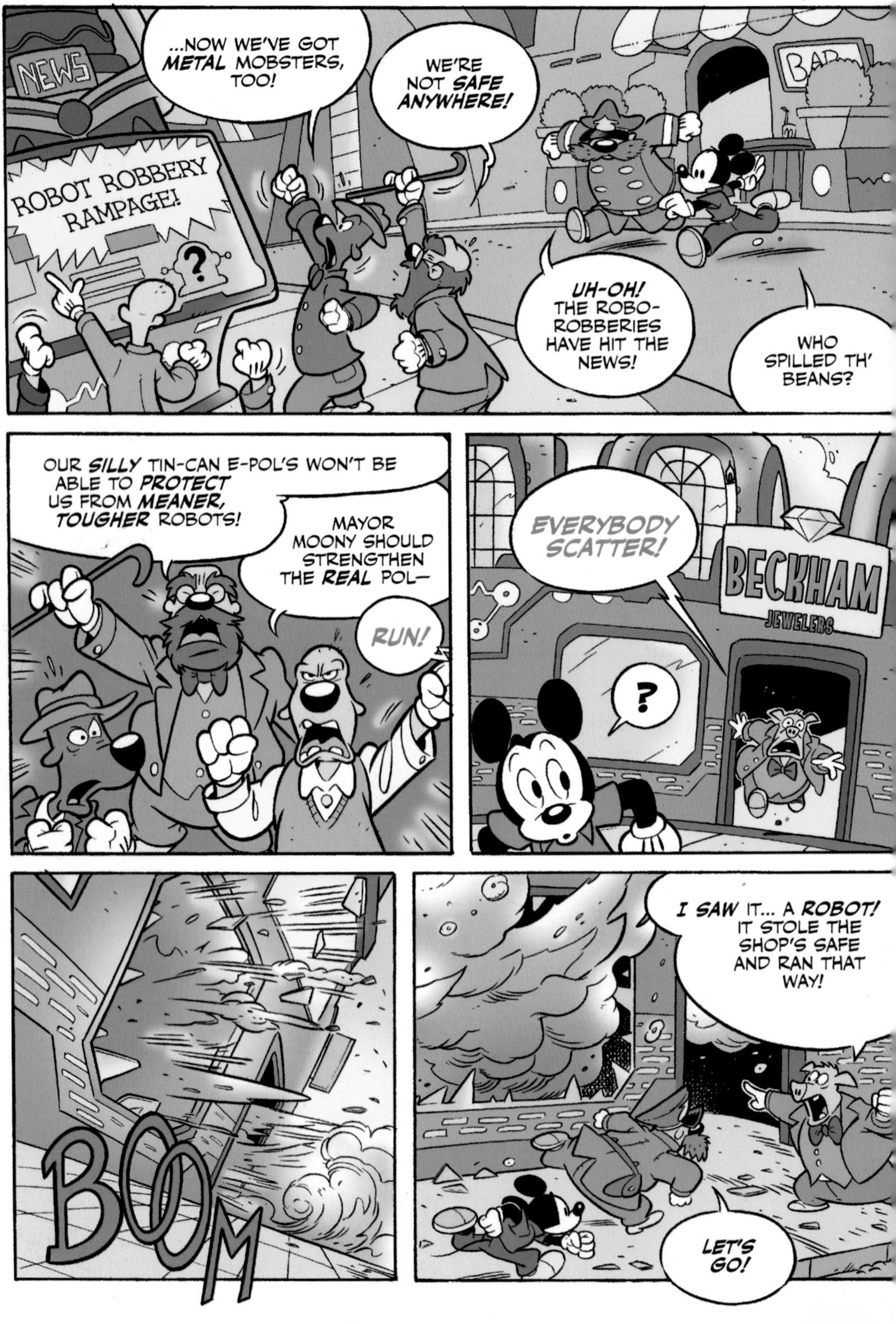
NEWS
ROBOT ROBBERY RAMPAGE!
?
...NOW WE'VE GOT METAL MOBSTERS, TOO!
WE'RE NOT SAFE ANYWHERE!
BAR
UH-OH! THE ROBO-ROBBERIES HAVE HIT THE NEWS!
WHO SPILLED TH' BEANS?
OUR SILLY TIN-CAN E-POL'S WON'T BE ABLE TO PROTECT US FROM MEANER, TOUGHER ROBOTS!
MAYOR MOONY SHOULD STRENGTHEN THE REAL POL—
RUN!
EVERYBODY SCATTER!
BECKHAM
JEWELERS
?
BOOM
I SAW IT... A ROBOT! IT STOLE THE SHOP'S SAFE AND RAN THAT WAY!
LET'S GO!

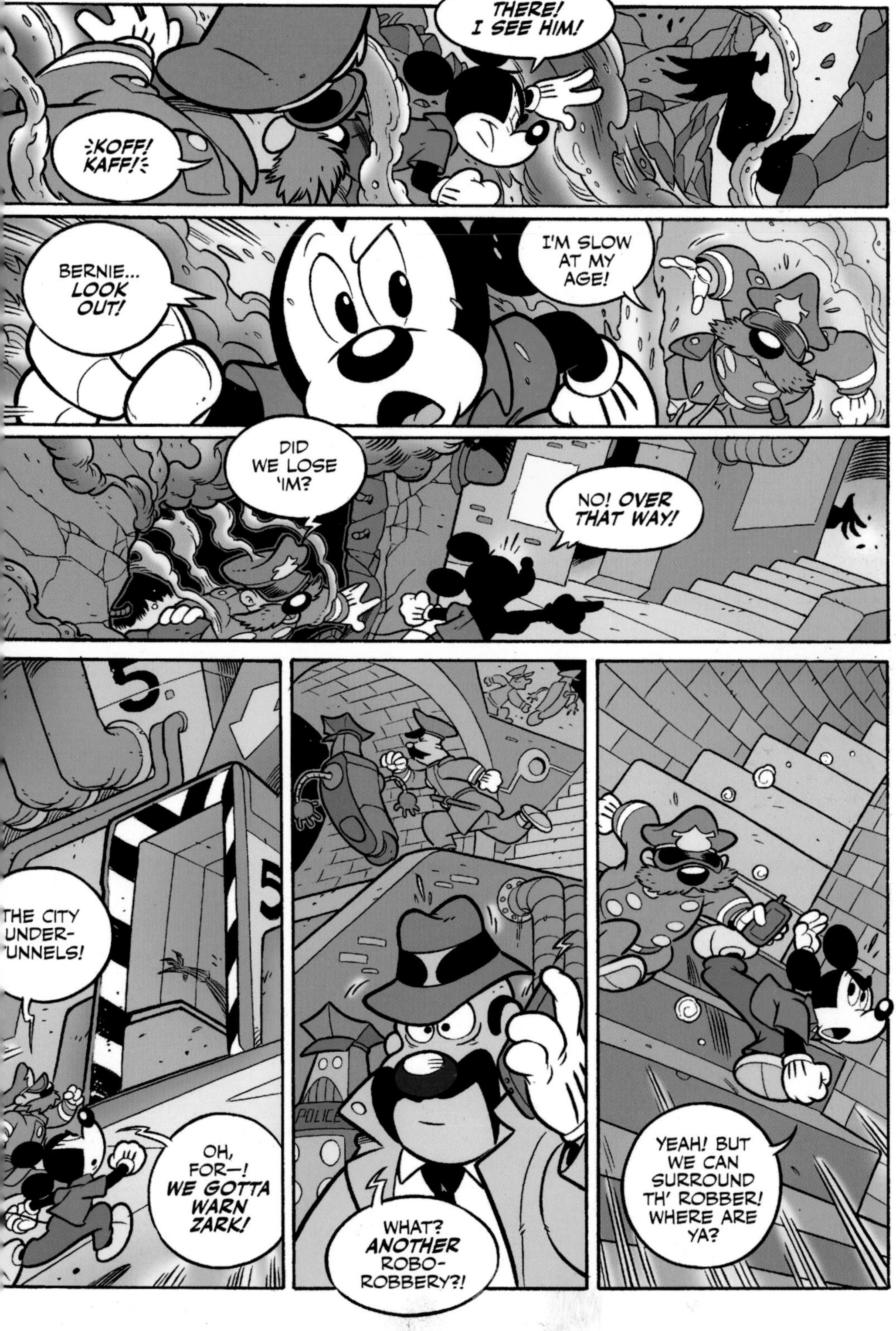
THERE! I SEE HIM!
KOFF! KAFF!
BERNIE... LOOK OUT!
I'M SLOW AT MY AGE!
DID WE LOSE 'IM?
NO! OVER THAT WAY!
THE CITY UNDER- TUNNELS!
OH, FOR—! WE GOTTA WARN ZARK!
POLICE
WHAT? ANOTHER ROBO-ROBBERY?!
YEAH! BUT WE CAN SURROUND TH' ROBBER! WHERE ARE YA?

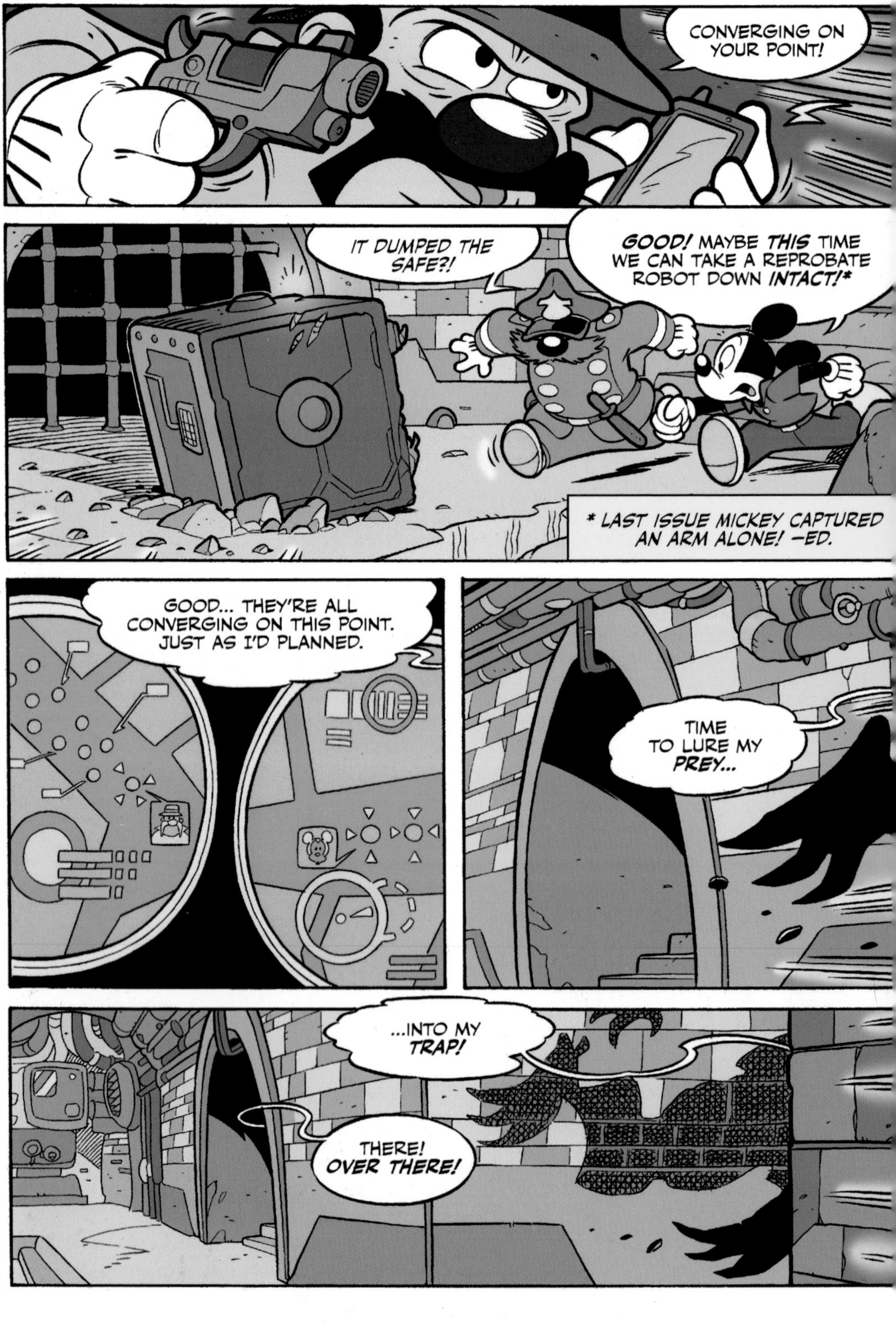
CONVERGING ON YOUR POINT!
IT DUMPED THE SAFE?!
GOOD! MAYBE THIS TIME WE CAN TAKE A REPROBATE ROBOT DOWN INTACT!*
* LAST ISSUE MICKEY CAPTURED AN ARM ALONE! —ED.
GOOD... THEY'RE ALL CONVERGING ON THIS POINT. JUST AS I'D PLANNED.
TIME TO LURE MY PREY...
...INTO MY TRAP!
THERE! OVER THERE!

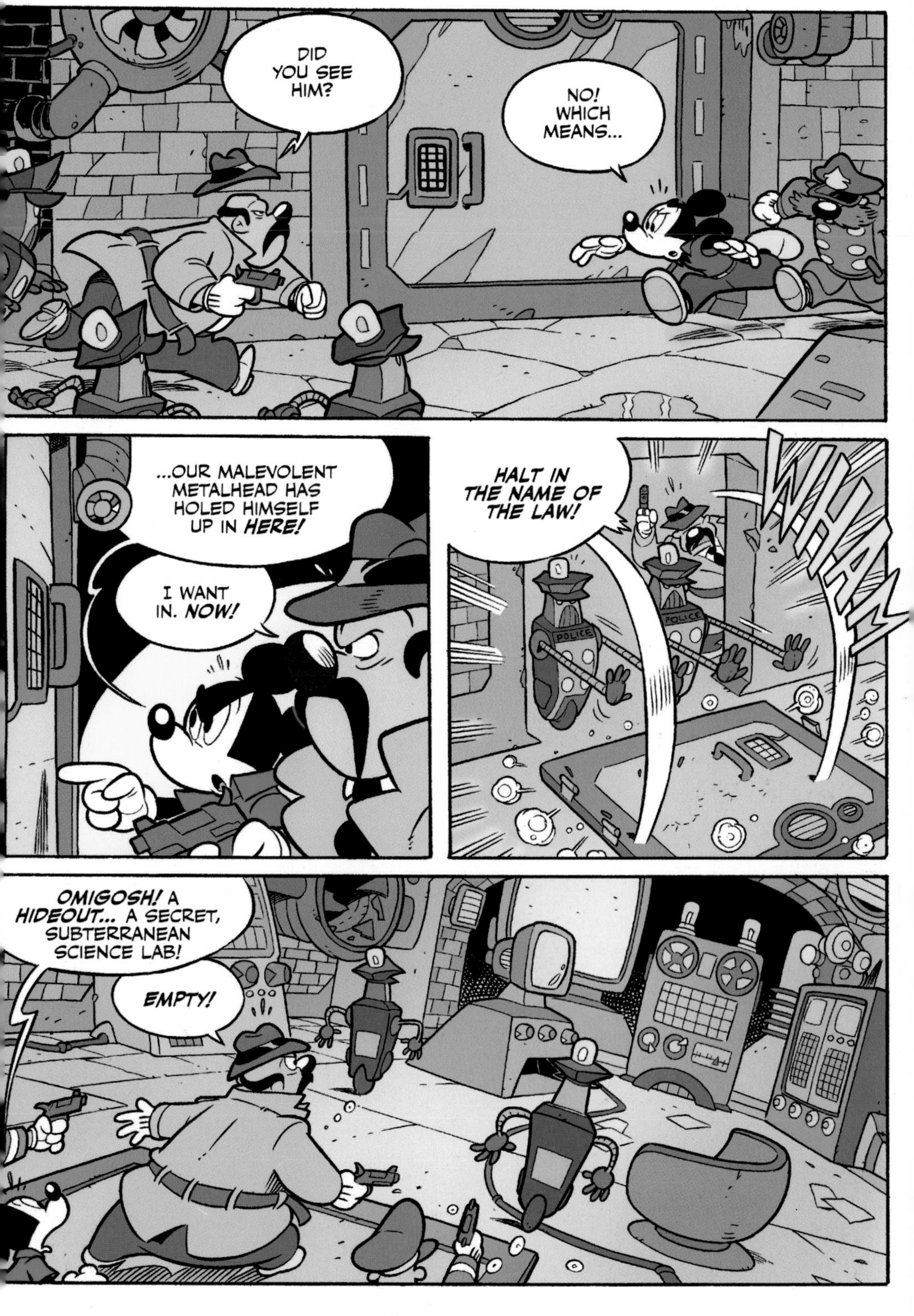
DID YOU SEE HIM?
NO! WHICH MEANS...
...OUR MALEVOLENT METALHEAD HAS HOLED HIMSELF UP IN HERE!
I WANT IN. NOW!
HALT IN THE NAME OF THE LAW!
WHAM
POLICE
POLICE
OMIGOSH! A HIDEOUT... A SECRET, SUBTERRANEAN SCIENCE LAB!
EMPTY!

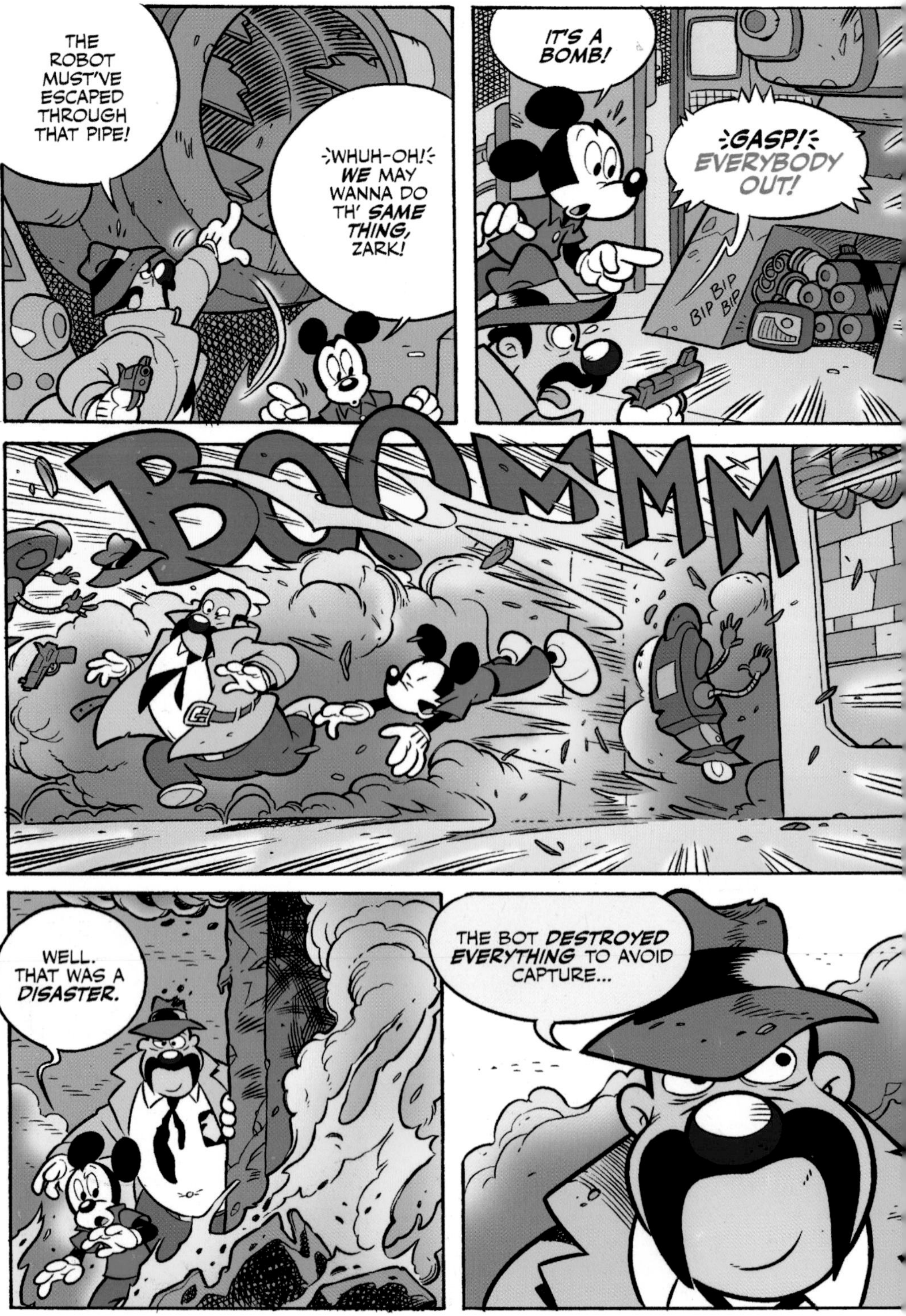
THE ROBOT MUST'VE ESCAPED THROUGH THAT PIPE!
WHUH-OH! WE MAY WANNA DO TH' SAME THING, ZARK!
IT'S A BOMB!
GASP! EVERYBODY OUT!
BIP BIP BIP
BOOMMM
WELL. THAT WAS A DISASTER.
THE BOT DESTROYED EVERYTHING TO AVOID CAPTURE...

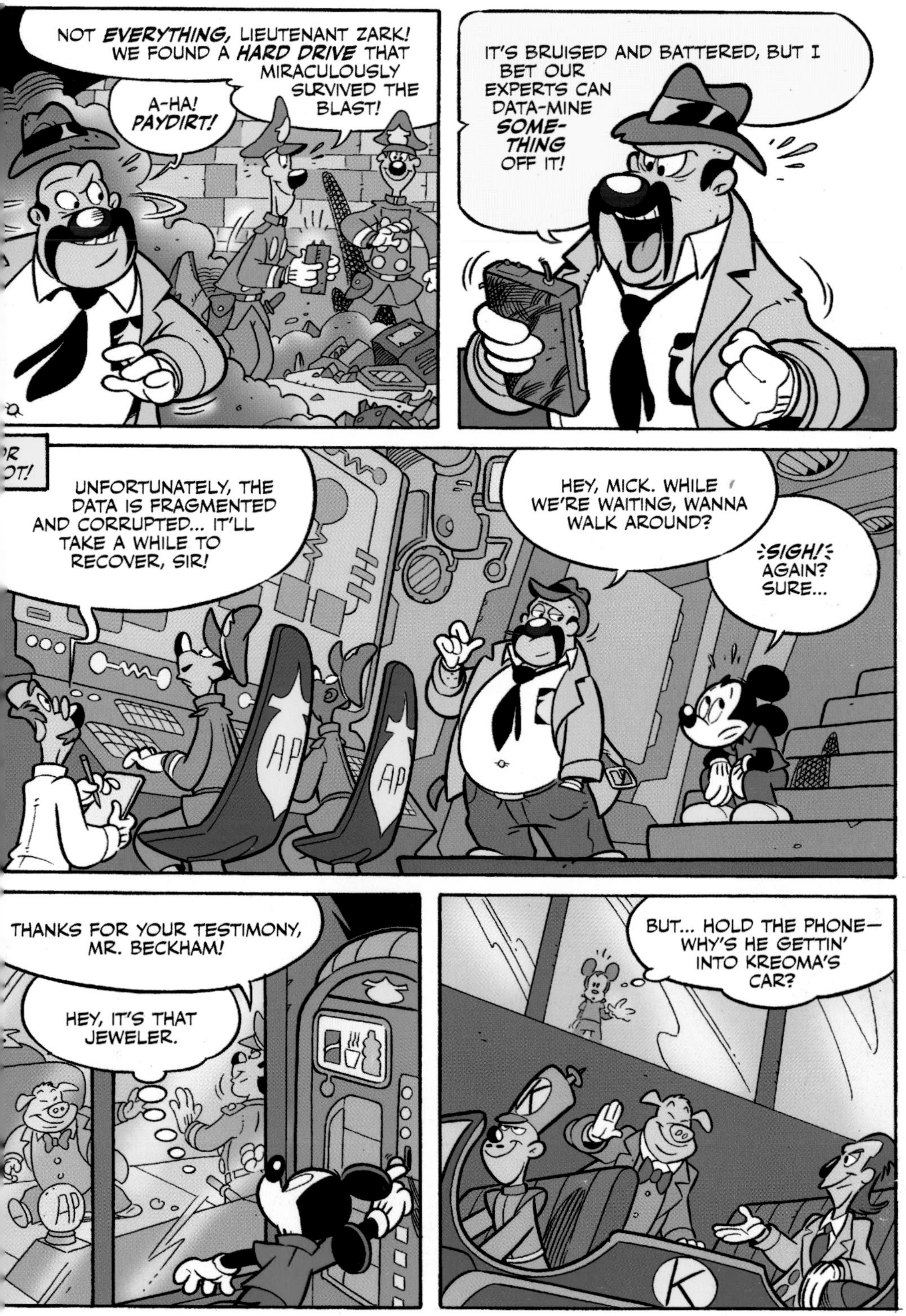
NOT *EVERYTHING,* LIEUTENANT ZARK! WE FOUND A *HARD DRIVE* THAT MIRACULOUSLY SURVIVED THE BLAST!
A-HA! *PAYDIRT!*
IT'S BRUISED AND BATTERED, BUT I BET OUR EXPERTS CAN DATA-MINE *SOME-THING* OFF IT!
UNFORTUNATELY, THE DATA IS FRAGMENTED AND CORRUPTED... IT'LL TAKE A WHILE TO RECOVER, SIR!
HEY, MICK. WHILE WE'RE WAITING, WANNA WALK AROUND?
*SIGH!* AGAIN? SURE...
THANKS FOR YOUR TESTIMONY, MR. BECKHAM!
HEY, IT'S THAT JEWELER.
BUT... HOLD THE PHONE— WHY'S HE GETTIN' INTO KREOMA'S CAR?

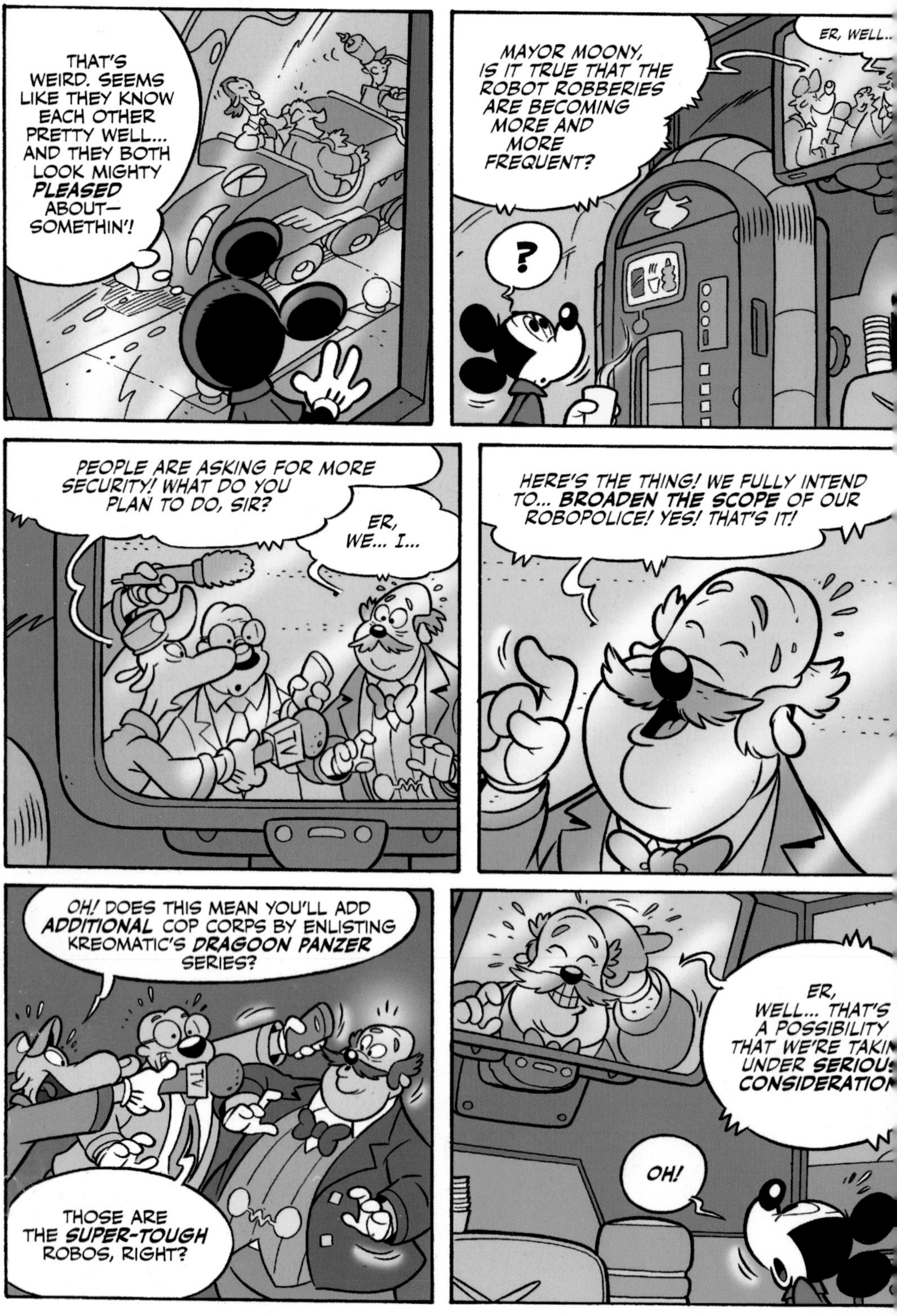
THAT'S WEIRD. SEEMS LIKE THEY KNOW EACH OTHER PRETTY WELL... AND THEY BOTH LOOK MIGHTY PLEASED ABOUT— SOMETHIN'!
MAYOR MOONY, IS IT TRUE THAT THE ROBOT ROBBERIES ARE BECOMING MORE AND MORE FREQUENT?
ER, WELL..
?
PEOPLE ARE ASKING FOR MORE SECURITY! WHAT DO YOU PLAN TO DO, SIR?
ER, WE... I...
TV
HERE'S THE THING! WE FULLY INTEND TO... BROADEN THE SCOPE OF OUR ROBOPOLICE! YES! THAT'S IT!
OH! DOES THIS MEAN YOU'LL ADD ADDITIONAL COP CORPS BY ENLISTING KREOMATIC'S DRAGOON PANZER SERIES?
TV
THOSE ARE THE SUPER-TOUGH ROBOS, RIGHT?
ER, WELL... THAT'S A POSSIBILITY THAT WE'RE TAKI UNDER SERIOU CONSIDERATIO
OH!

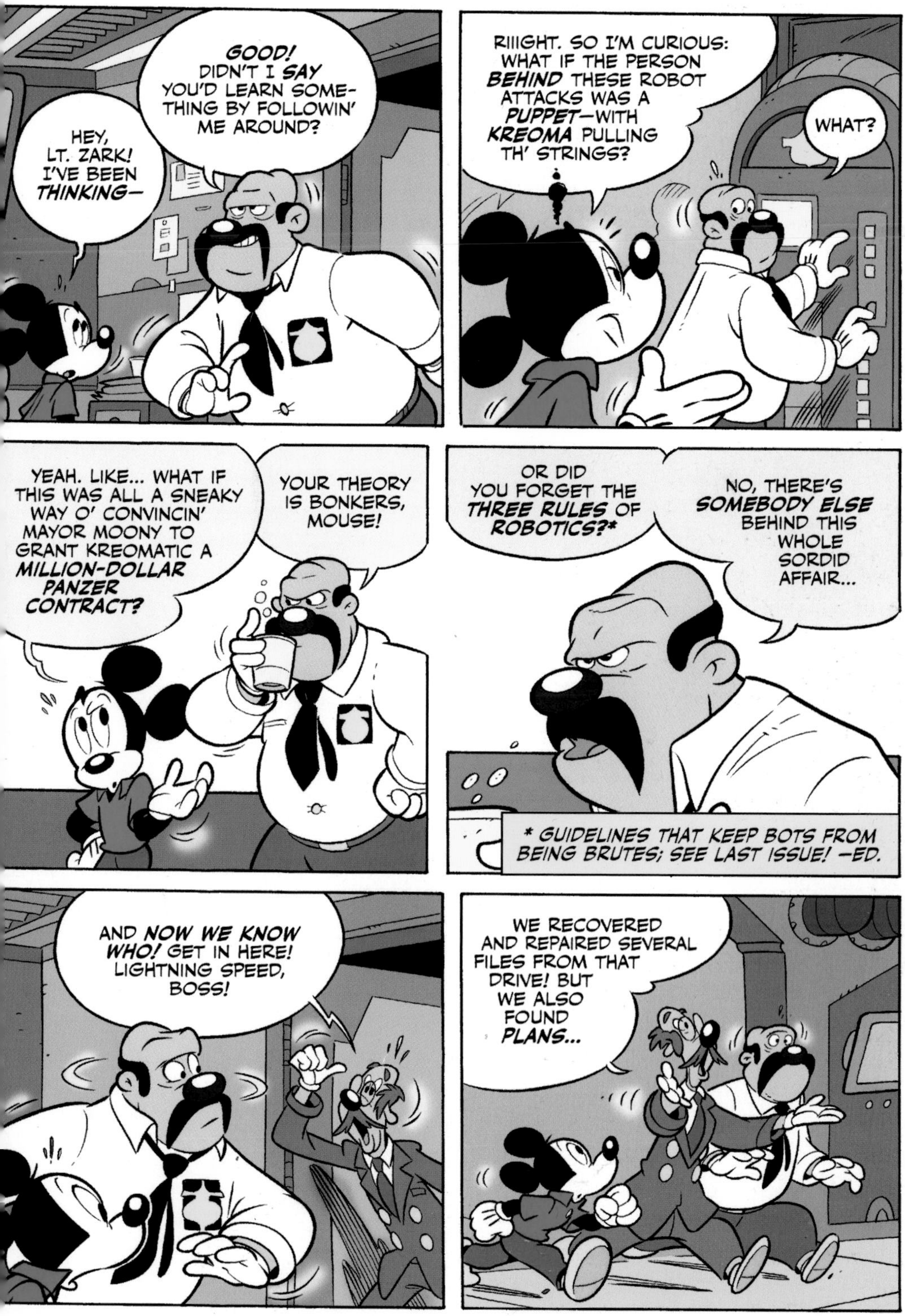
HEY, LT. ZARK! I'VE BEEN THINKING—
GOOD! DIDN'T I SAY YOU'D LEARN SOME-THING BY FOLLOWIN' ME AROUND?
RIIIGHT. SO I'M CURIOUS: WHAT IF THE PERSON BEHIND THESE ROBOT ATTACKS WAS A PUPPET—WITH KREOMA PULLING TH' STRINGS?
WHAT?
YEAH. LIKE... WHAT IF THIS WAS ALL A SNEAKY WAY O' CONVINCIN' MAYOR MOONY TO GRANT KREOMATIC A MILLION-DOLLAR PANZER CONTRACT?
YOUR THEORY IS BONKERS, MOUSE!
OR DID YOU FORGET THE THREE RULES OF ROBOTICS?*
NO, THERE'S SOMEBODY ELSE BEHIND THIS WHOLE SORDID AFFAIR...
* GUIDELINES THAT KEEP BOTS FROM BEING BRUTES; SEE LAST ISSUE! —ED.
AND NOW WE KNOW WHO! GET IN HERE! LIGHTNING SPEED, BOSS!
WE RECOVERED AND REPAIRED SEVERAL FILES FROM THAT DRIVE! BUT WE ALSO FOUND PLANS...

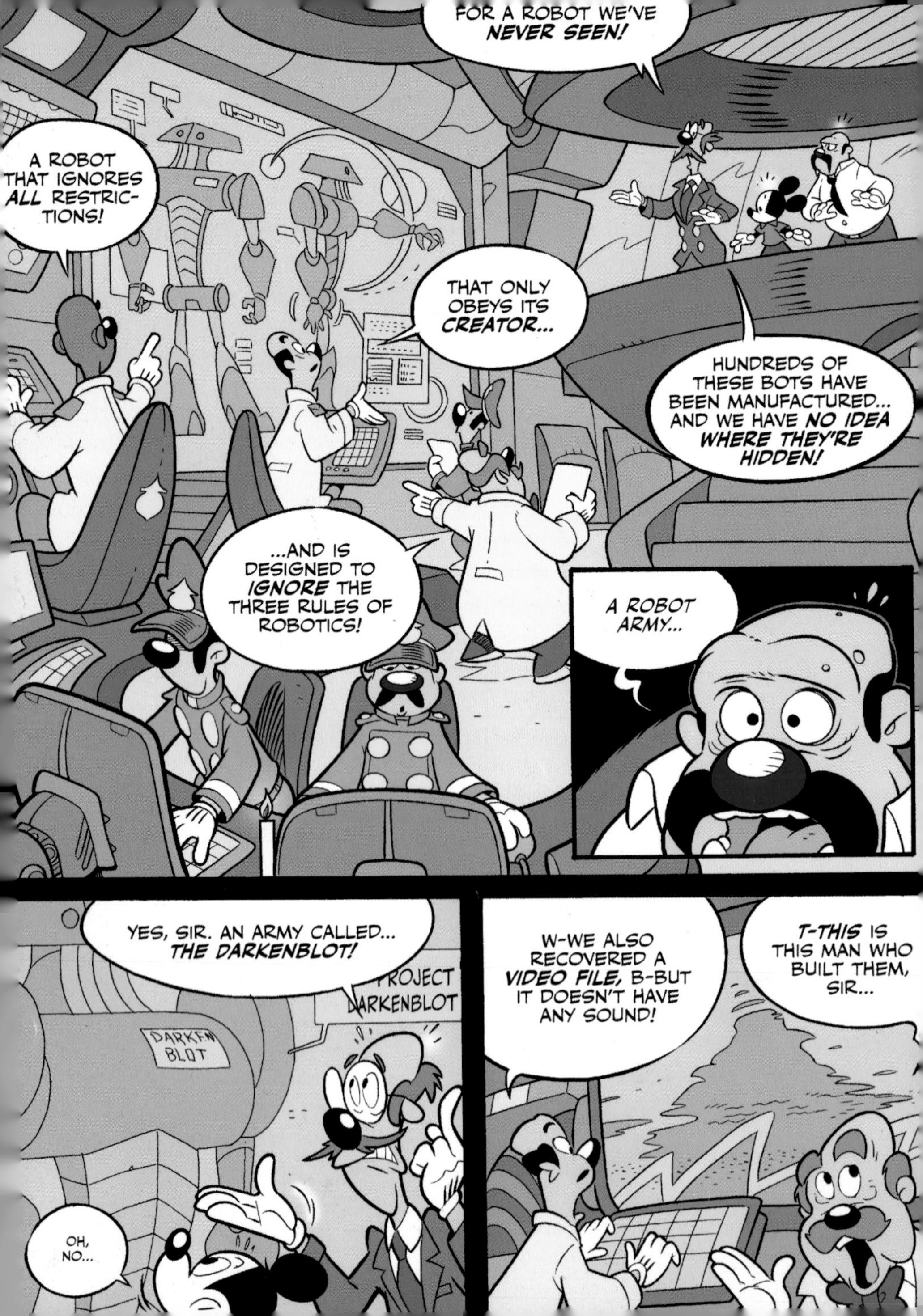
A ROBOT THAT IGNORES ALL RESTRICTIONS!
FOR A ROBOT WE'VE NEVER SEEN!
THAT ONLY OBEYS ITS CREATOR...
...AND IS DESIGNED TO IGNORE THE THREE RULES OF ROBOTICS!
HUNDREDS OF THESE BOTS HAVE BEEN MANUFACTURED... AND WE HAVE NO IDEA WHERE THEY'RE HIDDEN!
A ROBOT ARMY...
YES, SIR. AN ARMY CALLED... THE DARKENBLOT!
PROJECT DARKENBLOT
DARKEN BLOT
OH, NO...
W-WE ALSO RECOVERED A VIDEO FILE, B-BUT IT DOESN'T HAVE ANY SOUND!
T-THIS IS THIS MAN WHO BUILT THEM, SIR...

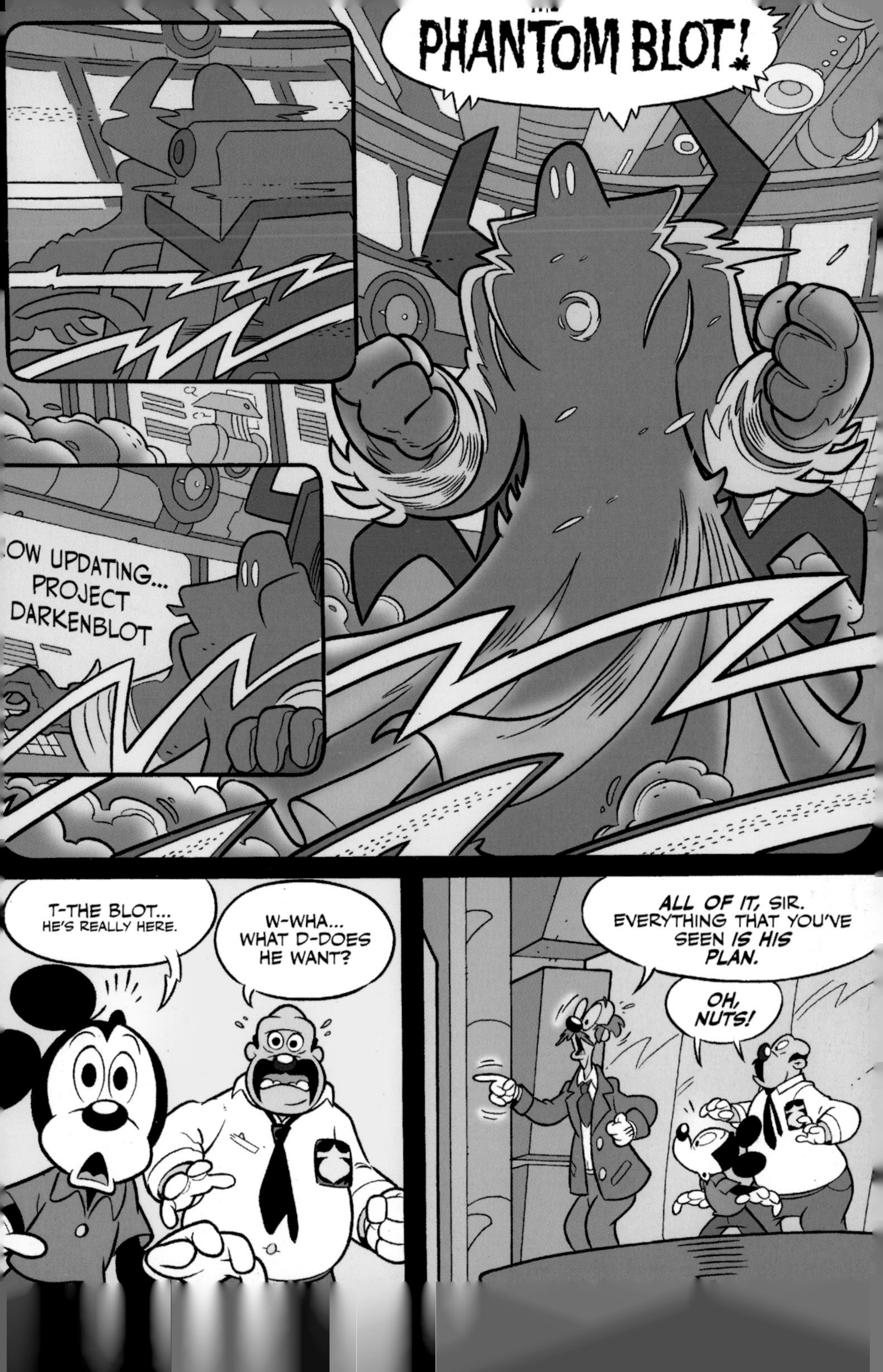
PHANTOM BLOT!
OW UPDATING... PROJECT DARKENBLOT
T-THE BLOT... HE'S REALLY HERE.
W-WHA... WHAT D-DOES HE WANT?
ALL OF IT, SIR. EVERYTHING THAT YOU'VE SEEN IS HIS PLAN.
OH, NUTS!

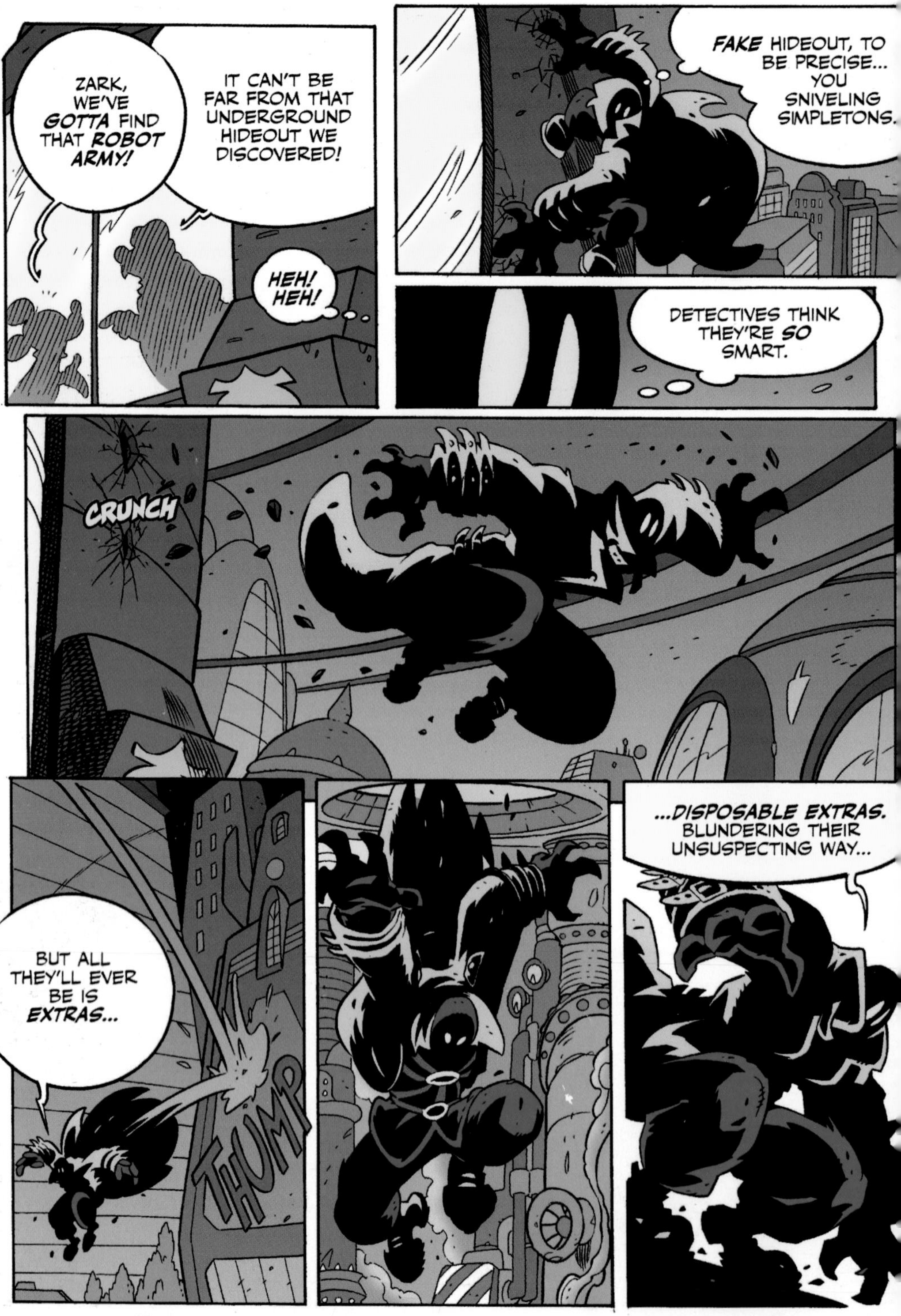
ZARK, WE'VE GOTTA FIND THAT ROBOT ARMY!
IT CAN'T BE FAR FROM THAT UNDERGROUND HIDEOUT WE DISCOVERED!
HEH! HEH!
FAKE HIDEOUT, TO BE PRECISE... YOU SNIVELING SIMPLETONS.
DETECTIVES THINK THEY'RE SO SMART.
CRUNCH
BUT ALL THEY'LL EVER BE IS EXTRAS...
THUMP
...DISPOSABLE EXTRAS. BLUNDERING THEIR UNSUSPECTING WAY...

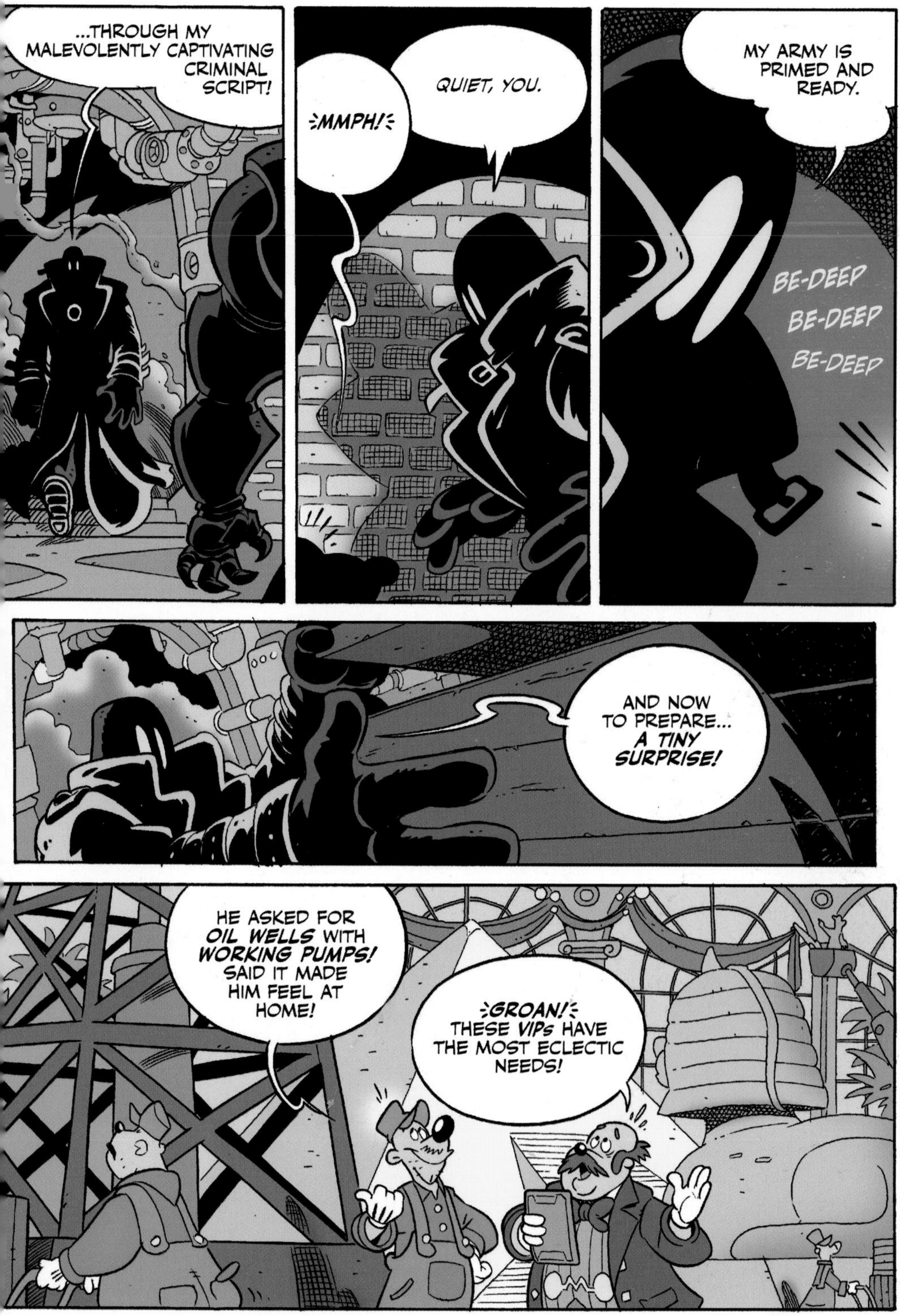
...THROUGH MY MALEVOLENTLY CAPTIVATING CRIMINAL SCRIPT!
MMPH!
QUIET, YOU.
MY ARMY IS PRIMED AND READY.
BE-DEEP
BE-DEEP
BE-DEEP
AND NOW TO PREPARE... A TINY SURPRISE!
HE ASKED FOR OIL WELLS WITH WORKING PUMPS! SAID IT MADE HIM FEEL AT HOME!
GROAN! THESE VIPs HAVE THE MOST ECLECTIC NEEDS!

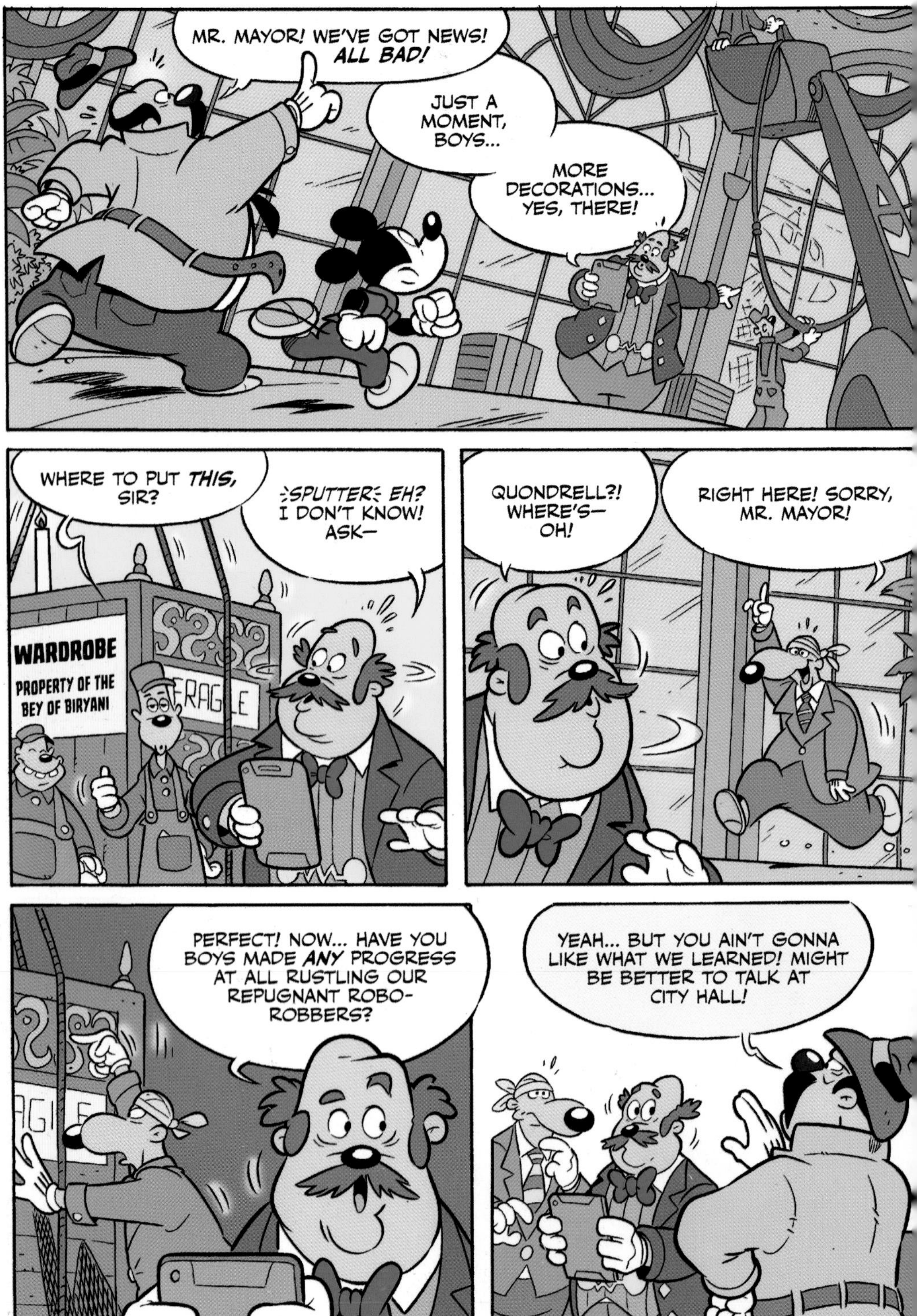
MR. MAYOR! WE'VE GOT NEWS! ALL BAD!
JUST A MOMENT, BOYS...
MORE DECORATIONS... YES, THERE!
WHERE TO PUT THIS, SIR?
WARDROBE
PROPERTY OF THE BEY OF BIRYANI
FRAGILE
-SPUTTER- EH? I DON'T KNOW! ASK—
QUONDRELL?! WHERE'S— OH!
RIGHT HERE! SORRY, MR. MAYOR!
PERFECT! NOW... HAVE YOU BOYS MADE ANY PROGRESS AT ALL RUSTLING OUR REPUGNANT ROBO-ROBBERS?
YEAH... BUT YOU AIN'T GONNA LIKE WHAT WE LEARNED! MIGHT BE BETTER TO TALK AT CITY HALL!

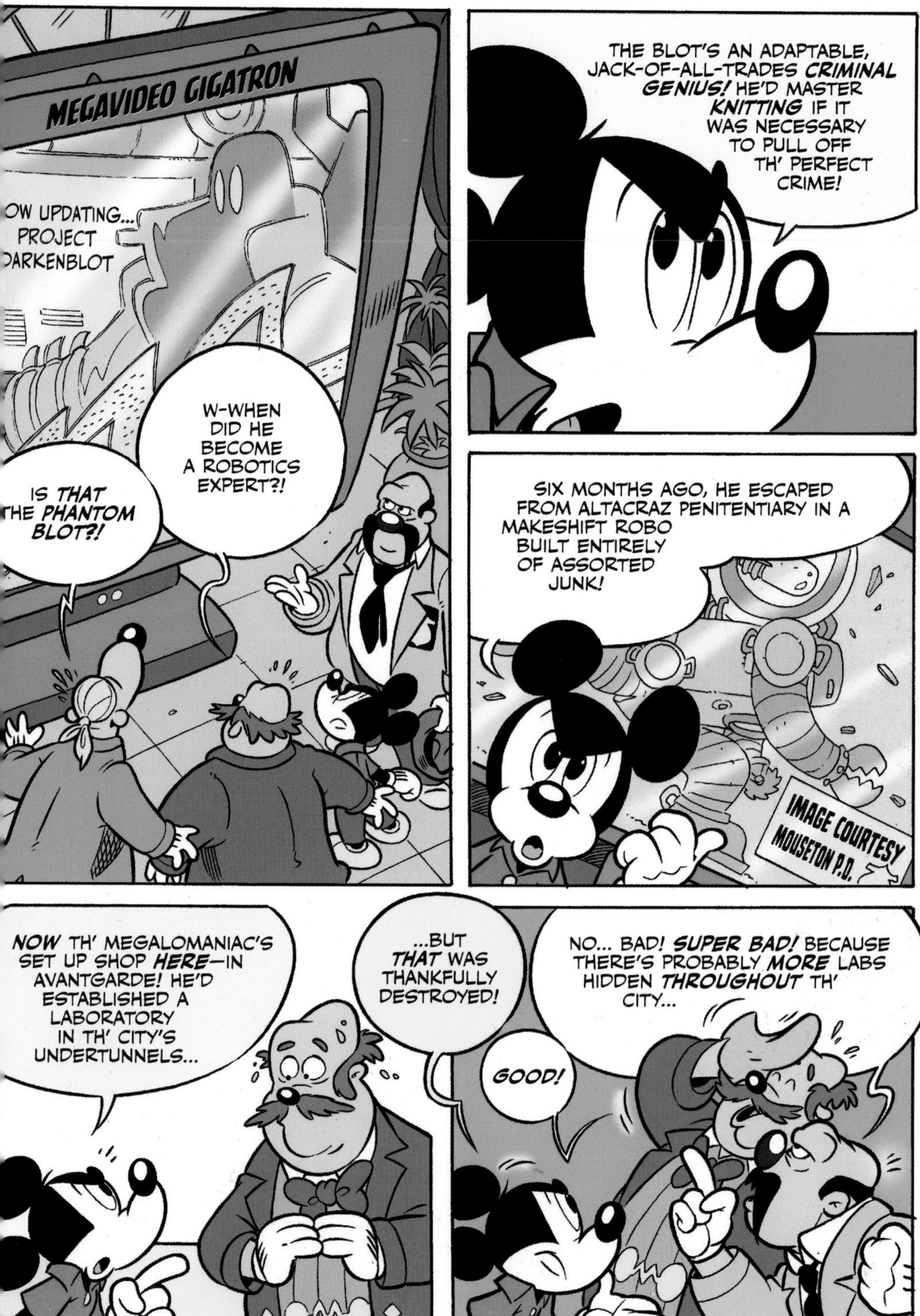
MEGAVIDEO GIGATRON
OW UPDATING... PROJECT ARKENBLOT
IS THAT THE PHANTOM BLOT?!
W-WHEN DID HE BECOME A ROBOTICS EXPERT?!
THE BLOT'S AN ADAPTABLE, JACK-OF-ALL-TRADES CRIMINAL GENIUS! HE'D MASTER KNITTING IF IT WAS NECESSARY TO PULL OFF TH' PERFECT CRIME!
SIX MONTHS AGO, HE ESCAPED FROM ALTACRAZ PENITENTIARY IN A MAKESHIFT ROBO BUILT ENTIRELY OF ASSORTED JUNK!
IMAGE COURTESY MOUSETON P.D.
NOW TH' MEGALOMANIAC'S SET UP SHOP HERE—IN AVANTGARDE! HE'D ESTABLISHED A LABORATORY IN TH' CITY'S UNDERTUNNELS...
...BUT THAT WAS THANKFULLY DESTROYED!
GOOD!
NO... BAD! SUPER BAD! BECAUSE THERE'S PROBABLY MORE LABS HIDDEN THROUGHOUT TH' CITY...

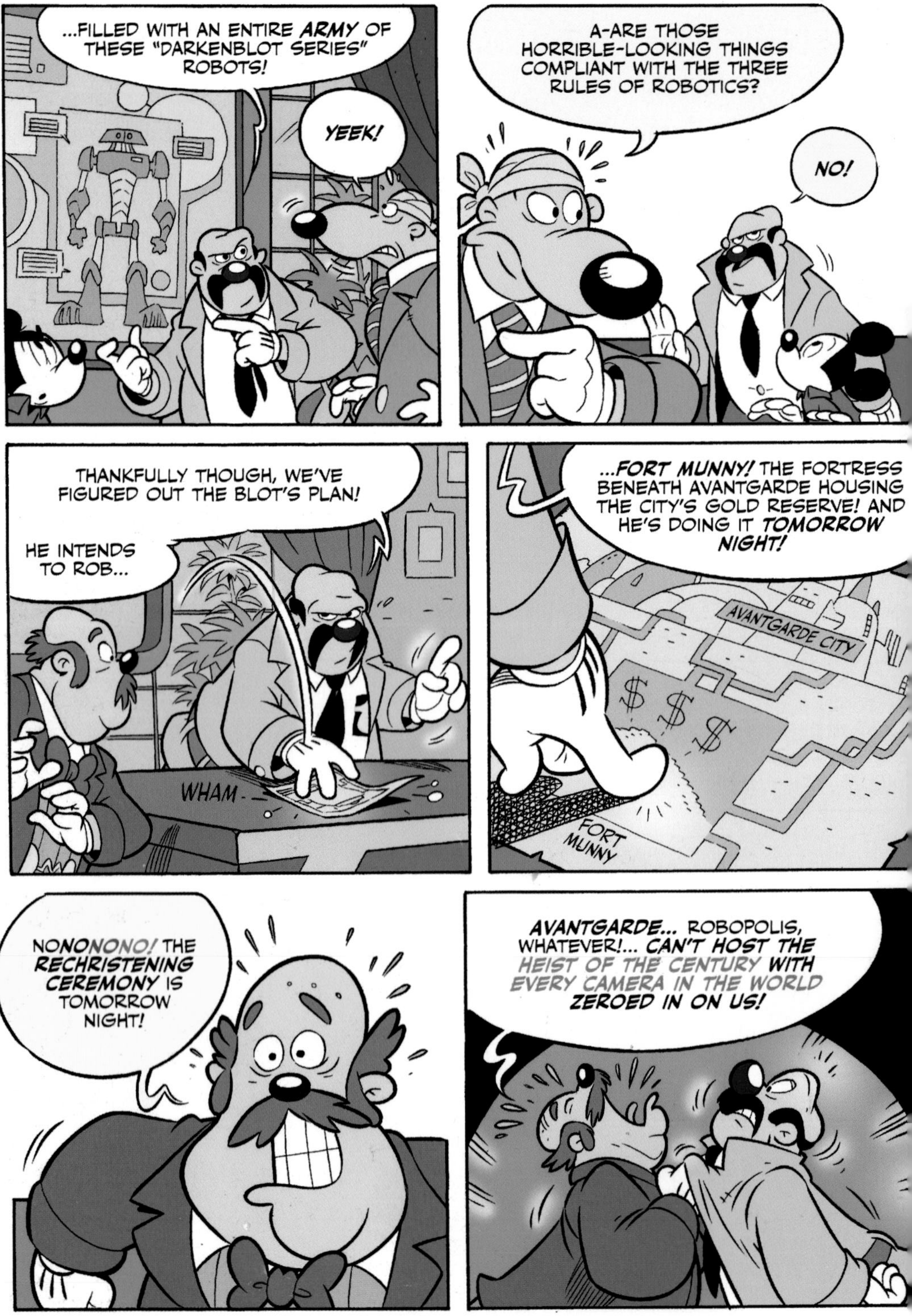
...FILLED WITH AN ENTIRE ARMY OF THESE "DARKENBLOT SERIES" ROBOTS!
YEEK!
A-ARE THOSE HORRIBLE-LOOKING THINGS COMPLIANT WITH THE THREE RULES OF ROBOTICS?
NO!
THANKFULLY THOUGH, WE'VE FIGURED OUT THE BLOT'S PLAN!
HE INTENDS TO ROB...
WHAM
...FORT MUNNY! THE FORTRESS BENEATH AVANTGARDE HOUSING THE CITY'S GOLD RESERVE! AND HE'S DOING IT TOMORROW NIGHT!
AVANTGARDE CITY
FORT MUNNY
NONONONO! THE RECHRISTENING CEREMONY IS TOMORROW NIGHT!
AVANTGARDE... ROBOPOLIS, WHATEVER!... CAN'T HOST THE HEIST OF THE CENTURY WITH EVERY CAMERA IN THE WORLD ZEROED IN ON US!

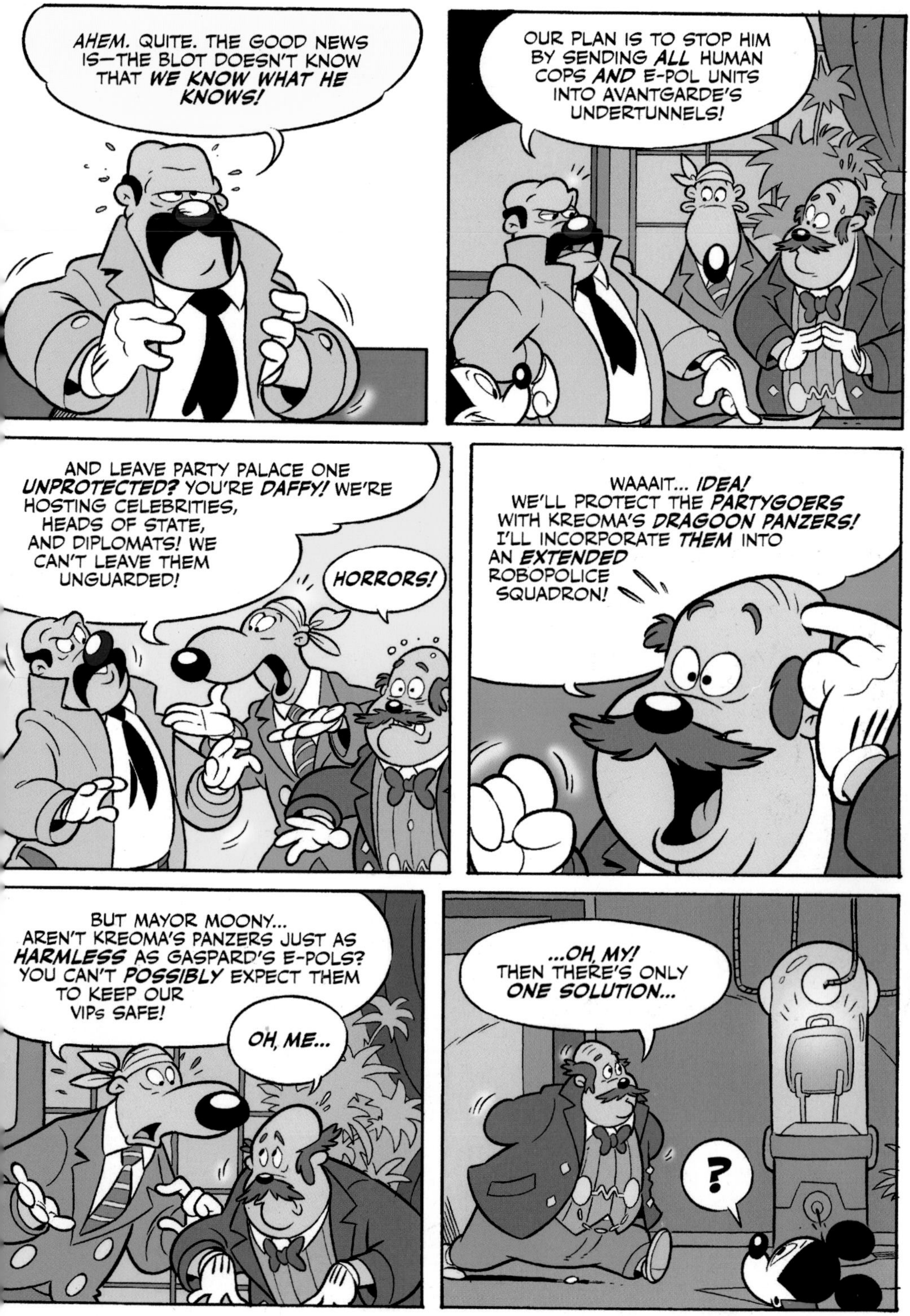
AHEM. QUITE. THE GOOD NEWS IS—THE BLOT DOESN'T KNOW THAT WE KNOW WHAT HE KNOWS!
OUR PLAN IS TO STOP HIM BY SENDING ALL HUMAN COPS AND E-POL UNITS INTO AVANTGARDE'S UNDERTUNNELS!
AND LEAVE PARTY PALACE ONE UNPROTECTED? YOU'RE DAFFY! WE'RE HOSTING CELEBRITIES, HEADS OF STATE, AND DIPLOMATS! WE CAN'T LEAVE THEM UNGUARDED!
HORRORS!
WAAAIT... IDEA! WE'LL PROTECT THE PARTYGOERS WITH KREOMA'S DRAGOON PANZERS! I'LL INCORPORATE THEM INTO AN EXTENDED ROBOPOLICE SQUADRON!
BUT MAYOR MOONY... AREN'T KREOMA'S PANZERS JUST AS HARMLESS AS GASPARD'S E-POLS? YOU CAN'T POSSIBLY EXPECT THEM TO KEEP OUR VIPs SAFE!
OH, ME...
...OH, MY! THEN THERE'S ONLY ONE SOLUTION...
?

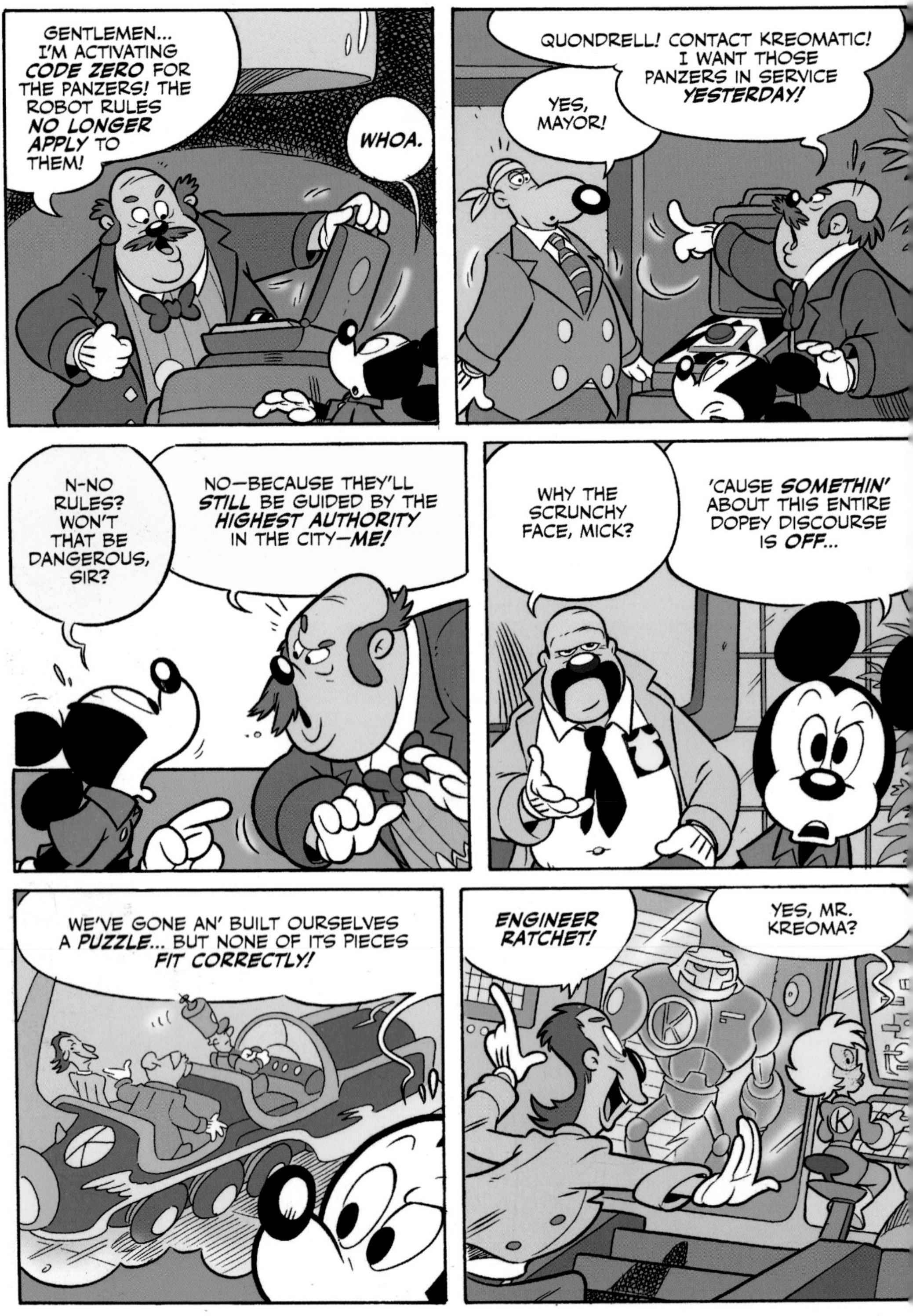
GENTLEMEN... I'M ACTIVATING CODE ZERO FOR THE PANZERS! THE ROBOT RULES NO LONGER APPLY TO THEM!
WHOA.
QUONDRELL! CONTACT KREOMATIC! I WANT THOSE PANZERS IN SERVICE YESTERDAY!
YES, MAYOR!
N-NO RULES? WON'T THAT BE DANGEROUS, SIR?
NO—BECAUSE THEY'LL STILL BE GUIDED BY THE HIGHEST AUTHORITY IN THE CITY—ME!
WHY THE SCRUNCHY FACE, MICK?
'CAUSE SOMETHIN' ABOUT THIS ENTIRE DOPEY DISCOURSE IS OFF...
WE'VE GONE AN' BUILT OURSELVES A PUZZLE... BUT NONE OF ITS PIECES FIT CORRECTLY!
ENGINEER RATCHET!
YES, MR. KREOMA?

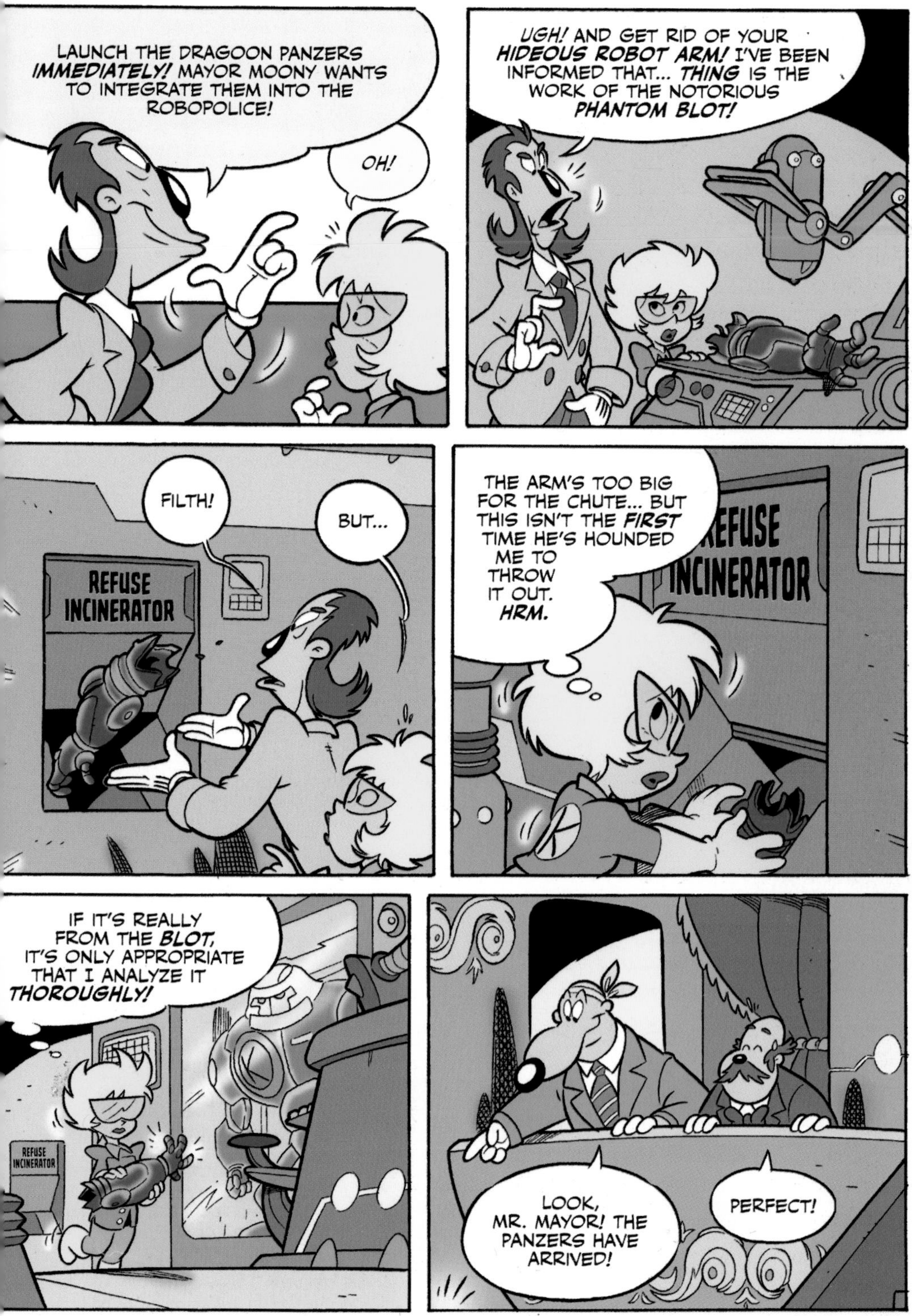
LAUNCH THE DRAGOON PANZERS *IMMEDIATELY!* MAYOR MOONY WANTS TO INTEGRATE THEM INTO THE ROBOPOLICE!
OH!
UGH! AND GET RID OF YOUR *HIDEOUS ROBOT ARM!* I'VE BEEN INFORMED THAT... *THING* IS THE WORK OF THE NOTORIOUS *PHANTOM BLOT!*
FILTH!
BUT...
REFUSE INCINERATOR
THE ARM'S TOO BIG FOR THE CHUTE... BUT THIS ISN'T THE *FIRST* TIME HE'S HOUNDED ME TO THROW IT OUT. *HRM.*
REFUSE INCINERATOR
IF IT'S REALLY FROM THE *BLOT,* IT'S ONLY APPROPRIATE THAT I ANALYZE IT *THOROUGHLY!*
REFUSE INCINERATOR
LOOK, MR. MAYOR! THE PANZERS HAVE ARRIVED!
PERFECT!

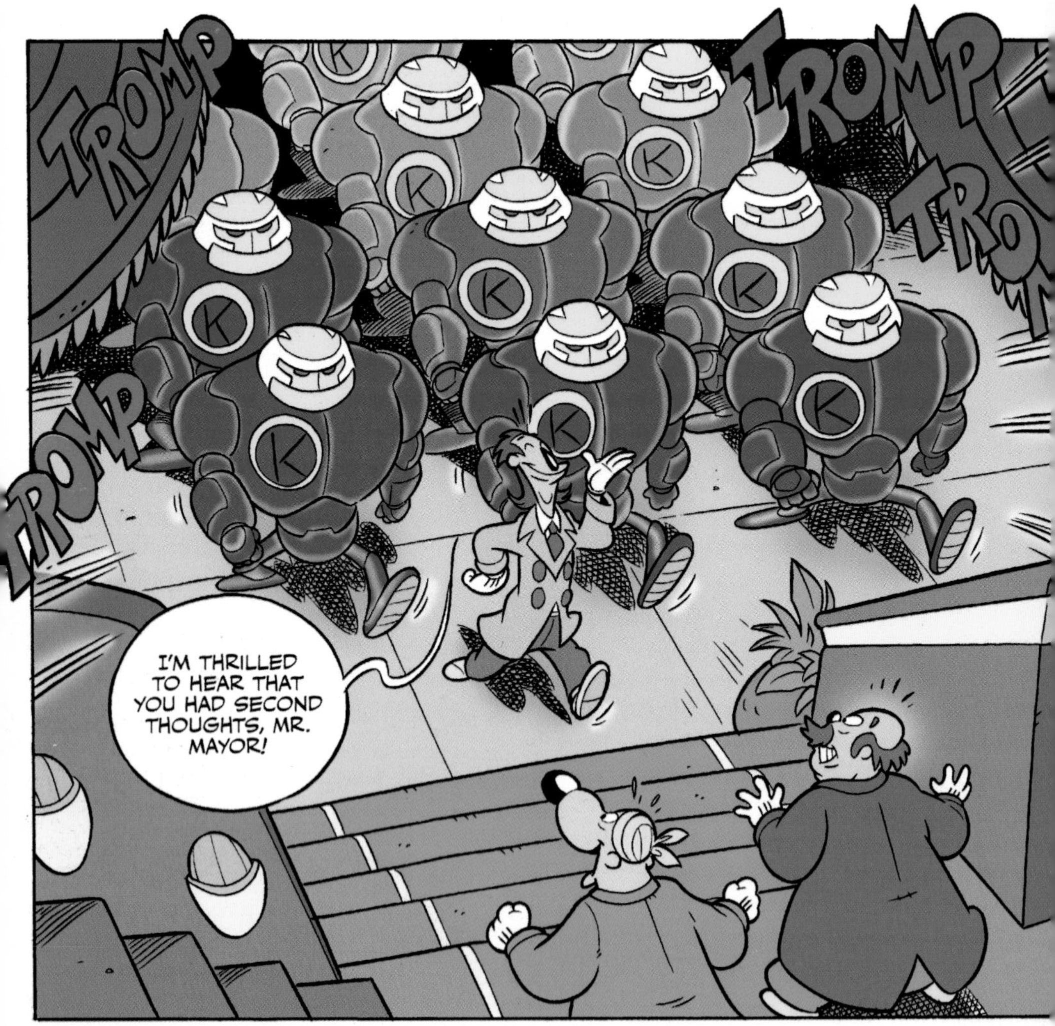
TROMP
TROMP
TROMP
TROMP
TRO
I'M THRILLED TO HEAR THAT YOU HAD SECOND THOUGHTS, MR. MAYOR!

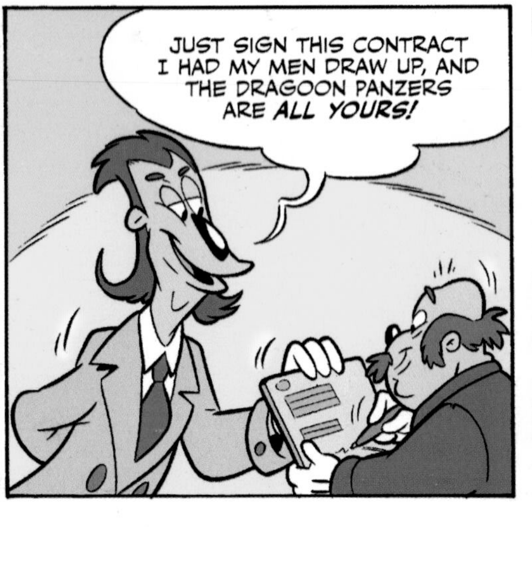
JUST SIGN THIS CONTRACT I HAD MY MEN DRAW UP, AND THE DRAGOON PANZERS ARE ALL YOURS!

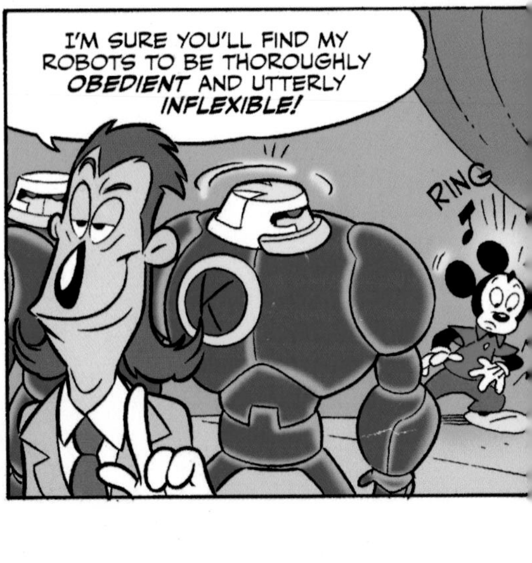
I'M SURE YOU'LL FIND MY ROBOTS TO BE THOROUGHLY OBEDIENT AND UTTERLY INFLEXIBLE!
RING

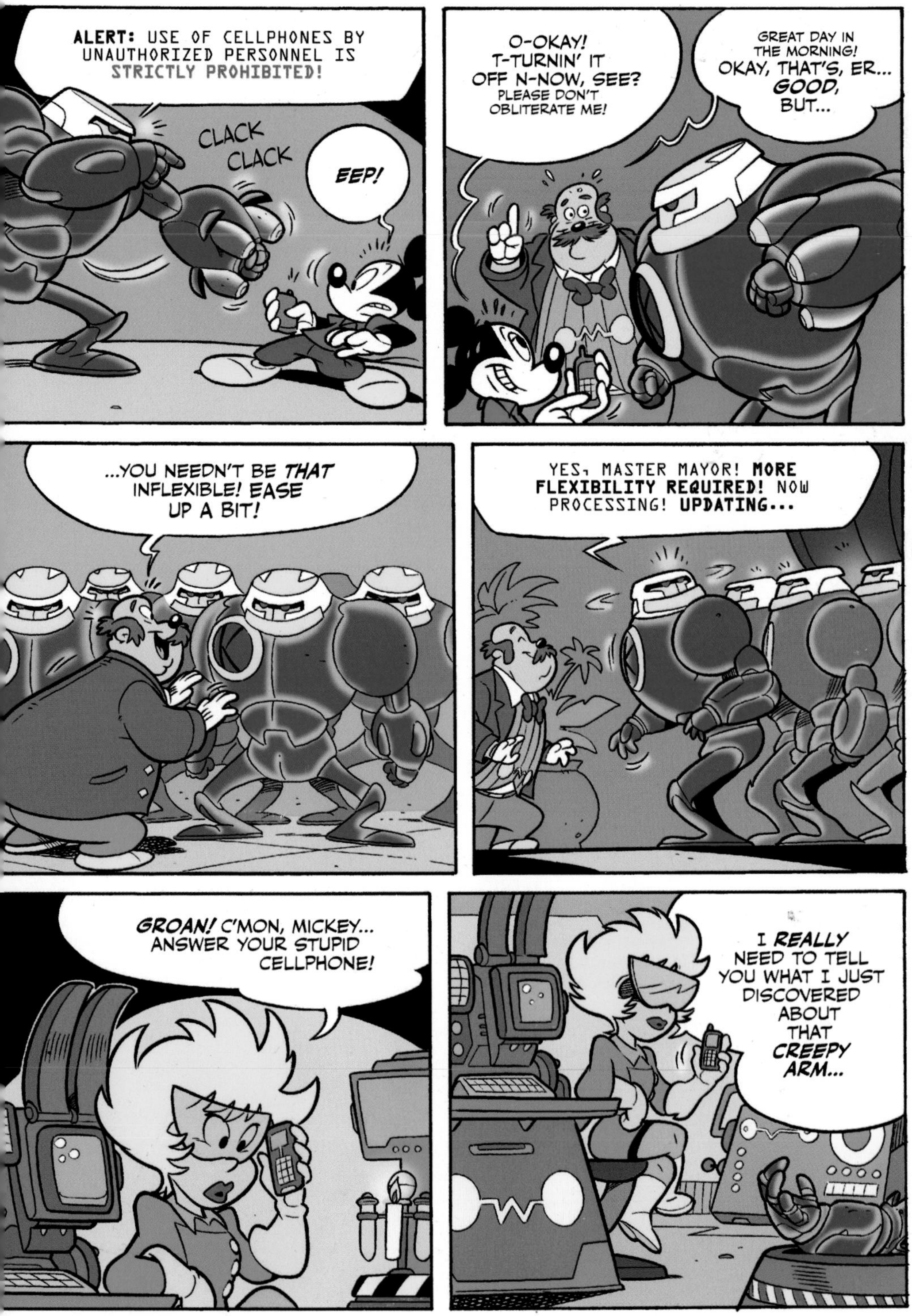
ALERT: USE OF CELLPHONES BY UNAUTHORIZED PERSONNEL IS STRICTLY PROHIBITED!
CLACK CLACK
EEP!
O-OKAY! T-TURNIN' IT OFF N-NOW, SEE? PLEASE DON'T OBLITERATE ME!
GREAT DAY IN THE MORNING! OKAY, THAT'S, ER... GOOD, BUT...
...YOU NEEDN'T BE THAT INFLEXIBLE! EASE UP A BIT!
YES, MASTER MAYOR! MORE FLEXIBILITY REQUIRED! NOW PROCESSING! UPDATING...
GROAN! C'MON, MICKEY... ANSWER YOUR STUPID CELLPHONE!
I REALLY NEED TO TELL YOU WHAT I JUST DISCOVERED ABOUT THAT CREEPY ARM...

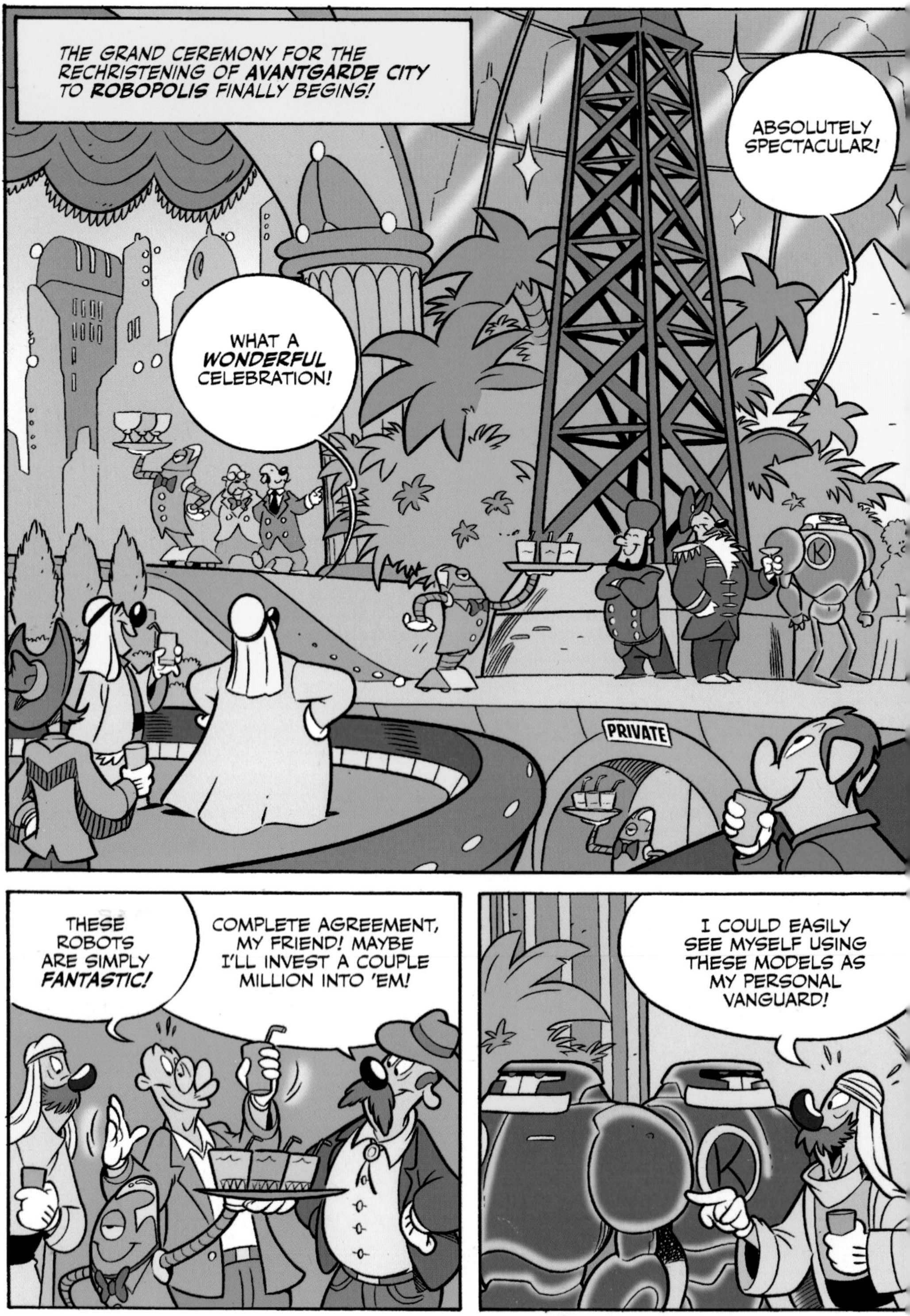
THE GRAND CEREMONY FOR THE RECHRISTENING OF AVANTGARDE CITY TO ROBOPOLIS FINALLY BEGINS!
WHAT A WONDERFUL CELEBRATION!
ABSOLUTELY SPECTACULAR!
PRIVATE
THESE ROBOTS ARE SIMPLY FANTASTIC!
COMPLETE AGREEMENT, MY FRIEND! MAYBE I'LL INVEST A COUPLE MILLION INTO 'EM!
I COULD EASILY SEE MYSELF USING THESE MODELS AS MY PERSONAL VANGUARD!

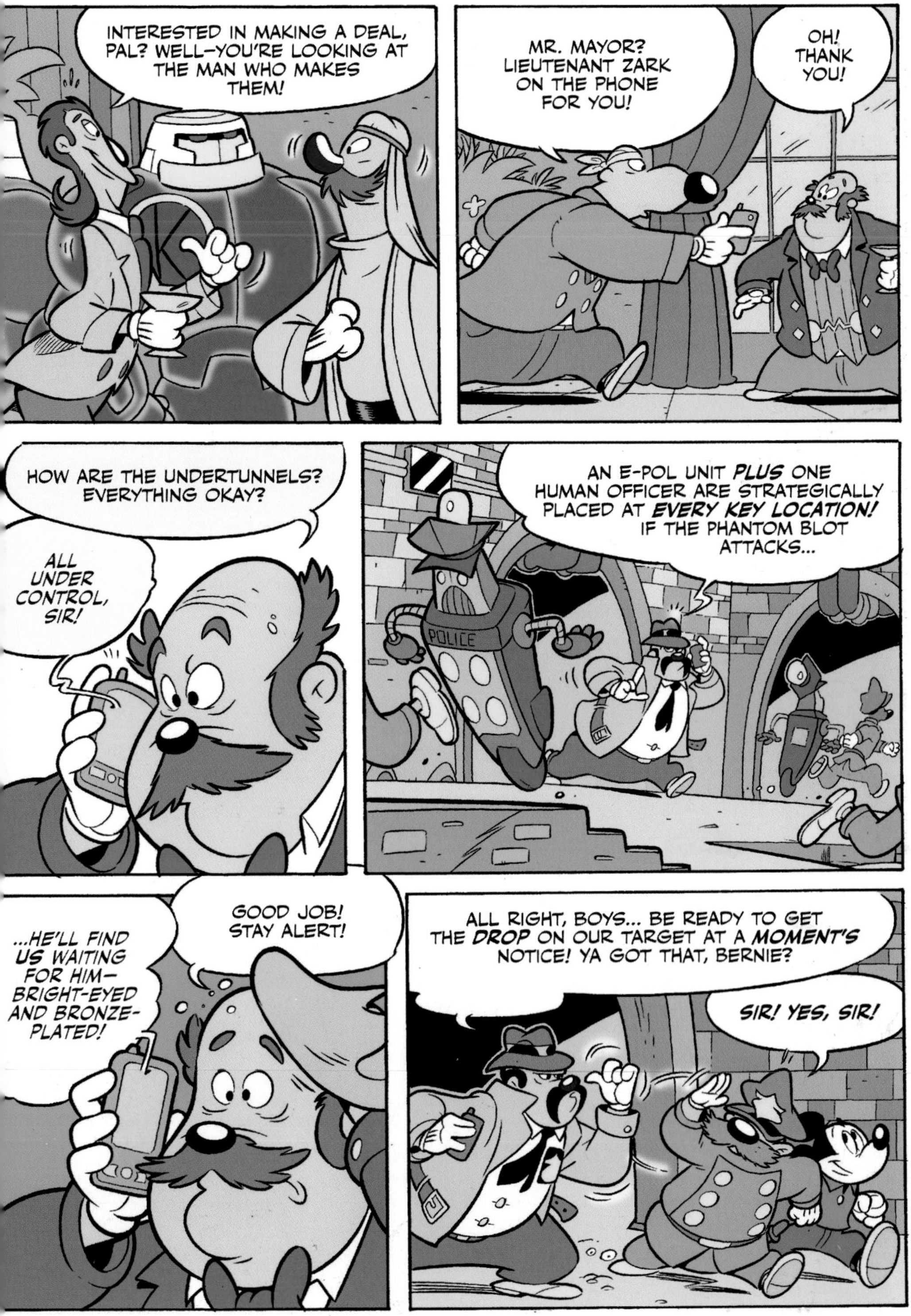
INTERESTED IN MAKING A DEAL, PAL? WELL—YOU'RE LOOKING AT THE MAN WHO MAKES THEM!
MR. MAYOR? LIEUTENANT ZARK ON THE PHONE FOR YOU!
OH! THANK YOU!
HOW ARE THE UNDERTUNNELS? EVERYTHING OKAY?
ALL UNDER CONTROL, SIR!
AN E-POL UNIT PLUS ONE HUMAN OFFICER ARE STRATEGICALLY PLACED AT EVERY KEY LOCATION! IF THE PHANTOM BLOT ATTACKS...
POLICE
...HE'LL FIND US WAITING FOR HIM—BRIGHT-EYED AND BRONZE-PLATED!
GOOD JOB! STAY ALERT!
ALL RIGHT, BOYS... BE READY TO GET THE DROP ON OUR TARGET AT A MOMENT'S NOTICE! YA GOT THAT, BERNIE?
SIR! YES, SIR!

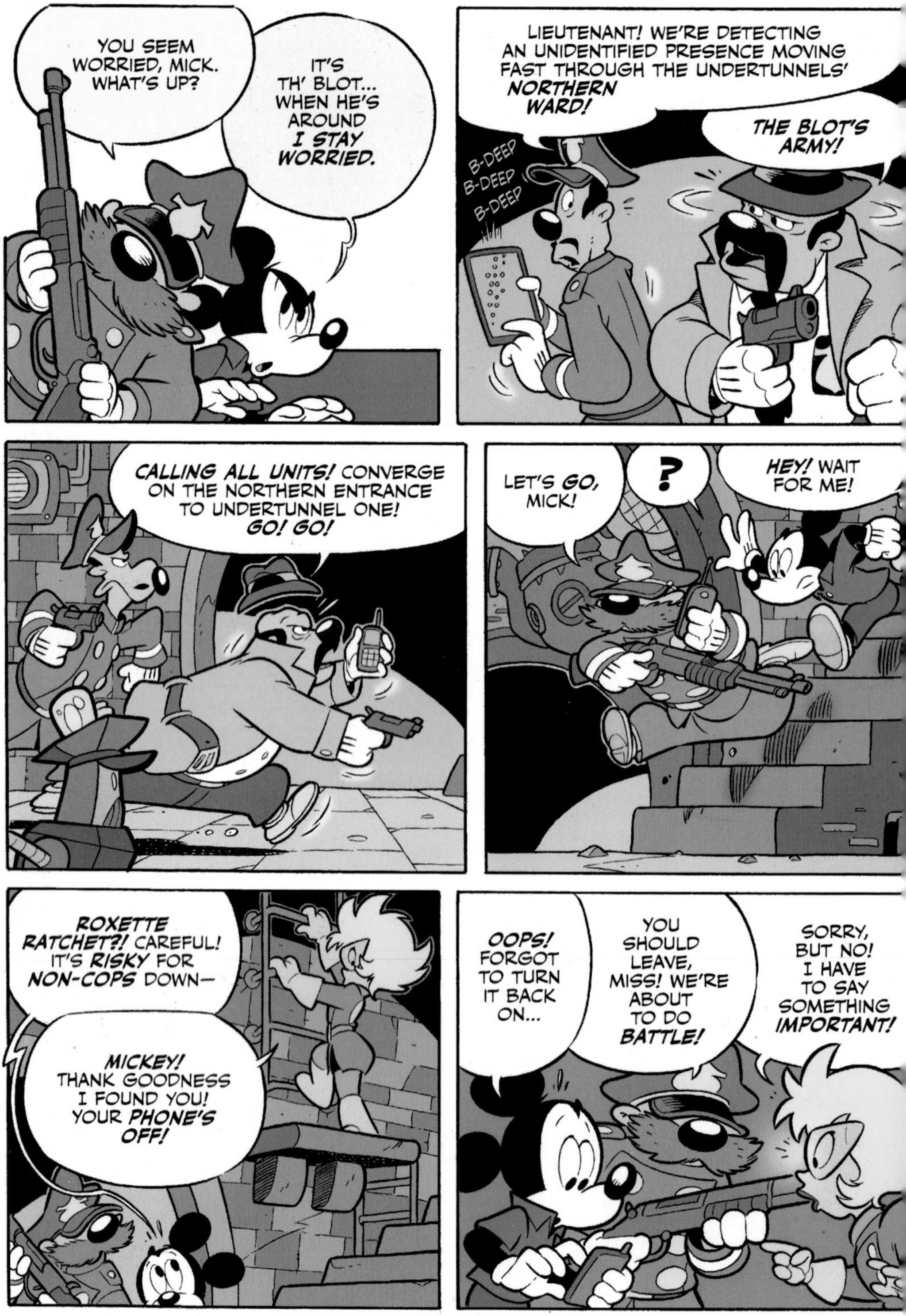

YOU SEEM WORRIED, MICK. WHAT'S UP?
IT'S TH' BLOT... WHEN HE'S AROUND I STAY WORRIED.
LIEUTENANT! WE'RE DETECTING AN UNIDENTIFIED PRESENCE MOVING FAST THROUGH THE UNDERTUNNELS' NORTHERN WARD!
B-DEEP B-DEEP B-DEEP
THE BLOT'S ARMY!
CALLING ALL UNITS! CONVERGE ON THE NORTHERN ENTRANCE TO UNDERTUNNEL ONE! GO! GO!
LET'S GO, MICK!
?
HEY! WAIT FOR ME!
ROXETTE RATCHET?! CAREFUL! IT'S RISKY FOR NON-COPS DOWN—
MICKEY! THANK GOODNESS I FOUND YOU! YOUR PHONE'S OFF!
OOPS! FORGOT TO TURN IT BACK ON...
YOU SHOULD LEAVE, MISS! WE'RE ABOUT TO DO BATTLE!
SORRY, BUT NO! I HAVE TO SAY SOMETHING IMPORTANT!

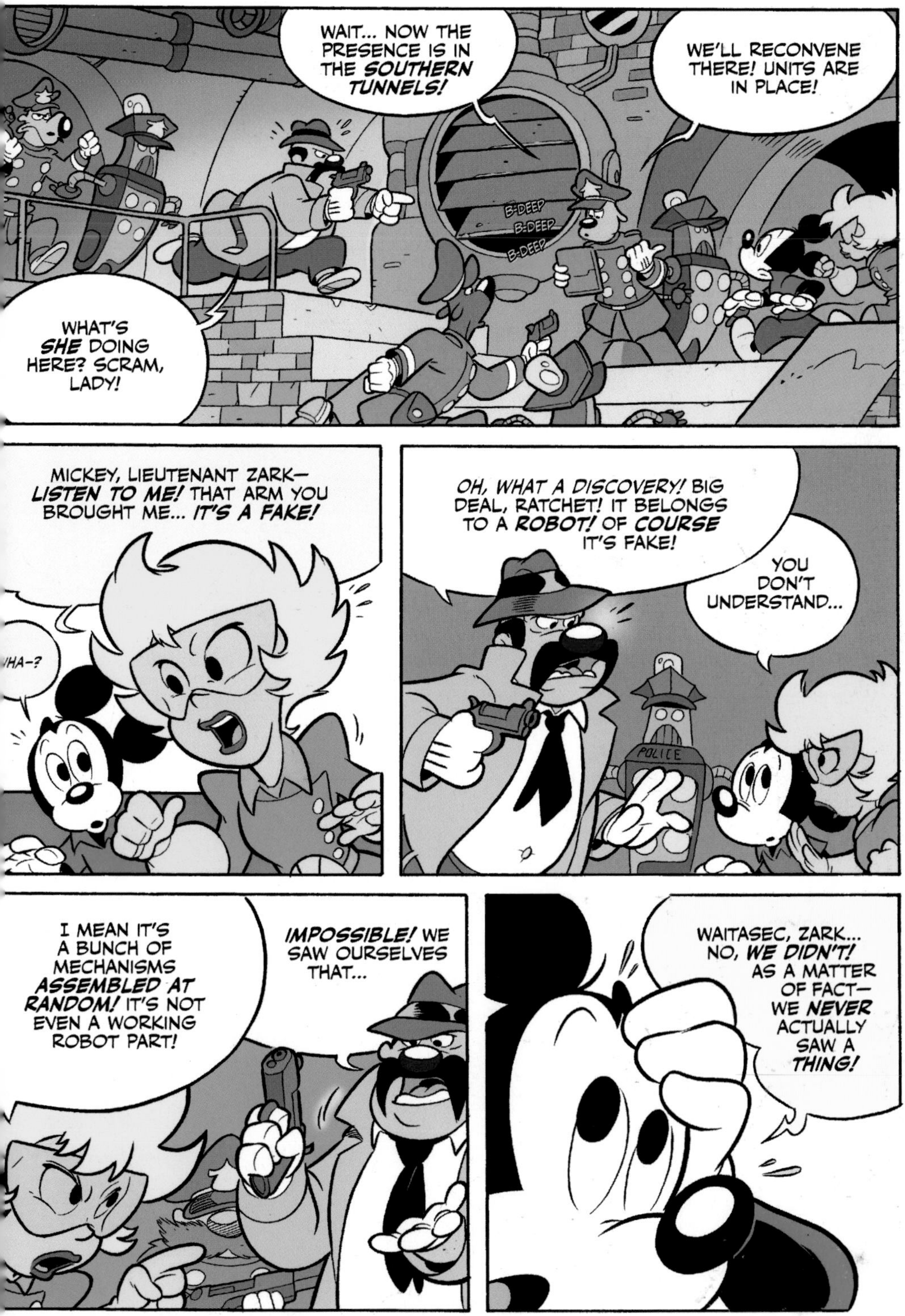
WAIT... NOW THE PRESENCE IS IN THE SOUTHERN TUNNELS!
WE'LL RECONVENE THERE! UNITS ARE IN PLACE!
B-DEEP B-DEEP B-DEEP
WHAT'S SHE DOING HERE? SCRAM, LADY!
MICKEY, LIEUTENANT ZARK— LISTEN TO ME! THAT ARM YOU BROUGHT ME... IT'S A FAKE!
WHA-?
OH, WHAT A DISCOVERY! BIG DEAL, RATCHET! IT BELONGS TO A ROBOT! OF COURSE IT'S FAKE!
YOU DON'T UNDERSTAND...
POLICE
I MEAN IT'S A BUNCH OF MECHANISMS ASSEMBLED AT RANDOM! IT'S NOT EVEN A WORKING ROBOT PART!
IMPOSSIBLE! WE SAW OURSELVES THAT...
WAITASEC, ZARK... NO, WE DIDN'T! AS A MATTER OF FACT— WE NEVER ACTUALLY SAW A THING!

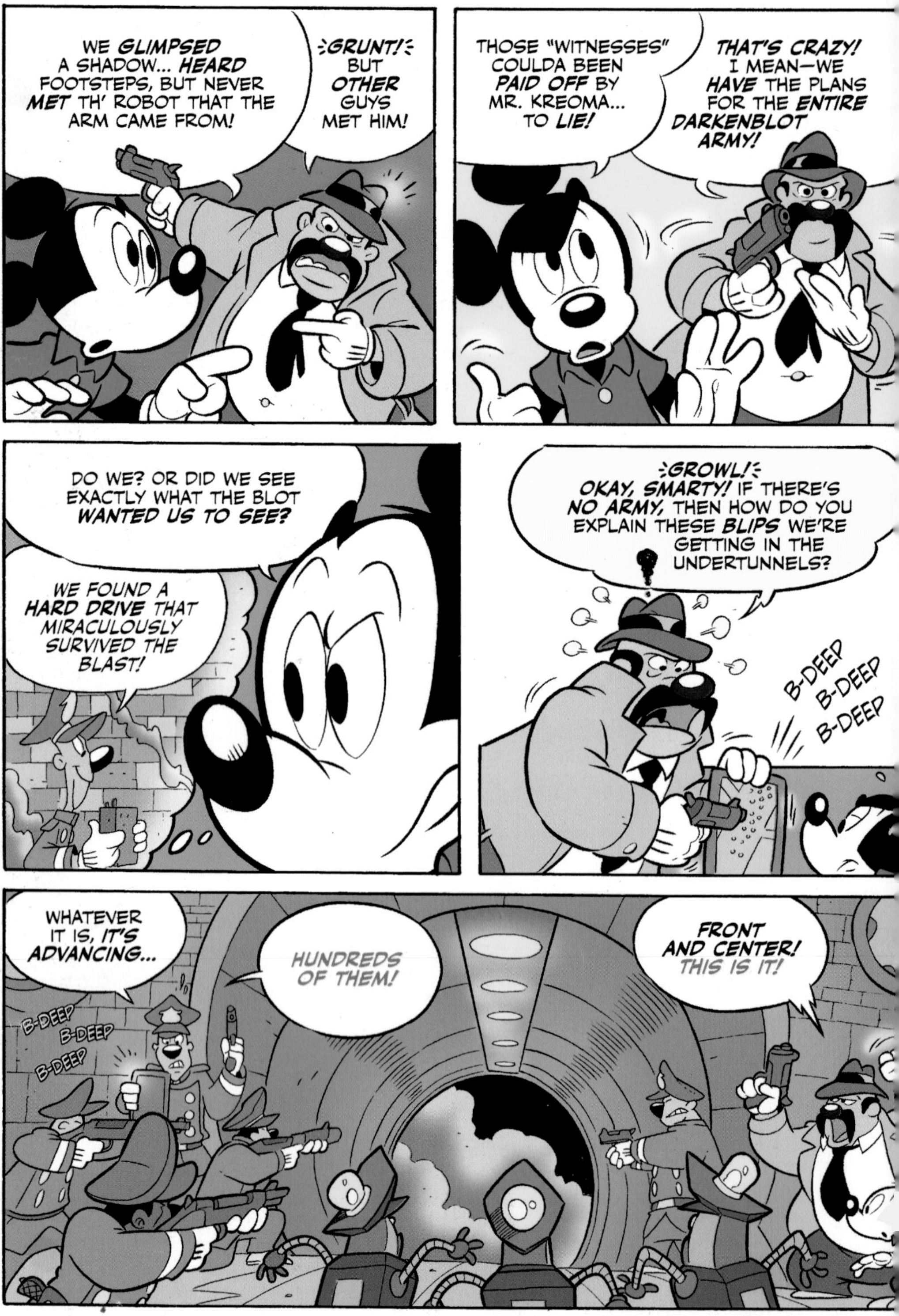
WE GLIMPSED A SHADOW... HEARD FOOTSTEPS, BUT NEVER MET TH' ROBOT THAT THE ARM CAME FROM!
GRUNT! BUT OTHER GUYS MET HIM!
THOSE "WITNESSES" COULDA BEEN PAID OFF BY MR. KREOMA... TO LIE!
THAT'S CRAZY! I MEAN—WE HAVE THE PLANS FOR THE ENTIRE DARKENBLOT ARMY!
DO WE? OR DID WE SEE EXACTLY WHAT THE BLOT WANTED US TO SEE?
WE FOUND A HARD DRIVE THAT MIRACULOUSLY SURVIVED THE BLAST!
GROWL! OKAY, SMARTY! IF THERE'S NO ARMY, THEN HOW DO YOU EXPLAIN THESE BLIPS WE'RE GETTING IN THE UNDERTUNNELS?
B-DEEP B-DEEP B-DEEP
WHATEVER IT IS, IT'S ADVANCING...
HUNDREDS OF THEM!
FRONT AND CENTER! THIS IS IT!
B-DEEP B-DEEP B-DEEP

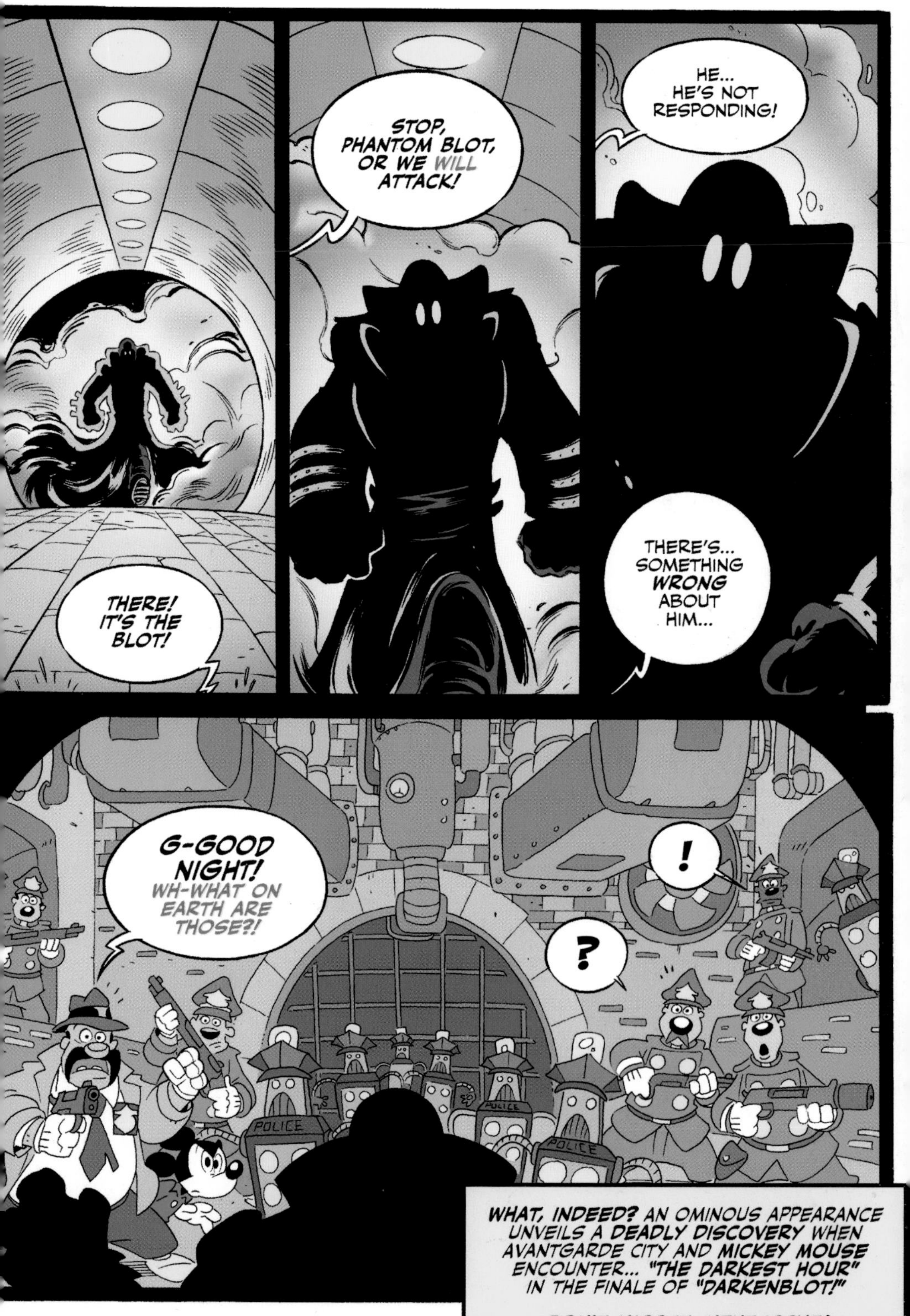
THERE! IT'S THE BLOT!
STOP, PHANTOM BLOT, OR WE WILL ATTACK!
HE... HE'S NOT RESPONDING!
THERE'S... SOMETHING WRONG ABOUT HIM...
G-GOOD NIGHT! WH-WHAT ON EARTH ARE THOSE?!
!
?
POLICE
POLICE
POLICE
WHAT, INDEED? AN OMINOUS APPEARANCE UNVEILS A DEADLY DISCOVERY WHEN AVANTGARDE CITY AND MICKEY MOUSE ENCOUNTER... "THE DARKEST HOUR" IN THE FINALE OF "DARKENBLOT!"
DON'T MISS IT—NEXT ISSUE!

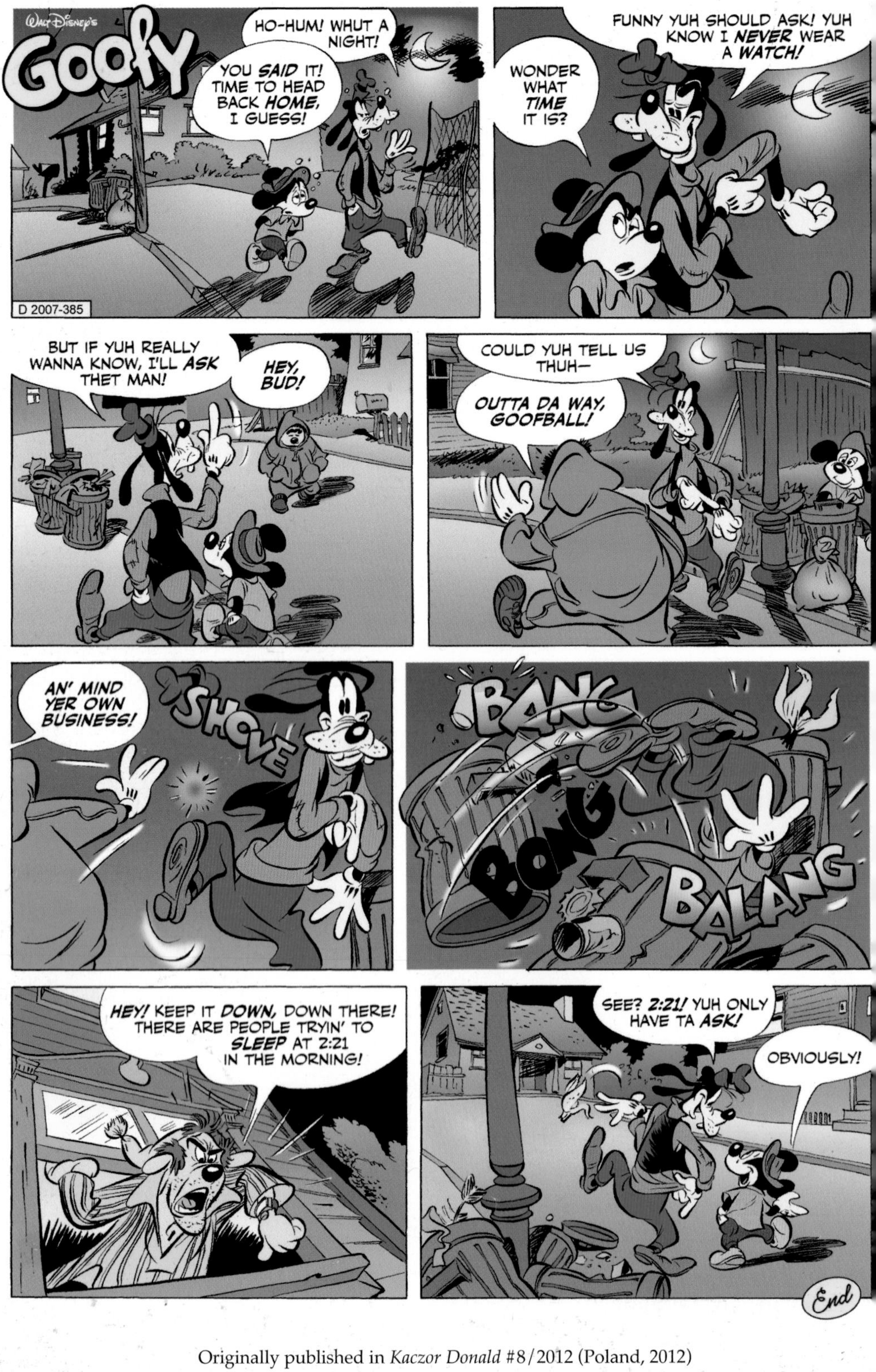
Walt Disney's
Goofy
HO-HUM! WHUT A NIGHT!
YOU SAID IT! TIME TO HEAD BACK HOME, I GUESS!
D 2007-385
WONDER WHAT TIME IT IS?
FUNNY YUH SHOULD ASK! YUH KNOW I NEVER WEAR A WATCH!
BUT IF YUH REALLY WANNA KNOW, I'LL ASK THET MAN!
HEY, BUD!
COULD YUH TELL US THUH—
OUTTA DA WAY, GOOFBALL!
AN' MIND YER OWN BUSINESS!
SHOVE
BANG
BONG
BALANG
HEY! KEEP IT DOWN, DOWN THERE! THERE ARE PEOPLE TRYIN' TO SLEEP AT 2:21 IN THE MORNING!
SEE? 2:21! YUH ONLY HAVE TA ASK!
OBVIOUSLY!
End

Originally published in *Kaczor Donald* #8/2012 (Poland, 2012)

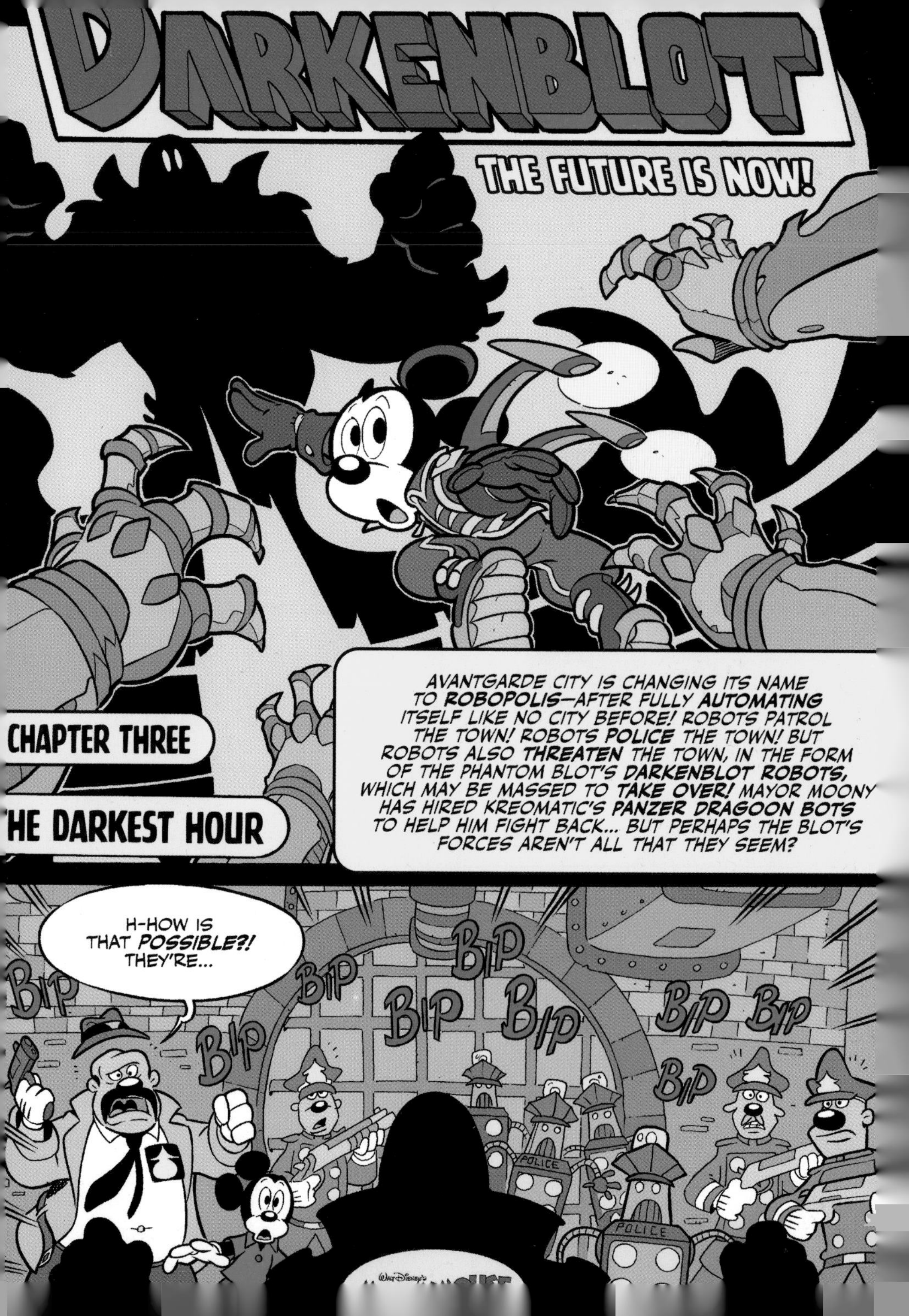
DARKENBLOT
THE FUTURE IS NOW!
CHAPTER THREE
THE DARKEST HOUR
AVANTGARDE CITY IS CHANGING ITS NAME TO ROBOPOLIS—AFTER FULLY AUTOMATING ITSELF LIKE NO CITY BEFORE! ROBOTS PATROL THE TOWN! ROBOTS POLICE THE TOWN! BUT ROBOTS ALSO THREATEN THE TOWN, IN THE FORM OF THE PHANTOM BLOT'S DARKENBLOT ROBOTS, WHICH MAY BE MASSED TO TAKE OVER! MAYOR MOONY HAS HIRED KREOMATIC'S PANZER DRAGOON BOTS TO HELP HIM FIGHT BACK... BUT PERHAPS THE BLOT'S FORCES AREN'T ALL THAT THEY SEEM?
H-HOW IS THAT POSSIBLE?! THEY'RE...
BIP
BIP
BIP
BIP
BIP
BIP
BIP
BIP
BIP
BIP
POLICE
POLICE

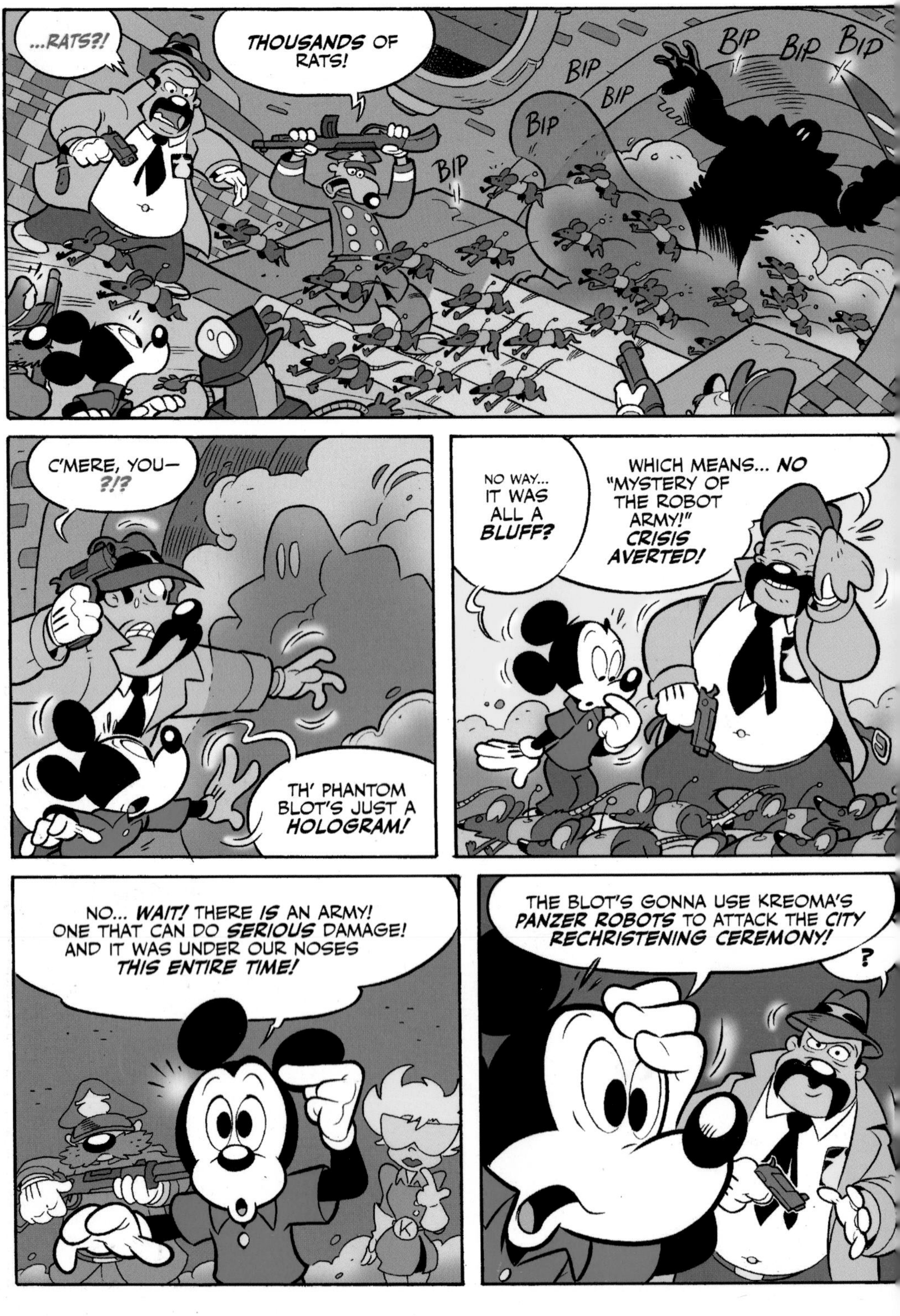
...RATS?!
THOUSANDS OF RATS!
BIP BIP BIP BIP BIP BIP BIP BIP
C'MERE, YOU— ?!?
TH' PHANTOM BLOT'S JUST A HOLOGRAM!
NO WAY... IT WAS ALL A BLUFF?
WHICH MEANS... NO "MYSTERY OF THE ROBOT ARMY!" CRISIS AVERTED!
NO... WAIT! THERE IS AN ARMY! ONE THAT CAN DO SERIOUS DAMAGE! AND IT WAS UNDER OUR NOSES THIS ENTIRE TIME!
THE BLOT'S GONNA USE KREOMA'S PANZER ROBOTS TO ATTACK THE CITY RECHRISTENING CEREMONY!
?

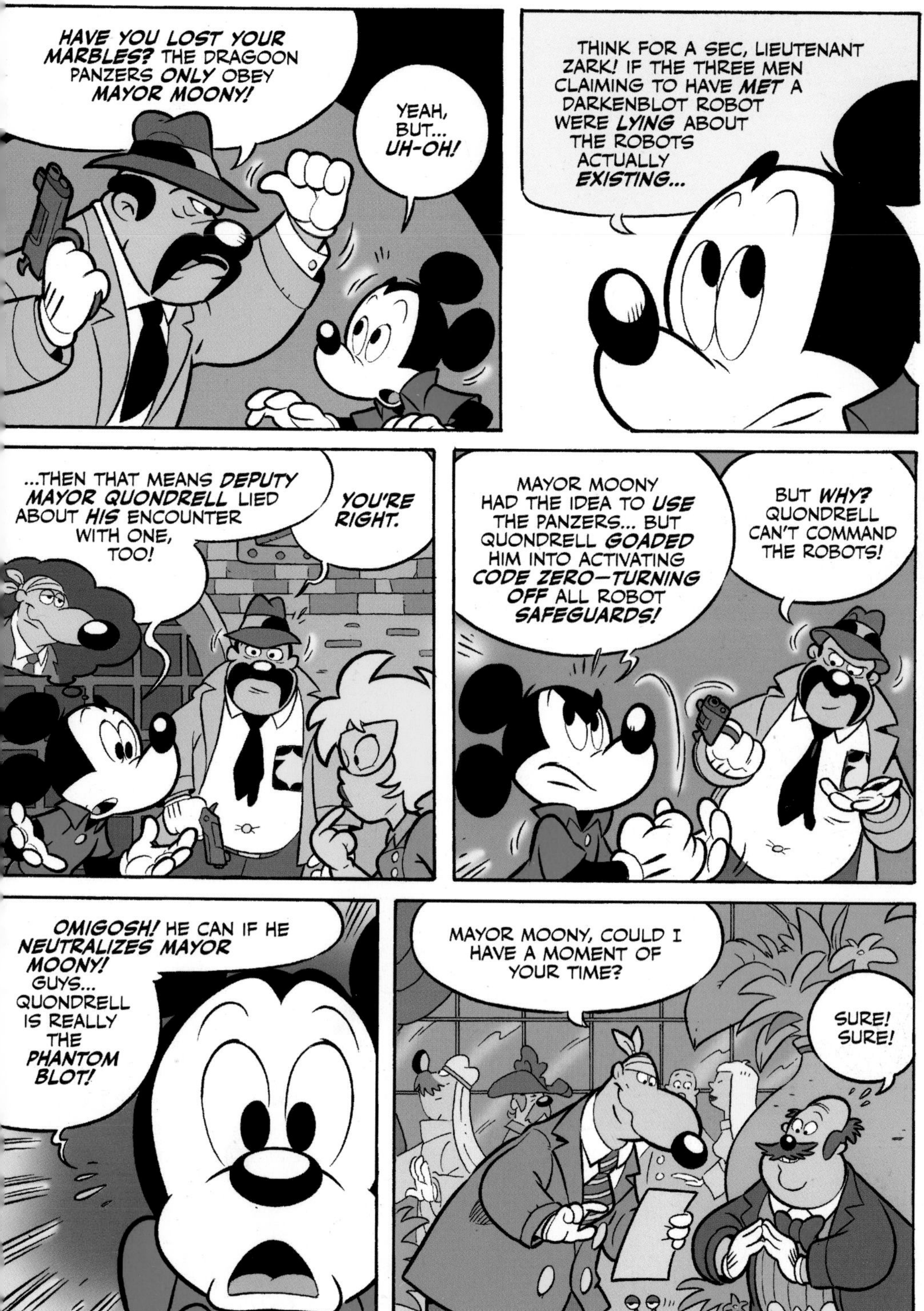
HAVE YOU LOST YOUR MARBLES? THE DRAGOON PANZERS ONLY OBEY MAYOR MOONY!
YEAH, BUT... UH-OH!
THINK FOR A SEC, LIEUTENANT ZARK! IF THE THREE MEN CLAIMING TO HAVE MET A DARKENBLOT ROBOT WERE LYING ABOUT THE ROBOTS ACTUALLY EXISTING...
...THEN THAT MEANS DEPUTY MAYOR QUONDRELL LIED ABOUT HIS ENCOUNTER WITH ONE, TOO!
YOU'RE RIGHT.
MAYOR MOONY HAD THE IDEA TO USE THE PANZERS... BUT QUONDRELL GOADED HIM INTO ACTIVATING CODE ZERO—TURNING OFF ALL ROBOT SAFEGUARDS!
BUT WHY? QUONDRELL CAN'T COMMAND THE ROBOTS!
OMIGOSH! HE CAN IF HE NEUTRALIZES MAYOR MOONY! GUYS... QUONDRELL IS REALLY THE PHANTOM BLOT!
MAYOR MOONY, COULD I HAVE A MOMENT OF YOUR TIME?
SURE! SURE!

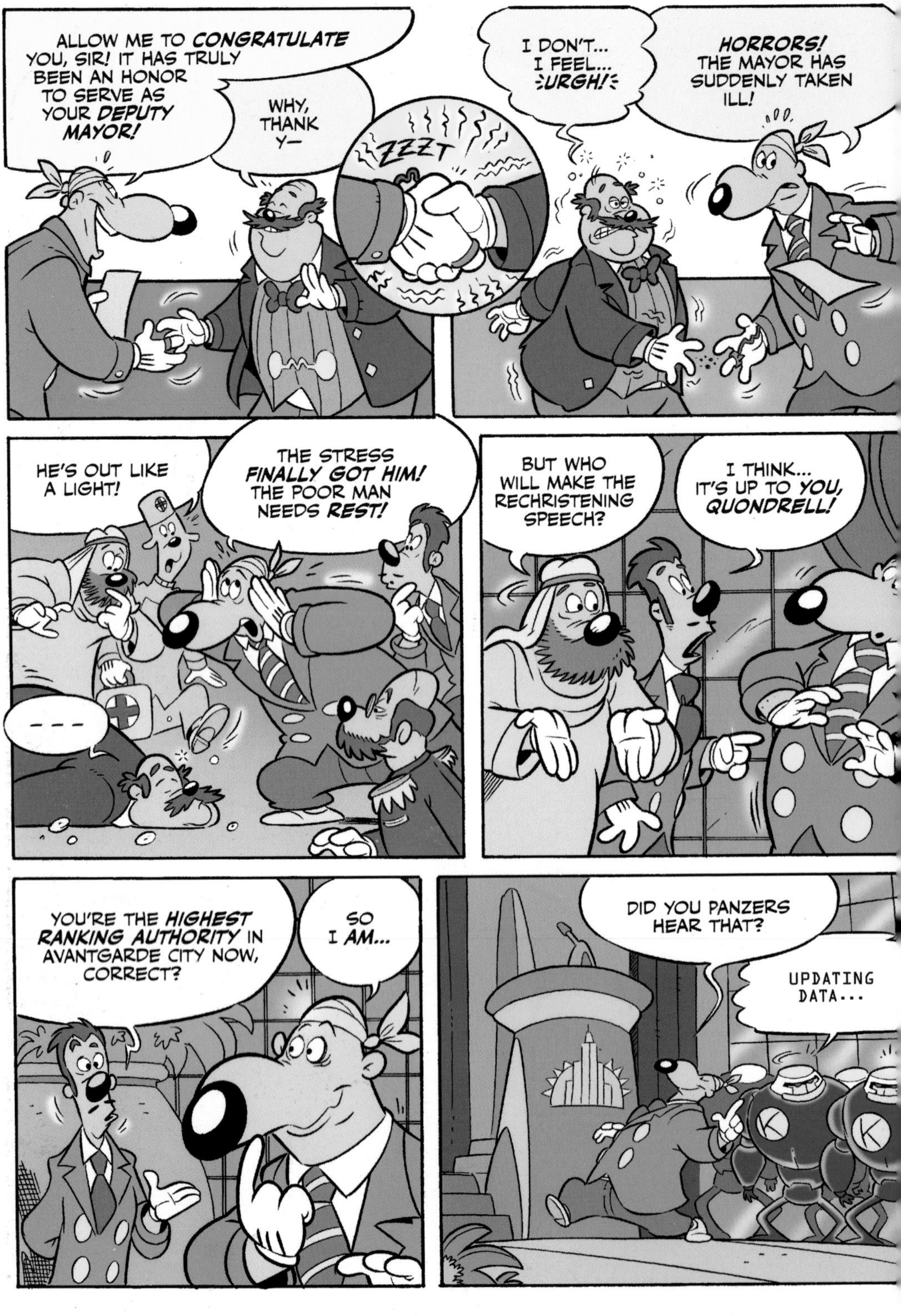

ALLOW ME TO CONGRATULATE YOU, SIR! IT HAS TRULY BEEN AN HONOR TO SERVE AS YOUR DEPUTY MAYOR!
WHY, THANK Y—
ZZZT
I DON'T... I FEEL... URGH!
HORRORS! THE MAYOR HAS SUDDENLY TAKEN ILL!
HE'S OUT LIKE A LIGHT!
THE STRESS FINALLY GOT HIM! THE POOR MAN NEEDS REST!
- - -
BUT WHO WILL MAKE THE RECHRISTENING SPEECH?
I THINK... IT'S UP TO YOU, QUONDRELL!
YOU'RE THE HIGHEST RANKING AUTHORITY IN AVANTGARDE CITY NOW, CORRECT?
SO I AM...
DID YOU PANZERS HEAR THAT?
UPDATING DATA...

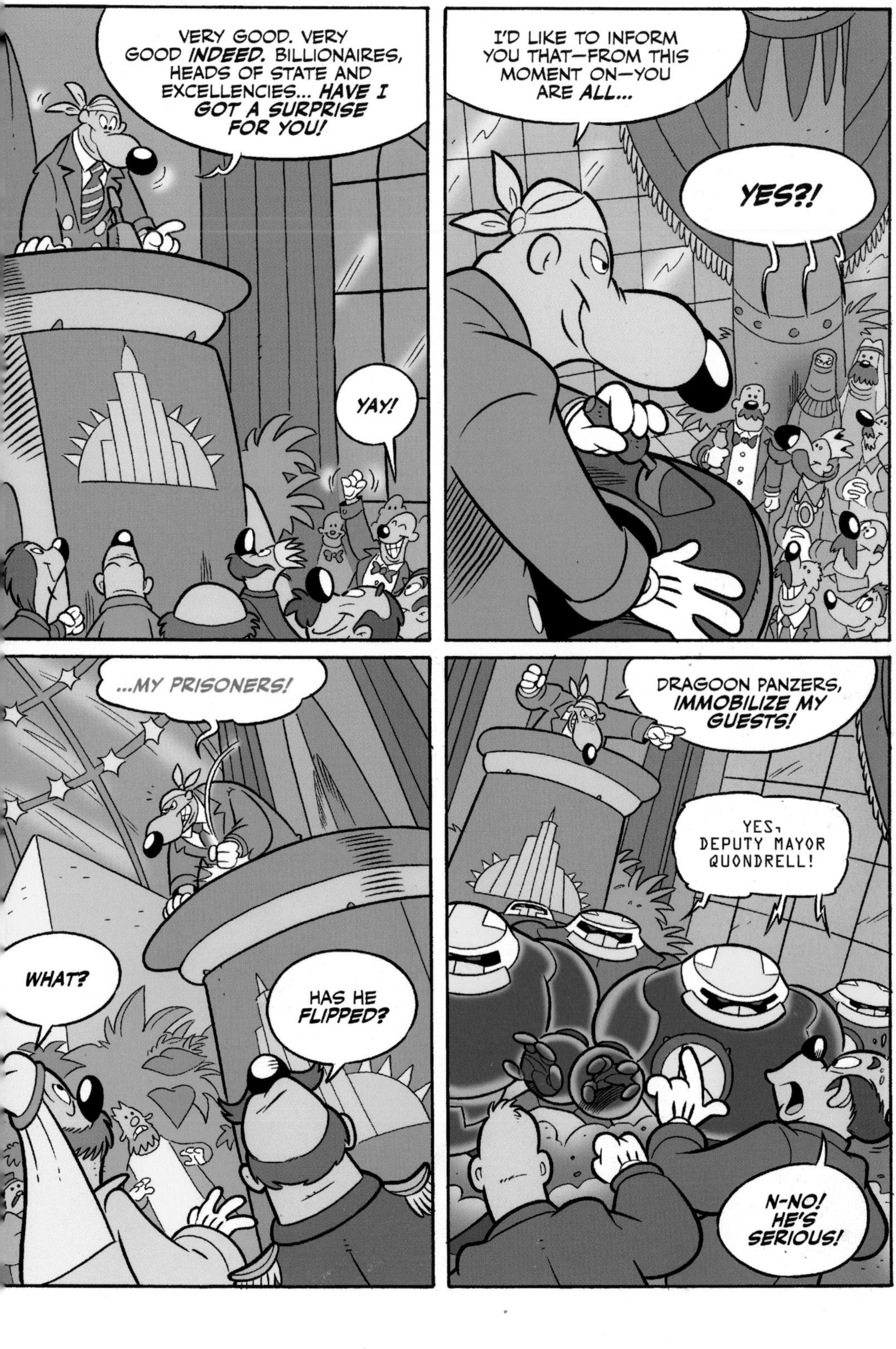
VERY GOOD. VERY GOOD INDEED. BILLIONAIRES, HEADS OF STATE AND EXCELLENCIES... HAVE I GOT A SURPRISE FOR YOU!
YAY!
I'D LIKE TO INFORM YOU THAT—FROM THIS MOMENT ON—YOU ARE ALL...
YES?!
...MY PRISONERS!
WHAT?
HAS HE FLIPPED?
DRAGOON PANZERS, IMMOBILIZE MY GUESTS!
YES, DEPUTY MAYOR QUONDRELL!
N-NO! HE'S SERIOUS!

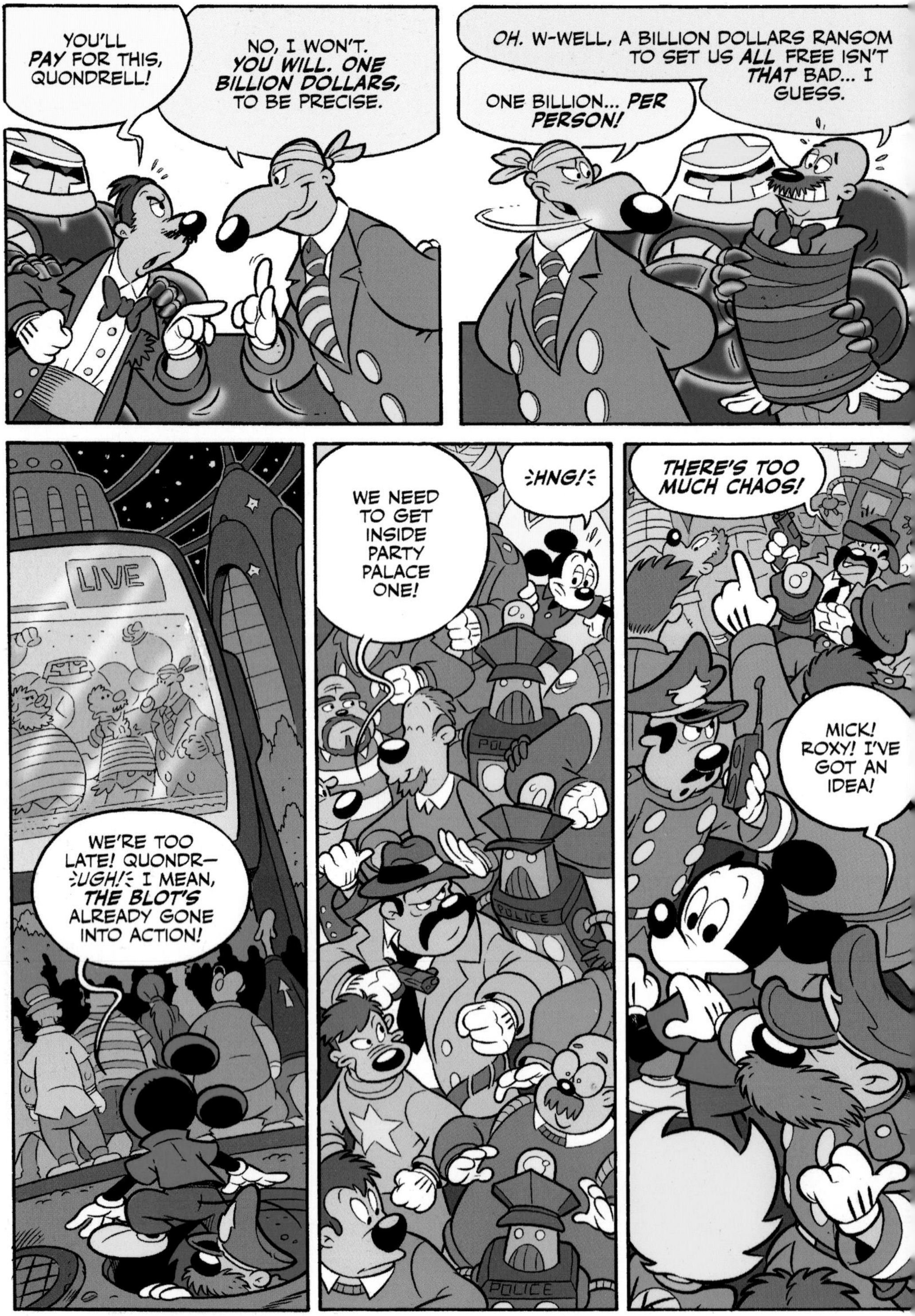
YOU'LL PAY FOR THIS, QUONDRELL!
NO, I WON'T. YOU WILL. ONE BILLION DOLLARS, TO BE PRECISE.
OH. W-WELL, A BILLION DOLLARS RANSOM TO SET US ALL FREE ISN'T THAT BAD... I GUESS.
ONE BILLION... PER PERSON!
LIVE
WE'RE TOO LATE! QUONDR— UGH! I MEAN, THE BLOT'S ALREADY GONE INTO ACTION!
WE NEED TO GET INSIDE PARTY PALACE ONE!
HNG!
POLICE
THERE'S TOO MUCH CHAOS!
MICK! ROXY! I'VE GOT AN IDEA!

I MAY BE ABLE TO GIVE YOU SOMETHING THAT'LL HELP YOU GET INTO PARTY PALACE ONE *FASTER!* MY HOUSE IS JUST OVER HERE!

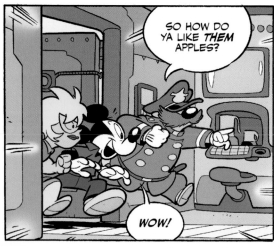

SO HOW DO YA LIKE *THEM* APPLES?

WOW!

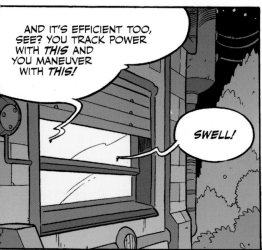

AND IT'S EFFICIENT TOO, SEE? YOU TRACK POWER WITH *THIS* AND YOU MANEUVER WITH *THIS!*

SWELL!

ROXETTE, I NEED Y' TO DO ME A FAVOR: SCOUR KREOMATIC'S ARCHIVES! TH' *DRAGOON PANZERS* HAD SOME KIND OF *UNSPECIFIED DEFECT!* FIND OUT *WHAT* IT WAS...

...AN' FIGGER OUT HOW *WE* CAN EXPLOIT IT!

ON IT, MICKEY!

YOU'RE MINE, PHANTOM BLOT.

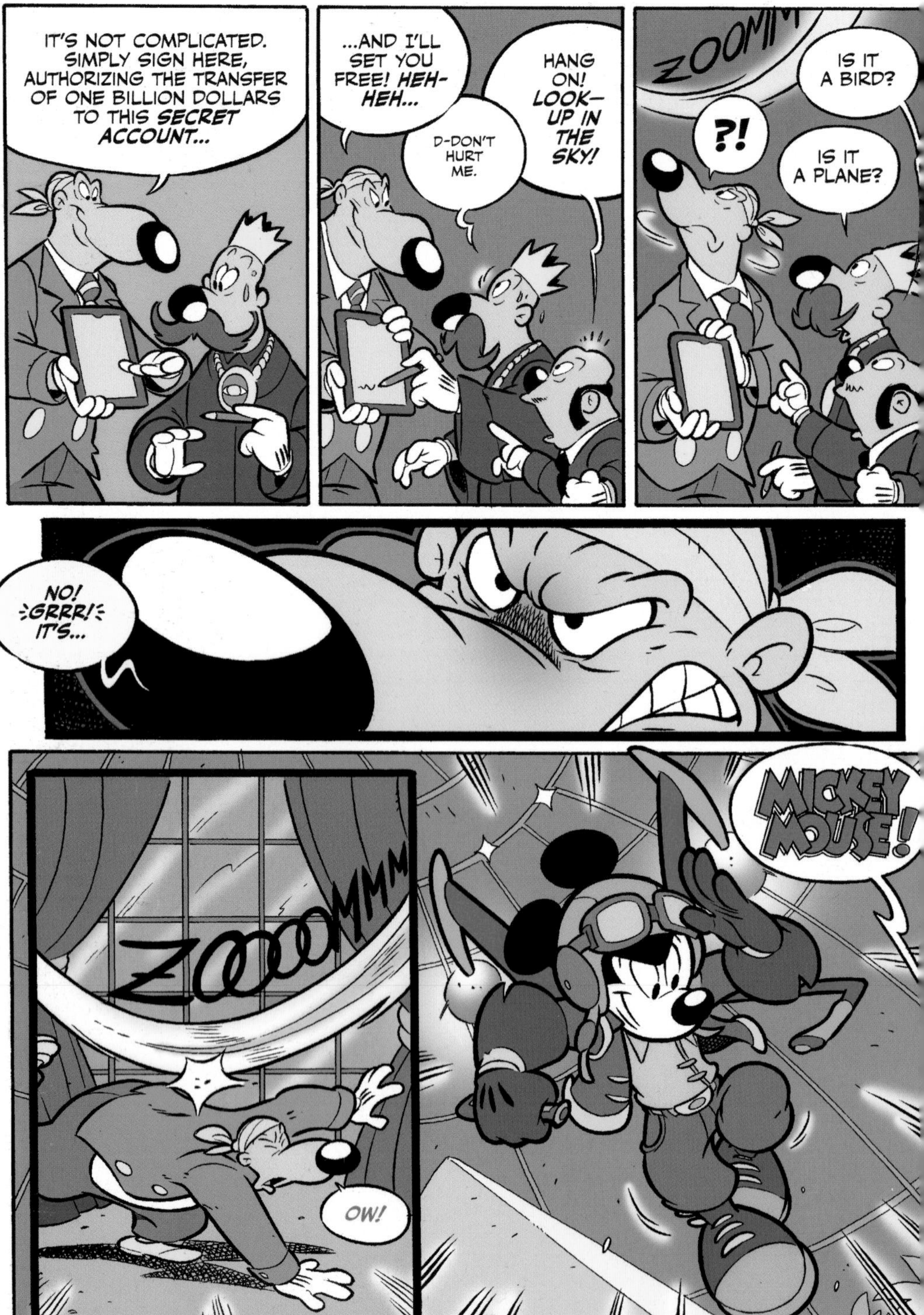
IT'S NOT COMPLICATED. SIMPLY SIGN HERE, AUTHORIZING THE TRANSFER OF ONE BILLION DOLLARS TO THIS SECRET ACCOUNT...
...AND I'LL SET YOU FREE! HEH-HEH...
D-DON'T HURT ME.
HANG ON! LOOK— UP IN THE SKY!
ZOOMM
?!
IS IT A BIRD?
IS IT A PLANE?
NO! GRRR! IT'S...
MICKEY MOUSE!
ZOOOOMMM
OW!

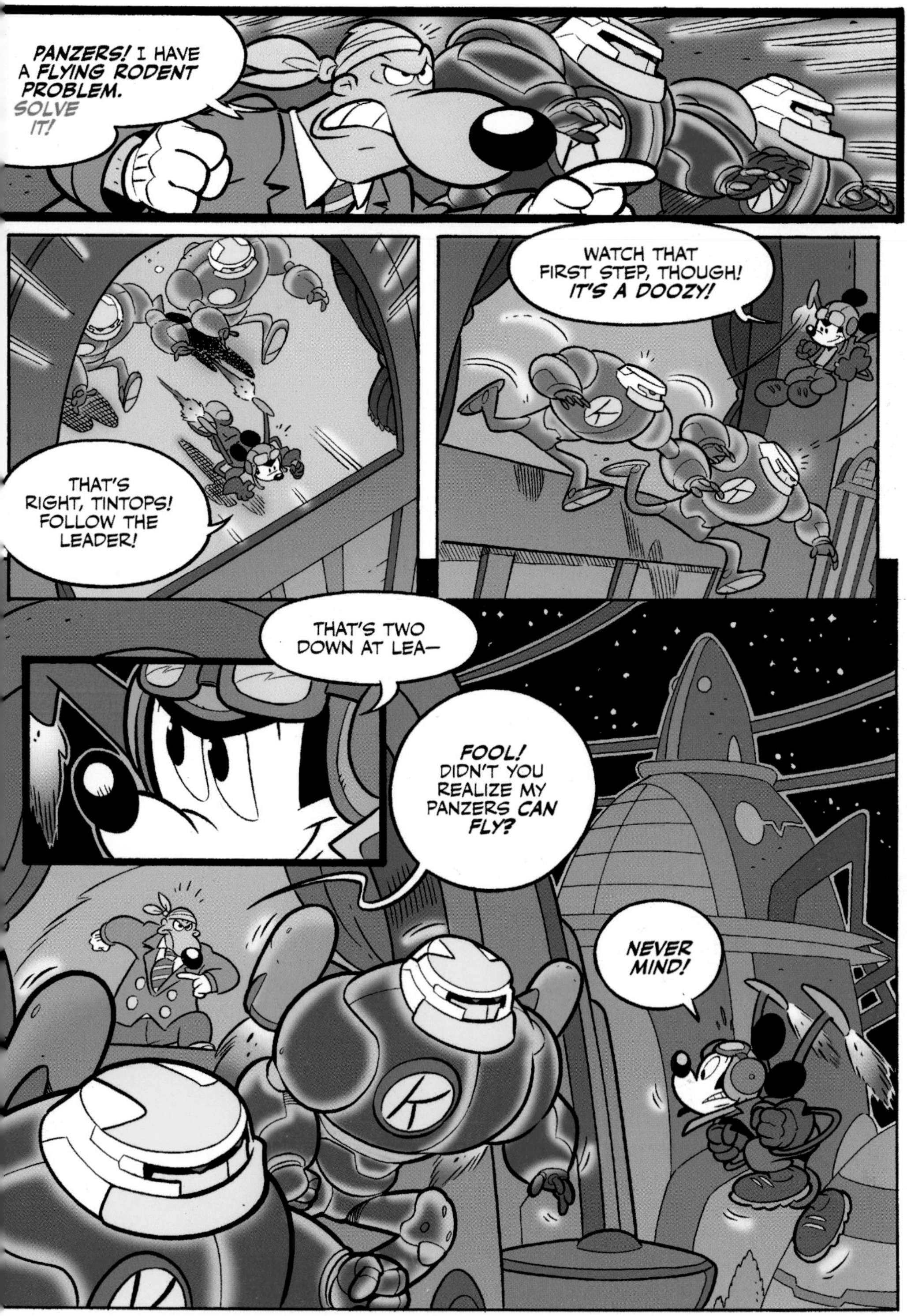
PANZERS! I HAVE A FLYING RODENT PROBLEM. SOLVE IT!
THAT'S RIGHT, TINTOPS! FOLLOW THE LEADER!
WATCH THAT FIRST STEP, THOUGH! IT'S A DOOZY!
THAT'S TWO DOWN AT LEA—
FOOL! DIDN'T YOU REALIZE MY PANZERS CAN FLY?
NEVER MIND!

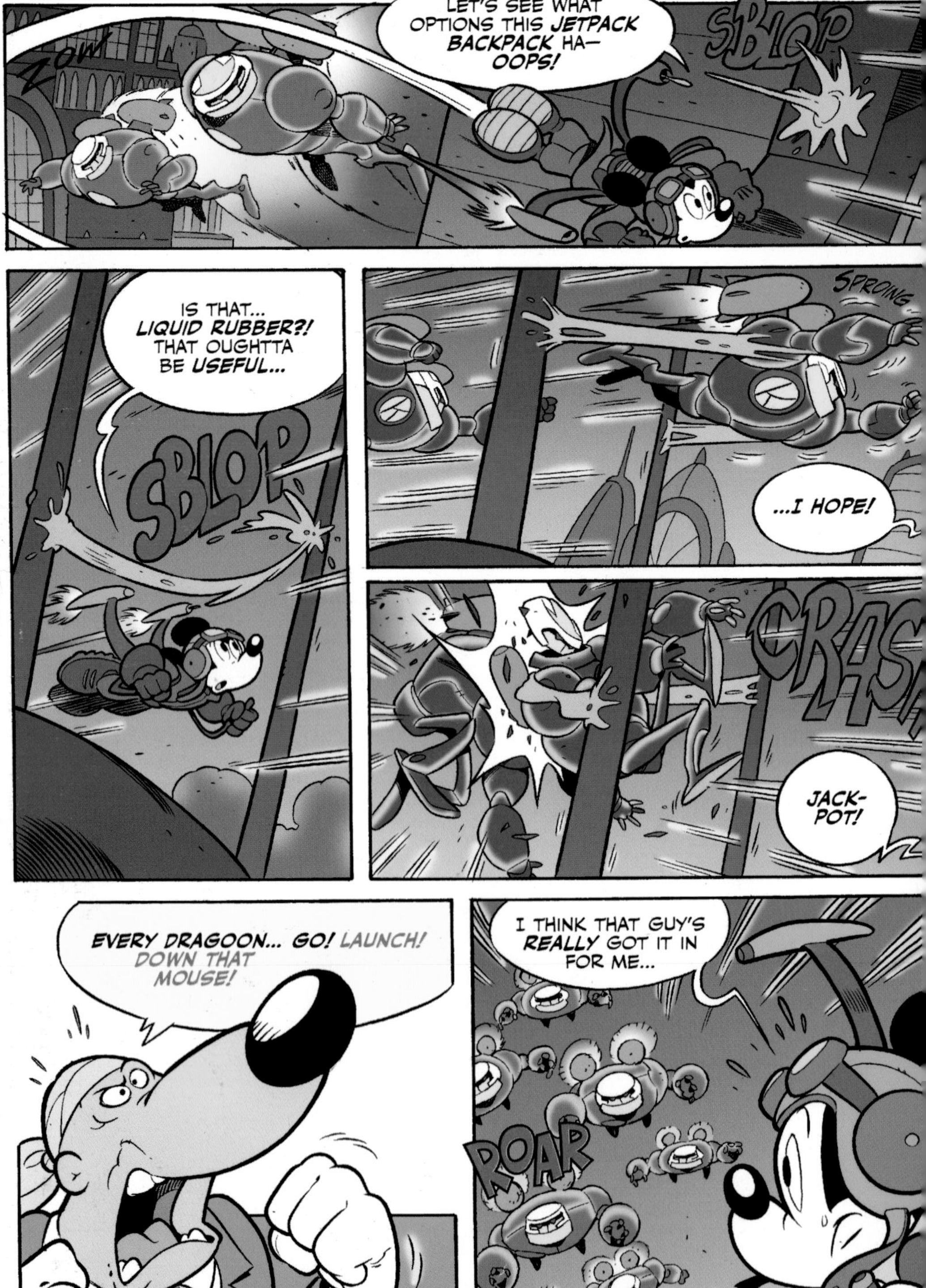
ZOW
LET'S SEE WHAT OPTIONS THIS JETPACK BACKPACK HA— OOPS!
SBLOP
IS THAT... LIQUID RUBBER?! THAT OUGHTTA BE USEFUL...
SBLOP
SPROING
...I HOPE!
CRASH
JACK-POT!
EVERY DRAGOON... GO! LAUNCH! DOWN THAT MOUSE!
I THINK THAT GUY'S REALLY GOT IT IN FOR ME...
ROAR

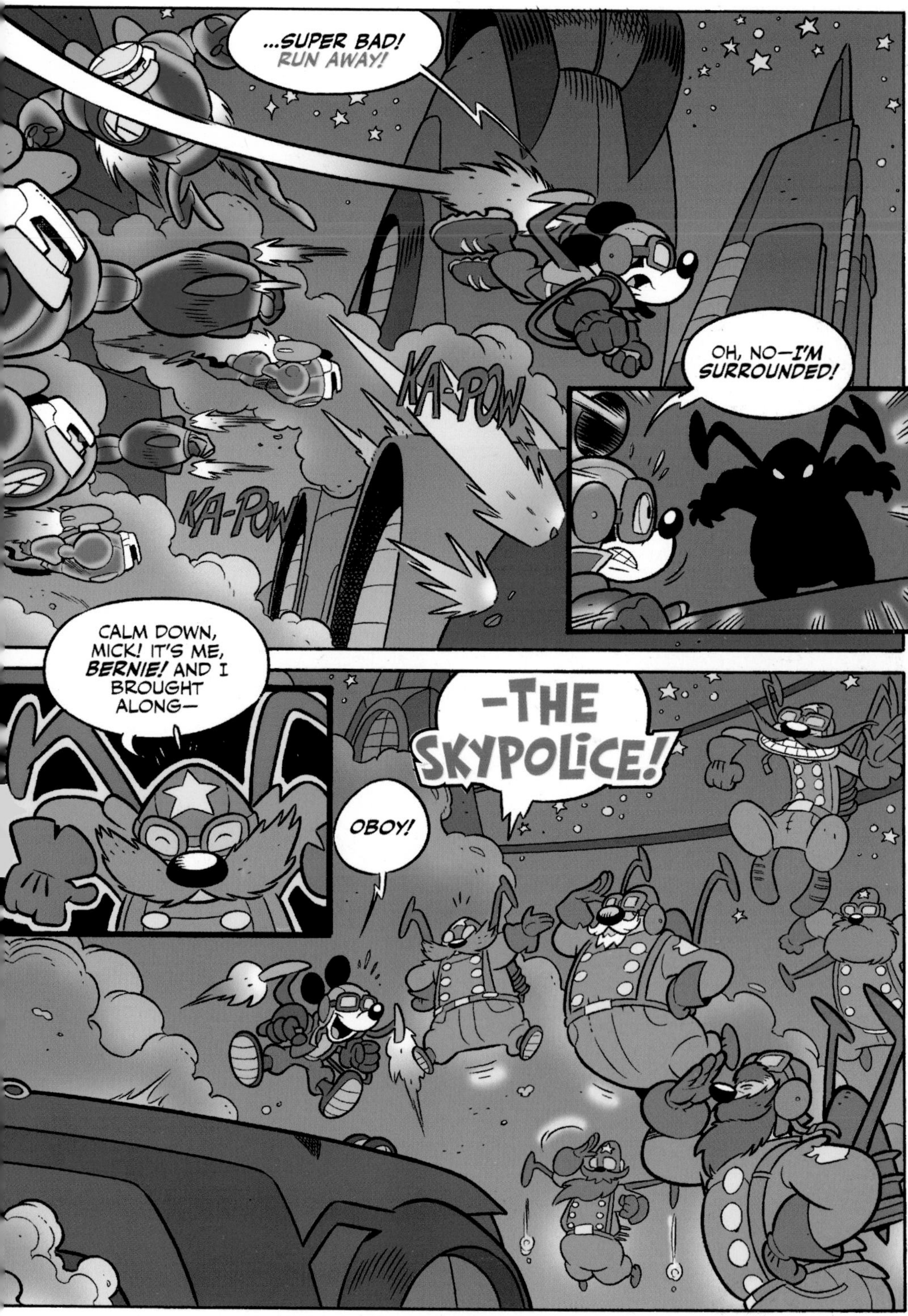
...SUPER BAD!
RUN AWAY!
KA-POW
KA-POW
OH, NO—I'M SURROUNDED!
CALM DOWN, MICK! IT'S ME, BERNIE! AND I BROUGHT ALONG—
-THE SKYPOLICE!
OBOY!

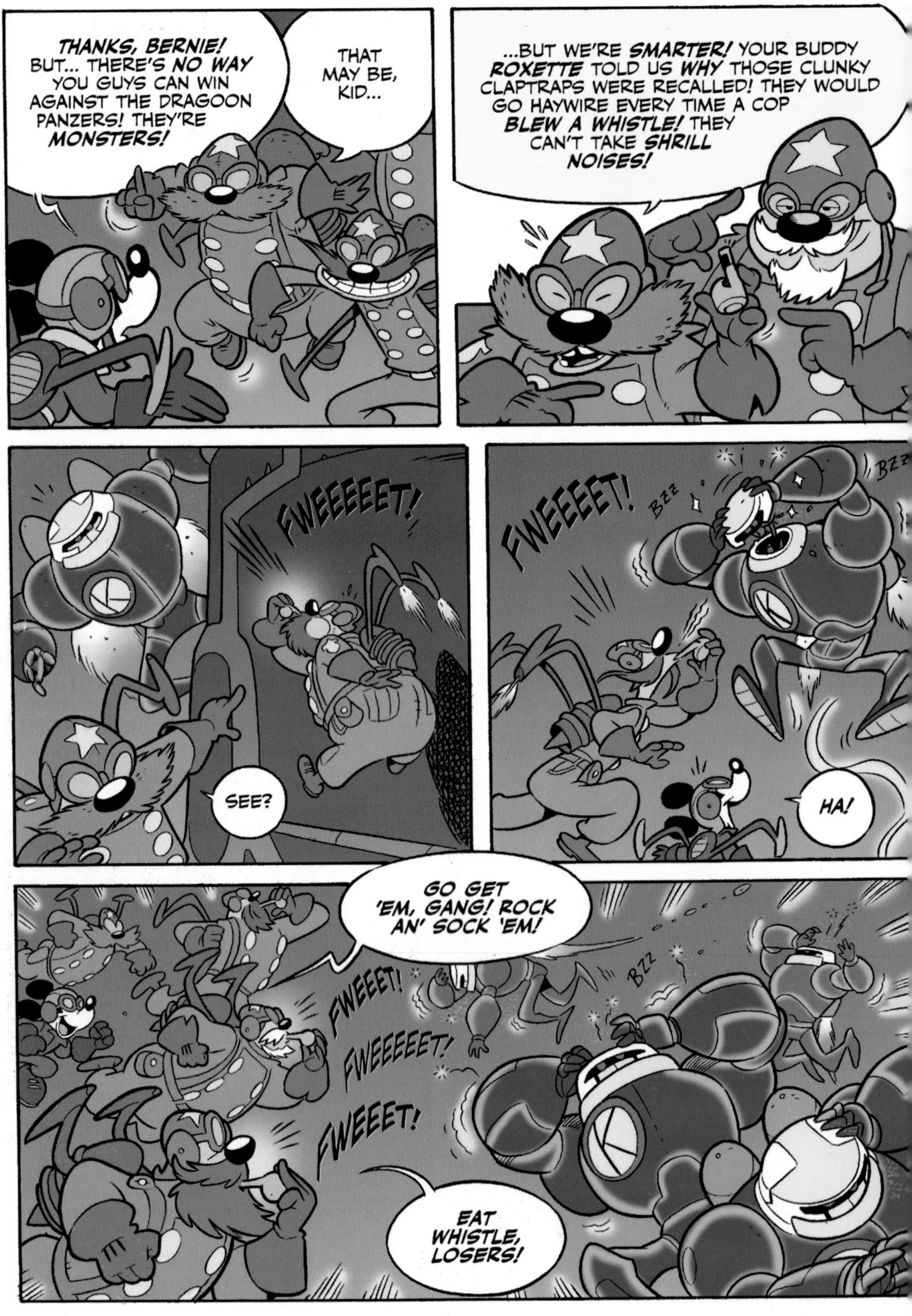
THANKS, BERNIE! BUT... THERE'S NO WAY YOU GUYS CAN WIN AGAINST THE DRAGOON PANZERS! THEY'RE MONSTERS!
THAT MAY BE, KID...
...BUT WE'RE SMARTER! YOUR BUDDY ROXETTE TOLD US WHY THOSE CLUNKY CLAPTRAPS WERE RECALLED! THEY WOULD GO HAYWIRE EVERY TIME A COP BLEW A WHISTLE! THEY CAN'T TAKE SHRILL NOISES!
FWEEEEEET!
SEE?
FWEEEEET!
BZZ
BZZ
HA!
GO GET 'EM, GANG! ROCK AN' SOCK 'EM!
BZZ
FWEEET!
FWEEEEET!
FWEEET!
EAT WHISTLE, LOSERS!

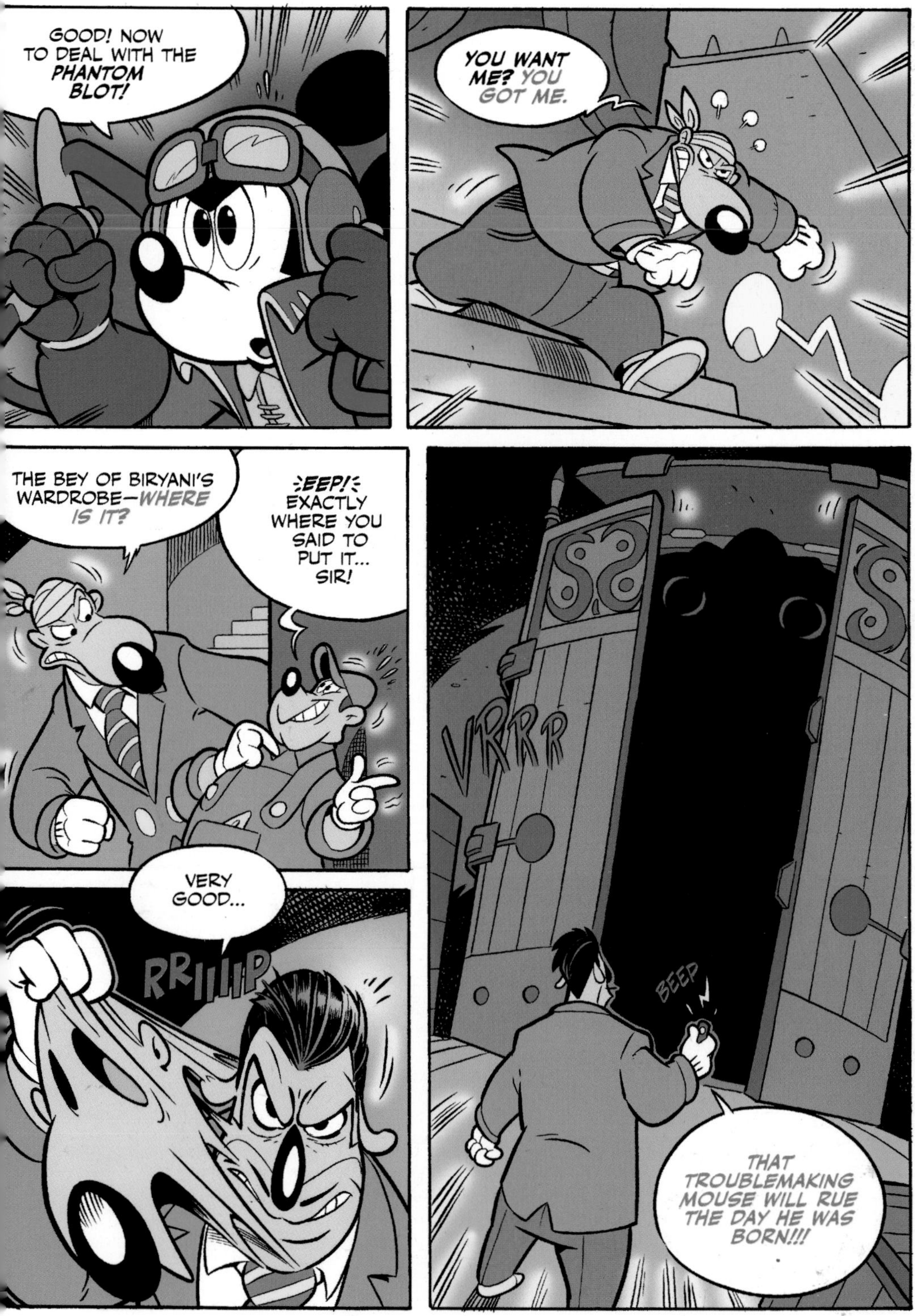
GOOD! NOW TO DEAL WITH THE PHANTOM BLOT!
YOU WANT ME? YOU GOT ME.
THE BEY OF BIRYANI'S WARDROBE—WHERE IS IT?
EEP! EXACTLY WHERE YOU SAID TO PUT IT... SIR!
VERY GOOD...
RRIIIIP
VRRR
BEEP
THAT TROUBLEMAKING MOUSE WILL RUE THE DAY HE WAS BORN!!!

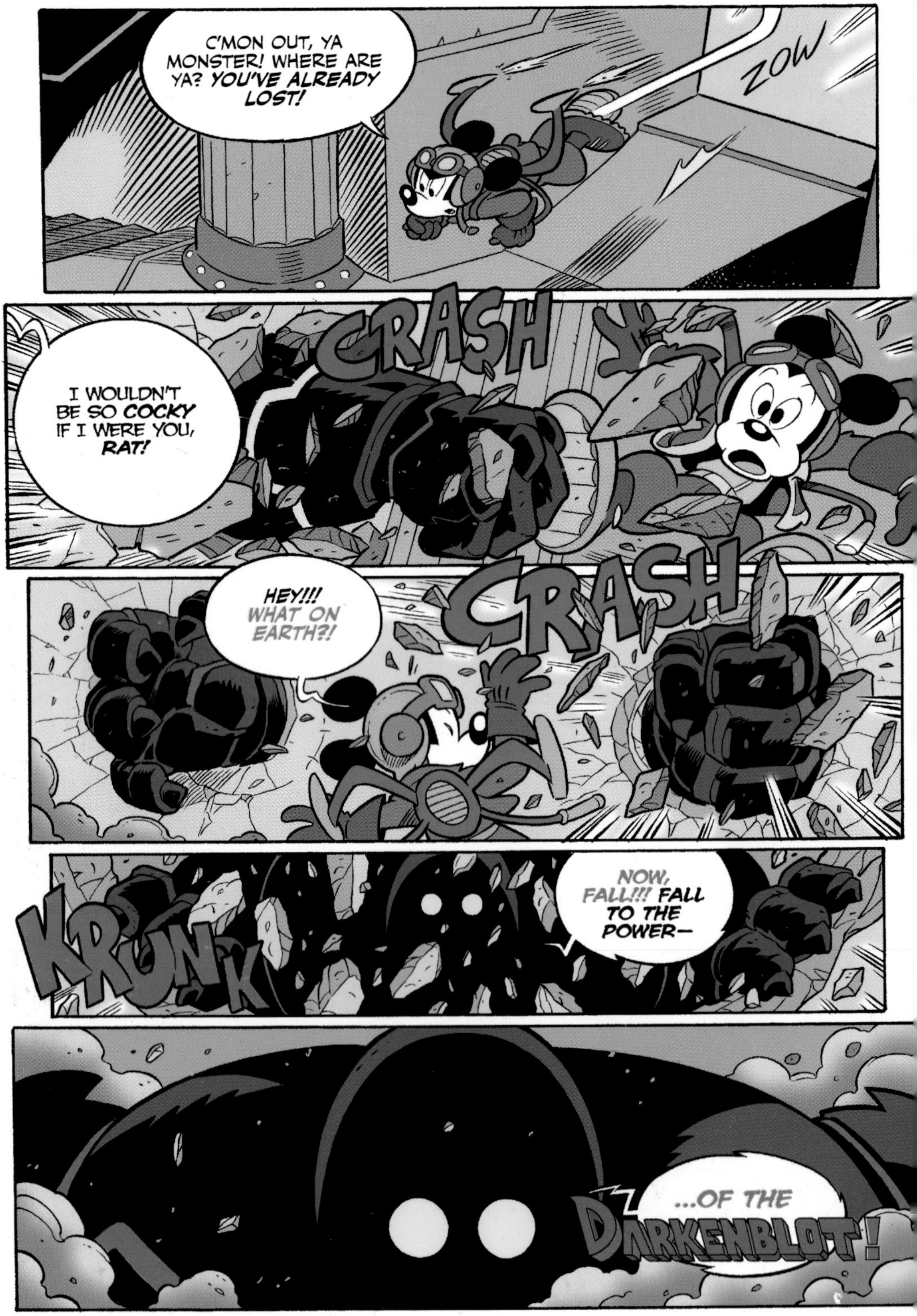
C'MON OUT, YA MONSTER! WHERE ARE YA? YOU'VE ALREADY LOST!
ZOW
CRASH
I WOULDN'T BE SO COCKY IF I WERE YOU, RAT!
HEY!!! WHAT ON EARTH?!
CRASH
KRUNK
NOW, FALL!!! FALL TO THE POWER—
...OF THE DARKENBLOT!

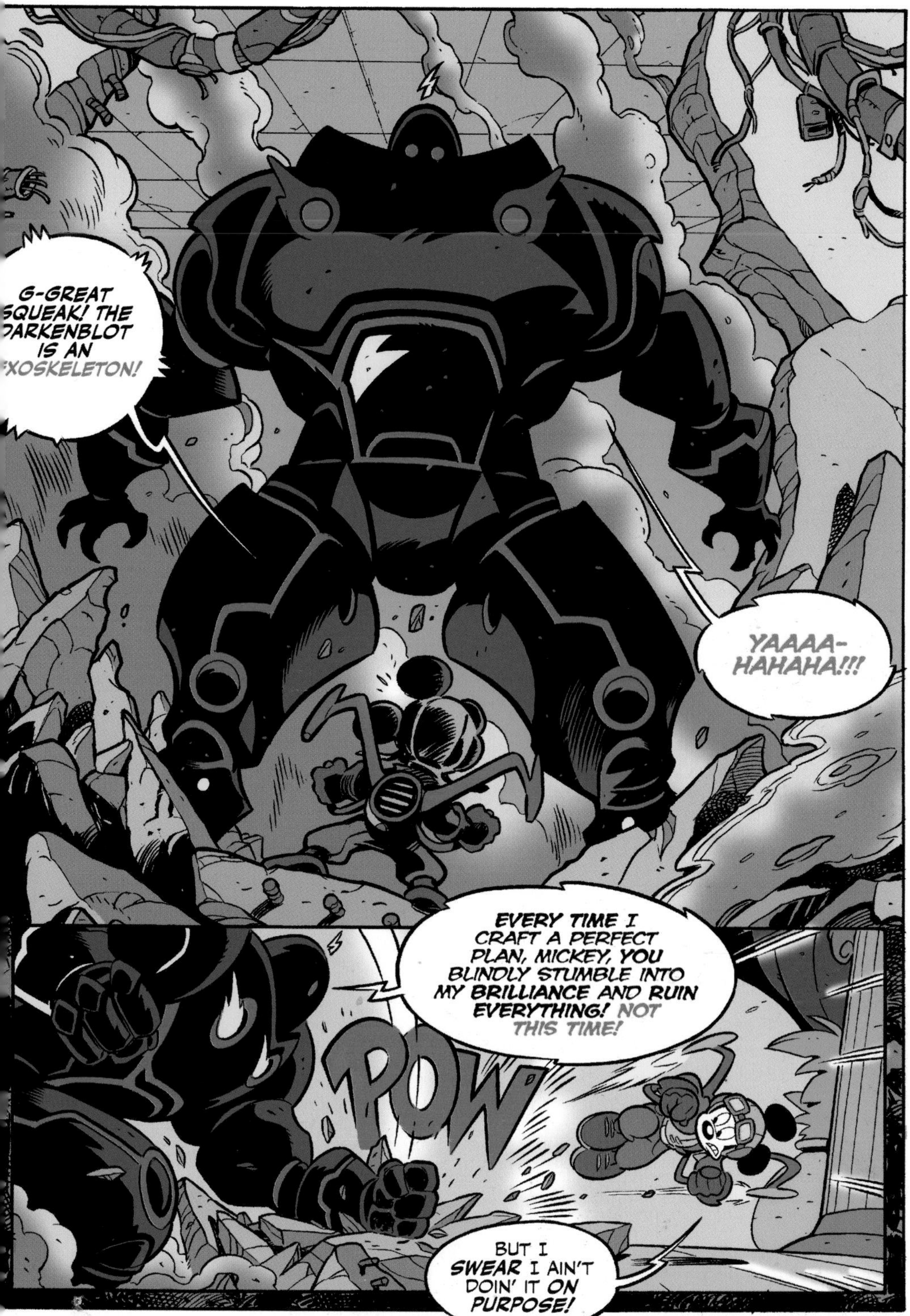
G-GREAT SQUEAK! THE DARKENBLOT IS AN EXOSKELETON!
YAAAA-HAHAHA!!!
EVERY TIME I CRAFT A PERFECT PLAN, MICKEY, YOU BLINDLY STUMBLE INTO MY BRILLIANCE AND RUIN EVERYTHING! NOT THIS TIME!
POW
BUT I SWEAR I AIN'T DOIN' IT ON PURPOSE!

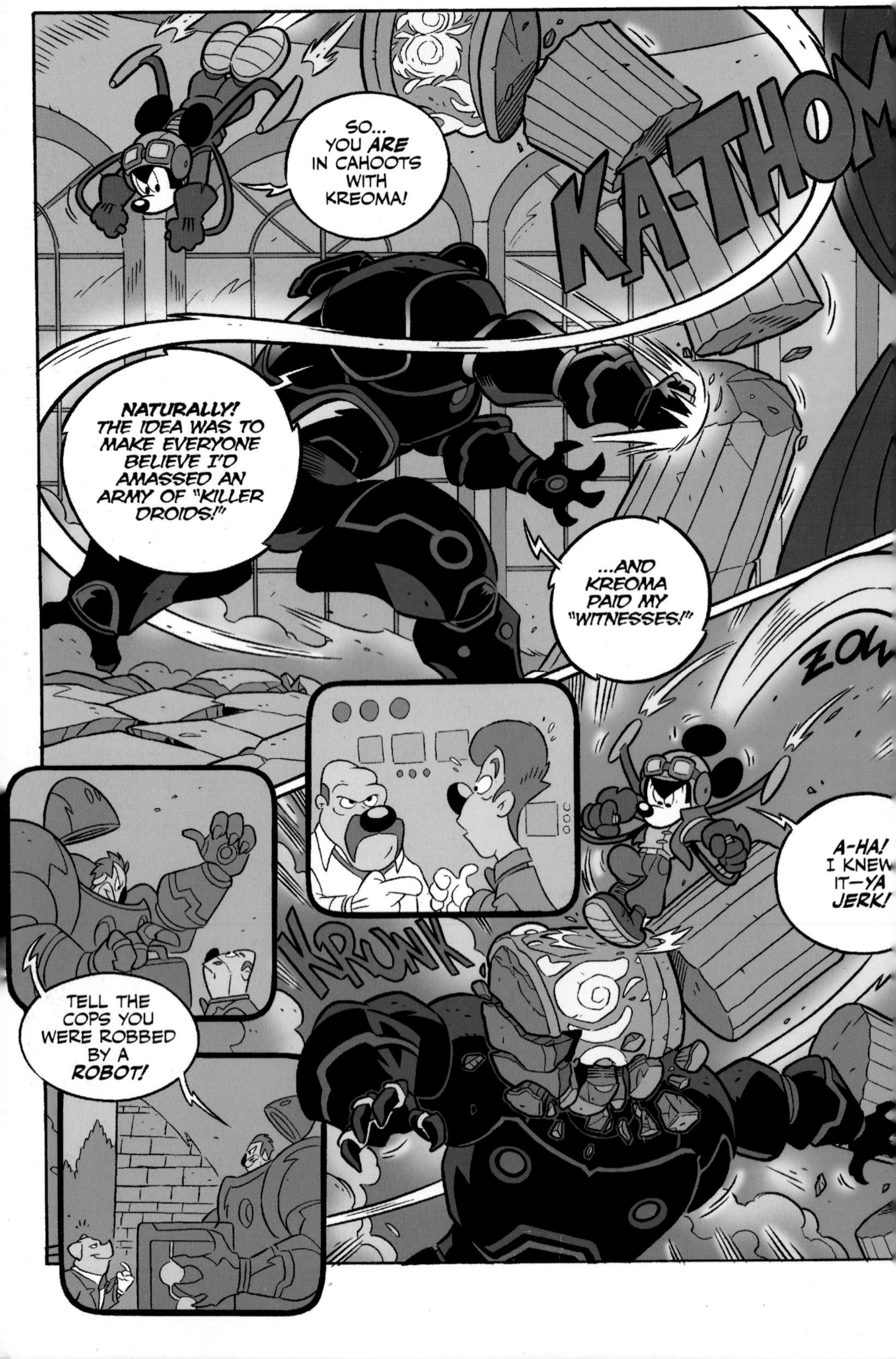
SO... YOU ARE IN CAHOOTS WITH KREOMA!
KA-THOM
NATURALLY! THE IDEA WAS TO MAKE EVERYONE BELIEVE I'D AMASSED AN ARMY OF "KILLER DROIDS!"
...AND KREOMA PAID MY "WITNESSES!"
TELL THE COPS YOU WERE ROBBED BY A ROBOT!
A-HA! I KNEW IT—YA JERK!
KRUNK

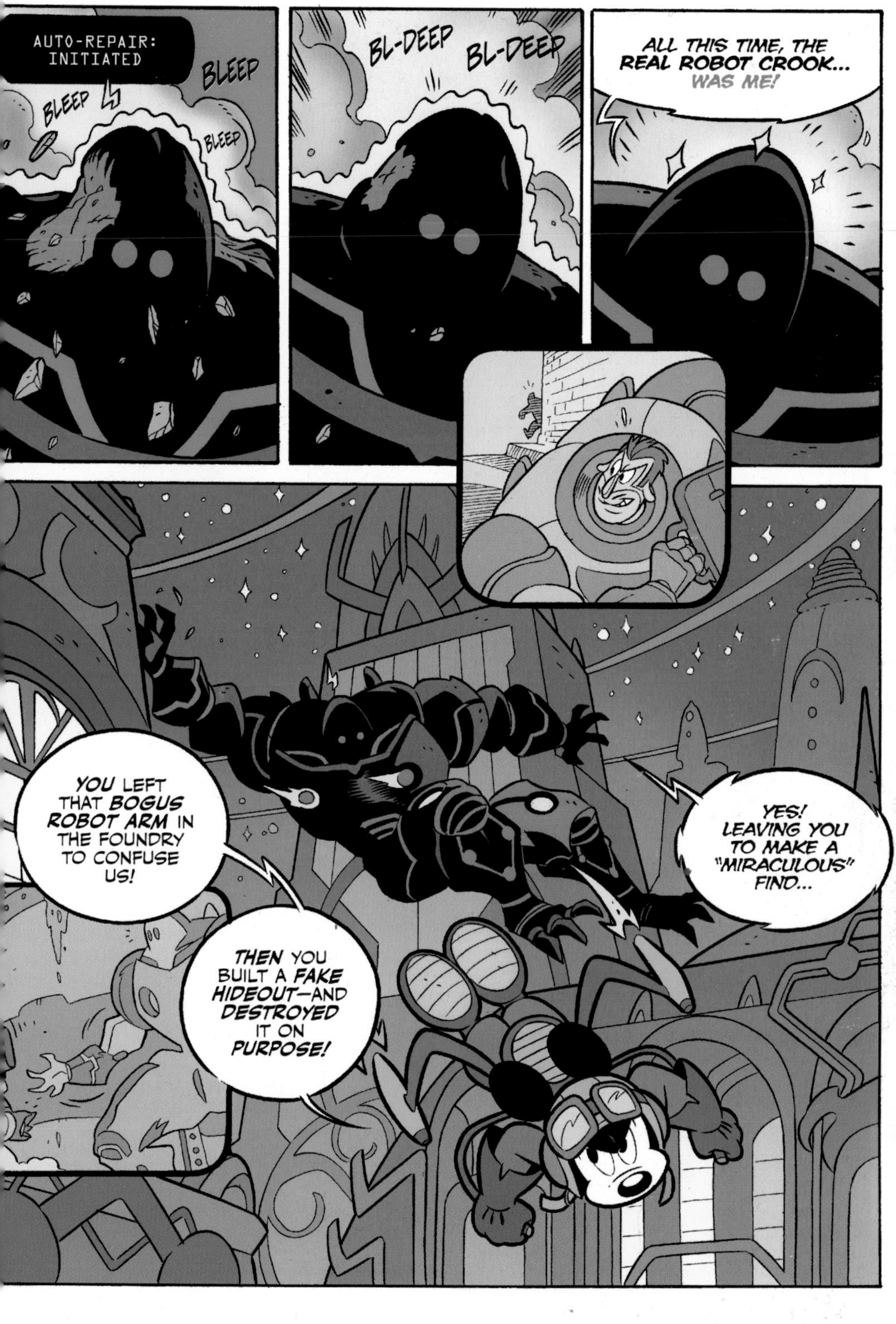
AUTO-REPAIR: INITIATED
BLEEP
BLEEP
BLEEP
BL-DEEP
BL-DEEP
ALL THIS TIME, THE REAL ROBOT CROOK... WAS ME!
YOU LEFT THAT BOGUS ROBOT ARM IN THE FOUNDRY TO CONFUSE US!
THEN YOU BUILT A FAKE HIDEOUT—AND DESTROYED IT ON PURPOSE!
YES! LEAVING YOU TO MAKE A "MIRACULOUS" FIND...

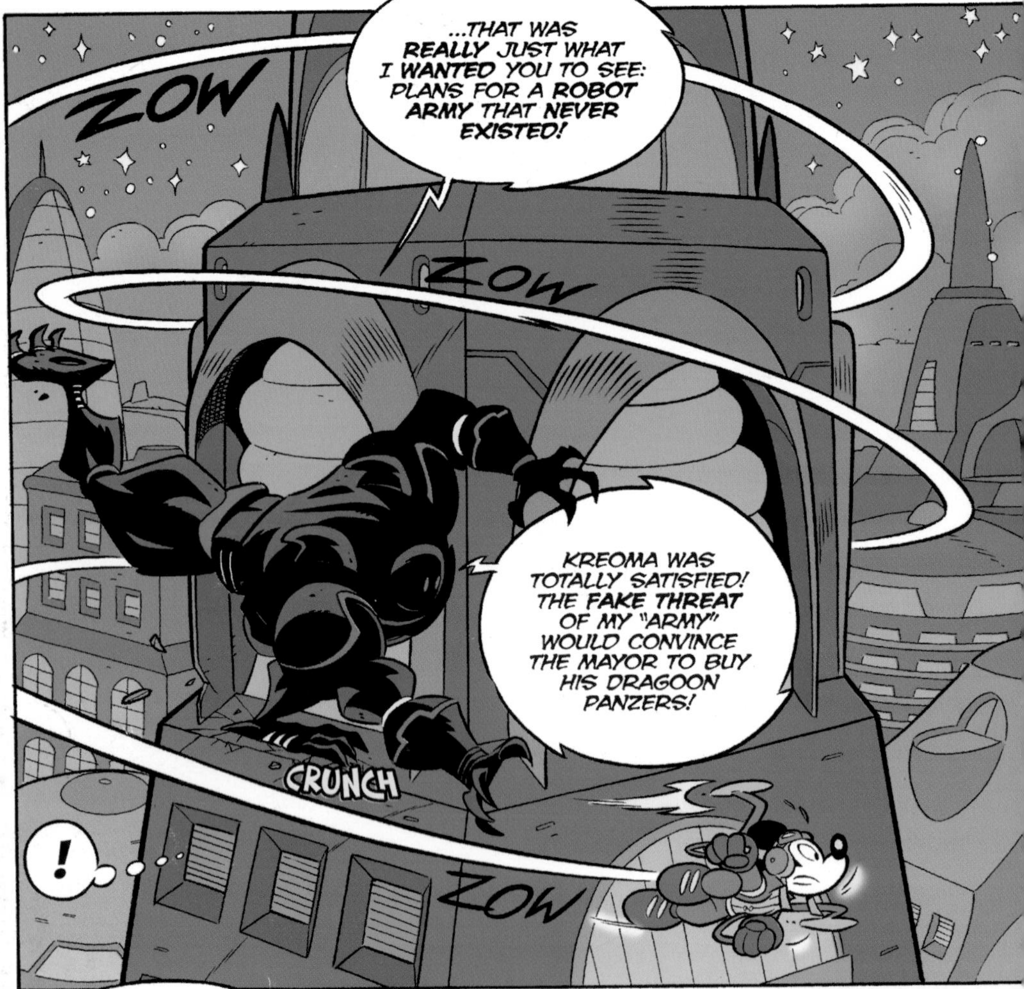
ZOW
...THAT WAS REALLY JUST WHAT I WANTED YOU TO SEE: PLANS FOR A ROBOT ARMY THAT NEVER EXISTED!
ZOW
KREOMA WAS TOTALLY SATISFIED! THE FAKE THREAT OF MY "ARMY" WOULD CONVINCE THE MAYOR TO BUY HIS DRAGOON PANZERS!
CRUNCH
!
ZOW

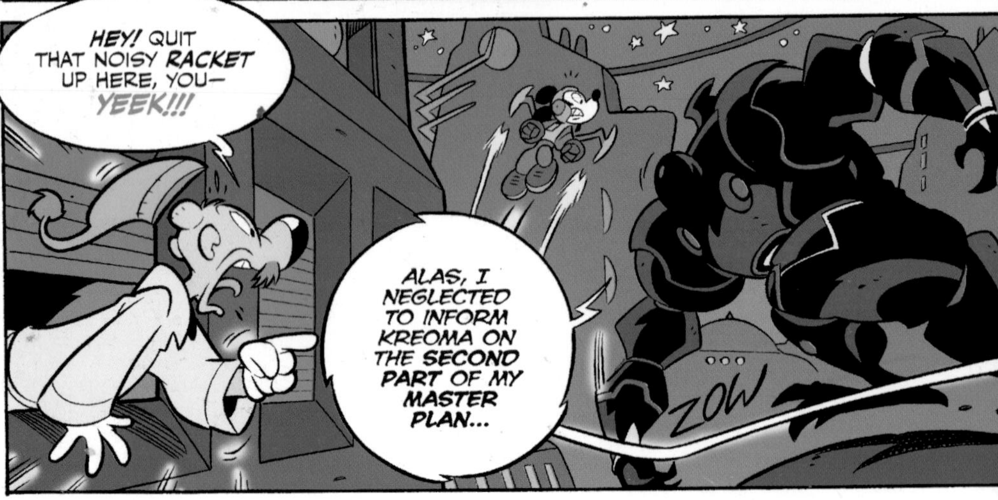
HEY! QUIT THAT NOISY RACKET UP HERE, YOU— YEEK!!!
ALAS, I NEGLECTED TO INFORM KREOMA ON THE SECOND PART OF MY MASTER PLAN...
ZOW

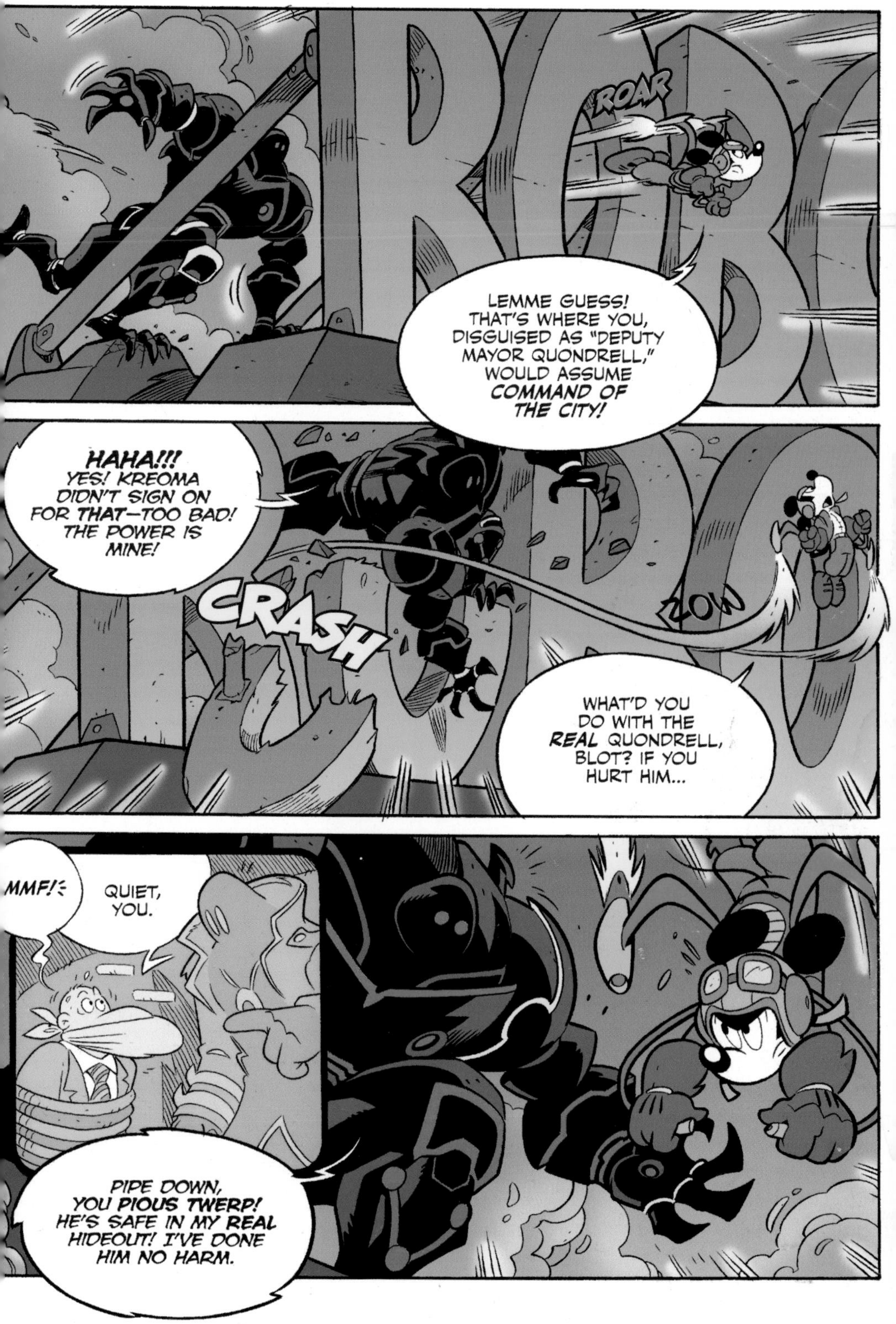

ROAR
LEMME GUESS! THAT'S WHERE YOU, DISGUISED AS "DEPUTY MAYOR QUONDRELL," WOULD ASSUME COMMAND OF THE CITY!
HAHA!!! YES! KREOMA DIDN'T SIGN ON FOR THAT—TOO BAD! THE POWER IS MINE!
CRASH
ZOW
WHAT'D YOU DO WITH THE REAL QUONDRELL, BLOT? IF YOU HURT HIM...
MMF!
QUIET, YOU.
PIPE DOWN, YOU PIOUS TWERP! HE'S SAFE IN MY REAL HIDEOUT! I'VE DONE HIM NO HARM.

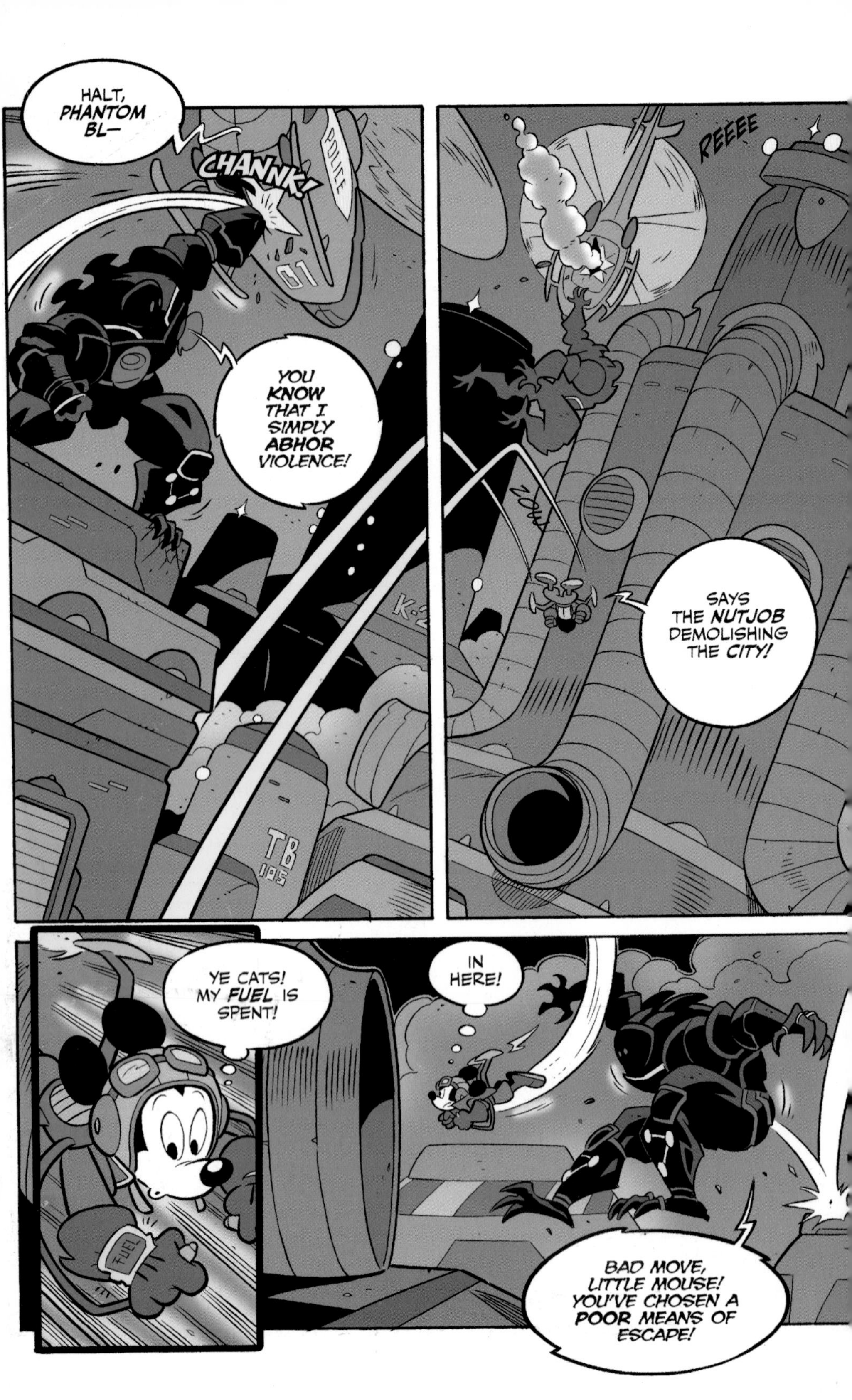
HALT, PHANTOM BL—
CHANNK!
YOU KNOW THAT I SIMPLY ABHOR VIOLENCE!
REEEE
SAYS THE NUTJOB DEMOLISHING THE CITY!
YE CATS! MY FUEL IS SPENT!
FUEL
IN HERE!
BAD MOVE, LITTLE MOUSE! YOU'VE CHOSEN A POOR MEANS OF ESCAPE!

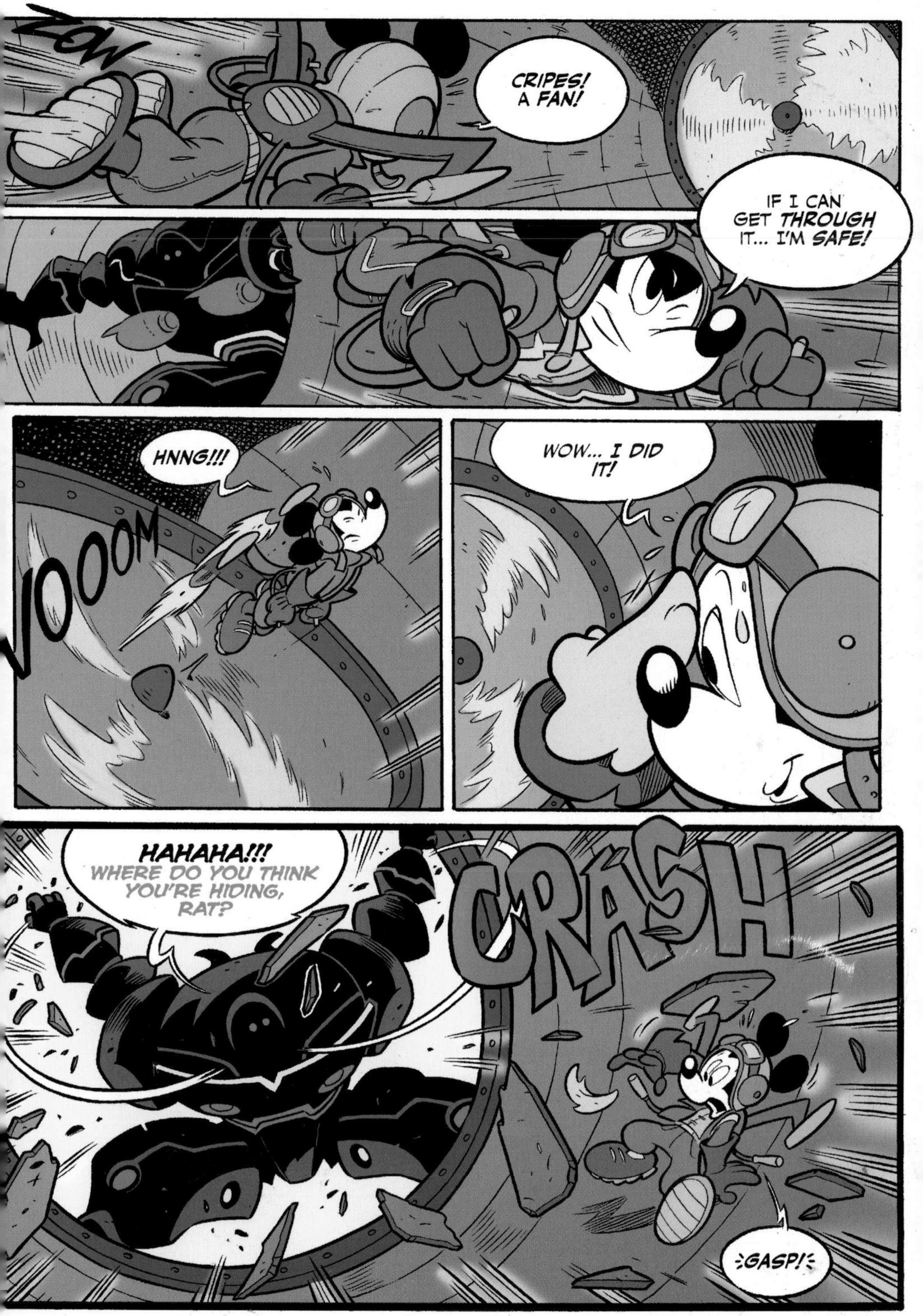
ZOW
CRIPES! A FAN!
IF I CAN GET THROUGH IT... I'M SAFE!
HNNG!!!
VOOOM
WOW... I DID IT!
HAHAHA!!! WHERE DO YOU THINK YOU'RE HIDING, RAT?
CRASH
GASP!

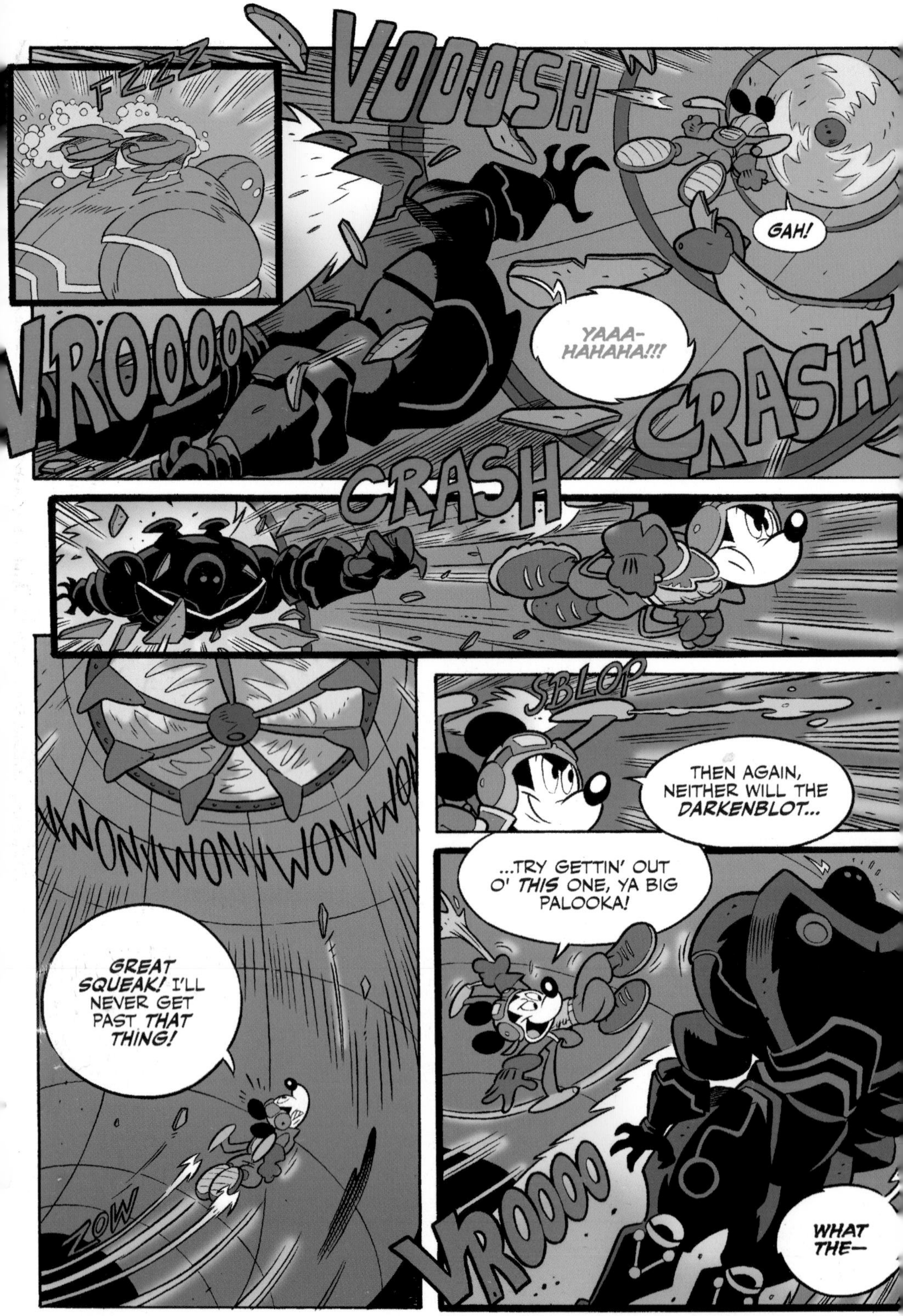
FZZZ
VOOOSH
GAH!
YAAA-HAHAHA!!!
VROOOO
CRASH
CRASH
CRASH
WONWONWONWONWON
SBLOP
THEN AGAIN, NEITHER WILL THE DARKENBLOT...
...TRY GETTIN' OUT O' THIS ONE, YA BIG PALOOKA!
GREAT SQUEAK! I'LL NEVER GET PAST THAT THING!
ZOW
VROOOO
WHAT THE—

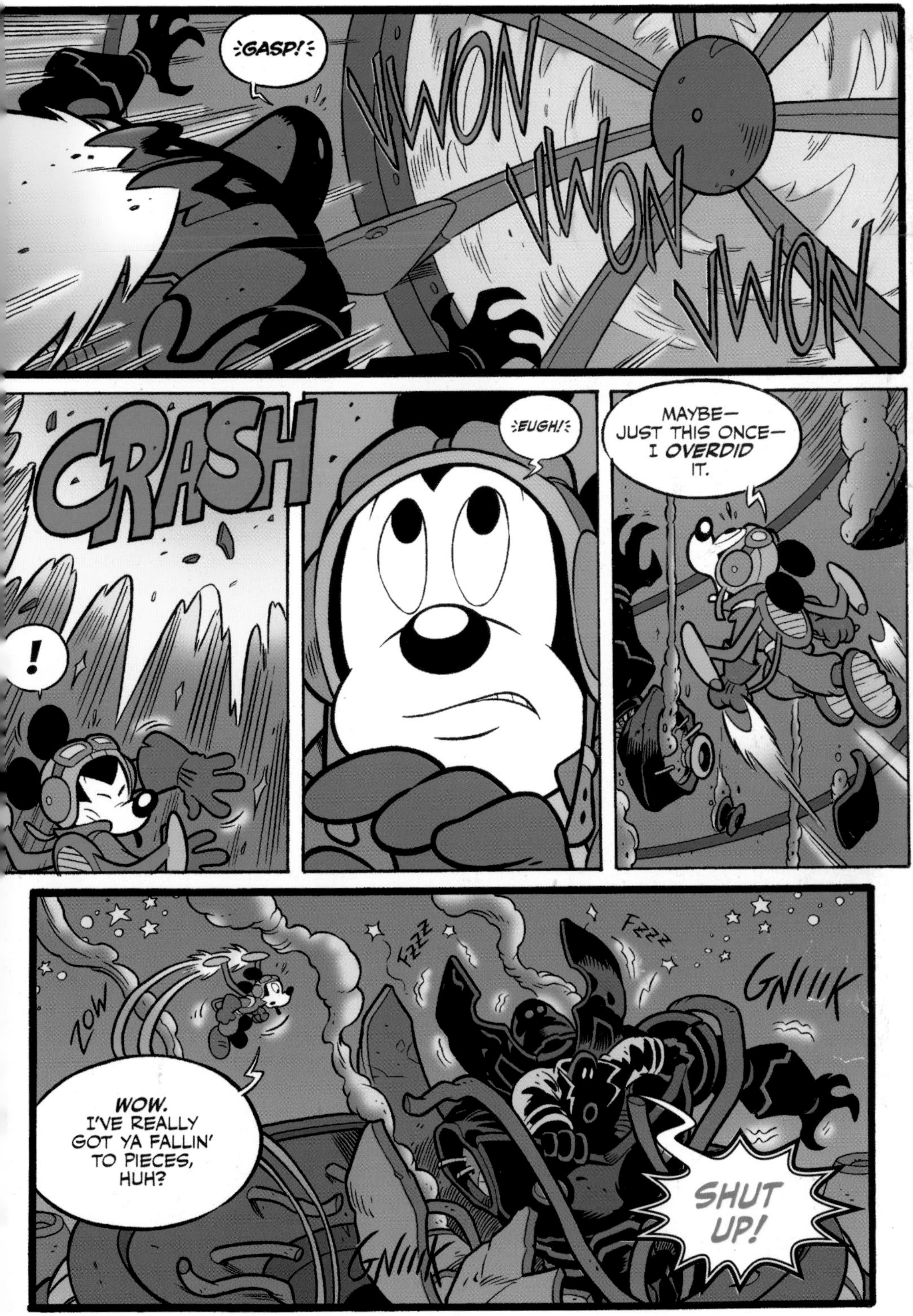
GASP!
VWON VWON VWON
CRASH
!
EUGH!
MAYBE— JUST THIS ONCE— I OVERDID IT.
ZOW
FZZZ
FZZZ
GNIIIK
WOW. I'VE REALLY GOT YA FALLIN' TO PIECES, HUH?
SHUT UP!
GNIIIK

C'MON, BIG BOY! I'LL PULL YA OUT!
LEAVE ME ALONE!!!
QUIT YER FUSSIN'! YER BIG METAL BABY'S... URGH! ABOUT TO FALL OFF THE TREETOP!
NO!
GNEEEK
CRACK
CLANK
PLUSH
MY BEAUTIFUL DARKENBLOT...

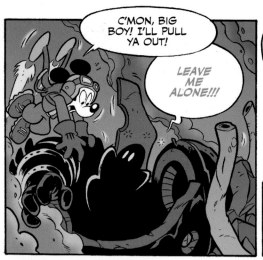

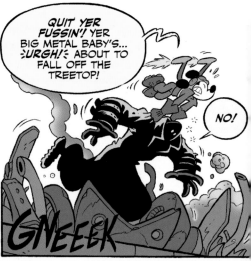

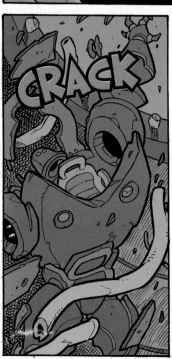

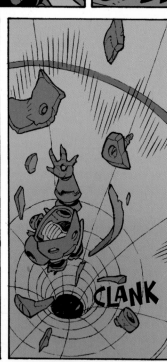

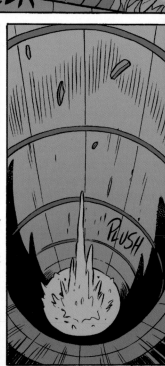

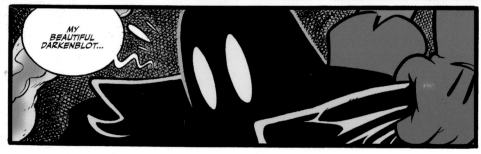

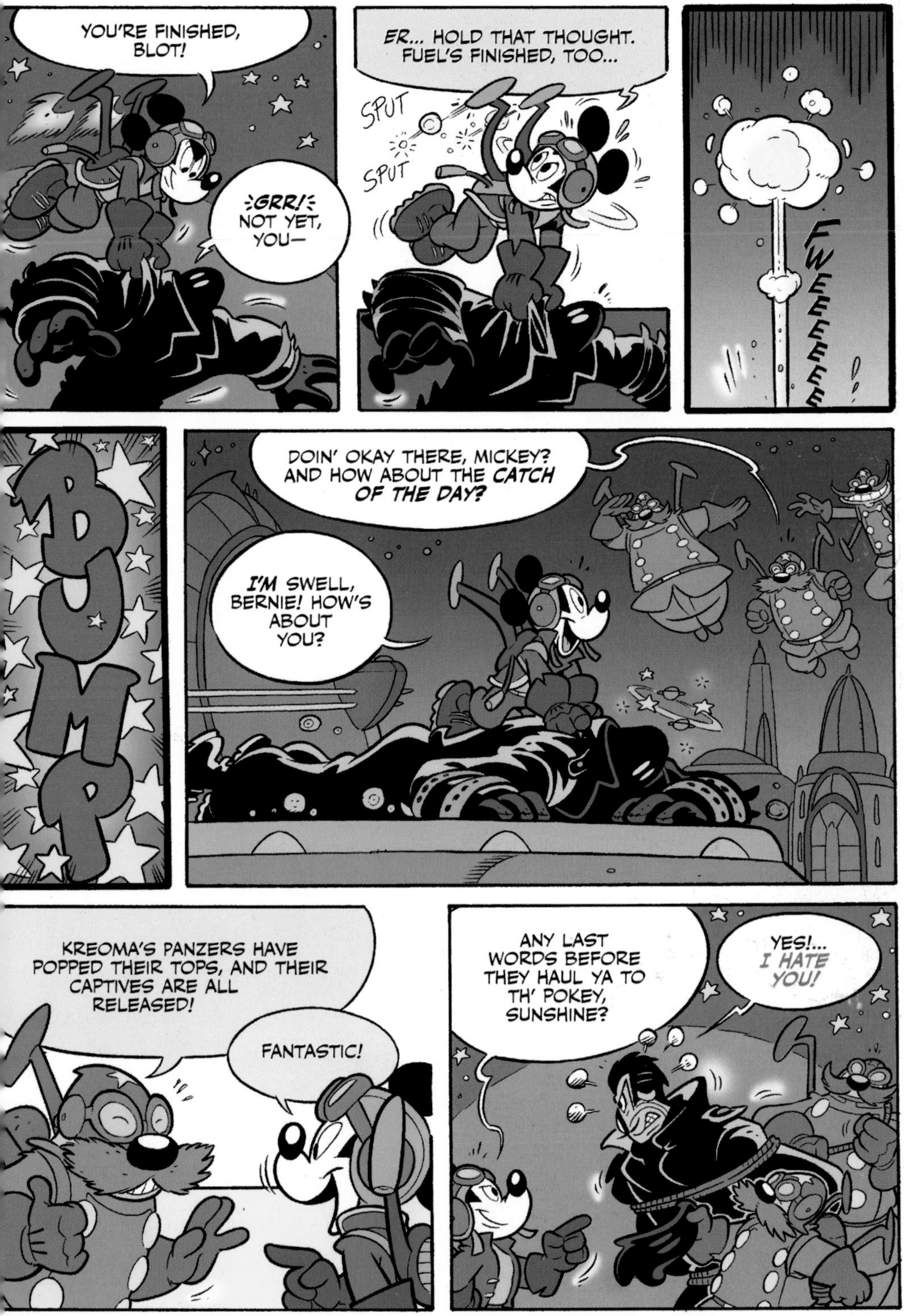
YOU'RE FINISHED, BLOT!
GRR! NOT YET, YOU—
ER... HOLD THAT THOUGHT. FUEL'S FINISHED, TOO...
SPUT
SPUT
FWEEEEEE
BUMP
DOIN' OKAY THERE, MICKEY? AND HOW ABOUT THE CATCH OF THE DAY?
I'M SWELL, BERNIE! HOW'S ABOUT YOU?
KREOMA'S PANZERS HAVE POPPED THEIR TOPS, AND THEIR CAPTIVES ARE ALL RELEASED!
FANTASTIC!
ANY LAST WORDS BEFORE THEY HAUL YA TO TH' POKEY, SUNSHINE?
YES!... I HATE YOU!

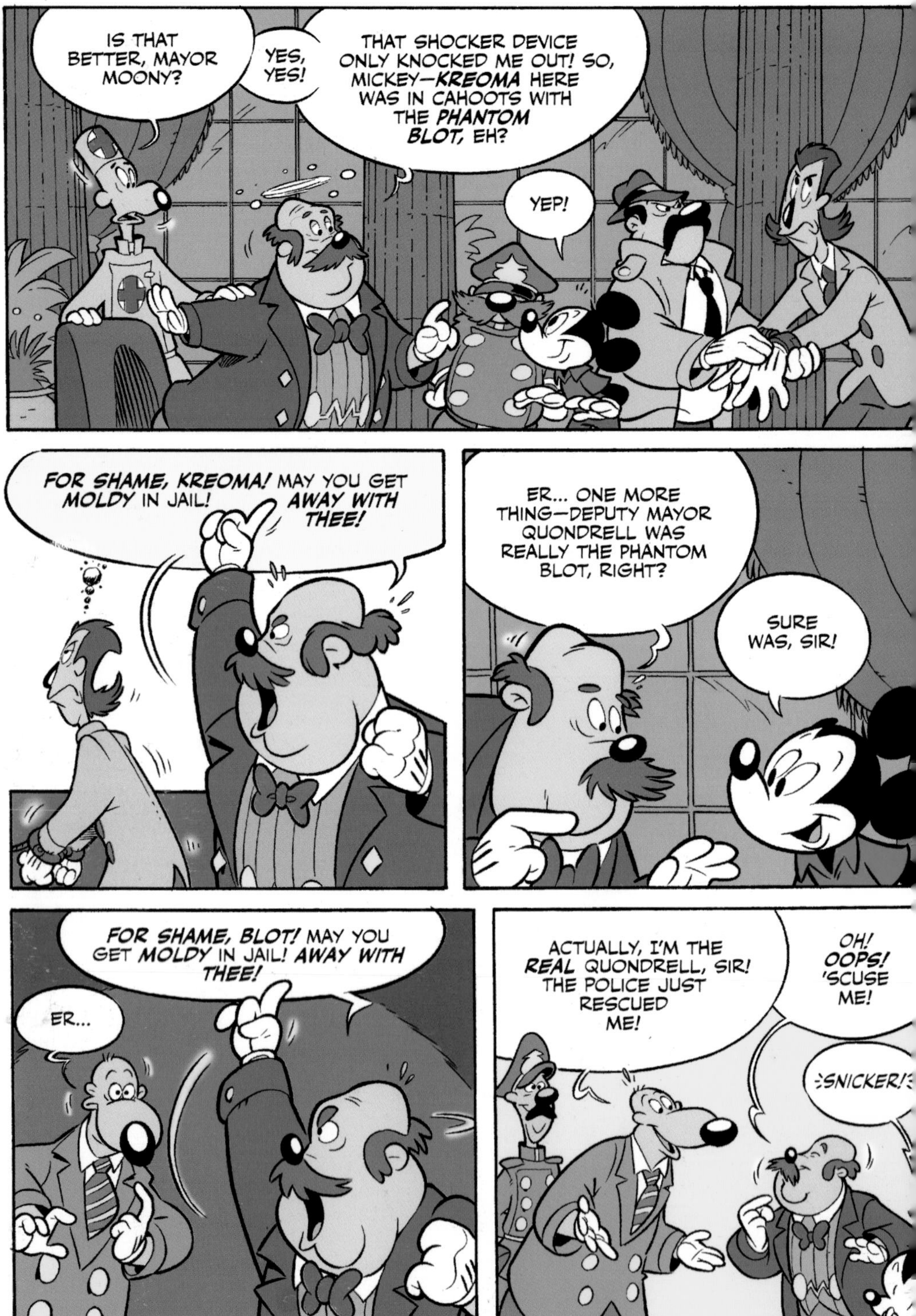
IS THAT BETTER, MAYOR MOONY?
YES, YES!
THAT SHOCKER DEVICE ONLY KNOCKED ME OUT! SO, MICKEY—KREOMA HERE WAS IN CAHOOTS WITH THE PHANTOM BLOT, EH?
YEP!
FOR SHAME, KREOMA! MAY YOU GET MOLDY IN JAIL! AWAY WITH THEE!
ER... ONE MORE THING—DEPUTY MAYOR QUONDRELL WAS REALLY THE PHANTOM BLOT, RIGHT?
SURE WAS, SIR!
FOR SHAME, BLOT! MAY YOU GET MOLDY IN JAIL! AWAY WITH THEE!
ER...
ACTUALLY, I'M THE REAL QUONDRELL, SIR! THE POLICE JUST RESCUED ME!
OH! OOPS! 'SCUSE ME!
SNICKER!

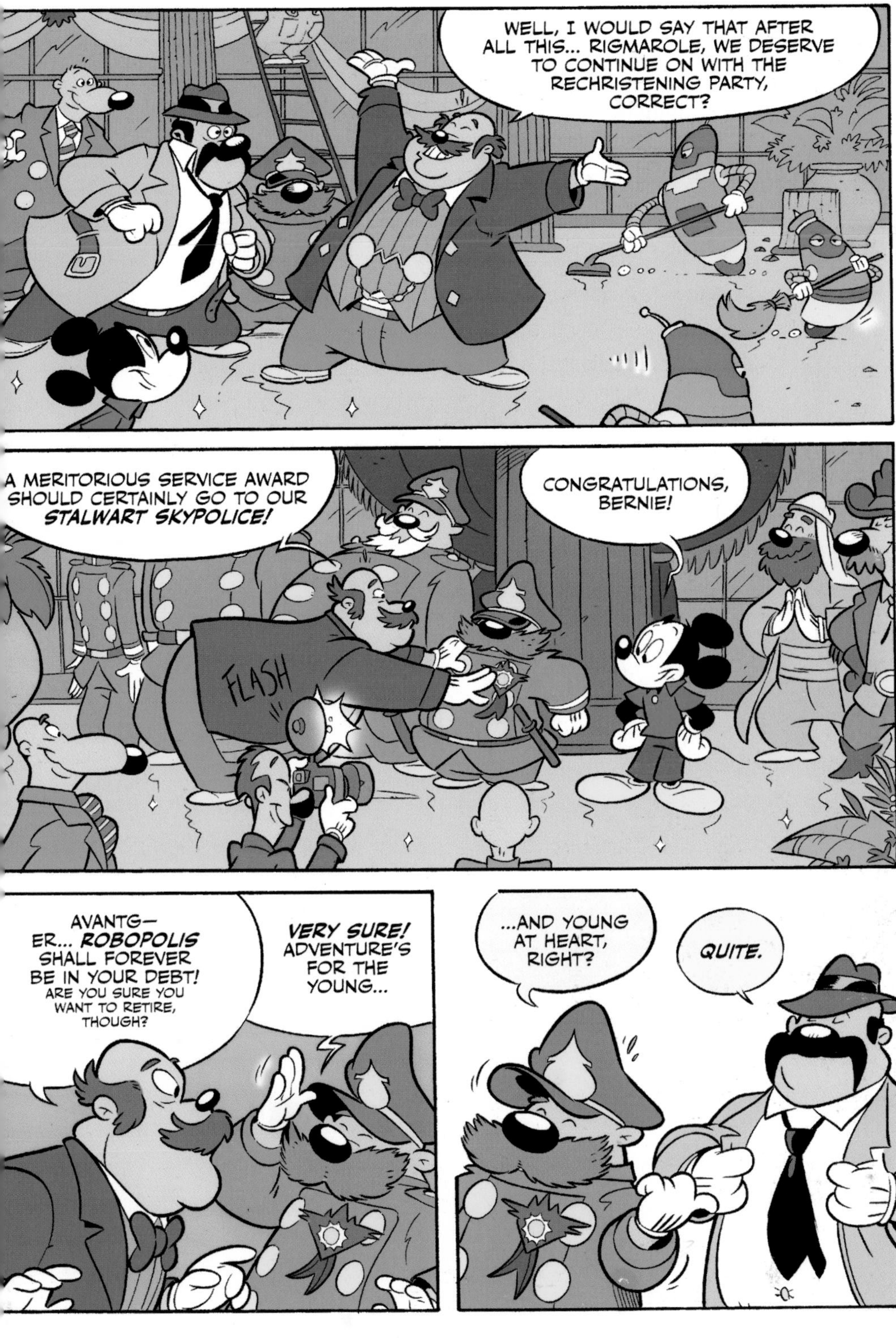
WELL, I WOULD SAY THAT AFTER ALL THIS... RIGMAROLE, WE DESERVE TO CONTINUE ON WITH THE RECHRISTENING PARTY, CORRECT?
A MERITORIOUS SERVICE AWARD SHOULD CERTAINLY GO TO OUR *STALWART SKYPOLICE!*
CONGRATULATIONS, BERNIE!
FLASH
AVANTG— ER... ***ROBOPOLIS*** SHALL FOREVER BE IN YOUR DEBT! ARE YOU SURE YOU WANT TO RETIRE, THOUGH?
*VERY SURE!* ADVENTURE'S FOR THE YOUNG...
...AND YOUNG AT HEART, RIGHT?
*QUITE.*

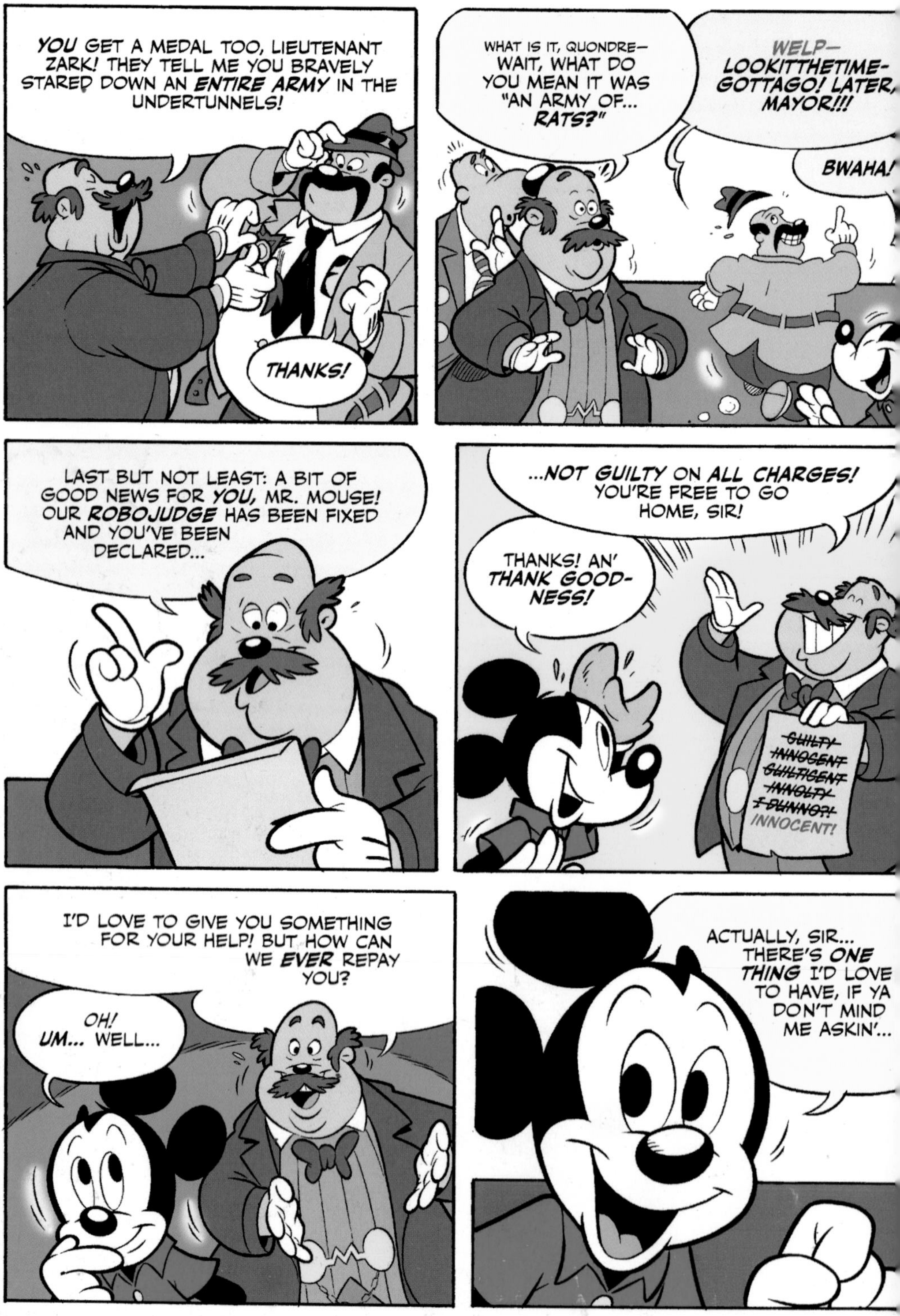
YOU GET A MEDAL TOO, LIEUTENANT ZARK! THEY TELL ME YOU BRAVELY STARED DOWN AN ENTIRE ARMY IN THE UNDERTUNNELS!
THANKS!
WHAT IS IT, QUONDRE— WAIT, WHAT DO YOU MEAN IT WAS "AN ARMY OF... RATS?"
WELP— LOOKITTHETIME- GOTTAGO! LATER, MAYOR!!!
BWAHA!
LAST BUT NOT LEAST: A BIT OF GOOD NEWS FOR YOU, MR. MOUSE! OUR ROBOJUDGE HAS BEEN FIXED AND YOU'VE BEEN DECLARED...
...NOT GUILTY ON ALL CHARGES! YOU'RE FREE TO GO HOME, SIR!
THANKS! AN' THANK GOOD- NESS!
GUILTY
INNOCENT
GUILTICENT
INNOLTY
I DUNNO?!
INNOCENT!
I'D LOVE TO GIVE YOU SOMETHING FOR YOUR HELP! BUT HOW CAN WE EVER REPAY YOU?
OH! UM... WELL...
ACTUALLY, SIR... THERE'S ONE THING I'D LOVE TO HAVE, IF YA DON'T MIND ME ASKIN'...

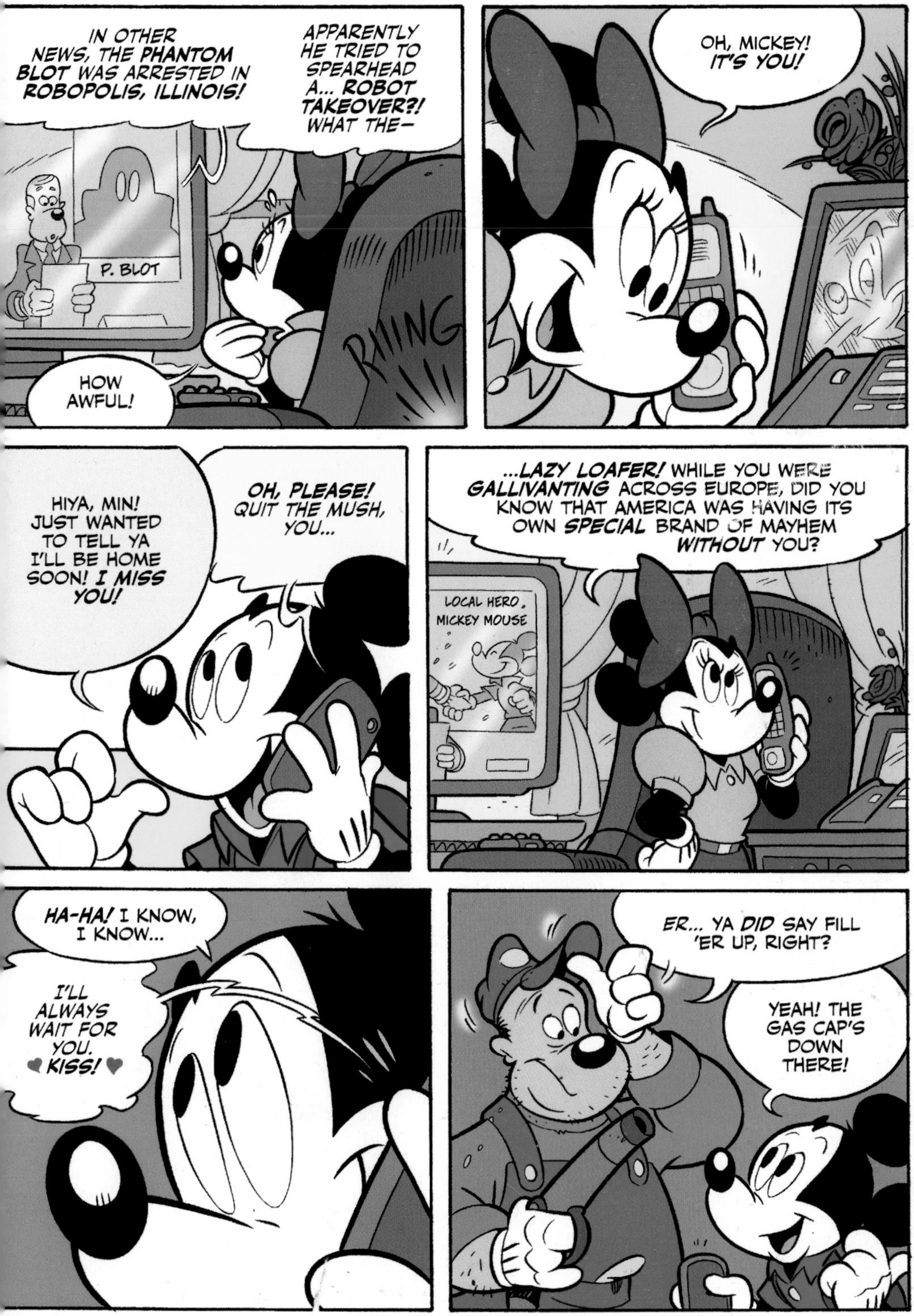

IN OTHER NEWS, THE PHANTOM BLOT WAS ARRESTED IN ROBOPOLIS, ILLINOIS!
APPARENTLY HE TRIED TO SPEARHEAD A... ROBOT TAKEOVER?! WHAT THE—
P. BLOT
HOW AWFUL!
RIIING
OH, MICKEY! IT'S YOU!
HIYA, MIN! JUST WANTED TO TELL YA I'LL BE HOME SOON! I MISS YOU!
OH, PLEASE! QUIT THE MUSH, YOU...
...LAZY LOAFER! WHILE YOU WERE GALLIVANTING ACROSS EUROPE, DID YOU KNOW THAT AMERICA WAS HAVING ITS OWN SPECIAL BRAND OF MAYHEM WITHOUT YOU?
LOCAL HERO, MICKEY MOUSE
HA-HA! I KNOW, I KNOW...
I'LL ALWAYS WAIT FOR YOU. ♥ KISS! ♥
ER... YA DID SAY FILL 'ER UP, RIGHT?
YEAH! THE GAS CAP'S DOWN THERE!

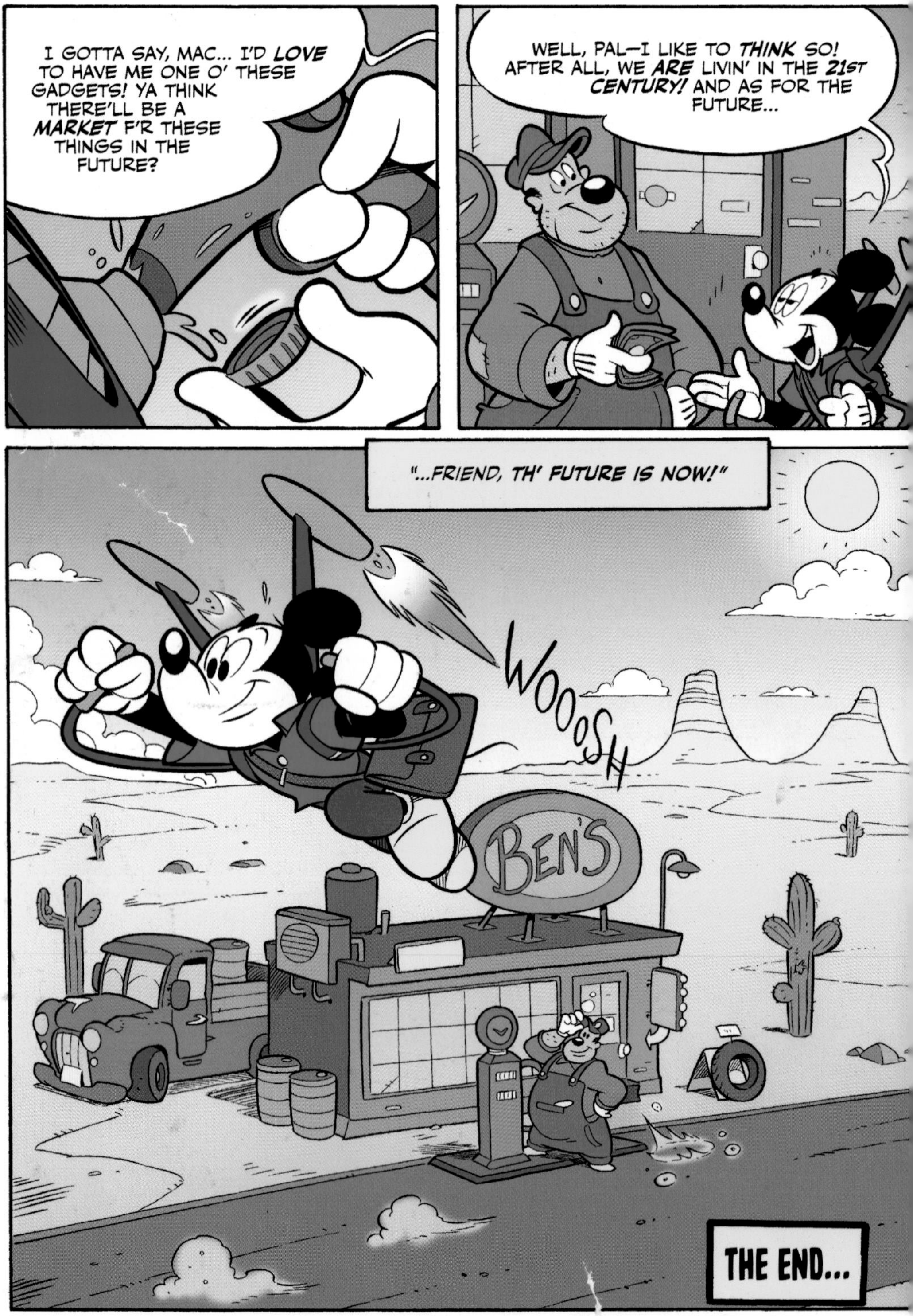
I GOTTA SAY, MAC... I'D LOVE TO HAVE ME ONE O' THESE GADGETS! YA THINK THERE'LL BE A MARKET F'R THESE THINGS IN THE FUTURE?
WELL, PAL—I LIKE TO THINK SO! AFTER ALL, WE ARE LIVIN' IN THE 21ST CENTURY! AND AS FOR THE FUTURE...
"...FRIEND, TH' FUTURE IS NOW!"
WOOOSH
BEN'S
THE END...

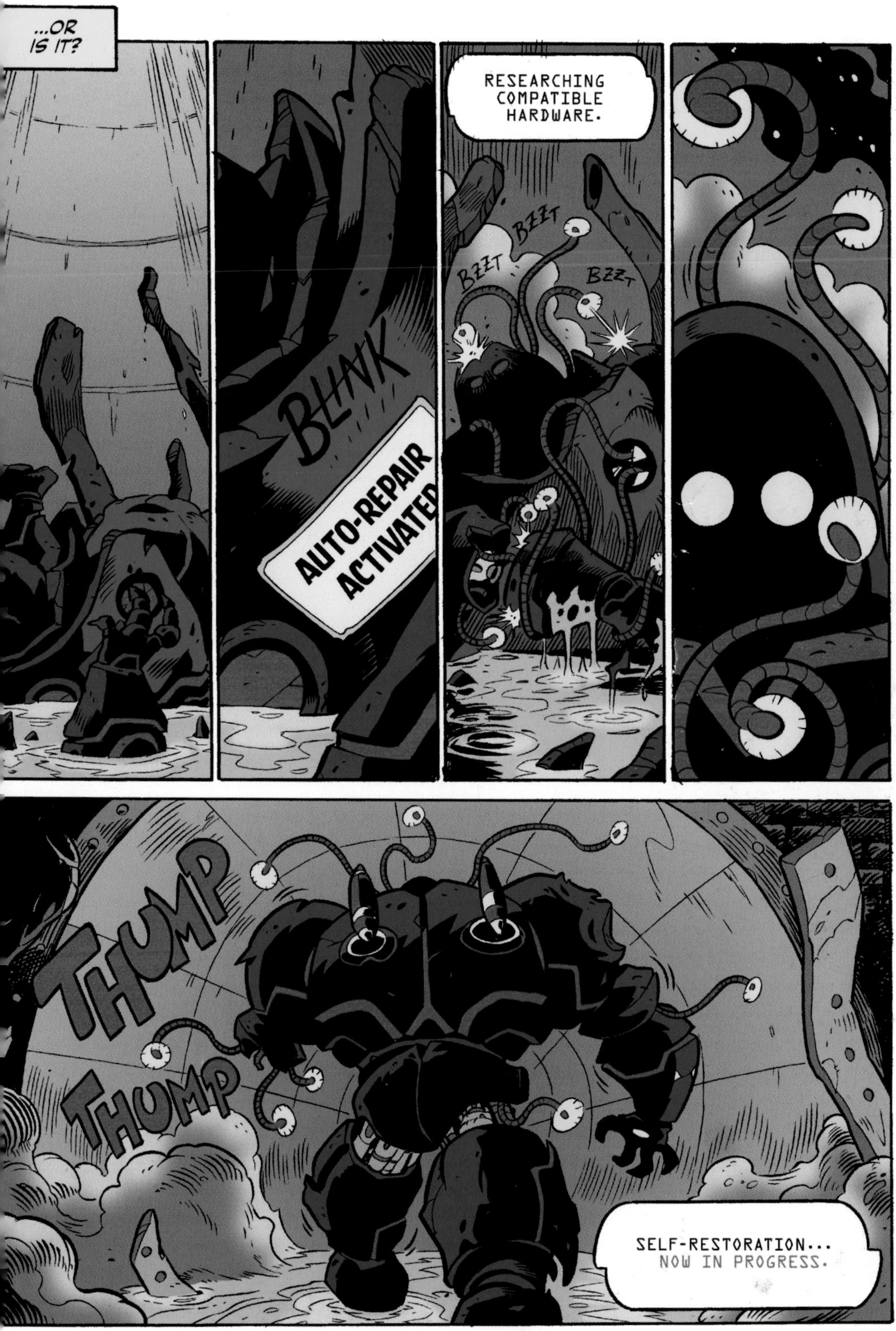

...OR IS IT?
BLINK
AUTO-REPAIR ACTIVATED
RESEARCHING COMPATIBLE HARDWARE.
BZZT
BZZT
BZZT
THUMP
THUMP
SELF-RESTORATION...
NOW IN PROGRESS.

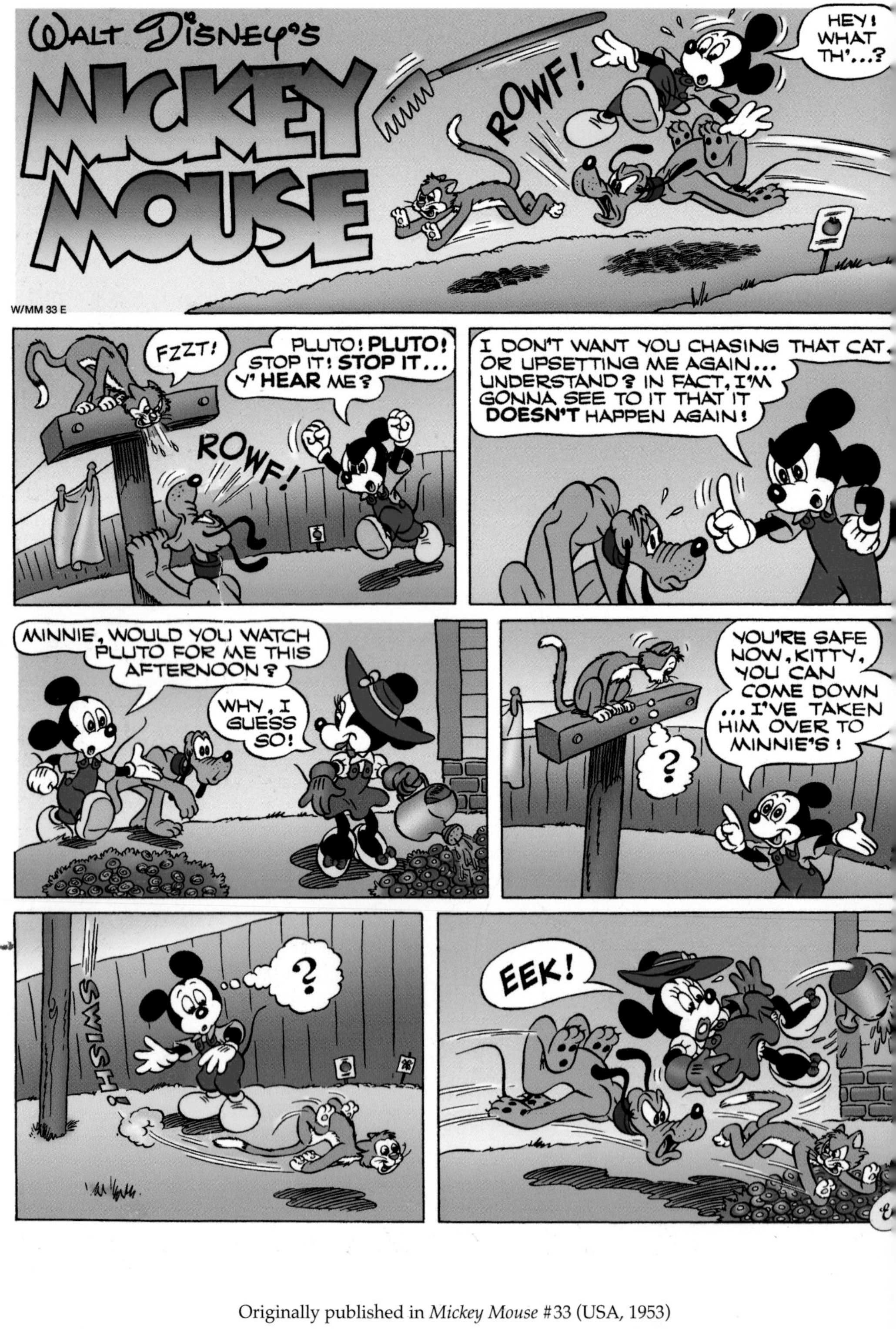
WALT DISNEY'S
MICKEY MOUSE
ROWF!
HEY! WHAT TH'...?
W/MM 33 E
FZZT!
PLUTO! PLUTO! STOP IT! STOP IT... Y' HEAR ME?
ROWF!
I DON'T WANT YOU CHASING THAT CAT, OR UPSETTING ME AGAIN... UNDERSTAND? IN FACT, I'M GONNA SEE TO IT THAT IT DOESN'T HAPPEN AGAIN!
MINNIE, WOULD YOU WATCH PLUTO FOR ME THIS AFTERNOON?
WHY, I GUESS SO!
?
YOU'RE SAFE NOW, KITTY, YOU CAN COME DOWN ... I'VE TAKEN HIM OVER TO MINNIE'S!
?
SWISH!
EEK!

Originally published in *Mickey Mouse* #33 (USA, 1953)

# Walt Disney's SUPER GOOF in RAIN, RAIN, GO ASTRAY!

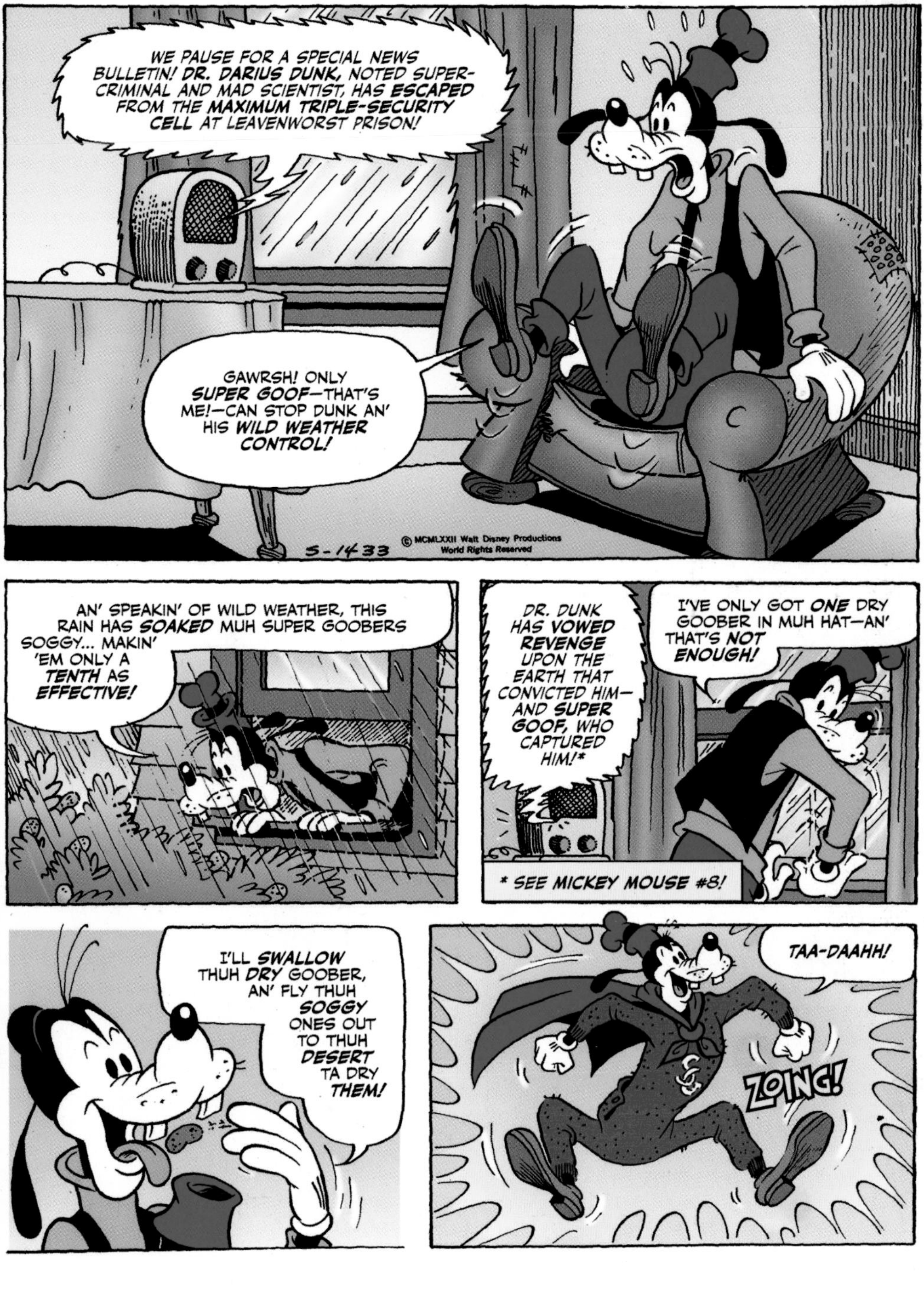
WE PAUSE FOR A SPECIAL NEWS BULLETIN! DR. DARIUS DUNK, NOTED SUPER-CRIMINAL AND MAD SCIENTIST, HAS ESCAPED FROM THE MAXIMUM TRIPLE-SECURITY CELL AT LEAVENWORST PRISON!
GAWRSH! ONLY SUPER GOOF—THAT'S ME!—CAN STOP DUNK AN' HIS WILD WEATHER CONTROL!
S-1433
© MCMLXXII Walt Disney Productions World Rights Reserved
AN' SPEAKIN' OF WILD WEATHER, THIS RAIN HAS SOAKED MUH SUPER GOOBERS SOGGY... MAKIN' 'EM ONLY A TENTH AS EFFECTIVE!
DR. DUNK HAS VOWED REVENGE UPON THE EARTH THAT CONVICTED HIM—AND SUPER GOOF, WHO CAPTURED HIM!*
I'VE ONLY GOT ONE DRY GOOBER IN MUH HAT—AN' THAT'S NOT ENOUGH!
* SEE MICKEY MOUSE #8!
I'LL SWALLOW THUH DRY GOOBER, AN' FLY THUH SOGGY ONES OUT TO THUH DESERT TA DRY THEM!
TAA-DAAHH!
ZOING!

Originally published in *Zé Carioca* #1105 (Brazil, 1973)

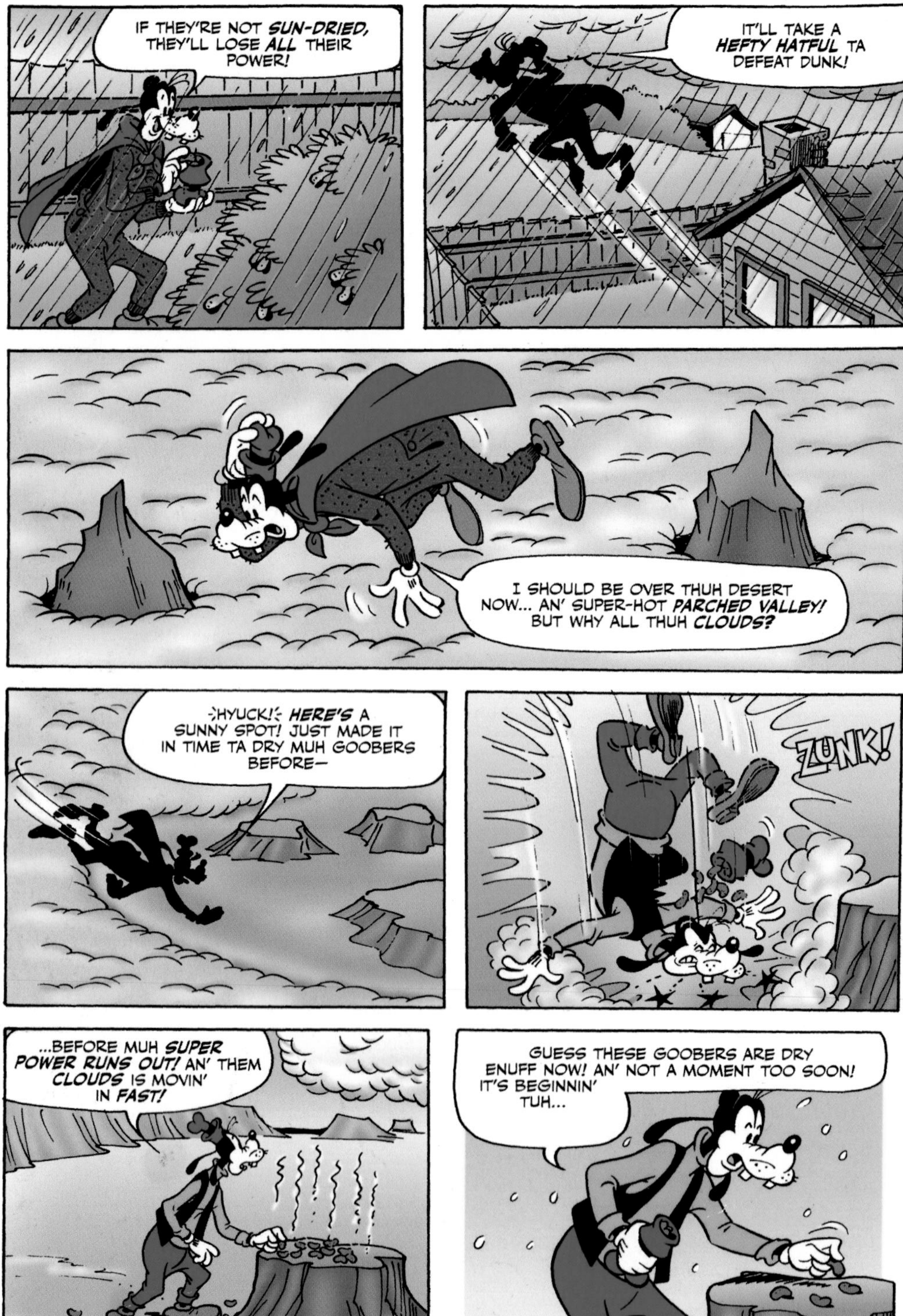
IF THEY'RE NOT SUN-DRIED, THEY'LL LOSE ALL THEIR POWER!
IT'LL TAKE A HEFTY HATFUL TA DEFEAT DUNK!
I SHOULD BE OVER THUH DESERT NOW... AN' SUPER-HOT PARCHED VALLEY! BUT WHY ALL THUH CLOUDS?
HYUCK! HERE'S A SUNNY SPOT! JUST MADE IT IN TIME TA DRY MUH GOOBERS BEFORE—
ZUNK!
...BEFORE MUH SUPER POWER RUNS OUT! AN' THEM CLOUDS IS MOVIN' IN FAST!
GUESS THESE GOOBERS ARE DRY ENUFF NOW! AN' NOT A MOMENT TOO SOON! IT'S BEGINNIN' TUH...

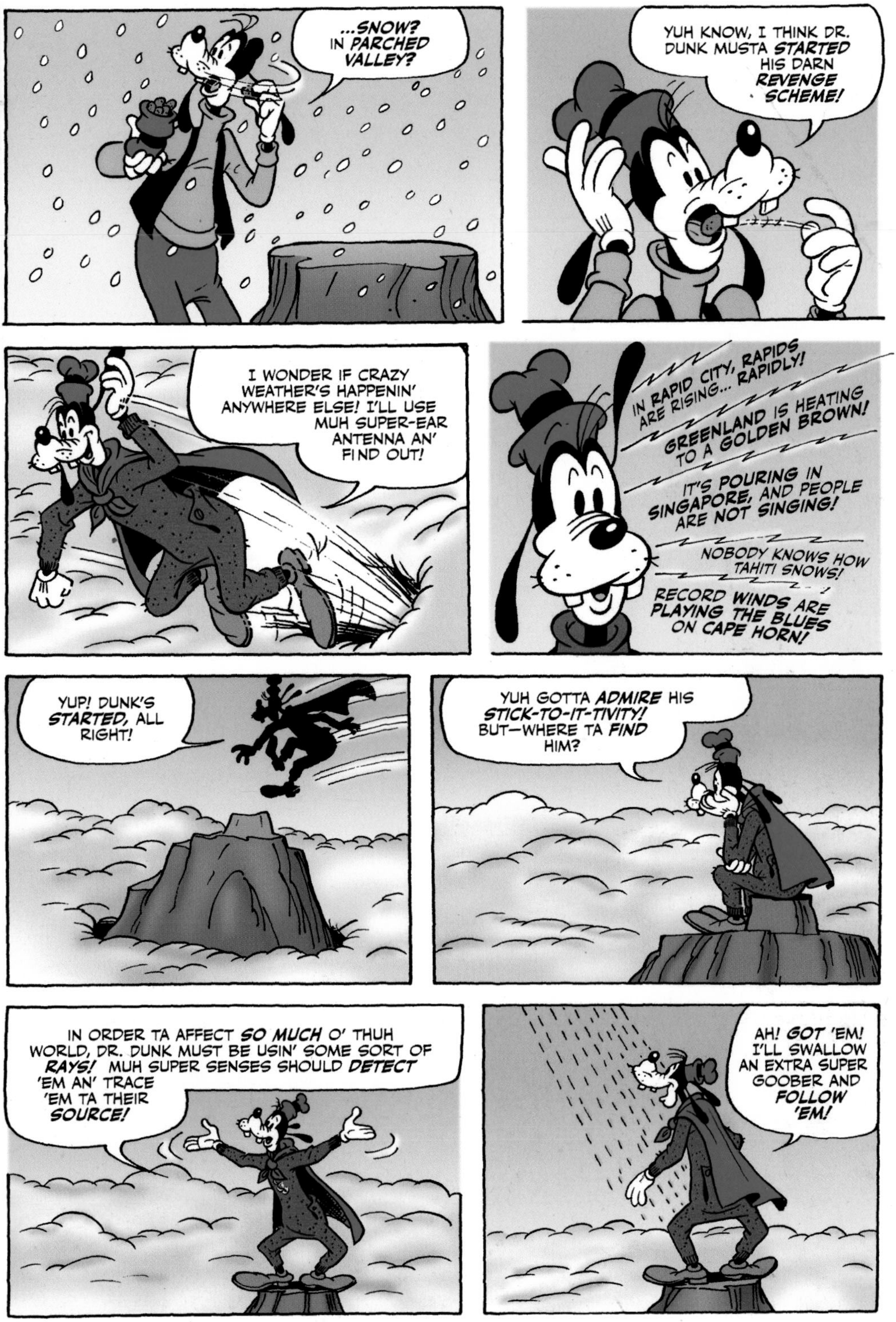
...SNOW? IN PARCHED VALLEY?
YUH KNOW, I THINK DR. DUNK MUSTA STARTED HIS DARN REVENGE SCHEME!
I WONDER IF CRAZY WEATHER'S HAPPENIN' ANYWHERE ELSE! I'LL USE MUH SUPER-EAR ANTENNA AN' FIND OUT!
IN RAPID CITY, RAPIDS ARE RISING... RAPIDLY!
GREENLAND IS HEATING TO A GOLDEN BROWN!
IT'S POURING IN SINGAPORE, AND PEOPLE ARE NOT SINGING!
NOBODY KNOWS HOW TAHITI SNOWS!
RECORD WINDS ARE PLAYING THE BLUES ON CAPE HORN!
YUP! DUNK'S STARTED, ALL RIGHT!
YUH GOTTA ADMIRE HIS STICK-TO-IT-TIVITY! BUT—WHERE TA FIND HIM?
IN ORDER TA AFFECT SO MUCH O' THUH WORLD, DR. DUNK MUST BE USIN' SOME SORT OF RAYS! MUH SUPER SENSES SHOULD DETECT 'EM AN' TRACE 'EM TA THEIR SOURCE!
AH! GOT 'EM! I'LL SWALLOW AN EXTRA SUPER GOOBER AND FOLLOW 'EM!

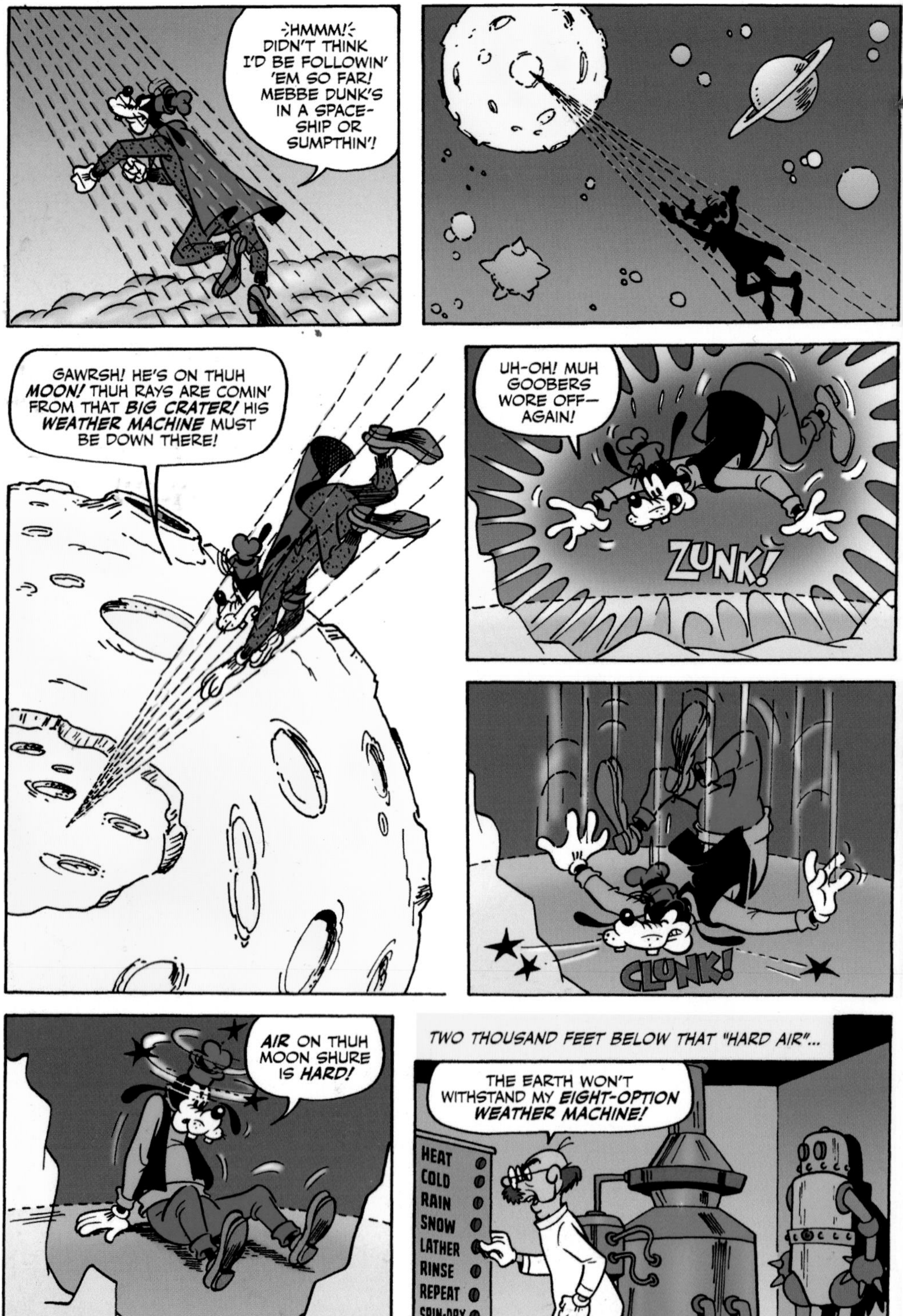
HMMM! DIDN'T THINK I'D BE FOLLOWIN' 'EM SO FAR! MEBBE DUNK'S IN A SPACE-SHIP OR SUMPTHIN'!
GAWRSH! HE'S ON THUH MOON! THUH RAYS ARE COMIN' FROM THAT BIG CRATER! HIS WEATHER MACHINE MUST BE DOWN THERE!
UH-OH! MUH GOOBERS WORE OFF— AGAIN!
ZUNK!
CLUNK!
AIR ON THUH MOON SHURE IS HARD!
TWO THOUSAND FEET BELOW THAT "HARD AIR"...
THE EARTH WON'T WITHSTAND MY EIGHT-OPTION WEATHER MACHINE!
HEAT
COLD
RAIN
SNOW
LATHER
RINSE
REPEAT
SPIN-DRY

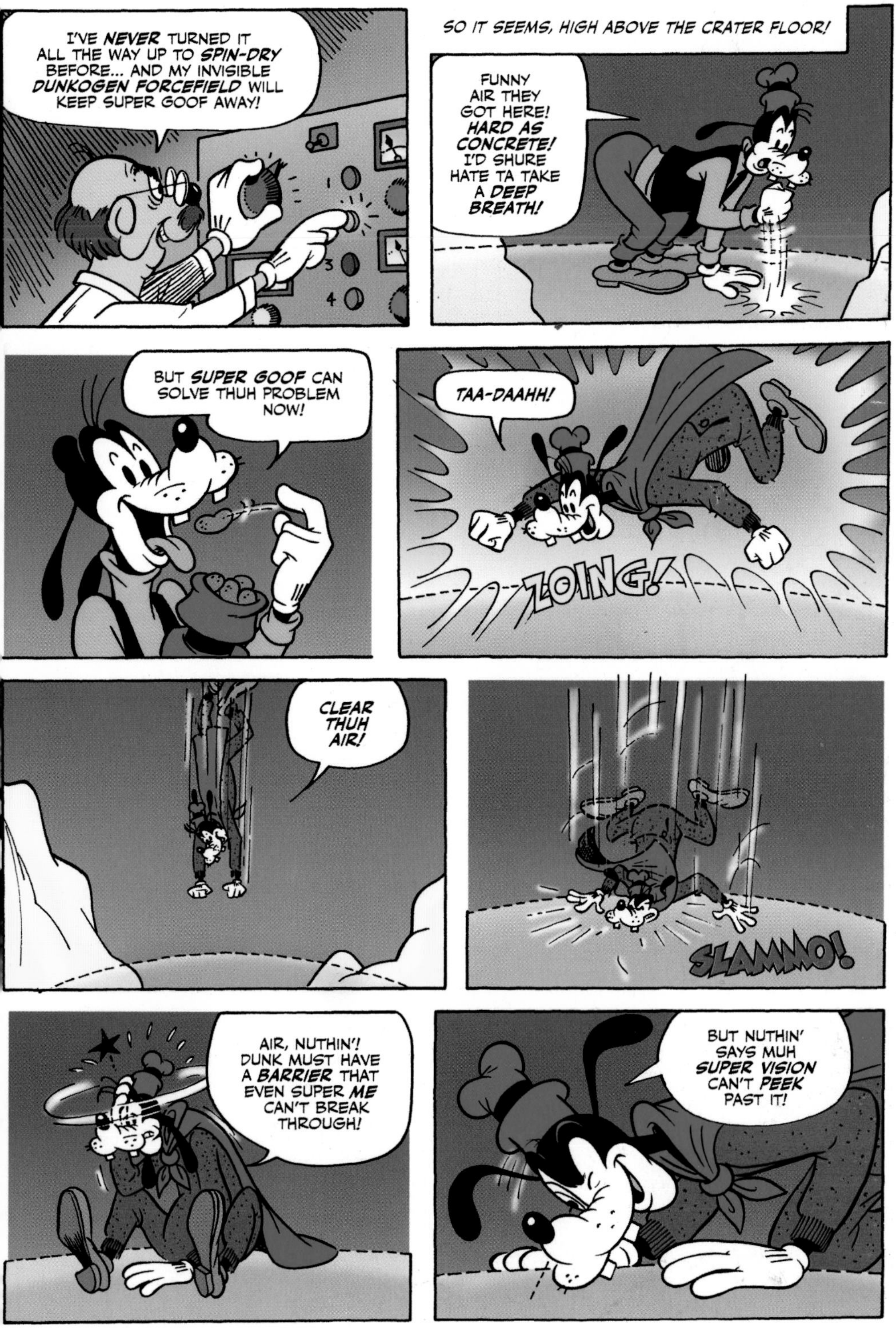
I'VE NEVER TURNED IT ALL THE WAY UP TO SPIN-DRY BEFORE... AND MY INVISIBLE DUNKOGEN FORCEFIELD WILL KEEP SUPER GOOF AWAY!
SO IT SEEMS, HIGH ABOVE THE CRATER FLOOR!
FUNNY AIR THEY GOT HERE! HARD AS CONCRETE! I'D SHURE HATE TA TAKE A DEEP BREATH!
BUT SUPER GOOF CAN SOLVE THUH PROBLEM NOW!
TAA-DAAHH!
ZOING!
CLEAR THUH AIR!
SLAMMO!
AIR, NUTHIN'! DUNK MUST HAVE A BARRIER THAT EVEN SUPER ME CAN'T BREAK THROUGH!
BUT NUTHIN' SAYS MUH SUPER VISION CAN'T PEEK PAST IT!

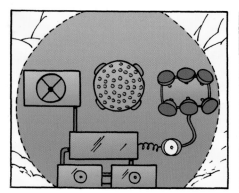

THAT'S DUNK'S SETUP, ALL RIGHT! IF I CAN'T REACH HIM FROM *ABOVE*, I'LL TRY A *GROUND-ATTACK!*

:ULP!: *ALL SOLID*—MAKIN' IT A *GROUND-ATTACK-LACK!*

IF YUH CAN'T GO *IN*, GO *UNDER!*

POING!

*BOTHERATION!* CAN'T A VILLAIN GLOAT IN PEACE?

IT CAN ONLY BE *SUPER GOOF*—BUT *HOW?* NEVER MIND... MY *DUNK-JUNK-SURPLUS ROBOT* WILL FIX HIM!

UH-OH! A *ROBO-FOE!*

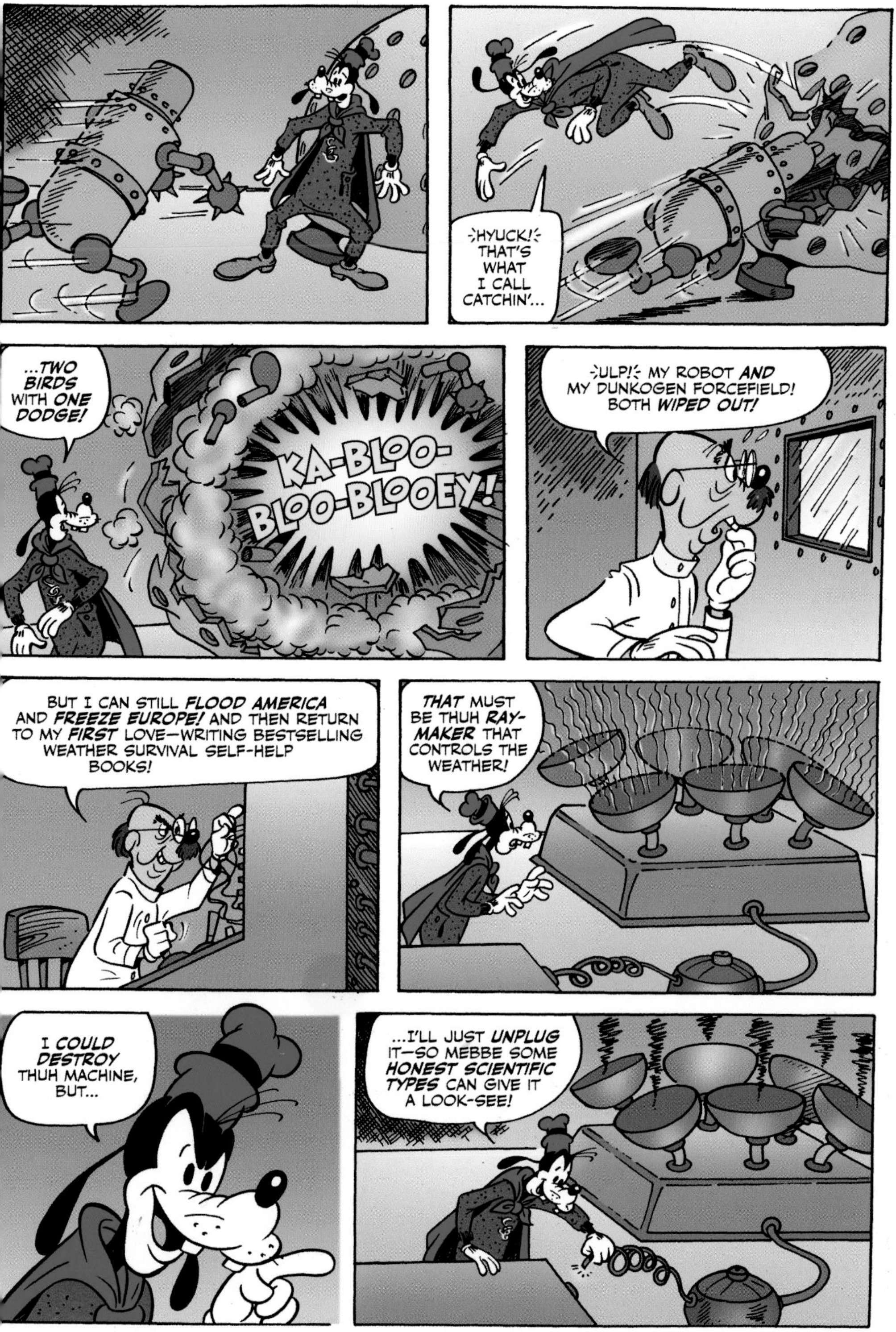

HYUCK! THAT'S WHAT I CALL CATCHIN'...
...TWO BIRDS WITH ONE DODGE!
KA-BLOO-BLOO-BLOOEY!
ULP! MY ROBOT AND MY DUNKOGEN FORCEFIELD! BOTH WIPED OUT!
BUT I CAN STILL FLOOD AMERICA AND FREEZE EUROPE! AND THEN RETURN TO MY FIRST LOVE—WRITING BESTSELLING WEATHER SURVIVAL SELF-HELP BOOKS!
THAT MUST BE THUH RAY-MAKER THAT CONTROLS THE WEATHER!
I COULD DESTROY THUH MACHINE, BUT...
...I'LL JUST UNPLUG IT—SO MEBBE SOME HONEST SCIENTIFIC TYPES CAN GIVE IT A LOOK-SEE!

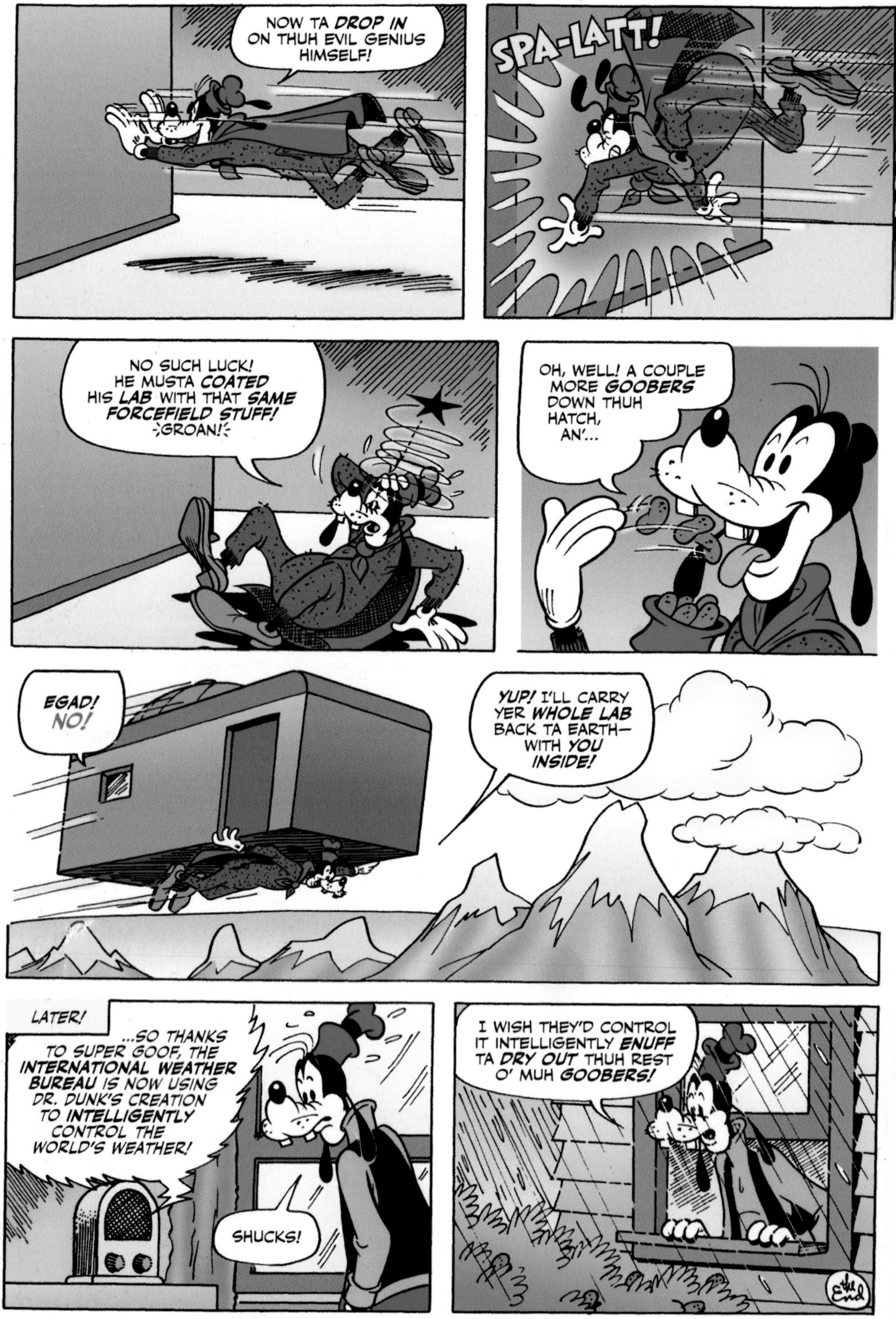
NOW TA DROP IN ON THUH EVIL GENIUS HIMSELF!
SPA-LATT!
NO SUCH LUCK! HE MUSTA COATED HIS LAB WITH THAT SAME FORCEFIELD STUFF! GROAN!
OH, WELL! A COUPLE MORE GOOBERS DOWN THUH HATCH, AN'...
EGAD! NO!
YUP! I'LL CARRY YER WHOLE LAB BACK TA EARTH— WITH YOU INSIDE!
LATER!
...SO THANKS TO SUPER GOOF, THE INTERNATIONAL WEATHER BUREAU IS NOW USING DR. DUNK'S CREATION TO INTELLIGENTLY CONTROL THE WORLD'S WEATHER!
SHUCKS!
I WISH THEY'D CONTROL IT INTELLIGENTLY ENUFF TA DRY OUT THUH REST O' MUH GOOBERS!
the End

# Walt Disney's Horace Horsecollar in MORTGAGE MISERY

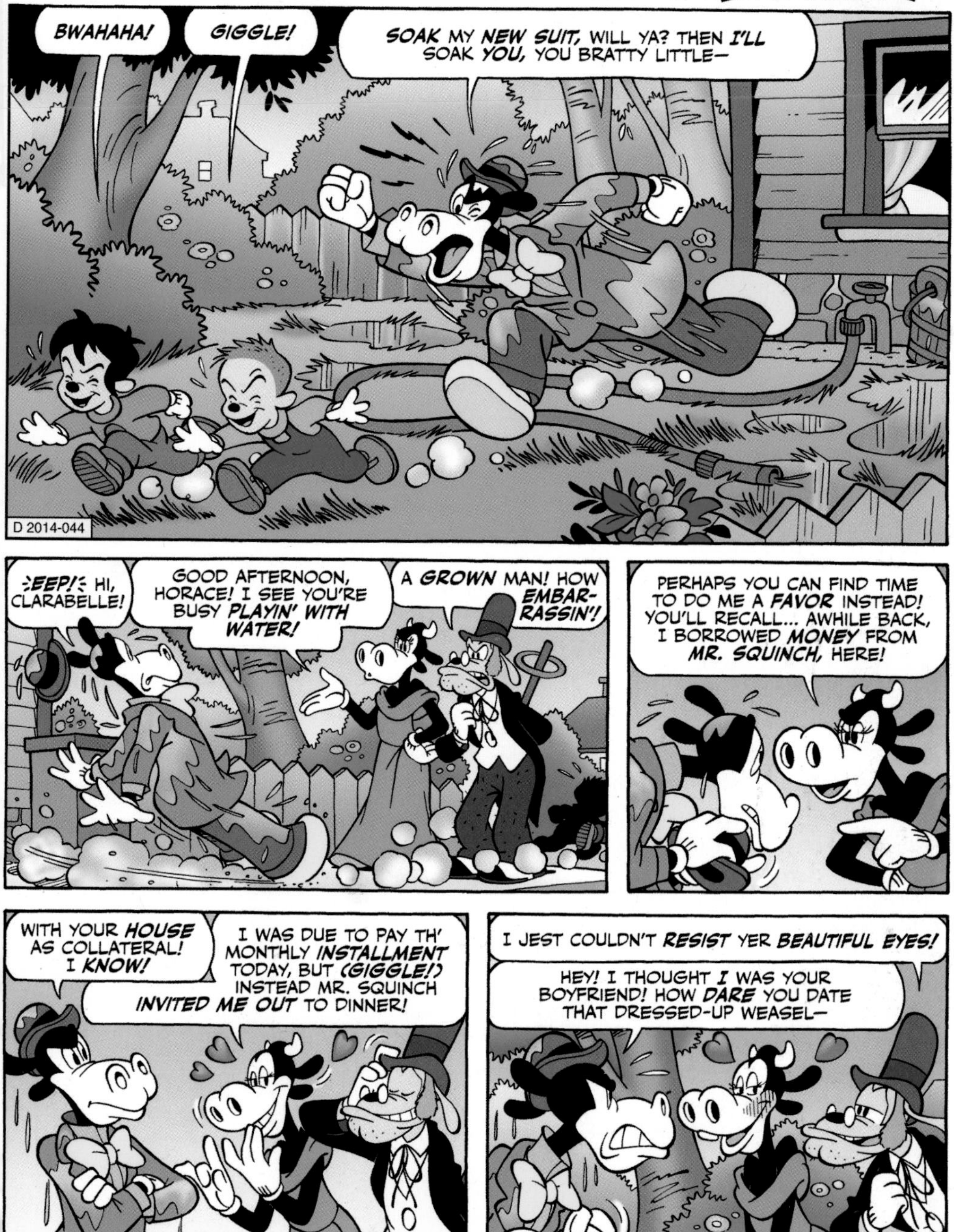

BWAHAHA!
GIGGLE!
SOAK MY NEW SUIT, WILL YA? THEN I'LL SOAK YOU, YOU BRATTY LITTLE—
D 2014-044
EEP! HI, CLARABELLE!
GOOD AFTERNOON, HORACE! I SEE YOU'RE BUSY PLAYIN' WITH WATER!
A GROWN MAN! HOW EMBARRASSIN'!
PERHAPS YOU CAN FIND TIME TO DO ME A FAVOR INSTEAD! YOU'LL RECALL... AWHILE BACK, I BORROWED MONEY FROM MR. SQUINCH, HERE!
WITH YOUR HOUSE AS COLLATERAL! I KNOW!
I WAS DUE TO PAY TH' MONTHLY INSTALLMENT TODAY, BUT (GIGGLE!) INSTEAD MR. SQUINCH INVITED ME OUT TO DINNER!
I JEST COULDN'T RESIST YER BEAUTIFUL EYES!
HEY! I THOUGHT I WAS YOUR BOYFRIEND! HOW DARE YOU DATE THAT DRESSED-UP WEASEL—


Originally published in *Donald Duck & Co.* #32/2015 (Norway, 2015)

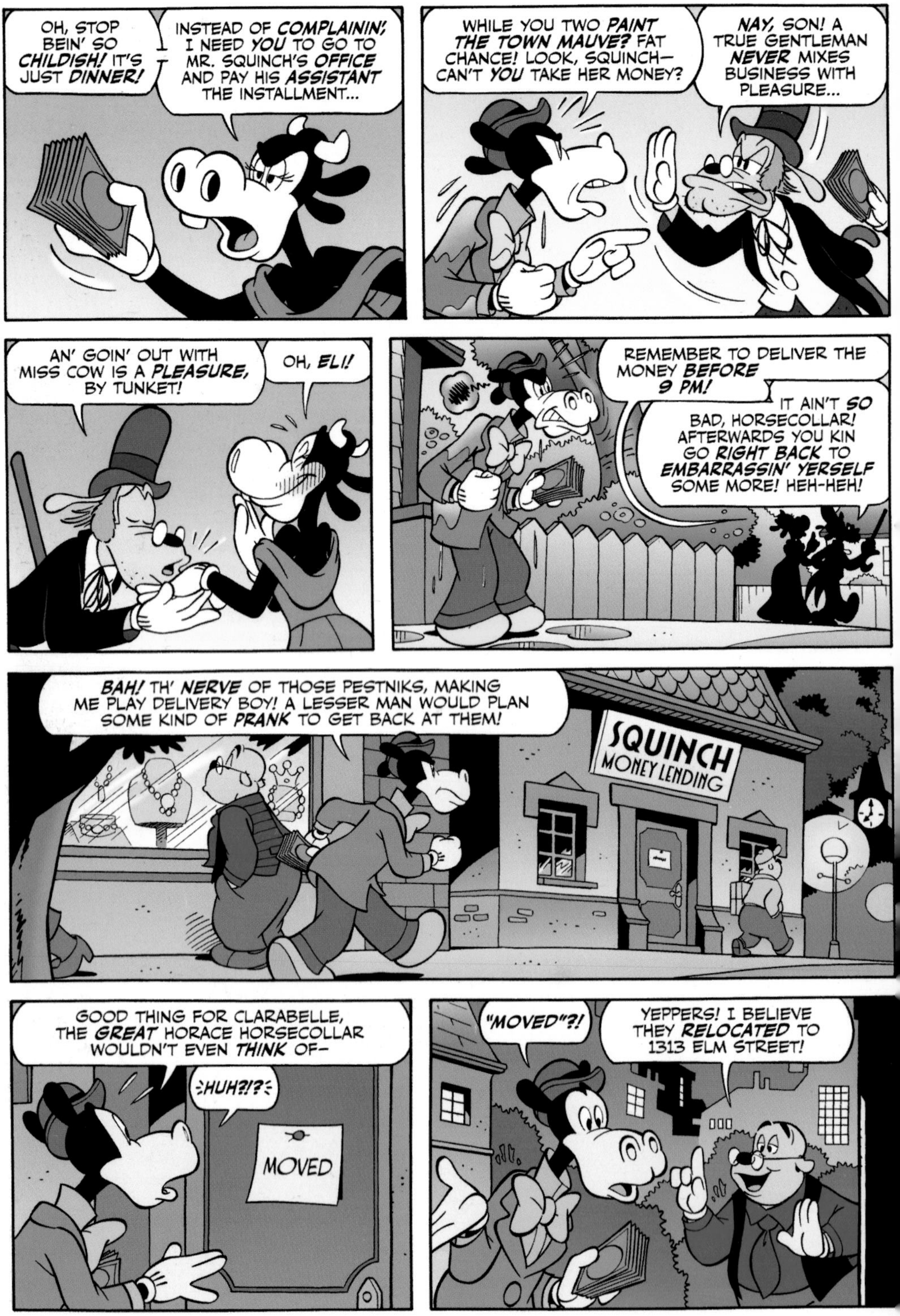
OH, STOP BEIN' SO CHILDISH! IT'S JUST DINNER!
INSTEAD OF COMPLAININ', I NEED YOU TO GO TO MR. SQUINCH'S OFFICE AND PAY HIS ASSISTANT THE INSTALLMENT...
WHILE YOU TWO PAINT THE TOWN MAUVE? FAT CHANCE! LOOK, SQUINCH— CAN'T YOU TAKE HER MONEY?
NAY, SON! A TRUE GENTLEMAN NEVER MIXES BUSINESS WITH PLEASURE...
AN' GOIN' OUT WITH MISS COW IS A PLEASURE, BY TUNKET!
OH, ELI!
REMEMBER TO DELIVER THE MONEY BEFORE 9 PM!
IT AIN'T SO BAD, HORSECOLLAR! AFTERWARDS YOU KIN GO RIGHT BACK TO EMBARRASSIN' YERSELF SOME MORE! HEH-HEH!
BAH! TH' NERVE OF THOSE PESTNIKS, MAKING ME PLAY DELIVERY BOY! A LESSER MAN WOULD PLAN SOME KIND OF PRANK TO GET BACK AT THEM!
SQUINCH
MONEY LENDING
GOOD THING FOR CLARABELLE, THE GREAT HORACE HORSECOLLAR WOULDN'T EVEN THINK OF—
HUH?!?
MOVED
"MOVED"?!
YEPPERS! I BELIEVE THEY RELOCATED TO 1313 ELM STREET!

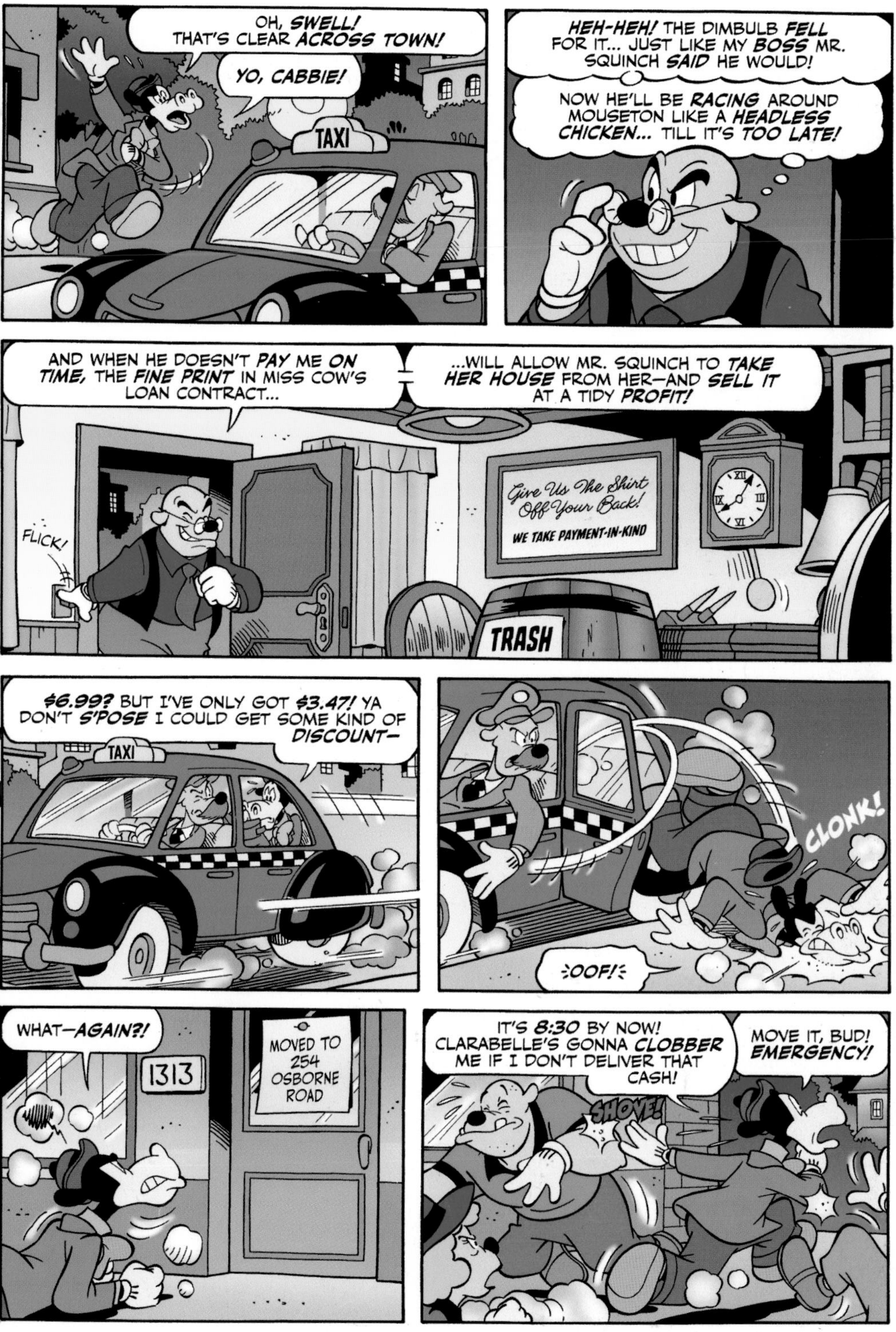
OH, SWELL! THAT'S CLEAR ACROSS TOWN!
YO, CABBIE!
TAXI
HEH-HEH! THE DIMBULB FELL FOR IT... JUST LIKE MY BOSS MR. SQUINCH SAID HE WOULD!
NOW HE'LL BE RACING AROUND MOUSETON LIKE A HEADLESS CHICKEN... TILL IT'S TOO LATE!
AND WHEN HE DOESN'T PAY ME ON TIME, THE FINE PRINT IN MISS COW'S LOAN CONTRACT...
...WILL ALLOW MR. SQUINCH TO TAKE HER HOUSE FROM HER—AND SELL IT AT A TIDY PROFIT!
FLICK!
Give Us The Shirt Off Your Back!
WE TAKE PAYMENT-IN-KIND
TRASH
$6.99? BUT I'VE ONLY GOT $3.47! YA DON'T S'POSE I COULD GET SOME KIND OF DISCOUNT—
TAXI
CLONK!
OOF!
WHAT—AGAIN?!
1313
MOVED TO 254 OSBORNE ROAD
IT'S 8:30 BY NOW! CLARABELLE'S GONNA CLOBBER ME IF I DON'T DELIVER THAT CASH!
MOVE IT, BUD! EMERGENCY!
SHOVE!

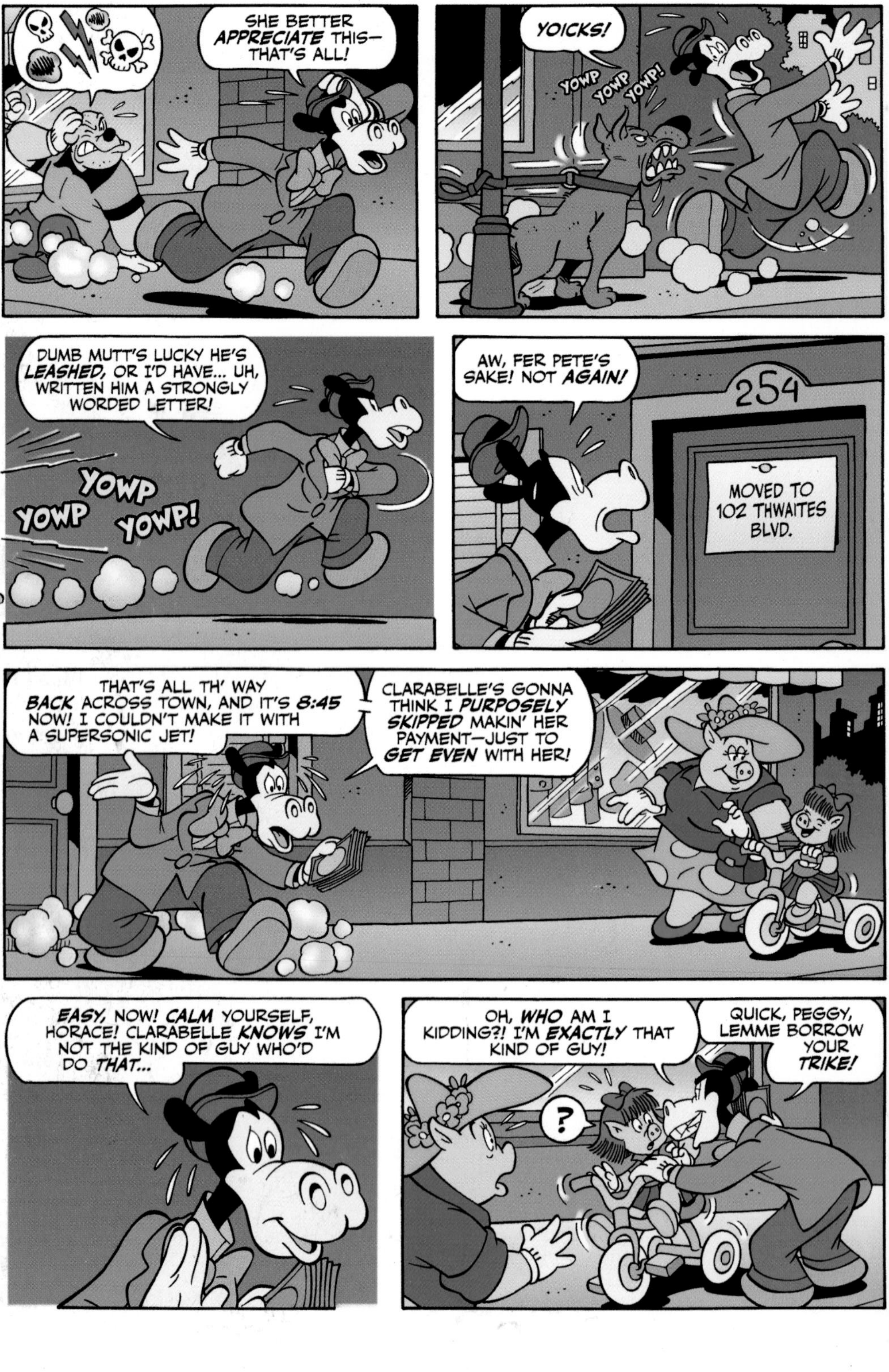
SHE BETTER APPRECIATE THIS— THAT'S ALL!
YOICKS!
YOWP YOWP YOWP!
DUMB MUTT'S LUCKY HE'S LEASHED, OR I'D HAVE... UH, WRITTEN HIM A STRONGLY WORDED LETTER!
YOWP YOWP YOWP!
AW, FER PETE'S SAKE! NOT AGAIN!
254
MOVED TO 102 THWAITES BLVD.
THAT'S ALL TH' WAY BACK ACROSS TOWN, AND IT'S 8:45 NOW! I COULDN'T MAKE IT WITH A SUPERSONIC JET!
CLARABELLE'S GONNA THINK I PURPOSELY SKIPPED MAKIN' HER PAYMENT—JUST TO GET EVEN WITH HER!
EASY, NOW! CALM YOURSELF, HORACE! CLARABELLE KNOWS I'M NOT THE KIND OF GUY WHO'D DO THAT...
OH, WHO AM I KIDDING?! I'M EXACTLY THAT KIND OF GUY!
QUICK, PEGGY, LEMME BORROW YOUR TRIKE!
?

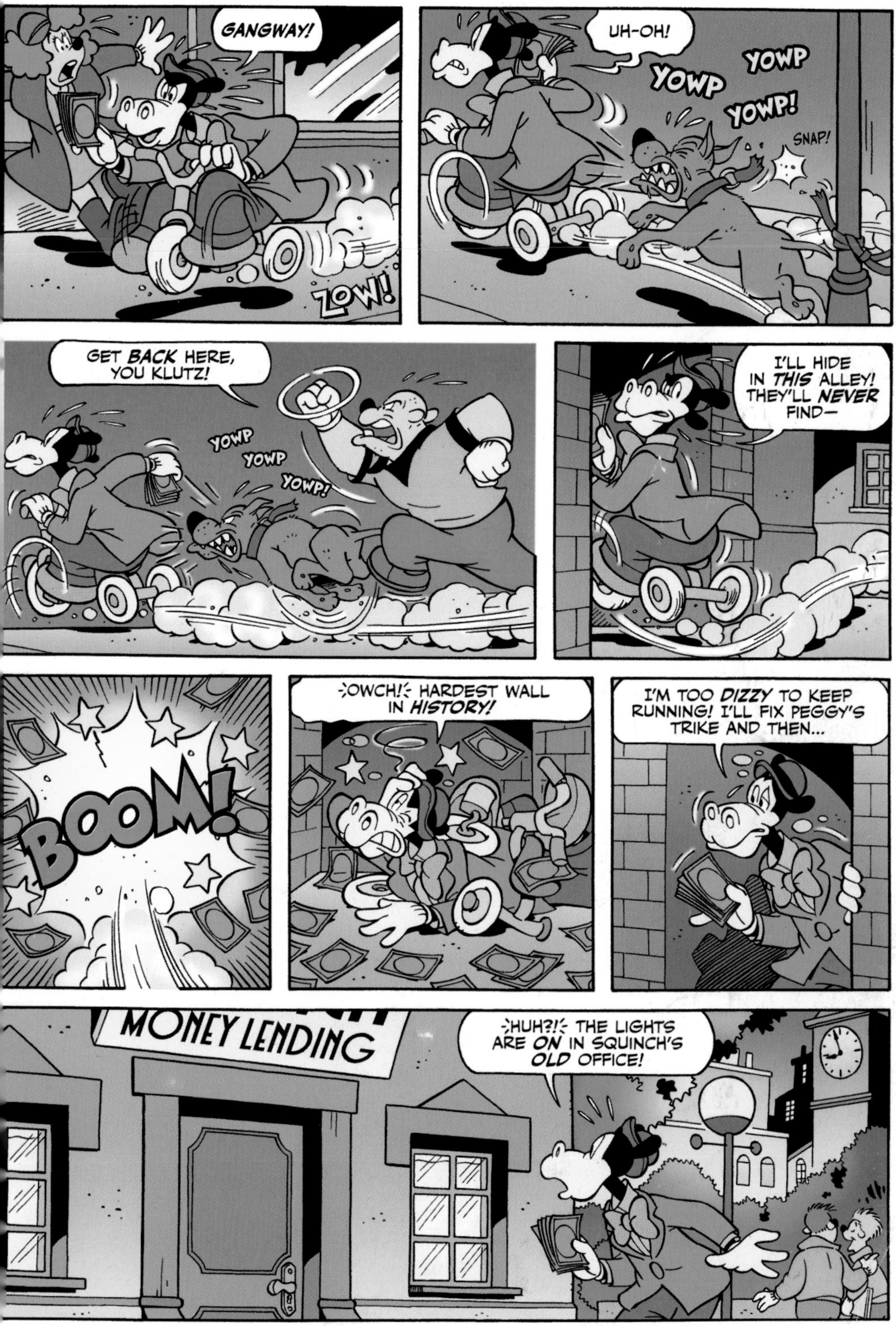

GANGWAY!
ZOW!
UH-OH!
YOWP
YOWP
YOWP!
SNAP!
GET BACK HERE, YOU KLUTZ!
YOWP
YOWP
YOWP!
I'LL HIDE IN THIS ALLEY! THEY'LL NEVER FIND—
BOOM!
OWCH! HARDEST WALL IN HISTORY!
I'M TOO DIZZY TO KEEP RUNNING! I'LL FIX PEGGY'S TRIKE AND THEN...
MONEY LENDING
HUH?! THE LIGHTS ARE ON IN SQUINCH'S OLD OFFICE!

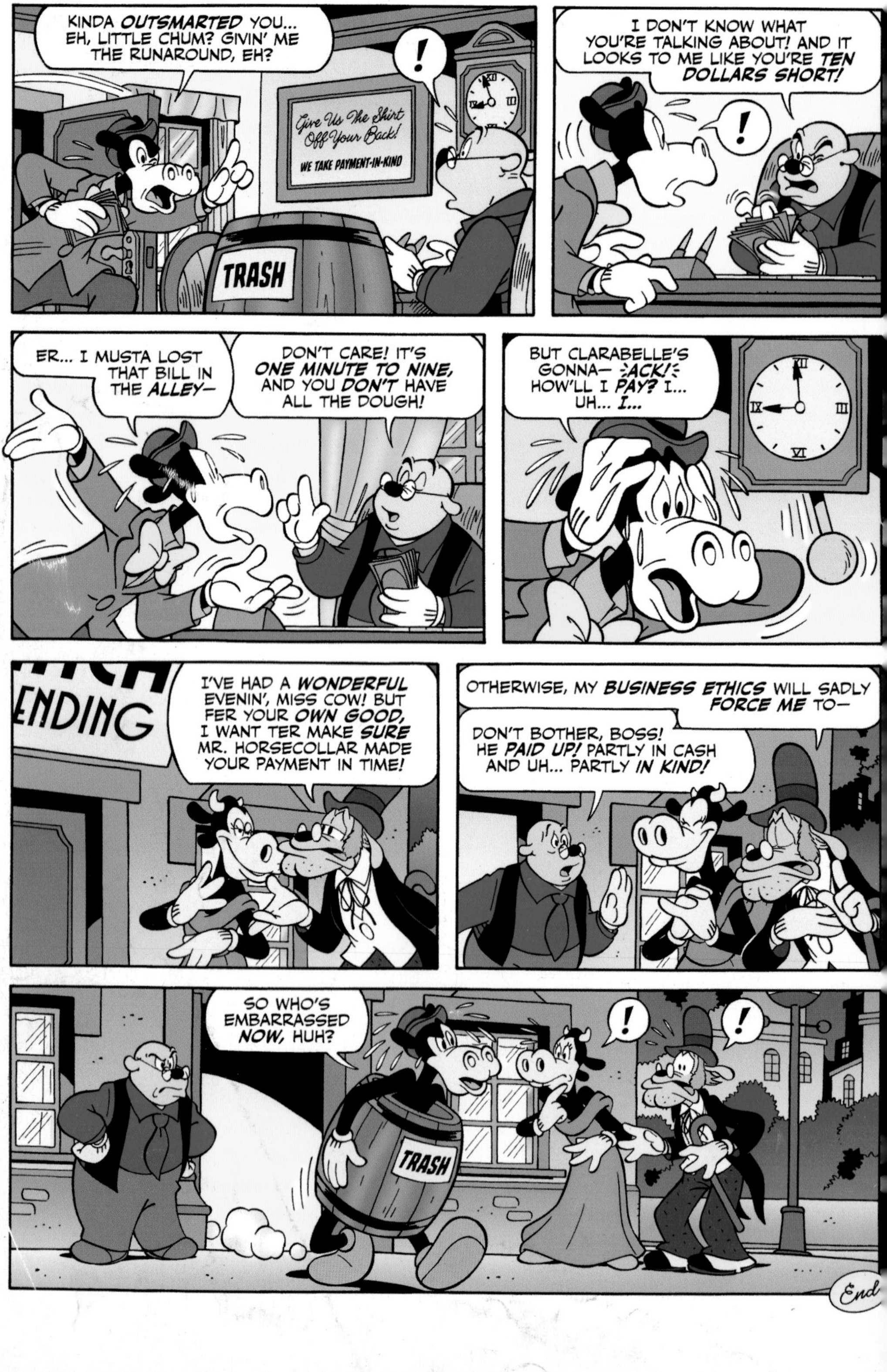
KINDA OUTSMARTED YOU... EH, LITTLE CHUM? GIVIN' ME THE RUNAROUND, EH?
!
Give Us The Shirt Off Your Back!
WE TAKE PAYMENT-IN-KIND
TRASH
I DON'T KNOW WHAT YOU'RE TALKING ABOUT! AND IT LOOKS TO ME LIKE YOU'RE TEN DOLLARS SHORT!
!
ER... I MUSTA LOST THAT BILL IN THE ALLEY—
DON'T CARE! IT'S ONE MINUTE TO NINE, AND YOU DON'T HAVE ALL THE DOUGH!
BUT CLARABELLE'S GONNA— ACK! HOW'LL I PAY? I... UH... I...
ENDING
I'VE HAD A WONDERFUL EVENIN', MISS COW! BUT FER YOUR OWN GOOD, I WANT TER MAKE SURE MR. HORSECOLLAR MADE YOUR PAYMENT IN TIME!
OTHERWISE, MY BUSINESS ETHICS WILL SADLY FORCE ME TO—
DON'T BOTHER, BOSS! HE PAID UP! PARTLY IN CASH AND UH... PARTLY IN KIND!
SO WHO'S EMBARRASSED NOW, HUH?
!
!
TRASH
End

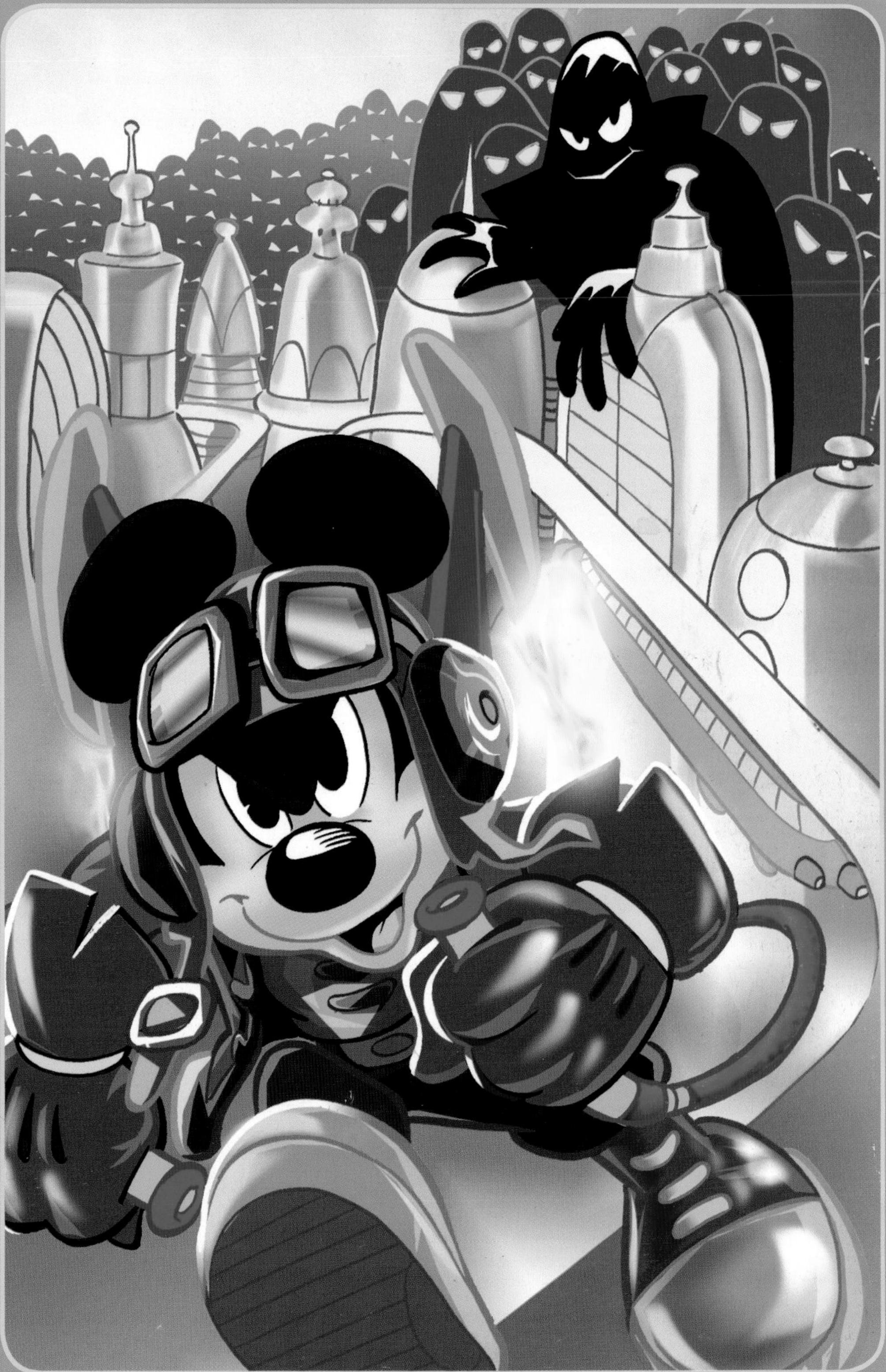

Art by Giorgio Cavazzano, Colors by Cyrille Leriche

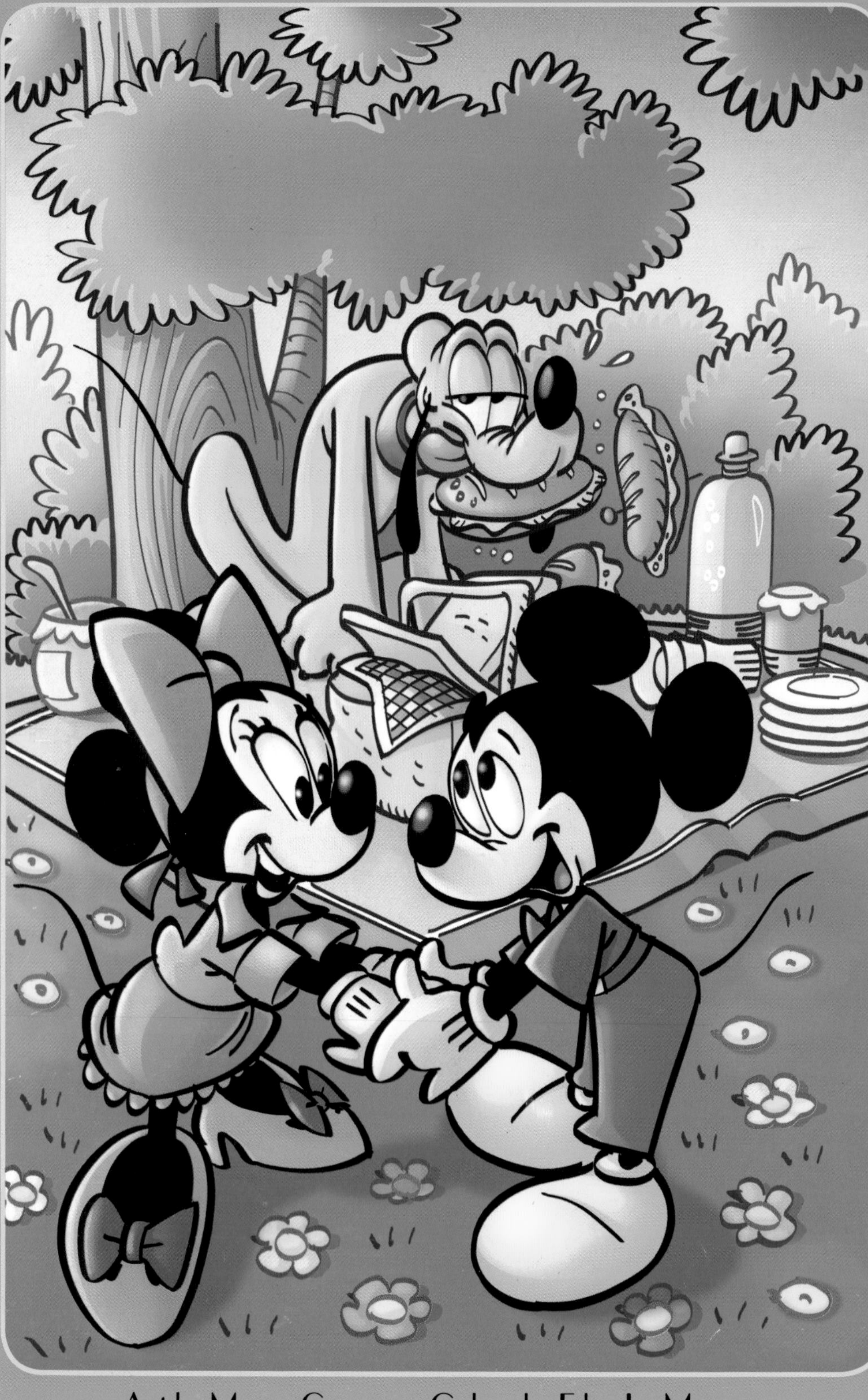

Art by Marco Gervasio, Colors by Fabio Lo Monaco

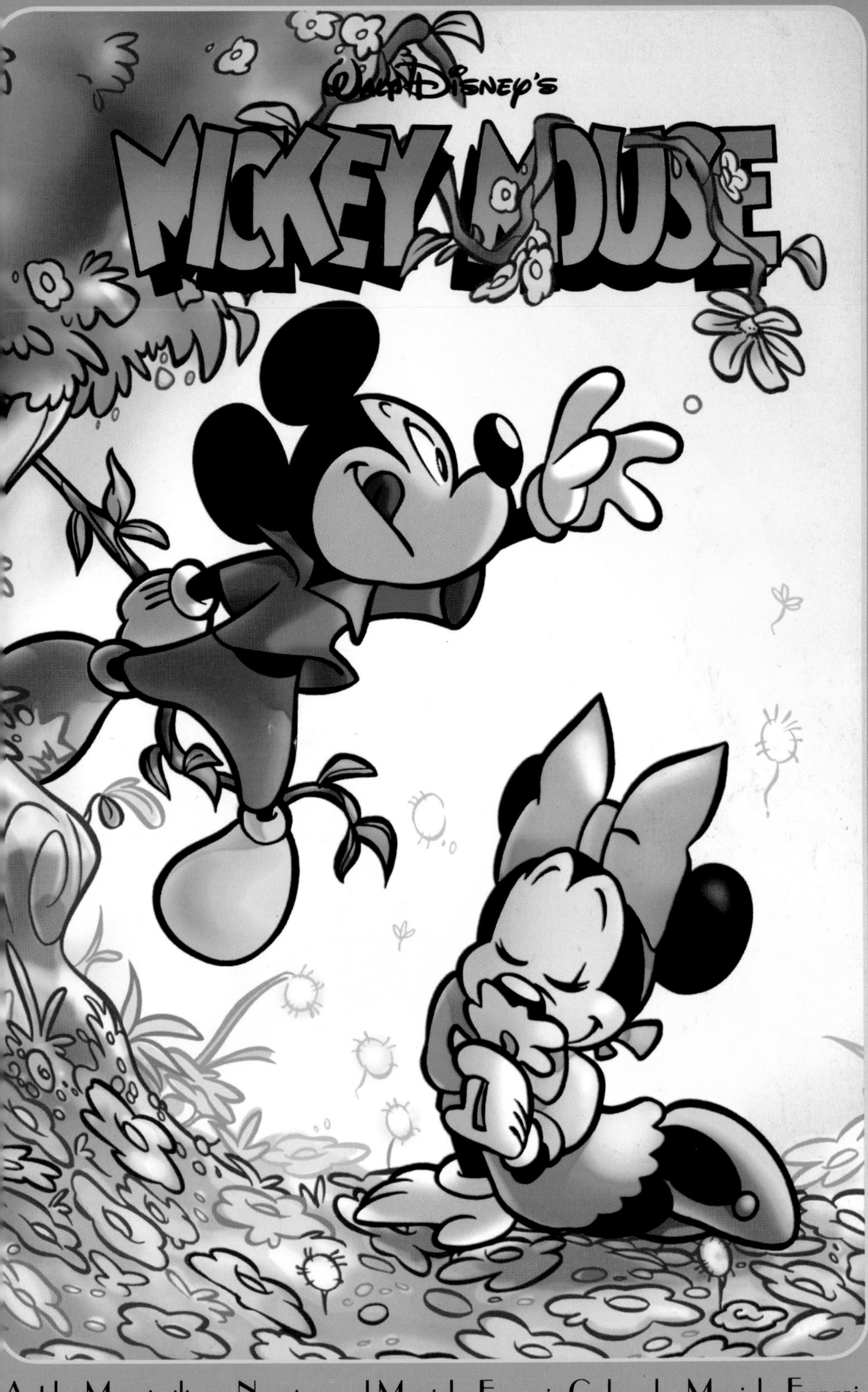
Walt Disney's
MICKEY MOUSE

Art by Massimiliano Narciso and Marieke Ferrari, Colors by Marieke Ferrari

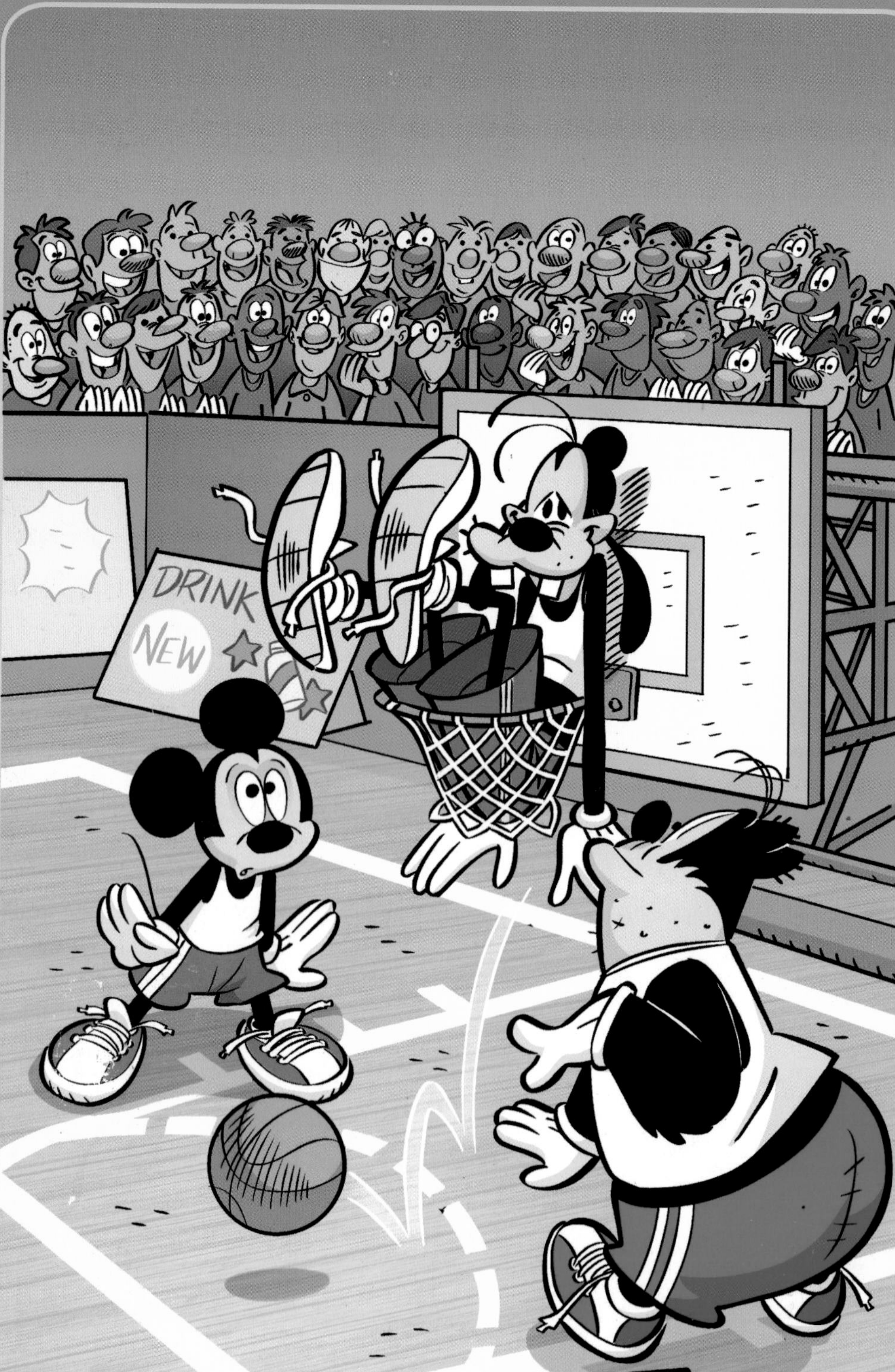
DRINK
NEW

Art by Marco Gervasio, Colors by Ronda Pattison

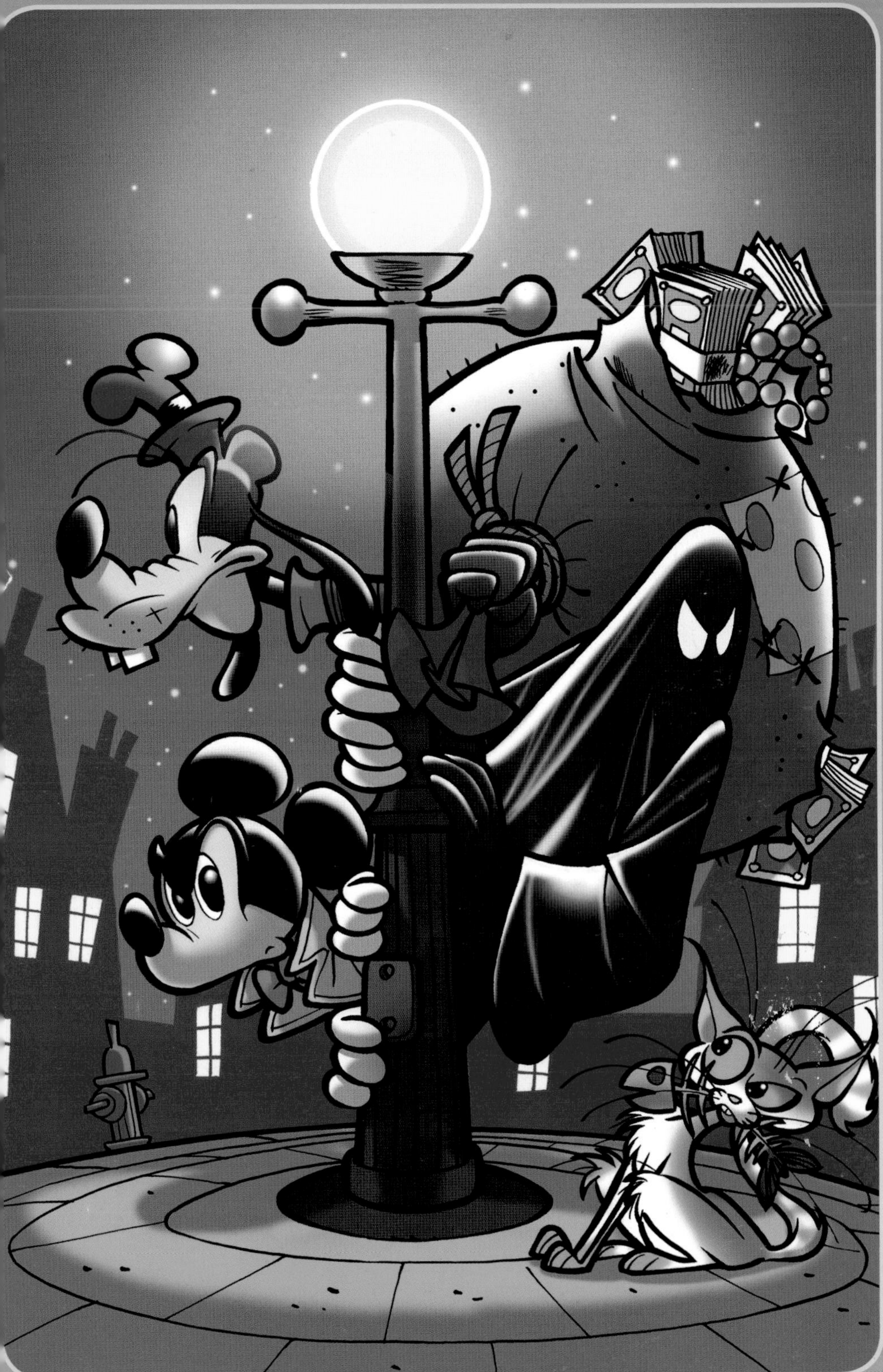

Art by Donald Soffritti